Broken Dream

Eden Maguire

A division of Hachette Children's Books

A Catalogue record for this book is available from the British Library

ISBN 978 1 444 90188 7

Typeset in Berkeley Book by Avon DataSet Ltd,
Bidford on Avon, Warwickshire

Printed and bound in Great Britain by
CPI Group (UK) Ltd, Croydon, CR0 4YY

The paper and board used in this paperback by Hodder Children's Books
are natural recyclable products made from wood grown in
sustainable forests. The manufacturing processes conform to the
environmental regulations of the country of origin.

Hodder Children's Books
a division of Hachette Children's Books
338 Euston Road, London NW1 3BH
An Hachette UK company
www.hachette.co.uk

For my editor, Naomi Pottesman —
delightful, enthusiastic and meticulous as ever.

1

Starry, starry night. I'm with Orlando in New York. Repeat slowly. I'm with Orlando. We're together again after two months apart.

The picture we're staring at shows a whirling, swirling, magical night sky. The midnight blue is like nothing you've ever seen, the stars are crazy, the painter is Vincent van Gogh.

New York in December. Two days ago Orlando flew into Bitterroot from Dallas and from there we took a plane to JFK. We gave ourselves five beautiful days to explore the city – time for me to attend a three-day film workshop and for us both to shop until we dropped, watch movies and walk, walk, walk these bright, buzzing city streets.

Fourteen days before Christmas and outside the gallery it's snowing. Earlier today the flakes froze on my eyelashes.

'How did Vinnie do that?' Orlando murmured. The colour, the texture, the light.

Especially the light.

I agreed that the painting was awesome beyond words.

We weren't alone in MoMA, obviously. Everyone who visits what must be the world's biggest collection of modern art wants to stand in line to see *The Starry Night*, buy the postcard and go home to tell their friends. But the painting lifts you out of reality – the shuffling crowds, the air con and the uniformed security guards. You're in a dream; it really feels like it's just you and Vincent's stars.

'Let's go.' In the end Orlando had to take me by the arm and steer me away.

'Aww!' I sighed.

'I know. But it's time for lunch. We need to eat.' He led me through the museum. I floated past magenta, cobalt-blue and chrome-yellow paint dribbled, splashed and thrown on to white surfaces, plus multimillion-dollar contemporary canvases that were pierced, slashed, scrunched up and scrawled on. I didn't care about any of them, only Vincent.

'Wow!' Orlando kept hold of my hand until we reached the exit.

'I know.' Starry skies, midnight swimming in Turner

Lake – that was how he and I first came together, in the mountains near our home. It was when he first told me he loved me and wanted to be with me always – under the stars in the cold, clear water. And now here we were in the heart of Manhattan, in a totally loved-up dream.

'Sorry,' he laughed. 'I can't seem to get past "Wow!"'

'Me neither.' Come back, words. Slot together and make sentences that prove we're more than three years old.

'I'm speechless.' Orlando shook his head.

Crazy, angry, tormented, inspired, possessed. Inside my head, the adjectives for Vincent's work floated free of verbs, definite articles and conjunctions. Pure genius. 'Come on, let's eat,' I said.

So we crunched along snowy sidewalks, scaled small mountains of slush dumped in gutters and crossed streets when the lights said 'Walk' until we came to Central Park.

'Look!' I told Orlando at the gates. I pointed to the snowflakes settling on my eyebrows and eyelashes. 'It's happened again.'

He laughed and kissed me, brushed the flakes from my eyes. Then we bought burgers and set off to watch the skaters on Wollman, the happy carousel riders further up the Mall, the relaxed lunchtime drinkers at the Tavern on the Green.

We reached the frozen lake in the centre of the park.

Crack! Someone fired a gun in broad daylight. Orlando and I flinched, fighting the instinct to duck and run because that would have looked stupid when no one in the crowd ahead of us had reacted.

There was another crack, and another. I noticed a helicopter parked on one of the empty volleyball courts and the orange and white crowd-control tape stretched across the path.

Who was shooting who here? Where were the cops? Why were people clapping?

As it turned out, this was another kind of shooting altogether.

'Cut!' a voice cried, to more loud applause.

Orlando wove through the crowd and I followed.

'Hey, back off!' someone protested.

'Yeah, we waited all morning to see this,' a chunky woman to my right agreed, her voice muffled by the red scarf wound round the lower half of her face. And she stepped across our path. 'You two don't get to elbow your way right to the front.'

'We were just trying . . . we only wanted . . .' I tried to explain.

'Stay right where you are. Can't you see they're filming?'

'Stand behind the tape.'

'Pushy little bastards.'

And so on. This is how Orlando and I found we weren't flavour of the month, that the gunshots weren't real and that somebody famous was attracting all the applause.

'Jack Kane,' a nearby kid took pity on us and explained. 'They're shooting a scene for *Siege 2*. Didn't you know?'

Orlando stood on tiptoe. At six three and on the balls of his feet he can see above most people's heads. 'Jesus – she's right,' he muttered.

'What can you see? Tell me.' The name Jack Kane equals blockbuster, equals squillions of dollars, bad boy headlines in every gossip magazine and a private army of security men wherever he goes.

'The bridge and the boathouse across the lake, cameras, sound equipment . . .' Orlando told me.

'Jack Kane?' I demanded.

'No – yeah, now I see him! They're setting up another sequence; he's sprinting down the steps on to the ice, he's fallen into the water – oh no, that must be a stunt double. More gunfire, can you hear it?'

The shots rattled out as Orlando kept up the running commentary.

'I can't see a frickin' thing,' the pitying girl sighed. She was a couple of inches shorter than me and I'm five ten. 'But I was in a great position when the helicopter landed. I got Jack Kane's autograph and snapped a picture of us together. How cool is that.'

'Cut!' the director yelled.

Orlando came down off his tiptoes. 'Pretty cool, actually,' he agreed.

'I'm Tania,' I told my new friend. 'This is Orlando.' The focus of the crowd changed from the boathouse to the stationary chopper. Heads turned. There was a fresh wave of oohs and aahs.

'I'm Macy Osmond – Jack's number one fan,' she mumbled. 'Looks like Jack's finished filming for the day. Natalia's waiting in the helicopter with the kids. They'll fly out to the hotel, even though it's only two blocks away on Park Avenue. The hotel has a landing pad on the roof. Natalia won't travel any other way – not with the kids in tow.'

'Security?' I asked, impressed by Macy's knowledge. She was pretty in a streetwise, heavy-kohl, tattoos and face-piercings kind of way. And she had zingy bright-red hair that shouted, 'Look at me!'

She nodded. 'See you later,' she muttered as the crowd swung and shuffled en masse towards the volleyball courts to say goodbye to Jack. 'Tomorrow maybe.'

'More filming?' Orlando asked.

Macy nodded. 'This movie is going to be massive,' she predicted. 'I want to tell my kids I was here.'

Hey, Holly. Hey, Grace. I texted my two best buddies back in Bitterroot. NY rocks. Saw Vincent's Starry Night in MoMA. So cool.

Hey, Jude. This was not Orlando breaking into the classic John Lennon riff, though we could see Strawberry Fields from where we stood and were able to pick out the Dakota building where he was shot dead. No, this was Orlando texting home. Hey, Jude. Jack Kane is in Central Park, shooting scenes for Siege 2. It's huge. But when he pressed Send, his BlackBerry told him that his battery was flat.

We stood at the edge of the frozen lake as the big star's chopper blades whirred. The crowd was splitting up. As Macy pushed past a gaggle of girls, she didn't notice the strap of her handbag slip from her shoulder. A young guy bumped into her. The bag fell to the ground.

'Wait – you dropped this!' Orlando called and he stepped forward to pick it up.

As he stooped, the giggling girls came between us and I lost sight of him. No problem. He would hand Macy her bag and reappear in ten seconds max.

I began a second text message to my mom and dad. Day 1 – MoMA a.m., Central Park p.m. Tomorrow workshop. Trip is excellent!

I glanced up. The girls had drifted away and there was no sign of Orlando, so I set off in the direction I'd last seen him. More Jack Kane fans crisscrossed the walkway. The chopper blades chugged and whirred, the engine roared, the star and his famous family rose into the sky.

'Orlando?' My voice was drowned out by the helicopter. I felt the force of the wind created by the rotating blades, leaned into it, pulled the hood of my quilted jacket low over my forehead.

The chopper rose like a giant dragonfly on skis, tilted clumsily then headed east towards Park Avenue. The actor's fans watched it leave, sucking every second of enjoyment out of the afternoon's gawk-fest.

'Orlando!' I didn't care if guys around me stared – I raised my voice and yelled his name as loud as I could. I crossed the empty volleyball courts, spotting a dozen tall young guys wrapped up in scarves, hats, leather jackets, gloves. But none of them was my tall young guy.

How can this happen? One second Orlando was there in the dying light of the late afternoon, stooping to pick up Macy's bag. The next second he was gone, all in the blink of an eye.

I took out my phone and tried to call him. Nothing. No reply. Then I remembered his dead battery.

OK. I told myself to stay calm. This was a minor crisis, but not one I couldn't handle. Somewhere, not far away, Orlando would be looking for me. I should stay on the spot, wait for the crowd to disperse.

The snow, which had eased since we came out of the gallery, began to fall heavily again. My heart started to race.

Orlando, come back! This time I didn't open my mouth, I just willed him to find me at the edge of the empty courts, standing by the security tape, which flapped in the wind. My stomach twisted, panic rose. Imagination (which is my strong point) kicked in and I went into a whole elaborate scenario – the shady-looking guy in a hooded jacket, the one who had made body contact with Macy, had done it deliberately. His plan was to snatch her bag but a stupid bystander – Orlando – had got in his way. The guy had a knife. He used it on Orlando. I pictured blood in the snow.

Take a deep breath.

I was alone by the frozen lake. Falling snow quickly covered the footprints made by the departing crowd.

Scenario two, minus my OTT imagination – Orlando had returned the bag to Macy without a hitch. She was super-grateful because it contained her camera with the precious photo of her and Jack Kane. He'd said no problem, given her one of his wide Irish smiles then made his way back to the spot where he thought he'd left me. Only he got confused and went to the wrong place. Then he started looking for me and the more he searched, the further away he drifted. It happens.

In that case, I reasoned, he would try to tune in to what I'd do next. What would be the sensible thing? Maybe he would figure I would go back to the entrance to the park and wait for him, so I should retrace my steps and hope to meet up with him there. Yeah, it was a plan and straight away I felt better as I set off south, with the Fifth Avenue traffic to my left and the multicoloured lights of the carousel twinkling up ahead.

You had to be brave to stay out in the cold but a few hardy tourists had paid their two dollars, or whatever, for the old-time Christmas treat. Inside the brick construction that sheltered the ride there was schmaltzy music and carved horses, rising and falling as they whirled by. It made me feel dizzy just to look at them. Then out of nowhere a short guy in a fur-lined hunter's hat and a black jacket zipped up to his chin stepped out of the shadows at the far side of the building. I registered him out of the corner of my eye as I trudged through the snow towards the park gates. When he ran at me and hooked his arm round my neck to drag me around the back of the carousel, it was as if my whole life went into slow motion.

The music played and the horses rose and fell. White horses with red and blue saddles, brown horses with carved manes and tails flying, black horses frozen in a full-out gallop, rising up and down on steel poles, going endlessly round.

The mugger's arm was round my neck. I was choking, staggering backwards in the snow, not even screaming or struggling.

The rafters of the carousel were painted red. Yellow lights were strung between them. The central support concealing the engine was pale blue. Round and round went the prancing horses, carved nostrils flared, sightless eyes staring.

My attacker tightened his hold. He had one arm round my neck, the other round my waist. I couldn't turn my head to look at him. I thought with a weird kind of mild surprise, Whoa, maybe this guy has a knife!

The horses stopped. I stared up at a rearing black stallion. *Slam!* My brain did its sickening dark angel thing of cutting out reality. A split second later it clicked back into action and shoved me into a nightmare vision of the black horse shape-shifting and coming alive, lunging at me and rearing with its heavy hooves flailing, its black neck flecked with white sweat.

I see its knotted mane caked with dirt and ice, its ears flattened, a bleeding cut across its nose. There is fear in its eyes as it rears over me. I roll to the side as its hooves thud down.

Slam – back into ugly reality.

The attacker in the black jacket threw me to the snowy ground and flipped me on to my stomach. He rammed a booted foot into the small of my back.

'Don't hurt me,' I begged. I was face down in untrodden snow. The woman who worked the carousel was turning out the lights.

'Phone,' he grunted. 'And your bag.'

Trapped by the foot grinding into my spine, I struggled to squeeze my hand into my pocket to pull out my phone. I had it halfway out when he stamped on my wrist and grabbed it. Then, instead of waiting for me to wriggle and raise the top half of my body to hitch my bag over my head, he wrenched at the strap and it broke. I was lying winded. My cheeks were frozen, my back and wrist hurt like hell. The mugger had what he wanted.

The black stallion rears again. I can smell him, hear his snorting anger and I feel the ground shudder as his front hooves land close to my face.

'Don't hurt me,' I pleaded a second time.

The guy was gone. He'd vanished into the snow with my possessions.

There was a click inside my head and the shiny stallion was back on the carousel, skewered on its steel pole, frozen in time.

I should take time out to explain. When my brain does that – splits and gives me two parallel versions of what's going on around me – it's a psychic, sixth-sense thing. You might call it a nightmare, only I'm awake.

Actually, it's me making a connection with a world most people can't tune into and sometimes I wish I couldn't either. I mean, how would you feel if objects changed shape before your eyes, came to life and scared the hell out of you? Would you be thrilled to be in contact with the huge forces of good and evil that govern this world, and to know that nothing and no one are what they seem?

That's exactly what happened to me when the mugger grabbed me and the carousel horse shape-shifted. I refused to make a big deal of it right then because I was in denial. I'd been blessed by a period without these visions for two whole months, travelling in Europe and free of my dark angel. The black stallion was a sign he might be back and thirsting for revenge. After all, I'm one of a very few gifted people standing between him and his planned victory.

Or maybe this carousel wasn't a psychic intimation that he was back, please God. Dark angel, twisted Cupid. His mission is to draw innocent lovers into his shadowy, tormented world and psychics like me are the only ones with enough energy to oppose him. If he gets rid of me, the door into the dark side stands wide open.

So no. I was in New York, convincing myself I was free, that I didn't need to warn or protect anyone, and that what had just happened was a city mugging, pure and simple. I got up from the trampled snow and, supporting my right wrist with my unharmed left hand, I stumbled out from behind the carousel.

'Hey, are you OK?' a voice asked.

A guy, a total stranger, strode towards me through the snow. I couldn't make out any details, only that he wore a dark padded jacket but no hat and that he sounded concerned.

Drawing a deep breath, I nodded. I didn't want to stop and talk, I was desperate to get to the park gates, where I was certain Orlando would be waiting.

'What happened to your hand?' the stranger asked. He was closer now – tall, dark-haired, out-of-this-world handsome – and I did a kind of double take.

It couldn't be . . . surely not!

'No, I'm not Jack Kane,' he confirmed as if he read

what was going on inside my muddled brain. 'A lot of people make the same mistake. I'm Charlie Speke, his stuntman double.'

My wrist ached and I could still feel the imprint of the mugger's boot in the small of my back. My jacket and jeans were caked with snow. 'The guy in the hat back there – did you see him?'

The stranger nodded.

'He stole my bag and my phone.' I broke down and sobbed helplessly.

Then the Jack Kane lookalike took my arm and led me to the carousel entrance, where the female operator was busy locking a metal grille. 'Stand here in the porch,' Charlie Speke told me. 'Take a deep breath and tell me exactly what happened.'

'The guy came out of nowhere, grabbed me from behind. I was looking for my boyfriend. I'd lost him in the crowd, back by the volleyball courts. He'll be waiting by the gates. I have to go.'

'Slow down,' Charlie said.

'Jeez!' The carousel worker had locked up, glanced at Charlie and made the usual mistake.

'Nope,' he said with a smile and a quick shake of his head. 'I'm not him. I'm nobody.'

The woman checked out his thick, short jet-black hair

15

and hazel eyes under strong, straight brows, his small, neat ears, angular jaw and high cheekbones. 'You got to be kidding,' she challenged.

'If only,' he shrugged. 'But believe me – I'm nobody. If I'm Jack Kane, where's my security team? Where's my helicopter?'

'Got you,' she agreed – an everyday, middle-aged woman in a dark-blue coat and black boots, not the type to be overly impressed by celebrity in any case. She glanced my way and saw the tears. 'You OK?'

'It's cool, I got it,' Charlie assured her and she nodded then headed for the walkway, taking the opposite direction to the one I wanted to go.

'What's your name?' He was helping me to brush the snow from the back of my collar.

'Tania. Tania Ionescu.'

'Tania, I'll come with you, make sure you're safe,' he offered, making small talk as we walked. 'You were in the park to watch the filming? Did you get a good look at the living legend? I guess you saw the first Siege movie? How did you rate it?'

Then, when I'd calmed down, he asked me again about the guy who had stolen my bag. 'Can you recall any details about how he looked?'

I shook my head.

'What he was wearing, how tall – that kind of thing?'

'Shorter than me, maybe only five eight. He had one of those hats that hunters wear, with the ear flaps. A dark leather jacket.'

'White? Black?'

'He looked mixed-race.'

'And he took your wallet, your money, everything?'

I nodded miserably.

'But your boyfriend is waiting for you at the entrance to the park?'

'Let's hope,' I said with an anxious sigh.

'So we'll soon find out.'

Stuntman Charlie was right. We were past the Wollman ice rink, almost at the gates. In the street beyond I could see the horse-drawn buggies waiting by the sidewalk, blowing steam into the cold dusk air.

I picked up speed, certain that Orlando would be there. It was still pretty crowded on the sidewalk, and messed up by piles of dirty snow, puddles of slush, overflowing trash cans, clouds of exhaust fumes.

'You see him?' Charlie enquired.

I shook my head, felt my heart falter. 'Maybe he's still back by the reservoir.'

'You remember his cell phone number?'

'Yeah, but that doesn't help. His battery's dead.' I was

in a rush to get away, ready to retrace my steps.

'Whoa, Tania. let's think this through. We're talking about eight hundred and fifty acres of parkland for your boyfriend to get lost in. It's a no-brainer – you could be running round there in the dark for hours like a headless chicken. It's better if you head back to your hotel and wait for him there.'

By now my pulse was racing again. I was listening to Charlie's idea partly because it was plain common sense and partly because I dreaded going back past the dark angel carousel. 'You sound like my dad,' I joked feebly.

He pulled down the corners of his mouth. 'Thanks.'

'He's Romanian.' I lowered my voice a couple of octaves. '"Running like headless chicken." That's how he talks.'

Charlie smiled. 'So going back to your hotel is a good idea?'

I didn't answer as I looked around for Orlando one last time, stepping aside as a family of shoppers bustled by loaded down with bulky Bloomingdale's bags. A cab pulled up in a nearby bay.

'Where's your hotel?'

'Way down in TriBeCa. It's a small B&B.'

'So take this cab,' Charlie told me, striding ahead and opening the door.

'I don't have any money, remember.'

'Give me the address.'

'86 Hubert Street, just off Twelfth Avenue.'

'You hear that?' Charlie asked the cab driver, taking bills out of his wallet and handing them over. 'This covers it, right?'

The driver nodded, glancing from Charlie to me before he took the money.

'Problem solved.' Charlie held open the door of the cab.

'But I can't . . . I mean, why would you do this?' He was just a guy walking through Central Park after a day's work.

'Let's say it's good for my karma,' he grinned, and as he did this the Jack Kane similarity sent me weak at the knees. I'll describe him again: hazel eyes that always seemed to find the funny side of any situation, plus perfect teeth and a quirky smile that puts a dimple in one cheek, which actually and coincidentally is one of the features I love most about Orlando's face – his dimple, his Irish smile.

'I want to pay you back,' I gabbled, leaning out of the window as the cab driver pulled away from the kerb.

'Don't even think about it,' my knight errant replied, striding off.

'Lucky you,' my driver grunted as he pushed into

the gridlocked traffic. He was looking in his overhead mirror, probably wondering what I'd had to do for my free taxi ride.

What could I say? I sat back and closed my eyes.

2

No Orlando, no phone, no money – it was so not good. But as the cab driver turned into Hubert Street, pulled up outside number 86 and I climbed the brownstone steps, I did actually begin to feel the band of anxiety loosen. The windows of my B&B glowed with a warm yellow light, there was a Christmas wreath on the door and a welcoming smile from my landlady as I walked into the cosy lobby.

'Had a good day?' she asked. She was straightening the Persian rugs in the hallway, turning on more lights.

'Until I went and lost my boyfriend. After that, not so good.' And I told her about the mugging, the loss of my bag and the fact that Orlando hadn't showed up yet. 'I was hoping he'd already be here.'

Mrs Waterman shook her head. She was small and slender, a widow in her fifties with a smart haircut and Botoxed brow.

'He's not?'

'No. Sorry, honey, I haven't seen him. But don't worry – he'll be here.'

I nodded and took the small elevator up to the third storey, found the old-fashioned brass room key in my jacket's inside pocket and turned it in the lock, still secretly hoping that Mrs Waterman was mistaken and that Orlando had made it back to the hotel before me.

I opened the door on our quaint room with its quilted bed throws and pretty floral drapes. *Be here!* I silently urged.

But no, the room was exactly the way it had been when we left it early that morning, with Orlando's clothes unpacked and laid neatly at the end of the bed and my stuff scattered everywhere. I sighed then turned on the TV.

I watched Fox News on politics, international unrest, bad weather in Maryland then a showbiz item about the on-location filming of Jack Kane's next movie. They showed the crowds in Central Park, Jack's helicopter and the briefest through-the-window glimpse of his wife, Natalia Linton, staring straight ahead as the chopper rose into the sky. Then there was follow-up stuff about the paparazzi harassing Natalia and the kids in the hotel lobby the previous day, footage of her in dark glasses trying to ignore the cameras and the avalanche of questions as they hassled her about rumours of her husband's latest affair with his current co-star, Angela Taraska.

I channel-hopped and tried not to look at my watch. If it got to eight p.m. and Orlando still hadn't showed up, I decided I would use the phone in my room to call home and ask my parents what to do next. Not very adult or independent, I agree. But in an emergency Dad never panics. He has the coolest, most practical of brains. And Mom has travelled all over the world – in her time she's lost luggage, cell phones, companions, maybe even boyfriends before she met my dad.

Seven forty-five p.m. I had fifteen long minutes to wait. Seven fifty came and went. At seven fifty-five I heard Orlando's key turn in the lock.

Suddenly it was as if all my Christmases had come at once.

I threw myself at him and clasped my arms round his neck, held him as if I would never let go.

'Hey, Tania,' he breathed, kissing the top of my head. 'Take it easy. Nobody died, did they?'

'You idiot!' I cried, flipping from relief into anger and pummelling his chest. 'What happened? Where did you go?'

'Where did *you* go?'

'I was there, in exactly the place you left me. I waited for ever. I didn't move from the spot.'

Orlando winced and caught me by the wrists. 'Ouch, that hurt.'

'Ouch!' I retaliated. He'd grabbed my sore arm. 'You didn't come back,' I sobbed into his chest.

'Sorry, sorry, sorry!' he told me when he understood my distress and saw the bruising on my wrist. 'How did you get this?'

'A guy jumped me. He stole my bag.'

'When? Tania, are you OK?' Now he held me at arms' length and looked into my eyes. 'Jeez, I'm beyond sorry. Sit down, tell me what happened.'

We sat on the bed and I began at the beginning, telling him everything, including the bad moments with the shape-shifting stallion, which is where he interrupted me.

'The spirit stuff has started over?' He frowned deeply and let his shoulders sag.

'Yes. No. Maybe. What can I say?'

Orlando shook his head then took a deep breath. 'Wait. This guy was attacking you, right?'

'He dragged me into the bushes at the back of the carousel, stomped on my wrist and put his foot in my back, right here.'

24

'Poor baby. You were scared out of your mind. And that's when the horse thing happened?'

I nodded. 'I just looked up and he – the stallion – came to life. You know how it is.' Carved masks jump off walls, painted forests are real, men in wolf cloaks are transformed into wild beasts. It's happened to me so often that I've stopped thinking how weird that must sound, written down like this.

'Wait . . . wait!' Orlando insisted. 'Maybe it doesn't mean what you think it means.'

'It's not my dark angel?' I asked in a tiny voice. My bottom lip quivered; I felt five years old.

'No, baby, it's not,' he said, slamming the door on the psychic stuff. 'You were under pressure, you lost control and your imagination went into overdrive – end of story.'

Hold it right there! Orlando's over-hasty protests plus my own sixth sense told me that I hadn't got it wrong. I always know when the fallen angels are gathering. I won't see them right away, might not identify them when I do, but I definitely sensed they were here in New York.

But Orlando's arms were round me, protecting me and persuading me to override my intuition so I chose the easy way out. 'You're right,' I whispered. 'I got rid of my dark angel for good when Turner Lake broke its banks.' In late fall, when the whole army of them shape-shifted into wolf men and fell howling into the flood.

'I'm here. You're safe,' Orlando promised.

I so wanted it to be true.

We turned down the lights and threw back the quilt. The bed was soft and narrow, all the better for moulding our bodies together and feeling the warmth, the smoothness of our skin.

'I love you,' I murmured, my lips against his chest so that the words blurred.

Orlando tilted my chin and kissed my mouth.

We were gentle and slow, cocooned in cool white sheets until he peeled them back to free our limbs. Then he leaned back and rested on his elbow, blocking out the soft glow of the bedside lamp. His face was in shadow – I could just make out his dark hair falling forward over his forehead and the gleam of his grey eyes.

'In Dallas,' he began.

I leaned in and kissed him.

'In Dallas I try to store up these moments in my memory and replay them – exactly the way you look, the shape of your body, the way your hair is spread out on the pillow, the angle your collarbone makes . . .'

'And?' I said, kissing him again.

'Sometimes I can do it, but other times it all just fades. The image goes and it feels like I'm losing you.'

'You're not,' I told him. There was no distance between us; my heart was always his.

We slept sweetly, Orlando on his back and me on my side with one arm resting on his stomach. All night long we hardly stirred.

It was still dark when we woke.

Here's one of the differences between us – Orlando always clicks straight into action, launches into the day, while I lie half asleep with a warm, fuzzy, floaty feeling, longing for ten more minutes in bed.

'You cancelled your bank cards, right?' he asked.

'Hmmm. What time is it?'

'Seven thirty. Visa. Amex. Tania, you called your bank?'

Slowly I opened my eyes and looked at him. He was wearing his jeans but his belt was unbuckled and he was still naked from the waist up. I carried on gazing at him and feeling happy.

'I guess you didn't.' Sliding off the bed, he unhooked his phone from its charger. 'We need to report your stolen cards. What time does your workshop start?'

'Nine o'clock.' The thought of making it uptown to the Lincoln Center in less than ninety minutes brought me fully awake. Day one of my three-day course was on transferring old 35 millimetre film to a digital format. We would finish at one thirty, leaving the afternoons free.

'So we need a small miracle to get you there on time.' Orlando had his phone pinned to one ear. He grinned as he watched me jump out of bed and head for the bathroom.

'I can do it!' I yelled. 'Five minutes in the shower, five to dry my hair, five to put on make-up, five more to get dressed.'

'Really? I never saw you get ready in under an hour.'

'Watch me.'

Five minutes later I was towelling myself dry and experimenting with the controls on the hotel hairdryer. 'What are your plans for today?'

'Number one – to buy you a new phone.'

'So sweet,' I murmured, finger hovering over the On switch. Orlando was more together than me over practical stuff and he enjoyed fixing this kind of problem.

Gently he took the dryer out of my hand and put me well behind schedule with a three-minute kiss.

'Number two on my tourist to-do list is take pictures from Brooklyn Bridge. Number three, visit the Flatiron and Empire State . . .'

'Meet me outside the Lincoln Center, one thirty?' I checked as he handed over twenty dollars for emergency spending.

OK, so it was more like thirty minutes before we made our way to the elevator, but still impressive. I was wrapped up in scarf, hat and gloves, planning our subway route as we exited into the lobby.

'You have a visitor,' Mrs Waterman told us from behind her desk.

We thought she'd made a mistake until she pointed to Charlie Speke waiting by the front door.

'Whoa!' Orlando cried.

We caught sight of Charlie in profile, hands in pockets, scanning the rules of the B&B pinned up on the wall.

'No – it's not . . .' I began to tell Orlando. 'It's his stuntman double, the guy who paid for my taxi fare – I think.' My voice tailed off. Really, the resemblance to Jack Kane was mind-blowing.

'Hey, Tania!' Charlie's greeting was warm and relaxed. 'And you must be the missing boyfriend, Orlando?' he added as he came across the Persian rug to shake hands. 'Glad you finally showed up. Listen, I can see you're all fired up and ready to go but I'm glad I caught you before you left the hotel. I have something for you.'

'Dude!' Orlando still couldn't take his eyes off Charlie's face.

'Sorry.' Charlie clicked his tongue against his teeth. 'I'm always pissing people off this way.'

'No, no problem.' Swallowing and trying to act normally, still Orlando couldn't help shaking his head in disbelief. 'Do you ever – I mean, have you?'

'Faked it? Pretended I'm really him?'

Orlando nodded.

Charlie gave us his dimpled Jack Kane smile. 'I'd be lying if I said no. Sometimes with girls I meet in a bar. Just at first – maybe for a couple of minutes before I fess up. It's so wrong, huh?'

'No,' Orlando assured him. 'Dude, anyone would.'

'But hey, here are the passes Natalia wanted me to give you.'

'Passes?' I took what Charlie was offering and read the print on the top card. '*Siege 2* – Crew', with a bar code beneath.

'These get you past Security,' Charlie explained. 'It's like an admission into the non-public areas. Natalia's idea.'

'Why?' I asked. 'What did we do?'

Charlie found my amazement funny. In fact, he seemed permanently amused. 'It's not what you did, it's what you had done to you. I met up with Jack and Natalia last night at their hotel. Me and a few other guys on the crew, we all got together for drinks in their private suite. I happened to mention the story about you and Orlando watching the shoot and how you two got split up. When Natalia heard about the attack, she was kind of upset. Natalia's like that – she hates violence of any kind. So she said why not try to put it right and give you special passes for today?'

'She really doesn't need to do this,' I pointed out. 'It totally wasn't her fault. Besides, I'm OK.' I held up my hand and wiggled my wrist to prove it.

'Good to hear it. But Natalia wants your trip to New York to be memorable for all the right reasons and she thought this might do it.' Charlie looked as if he'd carried out his instructions and was ready to leave.

'Cool!' Orlando said. He'd got over the lookalike situation and seemed eager to accept.

'Except I have my workshop,' I reminded him.

'Well, listen – you two can think about it,' Charlie cut in. 'You have the passes. You decide.' There was a cab waiting for him at the kerbside, throwing out clouds of exhaust, red tail lights winking.

'Thanks,' Orlando told him as he made his exit. 'Tell Natalia we really appreciate it.'

'Be good to see you there,' Charlie threw over his shoulder as he jumped into the cab.

Then he was gone.

My course wasn't actually in the Lincoln Center but in a smaller building between the giant theatre complex and the Julliard School. It was a small, poorly funded place that stored archives and ran courses for movie obsessives like me. On the ground floor there was a cinema seating eighty people, currently running a biographical film about Andy Warhol. The rest of the building was for storage, with a few rooms dedicated to a variety of courses on the history and preservation of film.

Our tutor for the morning was a guy named Adrian Ross, and a fellow student on the course was . . . Macy Osmond!

I stepped in the elevator to take me to the sixth storey and there she was, with silver studs in her nose and ears and wild magenta hair.

'Tania?' she asked as she checked me out from head to toe – my black jacket, my dime-store striped scarf with matching hat and fingerless gloves, circa 1975.

'Macy!'

'What are you doing here?' we asked simultaneously.

'I'm studying film preservation,' I answered. 'The weekend course.'

'Me too,' she said.

Honestly, what are the odds? Except, when you think about it, she was definitely a movie fan like me, committed enough to stand out the whole morning in sub-zero temperatures, waiting for Jack Kane to arrive. And not just blockbuster movies, it turned out. She was also into indie films from Eastern Europe and Italy, especially recent low-budget videos shot on camcorders, which she told me about as we went up in the elevator.

'So you live here in New York?' I asked as we stepped out and walked along the corridor to the room where the workshop would take place.

'I wish. No, I'm from Idaho – Nowheresville. How about you?'

'Likewise. Nowheresville in Colorado – actually a town called Bitterroot.'

'So where did you find a guy like – what's his name – Orlando?'

I laughed and held the door open for her to walk through. 'He's from my home town.'

'Jeez, are there any more like him on the shelf?'

I liked it that she openly admired my boyfriend but not in a threatening way. It made me feel that I had good

33

taste. 'Orlando is a one-off deal,' I solemnly told her.

She sighed. 'So thank him for chasing after me to give me back my purse.'

'You can thank him yourself if you like. He's meeting me after the workshop. Why not come for coffee?'

'Deal,' she replied as Adrian Ross began his talk on film decomposition, shrinkage and chemical disintegration.

The morning was everything I wanted it to be and I was learning a lot – all excellent information to help me in my college major except for a thirty-second blip when our lecturer showed us a piece of footage from a movie from the silent era.

We're talking pre-1920, a melodrama starring a fragile, eerily beautiful actress named Lillian Gish – a girl with a halo of curls, huge eyes in a pale, heart-shaped face and a small, baby-doll mouth. In the scene we were studying, the camera shows her in close-up, acting out a combination of fear and despair. She's totally expressive and surrounded by shadows. The 35mm film clicked and whirred through the projector. It started to jerk and falter. Lillian Gish's terrified face froze.

And yet I saw those celluloid shadows keep on moving, closing in on Lillian, sliding from the screen and across the floor towards me, enveloping me in darkness. I caught my breath.

'Are you sure you're OK?' Macy whispered. She was sitting next to me so she got a good look at my pale face and trembling hands. She handed me her bottle of water. 'You're not going to pass out?'

'No, I'm cool.' The projector whirred back into action. The film moved on.

At the end of the morning I kept to my plan of meeting up with Orlando, and Macy came too.

'I hope you don't mind,' she told him. 'If three's a crowd . . .'

'No way.' He said he was happy to buy her coffee. 'You heard what happened to Tania yesterday afternoon?' he asked. And he told her the story.

'Shoot, that was my fault,' Macy sighed. Beneath the piercings and the delicate unicorn tattoo on the inside of her wrist, she was old-fashioned and demure. She actually did soften the word to 'shoot'. 'Orlando, if you hadn't split from Tania to play the good guy and give me back my bag, none of that would have happened.'

He shrugged. 'There's a silver lining. Did Tania also tell you about our special passes?'

'No way!' she cried as he described Natalia Linton's

generosity. 'Do you guys know how lucky you are!' Then she paused to think it through. 'They might even include you as extras in the scene they're shooting today. You could be diners in the boathouse. You'll be in a Jack Kane movie!'

'Wait – this is only a pass to get through security,' I reminded her.

'No, no. You'll get to meet Natalia and the kids on set, maybe even Jack!' Macy began to gabble and hyperventilate. 'Yeah, you'll be doing what a million other people would kill to do – get up close and personal with movie royalty. I'm telling you, it's so worth having your bag stolen!'

She was serious but I was laughing. I pushed my piece of white card across the table. 'Here, you have it. Go on set with Orlando.'

She gasped, touched the magic entry into her dream world with her fingertips.

'Take it. I can see it means a hundred times more to you than it does to me. Me, I'm happy to spend the afternoon at MoMA with Vincent while you two schmooze with the stars.' I had my own starry night, plus my own dark angel reasons for not going anywhere near the park again.

I should have checked this out with Orlando first,

I realized. A glance his way made me see that. He was silent, avoiding eye contact and fiddling with his coffee spoon.

To her credit Macy picked up on it too. 'No.' She withdrew her hand from the card. 'Thanks, but no.'

'So why not come along with us; let's all three go,' Orlando suggested, realizing that he'd come across as mean and looking at me intently now to see if I approved. 'Maybe we can sneak Macy in with us.'

'I should be so lucky,' she sighed, following his lead out of Starbucks.

There was no fresh snow today and the heaped piles of slush looked tired and dirty. The puddles were deeper, the sidewalks if anything more treacherous than when the flakes first fell and covered the patches of black ice with a crunchy white layer. Christmas carols were piped from every gift shop and hotel lobby as we walked along Central Park West towards a different entrance. *While shepherds watched their flocks by night, all seated on the ground.*

'Watch out for the—' Orlando warned Macy as, distracted by a giant Mickey Mouse dressed as Santa Claus in a toy-shop window, she walked straight into an overflowing trash can attached to a lamp-post.

The angel of the Lord came down and glory shone around.

Macy backed off from the lamp-post then tripped over the kerb. She laughed as the choir sang on about mighty dread and troubled minds. 'Go ahead, disown me, I don't blame you. Pretend I'm not with you!'

'Fear not,' said he . . .

We laughed with her and made a big thing of guiding her the rest of the way to the park gates. Macy, who looked so urban-cool, was turning out to be anything but.

'No way should they let you out on your own,' Orlando told her with a grin. But once we were in the park, he turned to me. 'This way we avoid the carousel,' he confided as he squeezed my hand.

You can see why I love him and miss him when we're apart and want to be with him always.

We joined a steady flow of people converging on the lake to catch another glimpse of Jack Kane. Again there was security tape stretched across the volleyball courts, a helicopter at rest and in the distance a gang of movie technicians by the boathouse, preparing to go to work.

'Jack came early today,' Macy sighed when she saw the empty helicopter.

Obviously she realized she'd missed her best chance of getting close to her hero again and I felt for her. I joined Orlando in thinking maybe we could sneak her past Security. At the same time I found Macy's celeb worship a little surprising in someone who otherwise seemed pretty smart – take her knowledge of obscure Eastern European films as an example.

We were threading our way through the mass of people standing right against a metal barrier separating them from the lake, having to shove a little but this time ignoring the cries of protest. When we came to two guys guarding a gap in the fencing, Orlando and I waved our passes, simultaneously trying to hide Macy and slide all three of us through.

Guy number one took my pass and scanned it while guy number two did the same for Orlando. They were chatting to each other and didn't seem to be taking their job too seriously until envy struck someone in the huddled crowd.

'Hey, the one with the red hair – check her pass!' a woman cried. Although she wore a thick jacket and scarf, her nose was almost blue with cold. 'Would you look at that,' she muttered in pure disgust.

The security guys went up a gear. Keeping hold of the two valid passes belonging to me and Orlando, they hauled Macy into the open to demand hers.

Feebly she felt in her pockets. 'It's here somewhere.'

'Try looking up your ass,' someone else in the crowd

mocked, followed by other suggestions.

'No pass, no entry,' the first security guy told Macy. He joined shoulders with his co-worker – together, dressed in heavy black jackets and staring down at her, they were like a military tank facing down an unarmed civilian in an iconic Tiananmen Square moment.

'Is she with you?' the bigger of the two guards asked Orlando, looking as if he was tempted to turn us back too for attempting something so dumb.

'Are you kidding? I've never seen her before,' Orlando shrugged.

In case you're running away with the impression that my boyfriend is Mister Perfect, there are many times like now when he unhesitatingly looks after number one. 'Let's go,' he told me before the security duo could change their minds.

So we were through without Macy, treading the hallowed ground that Jack and Natalia had just trodden, taking a path around the side of the lake, heading for the film set for *Siege 2*.

3

With my rational head on I was telling myself not to be too impressed. After all, Jack Kane and Natalia Linton were only human.

A member of the crew wearing headphones walked quickly towards Orlando and me, warning us to step clear of cables. A lighting technician ran through cues, flicking lights on and off. Production staff glanced over their shoulders at us as we reached the Loeb Boathouse steps and hesitated.

I was doing OK, keeping a cool head, absorbing technical details about camera positions when Natalia appeared in the doorway to a trailer beside the boathouse.

Maybe it was the flashing lights, maybe the unacknowledged build-up of excitement – all I knew for sure was that it happened again. One second I was normal, seeing what everyone else sees. Next thing I'm plunged into nightmare.

The ice on the reservoir cracks and monsters rise. It's Lake Turner all over again. There are skulls beneath the surface, drowned souls who didn't deserve to die. There are black water serpents with scaly, hissing heads, a creature with broad shoulders and claw-like hands heaving himself on to the bank. I'm in my dark angel's presence and there is nowhere to run.

My breath came short, my heart raced. I looked again at the smooth white lake, its surface unbroken.

'You must be Tania.' Natalia came down the steps and out into the cold to greet us. 'And Orlando. So glad you made it.'

Shaken and tipped off balance, heart still beating dangerously fast, I turned my back on the lake and followed Orlando as Natalia Linton led us into her husband's trailer.

Time for a catch-up on Natalia. There was a period, ten years ago, when she was a bigger star even than Jack. Growing up in Bitterroot, I'd seen a thousand pictures in magazines, copied the Linton hairstyle, read a hundred interviews, watched all of her movies. But nothing prepares you for meeting an icon in the flesh.

She was one hundred per cent stunningly beautiful. It hits you, takes your breath away. Unbelievable, you think. How is it possible for a human being to be so perfect?

'So, Tania, this is your first time in New York,' Natalia began after she'd invited us to sit down on a sofa under a TV screen playing a kids' Power Rangers video with the volume turned down. In a whirl of primary colours, Lycra-clad superheroes turned robotic and lifted up trucks, scaled tower blocks, flew through the air. Spotting a red Power Ranger toy on the arm of the sofa, she sprang forward to move it out of Orlando's way.

Natalia Linton – beautiful in a smooth-as-porcelain way. Taller than you would imagine, even more slender than you expect, with a mass of dark-red hair piled on her head and unbelievable green eyes. Today she was dressed down in designer jeans, high-heeled black ankle boots and warm grey sweater, with a flame-coloured scarf wound loosely around her neck. A handbag that must have cost the same as a small car sat on the floor beside her chair.

'I feel so sad for what happened to you yesterday,' she confided, idly pressing buttons on the toy man's chest and turning him into a caped crusader. 'We like to think that they cleaned up the city, but I guess we'll always have crime on the streets. You'll have seen the warnings on the subways – keep your purses and bags safe.'

She was soft-spoken, warm and generous. And in the trailer where she spent so much time with the kids while Jack was filming she'd surrounded herself with luxurious things – silk cushions with delicate Japanese embroidery of birds and flowers, soft russet-red and jade-green rugs, Tiffany lamps casting warm pools of light.

'Lucky Charlie came by when he did,' she added.

I fell into heartfelt thanks, stumbling over my words, feeling myself blush. Any coherent idea that I might not be overawed by Natalia Linton's presence had disintegrated. A quick glance at Orlando told me he was suffering the same reaction and then some.

'This is so nice,' Natalia sighed, smoothing a cushion with long, white tapering fingers. 'To be sitting here chatting with someone who's not a journalist or a critic or any kind of media whore. Charlie told me how sweet you were, Tania. He said how much I would like you.' She offered us coffee, which we turned down and she said good because the coffee they made on set was the worst and she couldn't drink it herself; she stuck mainly to hot water with a squeeze of lemon.

Then she asked Orlando about himself and sighed with envy when she learned he wanted to be a costume designer for the theatre. 'Great job!' she declared enthusiastically. 'And you must design for movies too.

We need talented newcomers – ones who give us costumes that don't half kill you. You know, the male fantasy-driven shape that no woman ought to be or ever was, plus wigs and stupid hats for historical dramas that cut into your head and weigh fifty pounds.'

OK, again – beautiful and charming, funny, smart and easy to be with. Plus all of the above. We were under her spell, scared to pinch ourselves in case we woke up.

'Here, put your number into my phone,' she told Orlando, handing it to him. 'I'll keep it on my contact list. Maybe our costume designer or even our make-up people can offer you work experience. Would you be interested in seeing how that works?'

Orlando nodded then entered his name and number, eager as a puppy dog. 'About the media whores remark – I guess you're no fan of the press?'

Natalia arched her eyebrows. 'What's to like? Did you see them in the hotel lobby earlier this week? They're like hunters with dogs; they hound us everywhere we go.'

'Nobody believes what they read,' I said hastily, sensing a whole lot of backed-up emotion.

'Even with the kids,' Natalia sighed. 'You'd think they'd respect our privacy when we're on vacation, on the beach, by the pool, having a meal in a restaurant. But no, they're up in their helicopters, zooming in on us. And everybody on the street has a camera phone, all wanting a piece of us. Hey, it comes with the territory, I guess.' However strongly she felt, which she obviously did, I gave her credit that she managed to wave it aside.

'No, it's OK. We understand.'

'Which is why I reach out to people like you,' she explained.

People like us? Normal, everyday joes. She'd struck a wrong note and for the first time I felt patronized. The movie goddess was making the assumption that we were naive kids from out of town, not really able to take care of ourselves.

'Oh sorry, I didn't mean . . .' she began before I'd even formulated the negative reaction. 'That came out all wrong.'

She finished speaking just as the trailer door opened and the oldest of Natalia and Jack's kids charged in, followed closely by the other two. Adam, Phoebe and Charlie – all adorable – threw themselves at Natalia, trampling on her designer handbag and scrambling over the arm of her chair.

'What came out all wrong, Mommy?' Phoebe wanted to know, snatching the Power Ranger toy from her hands. She was three years old, with her mom's colouring – a little china doll.

'Nothing. It wasn't important. Adam, take your shoes off before you climb on the furniture. Charlie, why have you been crying?'

The baby of the famous family wiped his eyes and tried to explain, though his vocabulary didn't run beyond 'Momma' and 'down'.

'He slipped in the snow and fell down,' Phoebe interpreted. 'But it's OK. Uncle Charlie was there.'

It seemed Charlie Speke was on hand to rescue other people, not just strangers in the park. He came up the steps into the trailer, filling the doorway and smiling warmly when he saw Orlando and me. 'Hey, Tania, you made it. How was your course?'

'Interesting, thanks.'

'The kids want cookies from the catering trailer,' he told Natalia. 'I told them we had to check with you first.'

'That's cool, but make sure they have just one each,' she told him, taking little Charlie on to her knee.

'Hey, kids, Mommy says one cookie is OK!' Uncle Charlie caught Phoebe as she launched herself from the chair then he scooped up the baby from Natalia's lap. 'You coming, Adam?' he asked, heading for the door.

As Charlie waited for Natalia's eldest son to catch up, Jack Kane himself came up the steps and into the trailer.

For a second, body-double Charlie and movie-star

Jack stood face to face, neither stepping to one side. I had enough time to study them and see that the only possible way to tell them apart was in the way they dressed. Charlie wore a plaid shirt, blue jeans and well-worn, chunky lace-up boots. Jack was in costume – black shirt with small pearlized buttons, black pants and black leather vest. He had a three-day stubble and dull, unwashed hair.

I guess I have to admit right away that I was disappointed in Jack Kane. You meet the hottest movie actor on the planet and you expect genuine star quality. Instead we got someone who looked like he hadn't slept in a week, with bags under his eyes and definite grooming issues. Still, I supposed he was in character for the movie, playing a hit man on the run.

'The kids want cookies,' Charlie told him as they pushed past their dad and rushed out of the trailer.

Jack frowned, then pinched the bridge of his nose. Heading for a high shelf to the right of the TV screen, he took down a bottle and used it to gesture towards us. 'What are they doing here?' Then he put the bottle to its intended use, drinking straight from it with greedy gulps.

'I made some new friends,' Natalia told him with a bright tone that seemed suddenly forced. 'Jack, meet

Tania – I'm sorry, Charlie did tell me your second name but I don't recall.'

'Ionescu.'

'And Orlando . . . ?'

'Nolan.'

'You think I give a crap who you are?' Jack Kane snarled, still drinking as he turned his back.

I gulped and tried to disappear into the Japanese cushions. So either Jack was a serious Method actor so deeply into his role that he chose not to break out of character between takes (I've read that some of the biggest stars work this way) or else – and this was a million times more likely – he was a deeply unpleasant, angry alcoholic on a mission to humiliate anyone stupid enough to cross his path. I'm making this call on one swift first impression, I know.

'We'll go,' I said, quickly standing up.

'No, please!' Natalia stared at Jack's back as if she wished she could wave a wand and turn him into somebody who didn't snarl at strangers and swear and drink. 'Pay no attention. Jack's bark is worse than his bite.'

'"Jack's bark is worse than his bite!"' he mimicked in a high-pitched voice. 'Actually, my bite is much, much worse than my bark and she knows it.'

I was forced to swallow hard and decide which way to go. Should we stick with Natalia's request for us to stay or follow our natural urge to get the hell out of there? I was shocked, scared, even a little horrified.

I mean, the moment Jack Kane had lurched into the trailer he'd shattered my dreams of how a movie idol should be, which was bad enough. But worse still, how often did those small kids see their dad like this? Plus, how sad Macy would be when I told her. All this ran through my mind in the length of time it took Jack Kane to raise the bottle to his lips again.

'Ha!' Jack laughed harshly at the shocked silence then put the bottle back on the shelf. 'Hang around, you two little lap dogs. Stay with my wife as long as you like. Idolize her like every other poor sap, fall at her feet and give her a fresh topic next time she gets together with her ladies who lunch – you two country hicks look like good comedy value to me. I'm out of here.' Making as if to leave, he tripped over one of the kids' toys strewn across the floor then stumbled towards the sofa where Orlando and I sat. Hard-core swearing followed.

Now I was beyond shocked, moving rapidly towards repulsion and wondering how, if this happened on a regular basis, Jack's minders managed to sober him up enough to deliver his dialogue when necessary and how on earth his PR team kept his serious alcohol intake out of the public eye.

Still swearing, he slumped on to the sofa between me and Orlando. 'Have you any idea how frickin' bored I am making this movie?' he growled. 'The director's an asshole. He keeps me hanging around day after day in this crappy sub-zero climate when I could be spending the build-up to Christmas in the Bahamas. You think I'm kidding?'

'No,' I assured him. 'I believe you.'

Jack grunted and squinted at me from under hooded lids. 'They give me lines a frickin' parrot could say. All I basically get to do is play with guns, shoot a few guys and screw beautiful girls. Any moron could do it.'

At the far end of the couch, Orlando shrugged.

'Today I'm thinking, what the hell? Get Charlie to stand in for the action sequences and some of the close-up work too. I mean, who's going to know the frickin' difference?'

'You want to go back to the hotel?' Natalia asked quietly, picking up her phone to contact the helicopter pilot.

'No, I don't want to go back to the hotel.' Jack mimicked her again, making her sound prim and disapproving. 'What the hell do I do back there except stare at a TV screen and drink more whisky?' He sloppily shifted position to turn his back on Orlando and stare directly at me. 'What was your name again?'

I felt the full force of his gaze – hazel eyes flecked with amber, long dark lashes, thick stubble on his chin. 'Tania Ionescu,' I reminded him.

'What kind of frickin' name is that?'

'Romanian. My dad was born in Bucharest.'

'Where the hell's that? Russia, right? Don't tell me – your dad's an oil zillionaire. Yeah, they're crawling all over the city in their Armani shades and Louboutin heels.'

'Romania's on the Baltic coast. My dad got American citizenship when he married my mom. He works in construction.'

'Well, there ain't a whole lot of that happening right now, not with the economy down the pan.' As Jack went on staring at me, his voice grew less slurred and he eased off the cuss words. 'Are all Romanian girls as beautiful as you?'

I stared back, unable to find a response. Really, the guy took my breath away for bare-faced sleaze.

He didn't seem to notice my reluctance to engage. 'Long black hair – that looks kind of Italian,' he went on. 'And you've got good skin, a great body. Hey, now I get it – you wormed your way in here because you're a waitress/wannabe actress and you see this as the fast route to fame!'

'Jack!' Natalia interrupted as he slid closer towards me. His knee was touching mine and his arm crept along the back of the sofa.

'Move right to the top of my list,' he went on, breathing in my ear. 'And I can see you're a smart kid – you know there's only one hoop you need to jump through to be an extra in my movie.'

'Jack!' This time Natalia stood up to make her point. 'I invited Tania on to the set today. She's not interested in anything you have to offer!'

He flicked his beautiful wife away with the back of his hand, not for a second taking his eyes off me. 'Hey, Tania, I'm serious – maybe you'll even get to speak a line or two. And take no notice of Natalia. My wife has a dirty mind. I'm talking about your acting experience – I'm not asking you to screw me.'

'Let's go.' This was too much for Orlando, who jumped up and headed for the door. Anyone would react like this if another guy made this sick-making move on his girl and it made no difference to Orlando that his 'rival' was a world-famous movie star.

'We're out of here.' I stood up in disgust, leaving Jack to topple sideways into the vacant space.

'Thanks for inviting us,' Orlando told Natalia as I joined him by the door.

Her eyelids flickered nervously. 'You're welcome,' she said with a forced smile. Behind that façade it felt to me as if she was begging us not to leave her alone with her drunken husband.

'Aw, come on!' Unsteadily Jack pushed himself up from the soft cushions. 'Why leave the party before it starts?' he asked Orlando and me as the door opened and an icy blast entered the trailer. 'Hey, look – here comes Charlie, right on cue!'

Natalia shivered then quickly recovered. The build-up of tension collapsed. She smiled and said hi to the girl who followed Jack's body double up the steps. 'Tania, Orlando, this is Charlie's sister, Gwen Speke. Gwen is a make-up artist.'

Breathing more easily and feeling Orlando relax beside me, I smiled at the newcomer, who looked nothing like her brother. Small, with fair curls escaping from beneath her suede, fur-lined hat, she was dainty and delicate where Charlie was strong and muscular, shy where he was open and laid back.

'Dude, that was good timing,' Jack told Charlie. 'Tania wants a part in my movie. You can fix that for her, can't you?'

'Actually, I don't,' I said before the situation ran away from me a second time. 'Orlando and I have to leave.'

'Oh my God, Tania the beautiful Romanian wannabe turned me down!' Jack wailed.

'So not funny,' Charlie muttered. He saw Jack heading towards the shelf with the whisky bottle and stepped across his path. 'Time to take a shower and straighten up, Jack. They need you on set in fifteen.'

'Tell them to go fuck themselves.'

'You tell them.' Charlie didn't miss a beat. 'You're the one with the multimillion-dollar contract. See how they like it if you screw this up one more time.'

Taking a step back, Jack smiled uneasily. 'Don't tell me my business. You and I both know they can't make this movie without me.'

Charlie gave an imperceptible shake of his head. 'So take a shower,' he insisted. Then he turned to his sister. 'Hey, Gwen, why don't you walk Tania and Orlando around the set,' he told her, 'while I straighten Jack out and take care of Natalia.'

'Sorry about that,' Gwen Speke told us at the steps to the boathouse. Across the lake the usual horde of Jack Kane fans still stood waiting for him to appear. 'You caught him on a bad day.'

'He has good ones?' Orlando asked sceptically.

'Oh yeah. Some days he can be totally charming. My brother swears he's witnessed him go up to fans to sign autographs and kiss their babies.'

'Sounds like you don't believe it,' I checked.

'I haven't seen it myself,' she confessed. She bit her lip and considered something for a while. 'Now that you're out of Jack's evil clutches, why not stick around and catch some filming?'

'What about . . . ?' Orlando jerked his thumb towards the Kane trailer.

'Charlie will fix him, no problem. Anyway, Jack's short-term memory is shot. By the time he makes it down those trailer steps, he'll have forgotten you two exist.'

We believed her and went with her for coffee in the catering trailer. The coffee was as bad as Natalia had said, but we soon warmed to Gwen, who told funny stories about the famous actors she'd worked on, giving us the gory lowdown on various cosmetic procedures until the Kane kids came running up to her.

'More cookies!' Phoebe pleaded.

'More!' little Charlie mouthed.

But Adam, at five, wrecked their high hopes. 'Mommy said just one,' he told them sternly.

Gwen spread her hands and pulled a face. 'Sorry, kids.'

So the little ones groaned and ran off again to pester a guy with a pair of headphones hung around his neck.

'Poor kids – I know,' Gwen confided as Adam drifted towards a window, pressed his nose against the cold surface and stared out over the frozen lake. 'People think they have everything they want, but really they live inside a bubble. They can't go anywhere, do things normal kids do. I'm not saying that Natalia isn't a good mom,' she added quickly. 'And thank God for my brother – he's her rock. She even named the baby after him.'

Frowning, I secretly wondered how that had gone down with Jack.

'Oh no!' Gwen seemed to follow my train of thought and laughed as she protested. 'That's funny. Charlie and Natalia – no way! I mean, how weird would that be?'

'For her to have an affair with a guy who's the body double of her husband?' Orlando caught our thread.

'Yeah,' I said, watching Phoebe run from the sound man to a girl with a clipboard and start the cookie thing over while Adam still stared out of the window. 'Very weird.'

But not impossible, I thought.

Spending the rest of the afternoon with Gwen was fun. Together we watched Lucy Young, an assistant director, run through a scene with fifty or so extras. It was a thirty-second sequence inside the boathouse café, which ended with Jack's character entering then getting into a brawl with an undercover cop, a role played by an actor named Rocky Seaton. We'd got close to Rocky when Gwen worked on him in the make-up trailer and found he didn't live up to his tough screen image, sitting there reading Tolstoy and talking politics with anyone who would listen.

He was good in his role though. When he walked on set and the lights came on, he transformed into a cold, calculating cop.

'Cool!' Orlando breathed as we watched Rocky narrow his eyes and alter the set of his jaw. We saw him tense up as Jack Kane's character walked through the door and began to make his way between the café tables. The camera caught Jack's back view – black-shirted, broad-shouldered.

'Jack or Charlie?' I whispered to Orlando. 'What's your guess?'

Orlando shrugged. Who knows?

Rocky stood up from his flimsy chair, full of menace. Jack/Charlie swayed and lurched against a table as he walked forward.

'Jack,' I muttered.

Cut!' the director barked and prepared everyone for take two.

After thirteen takes of Jack stumbling into things and fumbling for his gun, Orlando and I went back to find Gwen.

'You're leaving already!' she exclaimed, pouting as she glanced up from a magazine.

'It's four thirty,' Orlando pointed out.

'You're right. They'll soon have to quit – not enough daylight. How did Jack do?'

We both grimaced but said nothing.

'So thanks,' I told her, quickly moving on. 'And please thank Charlie when you see him.' It had been a fascinating afternoon. A few dreams had been shattered and I'd learned a lot, but on the whole neither Orlando nor I was sorry to be leaving.

Gwen put down her magazine, zipped up her jacket and put on her suede hat to walk with us down the row of trailers. She'd been right – the light was fading and it was growing colder. 'Come again tomorrow?' she enquired brightly, aiming the question at Orlando rather than me.

I tried not to bristle and say thanks, but no thanks.

'Tomorrow's Saturday, right?' Orlando checked.

'Yeah. We work twenty-four–seven until we get what we need.'

'So Tania has a workshop.'

Gwen dipped into her pocket and drew out two familiar-looking pieces of card – more crew passes, dated for the next day. She had her back to me so I had to imagine the bright smile to match her light, childlike voice. 'Which means you have time on your hands,' she told Orlando. 'Here, take these, why don't you?'

She said goodbye and turned back to the trailers before he had time to reply. We went on by the side of the lake until we reached the striped tape. 'Did you see that?' I exclaimed. By now I was bristling unashamedly.

'See what?'

'Gwen came on to you,' I complained. 'With me standing right there beside you.'

'No way,' he argued. He nodded thanks at the guy who let us through the tape then led the way through the crowd of hopeful spectators. 'Why would she come on to me?'

'Doh!' Because you're easily as good-looking as any guy on that movie set, I thought. And maybe Gwen likes your type – someone who keeps in the background, without the huge ego she's gotten used to dealing with in every actor she ever worked with. And your eyes – you just have to look at a girl and her knees turn to jelly. Orlando didn't know the power he had. I thought these things but kept them to myself in case he accused me of acting like a jealous bitch.

'Where do you want to eat?' he asked. 'Here or back in TriBeCa?

'I don't care,' I said. He seemed to have forgotten all about my carousel phobia and was walking towards the south gate. I was sore that he'd cut off any discussion about Gwen.

Music played, lights winked, the painted horses went round and round. I shuddered as I relived the moment of my mugging.

'Let's ride the subway to Hubert Street,' Orlando decided.

He knows but had ignored the fact that subways freak me out.

I don't like being below ground.

A million people ride the subways of New York without even thinking – more than a million; who knows how many each and every day. They read their ebooks and newspapers, step on and off without any of the knotted-up anxiety I feel about taking the right train and getting off at the correct stop. I don't like being rammed in, shoulder to shoulder with a thousand office and shop workers, staring into their armpits and breathing their stale air. As Natalia said back there in a different context: what's to like?

Unfortunately, Orlando and I hit the rush hour. We stood for ages on the platform, shuffling forward and finding that the doors slid closed on us just as we were about to step into the train. This happened twice.

'Let's go back up, take a cab,' I suggested.

Orlando shook his head. 'We'll get on the next train, no problem,' he assured me.

The next train rattled by without even stopping.

'Or we could walk,' I said. This is a rabbit warren. Crazy people throw themselves on to the tracks.

'We'll definitely make it on to the next one,' he promised.

A train appeared and shuddered to a halt. Passengers stepped out then we were carried forward in an impatient, jostling surge. We found standing room inside the coach. The doors closed and the train slid, clicked, rattled onward.

We were far from the surface, hurtling through a tunnel. There were hundred-storey tower blocks bearing down on us, the ground above our heads was a honeycomb of sewage systems and air vents as well as these snaking subway tunnels and cavernous stations. And bear in mind that the engineering of these subway trains is almost a hundred years old. Shake, rattle, roll.

When our train slowed down between stations, fellow passengers didn't even look up. When it ground to a halt and the lights began to flicker, a couple of people groaned at the delay.

Then the lights went out. We were in total darkness.

I feel the crushing weight of the earth above. I'm trapped.

The ground around me heaves with subterranean life. Pale, bloodless beings writhe, neither animal nor human. Their faces are white, the place where their eyes should be are dark holes. They surround me.

I struggle to get away but I can't move. It's the weight of the crumbling black earth. My ribs are crushed.

What are these silent creatures with empty eye sockets and open, wailing mouths? How long have they been in the earth?

And I recall the three words that accompany my dark angel wherever he goes – death, darkness, suffering.

Machines cut through rock, men without safety helmets hack out a tunnel, lay down mile after mile of steel rails, die when the roof collapses. They look up in terror as the rock shifts and splits. Boulders thud down from above. They smash skulls and crush ribs. All is darkness.

63

I'm pressed down, there is soil in my eyes, my mouth, my nose. I am buried alive.

The train lost power for thirty seconds – no more. When the lights came back on, Orlando took one look at me and knew he had to get me off the train. 'Next station,' he promised. 'Can you hang on until then?'

I could only nod and close my eyes. I heard the click of the wheels on the tracks, felt the coach jerk forward. My skin ran with cold sweat.

I have no recollection of how Orlando got me off the train and out of the station, up in the elevator on to the street.

'It's OK,' he said. 'Look, Tania, everything is OK.'

The streets were lit up for Christmas, frost sparkled on the sidewalks. There was a happy Friday night buzz in the air.

But everything wasn't OK.

'He's back,' I told Orlando.

He walked me across the street, out of my nightmare.

'He's inside my head.'

There was no longer any doubt in my mind – my dark angel had followed me to New York.

4

Who needs words when body language tells you all you need to know?

The moment I made my dark angel confession, Orlando held back from physical contact, walking towards our hotel with his head down, hands in pockets.

Meanwhile, I was under a dark shadow, fearing the swoop of eagle wings, the jaws of the wolf man.

'I'm so sorry,' I sighed when we reached the safety of our room. 'This is the last thing I wanted to happen.'

To be pursued across the country because I was born psychic, to feel that my battle with dark angels would never end.

Orlando shook his head and went to the window to stare down at the parked cars, the heaps of shovelled snow. 'I don't know, Tania. I'm just not sure.'

'What don't you know?' I kept my distance, had a

prickling sensation at the back of my neck that the axe might be about to fall on our love affair. If you think I'm overreacting, just bear in mind my extra-sensory gift.

'If I can go through this again.'

Think about it – one, two and now three attacks. The first time my dark angel made me his target was through Zoran Brancusi at Black Eagle Lodge. That's what the twisted, tormented spirit does – he finds a human form and enters it, builds his power base, prepares to ensnare innocent souls and drag them from their lovers and their families. He's flanked by fallen angels, also in disguise. He shape-shifts and creates a world of monstrous creatures; he's into total mind control.

And with Zoran it was fire. Flames leaping into the night sky, smoke billowing across mountains, and only me with my psychic powers to warn and try to rescue his victims – first my best friend, Grace, then Holly.

Yes – second time round it was Holly, and not fire but water. On that occasion Aurelie and Jean-Luc Laurent were dark angels in disguise, a twin threat. Their nightmare visions emerged from Lake Turner. Beneath the surface lay a sunken town. Corpses rose from the graveyard to entice the living into the icy depths.

I saw all this and suffered, fought back against the wolf-man vision until I discovered the double mask my dark angel was hiding behind. Through it all Orlando had been there at my side. He'd believed me, put himself through incredible dangers to protect me.

Fire and water. And now this third time I was convinced that my dark angel belonged to the earth. That's where he was hiding – crawling, writhing, emerging from the subways of New York City. And this totally sucked because I was a long way from home and he existed in total, suffocating darkness, so far without any human shape.

But worse than anything, here in this hotel room on Hubert Street my one and only love, my soul mate Orlando was warning me he couldn't take it; he'd had enough.

I sat on the bed and put my hands to my head.

'Maybe you're imagining it.' Still with his back turned, he denied the hell that I'd described. 'This could be some kind of panic attack.'

'So we're back to the old routine – you're saying I'm ill and I should see a doctor?' My voice was hollow. I felt my strength drain away.

'I tell you I don't know, Tania. I mean, you've been through a lot lately. Maybe it's messed with your mind more than we think. You could ask for help.'

I groaned because we'd been here before: anti-anxiety

pills and sessions with a shrink re-entered the frame. This is what Orlando was saying, though I know he didn't mean for it to wound me like it did. 'You don't believe me,' I said flatly.

He let out a long sigh. 'The truth is, I don't *want* to believe you,' he acknowledged. 'I want us to be free.'

Free of destroyers who gather at the shoulder of my dark angel, all driven by malice, all tormented since they fell from heaven. They are part of the cosmic battle between good and evil – an army of fallen angels.

'How can we be free?' I asked.

The axe hovered over us all evening but didn't fall. After we'd undressed and showered then got into bed Orlando relented and didn't give up on me after all.

'I will be here,' he promised, digging deep to find the strength he needed. 'It was my head telling me to back off and get you checked out by a doctor, but you know how I feel in my heart.'

'I wouldn't blame you,' I tried to tell him.

He put his arms around me and drew me to him, skin against skin, smooth and warm. 'I would. I'd blame myself. Tania, it's only with you that I feel . . . like a whole person. Without you I can't make sense of this crazy world. You know how much I love you.'

I smiled through tears. 'You really do?'

'I'm here. I'll stay. And promise me not to fall apart when I tell you this – I'm hoping, really, really hoping that this time you have got it wrong.'

I breathed out then laughed and caught my lip between my teeth. 'Wouldn't that be cool?'

He nodded and kissed me softly on my lips.

'I'll call home, ask my mom to make me an appointment with the doctor.' It would make Orlando feel better and anyway what harm could it do?

'You're not just saying that for my sake?' More kisses as we talked, and a falling backwards on to the pillows.

'Yep,' I confessed with a sad smile. I sank back on the bed and welcomed the weight of his body on top of me.

We made love, slept and woke early. Then, still snuggled under the warm quilt, we backtracked, talking through our action-filled stay in New York, discussing Jack Kane and wondering why Natalia didn't file for divorce.

'It's not the money,' Orlando said. 'I read a feature in a magazine: she's still up there with the top earners. Every time she makes a movie she banks millions of dollars.'

'Maybe it's better for the kids if she stays.' I came up with a major reason couples stay together.

'It didn't look that way. How is it better to see your

dad cussing and falling down drunk every day?'

'So maybe Charlie is part of the deal. If Natalia splits from Jack, she loses Charlie too? And you saw how much she depends on him.'

'Yeah, that complicates things.' Orlando sat up and swung his legs over the side of the bed.

'We don't know from the outside how it really is on the inside.' I happily fell into the safety of discussing other people's problems and avoiding our own.

Orlando agreed then switched to the practical. 'I spoke to the insurance company about your stolen phone.'

'You did? Thanks.'

'The bad news is, they said we need a crime number.'

'But I didn't report it to the cops.'

'We still could.'

I shook my head. 'I missed my chance. They'll ask why I left it so long.'

'"Because you don't have a snowball in hell's chance of finding the guy,"' Orlando quoted what he would have told the cops. 'They'll say, "We have killers and terrorists to pursue. Why are you wasting valuable NYPD time?"'

'So the insurers won't pay out. Every day you learn something useful.' I shrugged then wriggled across the bed, put my arms around his waist and tried my hand at a none too subtle piece of emotional blackmail. 'So last night I said yes to popping a few pills, right?'

'Ye-es?' he mumbled. Turning towards me, he twisted a lock of my hair round his finger and for once he didn't see where I was going.

'That means I'm due payback – I can ask you to do something for me.'

'Anything!' he sighed recklessly. 'What do you want me to do – run through fire? It wouldn't be the first time.'

'Hush.' I reached up and put my hand to his lips. 'I'm serious. What I'm asking, it's not huge.'

'Ask away.'

I hesitated, pulled back and made him look me in the eyes. 'I'm asking you: don't shut me out. Let's at least keep on talking about the dark angel thing – the possibility that he's back in my life.'

Orlando closed his eyes then slowly opened them and held my gaze.

'Say yes,' I pleaded. 'Right now I'm so scared, I need you to be with me every step of the way.'

He nodded slowly. 'Go get a shower,' he sighed. 'We'll talk later.'

I pushed too hard – I know it.

'I've been thinking,' I told Orlando over breakfast.

'Uh uh.'

In the dull early morning light of a New York winter, Orlando and I were in a small kitchenette across the hallway from Mrs Waterman's reception desk where we could help ourselves to fresh bread rolls and coffee. 'I've been looking back over the last couple of days and I can definitely identify when I got my first contact.'

'It's seven thirty a.m.,' he mumbled. 'And already you want to talk?'

'Yeah, and you promised.' After feeling scared and majorly sorry for myself, I'd got my head together and started to run through all the dark angel possibilities. 'So I'm obsessed,' I admitted. 'Fixated even. But you did say we could discuss this.'

'I guess this is later,' Orlando agreed reluctantly, perching on the stool by the breakfast counter, looking about as hot as it's possible for any guy to look in a white T and blue jeans, with Timberland boots and a black fleece jacket slung over one shoulder as he sipped his coffee. 'Shoot.'

'I was by the carousel, and it came to me as clear as any of the other times. Something scary was in the air and I picked it up in a flash. I got the cold sensation that makes my flesh creep. My head started to spin. That's when the carved horses came to life.'

Orlando thought it through with me then tried out a

theory based on the evidence I was giving him. 'So it's the mugger – he's the dark angel? We're not looking for the leader of a cult or anyone with power and charisma. This time, he's totally anonymous.'

'It's possible.' I was so deep in thought that I didn't even see our landlady walk down the hall with today's *New York Times*.

'They closed JFK and LaGuardia,' she commented as she passed by. 'Fresh snow on the runways. All flights cancelled.'

Practically ignoring Mrs Waterman, I hurried on with my train of thought. 'Then there was something else I didn't tell you about. It happened during yesterday's workshop.'

'Really?' Orlando's one-word question came across as a rebuke.

'I didn't mention it because when we met up at lunchtime Macy was with us,' I reminded him. 'I wasn't going to say in front of her, "By the way, evil shadows slipped off the movie screen and crept right into the lecture room where I was sitting. They surrounded me and make me shake with terror."'

'Ssh!' he warned as the landlady crossed the hall again.

'So now I'm telling you,' I hissed. 'The film projector broke down and the shadows came off the screen. It was so scary I almost passed out. Macy asked me if I was OK.'

'So this has nothing to do with the guy who attacked you in the park?' Orlando checked. 'There's no connection.'

'No, totally separate. And then there was a third time when we were walking across the film set, right by the reservoir, just before we met Natalia. I got a vision of the ice cracking and these horrible creatures rising out of it . . .'

'Are you done?' Orlando cut right across me. With a meaningful glance towards the landlady he finished with his coffee cup, put on his jacket and led the way out on to the street.

'Actually, I'm not,' I protested. 'There was also the time on the subway when I couldn't breathe . . .'

'I hear you.' Stopping at the bottom of the brownstone steps, he took my hand and spoke more gently. 'And so, as it happens, did Mrs W.'

I shook my head. 'How could she hear me? I was whispering.'

'Maybe she can lip-read.'

'Seriously?'

'No. Yes. I don't know. Anyway, she was tuned into our conversation,' he insisted. 'And she was giving us a weird look when we left – like we were

74

aliens or something. Didn't you see?'

'So now you're saying we'll be thrown out of our room, we'll have to spend our last nights in New York on the street and it's all my fault.' I marched angrily down Hubert Street, slipping and sliding as I went.

Orlando soon caught up with me. 'Jeez, Tania, what's eating you today?'

'You know what's eating me.' I was seeing dark angels in every shadow, round every corner. I shook when we entered the subway; they were on the train with me, lurking in the tunnels – creatures you only see in nightmares and which wake you up with a scream.

'So?' Macy stood at the classroom door and greeted me impatiently.

'So this is the second day of our course.' I grinned, deliberately sidestepping the obvious question and trying to lighten my mood after the early morning, intense conversation with Orlando. 'Let's hope we learn something interesting.'

'So, in the flesh . . . ?'

'What? Who are we talking about? Oh, you mean Jack Kane!'

She blocked the doorway, desperate for details. 'Come on, Tania, quit fooling. After you and Orlando

75

got through Security, how close did you get to the main man?'

'This close.' I teased her by showing a distance of about four centimetres between my thumb and forefinger.

'Jeez! Really? That close!'

'Jack sat on the same sofa, right next to me.' I couldn't help laughing at Macy's expression – a mixture of amazement, envy and disbelief.

'Where were you? How come? What did he say to you?'

'We were in his trailer with Natalia. We met his kids. Then we spoke with the screen god himself.'

'Oh my God, Tania! His trailer! Are you for real?'

'I know – totally cool, huh?' At first I'd planned to play along with Macy's hero worship of Jack Kane only for a short time, before I gave her the real picture, alcoholic warts and all. But as we got deeper into the conversation, I found I was in no hurry to smash her precious dream into sharp, nasty little pieces. It was her face that stopped me – so shiny, bright and full of little-kid wonder beneath the kohl and mascara – that I knew it would be too cruel.

'So what did Jack say?'

'He asked our names. Yeah, and then he offered me a role in the movie.' I threw this in casually, knowing her jaw would drop still further.

'Tania, no! Didn't I tell you that would happen?'

'I said no.'

'You said no! But you have a great face for the screen – so photogenic.'

'I told him we were only in town until Monday.'

'B-b-but . . . you're missing a chance in a million – you know that.'

'I guess I wasn't thinking straight,' I said, still trying to keep up the illusion.

'And close up, was he drop-dead, you know, gorgeous – even hunkier than in his movies?'

Luckily at this point I spotted our lecturer, Adrian Ross, heading down the corridor. Here was my escape from a game that was getting out of hand. 'Jack was . . . unbelievable,' I told Macy as I stepped by her into the classroom.

And one over-the-moon Jack Kane fan followed behind with her dream intact.

By coffee time both Macy and I had had our fill of Adrian's two major topics for the day: abstract art house movies and East Village grunge flicks. We stood in the small, sixth-floor lobby next to the elevator, close to the Coke machine.

'So what are you doing for Christmas?' My question was a time-filler before we returned to the classroom for more grunge.

'I don't know yet. I haven't decided.' Macy looked down and fiddled with the ring-pull on her Coke can.

'I'll be in Bitterroot with Orlando – Christmas and New Year.'

'You're lucky. I don't have anyone like him in my life right now.'

'So you'll spend time with your family?'

'No family either,' she muttered. 'My dad left home when I was eight. My mom died.'

'Oh, Macy, when?'

'January this year.'

'That's so sad. I'm sorry.'

'Hey.' She threw her can into the trash with a sudden movement. 'I still have Mom's house, so at least there's a place to call home after I'm done with New York.' She looked up at me with a defiant tilt of her head. 'No pity, please. I'm totally fine where I'm at in my life – free to visit with friends, free to study.'

'That's cool,' I agreed. But all through the next session I was distracted by the sad thought of Macy home alone on Christmas Day.

*　*　*

I stuck with her as the lecture finished and the classroom emptied out. 'Come for coffee,' I told her, pressing the elevator button and hearing it whir between floors.

'No – you and Orlando, you guys need time together.'

'Come!' I insisted, stepping into the elevator.

But then a bunch of fellow students pushed ahead of Macy, leaving her stranded in the lobby as the doors closed and we went down to ground level. Planning to go back up to the sixth floor to collect her, I waited for the elevator to empty then pressed six on the control panel. There was a jolt. Instead of rising again, the arrow on the panel told me that we were headed for the basement. I frowned, wondering how long Macy would wait before she gave up on the elevator and headed for the stairway.

Another jolt prepared me for the doors to open. Sure enough, I was below ground, staring out at a dimly lit, empty car park. No one waited to step into the elevator so I chose the sixth floor and pressed again. The door stayed open. Nothing happened.

Great! I stepped outside, took a look around, stepped back in and tried the control panel again. Taking a second look at the concrete pillars and oil-stained floor, and the absence of cars, I knew there was something odd but it took a while for me to work it out – the car park must be empty because the elevator up to street level was out of order. Except that, weirdly, it had decided to bring me down here in the first place. That was when the first creepy, skin-crawling sensation began.

It started at the back of my neck as I finally gave up on the lift buttons and set out to find a stairway out of there. Then, just as I was crossing an open area towards what looked like a pedestrian exit, the yellow safety lights started to flicker and cold panic spread through my whole body. With a final glimmer the lights went out. I was in total darkness.

I hear voices yelling out a warning. Rocks fall, the roof caves in.

I see a faint beam of light and crawl towards it. Behind me, boulders scrape and grind, falling and forming a barrier. Ahead there is a pocket of air. Three men lay curled on their sides. Their faces are bruised and cut. Their eyes are dark with fear. One has a flashlight. He shines it on my terrified face.

'We're dead men,' he gasps. 'We're dust.'

All around us there are creatures who never saw the light. Bloodless, the same as the first time I saw them, but now I have longer to breathe in the dust and see them advance, writhing like snakes, burrowing through the earth towards me. They want me and I can't run, I can't move. I'm staring at death.

The lights in the basement car park flickered back on.

In my panic I saw that I'd lost my sense of direction, turned away from the exit and blundered towards a support pillar. Now I leaned against its rough, cold surface, my breathing shallow, my heart hammering against my ribs.

I didn't see but I sensed that there was someone down here with me, close to where I stood. I picked up small movements, body heat and almost inaudible breathing.

Still no one emerged from the shadows. I swallowed hard to beat the constriction in my throat then tried to take a deep breath. Fixing my sights on a red Exit sign beyond the parking bays, I inched towards the door.

He sprang from behind the nearest pillar, bare-headed this time and wearing a black T and jeans, planting himself in front of me, blocking my way. It was the same small but stocky mixed-race guy minus the hunter's hat and leather jacket. And today he held a knife.

He stood three paces from me, his face blank of expression, the hand with the blade raised slightly.

I had enough time to register a few thoughts. How unexpected this was, after rock star Zoran Brancusi and the charming, elegant Laurent twins. This guy was nobody – a punk with a knife. I hadn't expected this, then I realized how clever it was for my dark angel to take an everyday shape, lurk in the shadows and finally corner me without fireworks or fanfare in an underground car park, alone and helpless. I knew with total clarity that this could be the end.

My oh-so-ordinary dark angel didn't open his mouth to gloat or deliver a victory speech. Instead, he stared at me with expressionless eyes, keeping the knife raised.

The only thing I could do was cut and run. I turned back the way I'd come, away from the Exit sign towards what I hoped was the elevator shaft. I sprinted in the dark between concrete pillars, across empty parking bays. When I didn't hear my attacker's footsteps coming after me, I glanced over my shoulder to see that he was in fact right there behind me. I stopped suddenly, turned and swung my bag at him. Its buckle caught the side of the face and I was shocked to see blood spurt from a cut above his eye.

It ran down his cheek and into his mouth. He touched it with his fingertips, giving me a split second to run on ahead and hope that he would lose track of me beyond the next pillar. I got my bearings, spotted the sign for the elevator, allowed myself to hope.

Then the doors opened and Macy stepped out.

'There you are, Tania!' she cried. 'I've been up and down, up and down in the elevator trying to find you. What the hell happened to you?'

5

Macy appeared and the guy with the knife ran off. White striplights came on and flooded the underground car park.

'You look terrible. What happened?' she asked.

I stumbled into the elevator with her. The door closed behind us and I felt the lift judder then rise. 'I just ran into the guy who stole my phone – the one in Central Park. He had a knife.'

'You're sure it was the same guy?'

'One hundred per cent.' I still shook with fear and felt a big knot form in my stomach and threaten to rise into my throat.

'You have a stalker!' Macy cried, pulling me out of the elevator through the ground-floor lobby and out on to Lincoln Plaza.

'Oh God, I feel nauseous!'

'Take deep breaths. Is that better? OK, now quickly, Tania – call the cops!'

'Wait. First let me speak with Orlando.' Before I did anything else, I needed to hear his voice. But when I called his number, it went straight on to not-available-and-speak-after-the tone. 'Orlando, it's me,' I said hurriedly. 'Call me. I want you to meet me outside the Lincoln Center.'

'Now the cops,' Macy insisted. While I'd been trying to contact Orlando she'd had a better idea than dialling 911. 'We get a cab to drive us to the nearest station. You tell them face to face.'

I was too shocked and confused to argue and soon I found myself in a taxi with Macy beside me asking the driver which precinct we were in and telling him to drive us the fastest route to the cop station.

But you get nowhere fast in Central Manhattan. We hit all the red lights and got stuck behind guys riding Harleys all dressed up as Santa Claus – a phalanx of them stretched out across the street. The cab driver had seen all that city life has to offer so eight office-party Santas on motorbikes drew no reaction.

'How far now?' Macy demanded. She kept checking to see if I was still about to vomit or pass out. 'Preferably the latter,' she muttered, uncertain of the level of sympathy we'd get from our driver if I puked all over his cab.

Looking in his mirror and judging the situation on the back seat, he cut down a couple of side alleys and when he found a delivery van blocking our way he swore and blasted his horn. No one came so he gave a second blast, again without a result. He turned and told us it would be faster to get out and walk. 'Take a left. Walk two blocks and you're there.'

Macy thanked him, paid the fare and dragged me down the alley. Five minutes later we were facing a female cop across a high counter.

'My buddy is being stalked by a maniac with a knife,' Macy announced.

The cop didn't look up from her computer screen. 'Anybody get hurt?' she asked. She had a great figure and wore her uniform well. Her blonde hair was held back in a neat ponytail and her face had a Scandinavian look – high forehead, small nose, strong cheekbones, pale-grey eyes.

'He had a knife,' Macy repeated. 'If it hadn't been for me stepping out of the elevator and messing with his plan, he'd totally have used it.'

A click of the mouse told us the good-looking cop had finished her task and logged off. 'Anything stolen?' she enquired.

'Yesterday he snatched her phone and her bag – the same guy.'

'And today?'

'Zilch,' Macy admitted. 'But you heard what I said about the knife?'

The cop ignored Macy and focused on me. 'You have his name?'

I shook my head.

'Any means of identification?'

Another shake of my head made her sigh so I did my best to fill in some details. 'He was about nineteen or twenty, I guess. Around five eight or nine, mixed-race, a bodybuilder type.'

'Is that all?'

This time I nodded.

'So you want me to arrest the half-million kids in Manhattan who fit this description?'

'No, but she needs some protection,' Macy cut in. 'When I showed up, the stalker took off. He's still out there somewhere.'

Seeing how pale and shaky I was, the cop decided to go easy on me. 'You're from out of town, right? What's your name and how old are you?'

'I'm Tania Ionescu. I'm eighteen and I'm from Bitterroot.' I was trying hard to stay calm but my voice croaked and my hands shook.

'That's Colorado, right? Actually, I have an uncle in Bitterroot. It's a pretty place. And you're here in town with your buddy . . . ?'

'My name's Macy,' she volunteered. 'No, I just met Tania on a film course. She's here with her boyfriend, Orlando.'

'Orlando . . . ?'

'Nolan,' I told her.

'And Orlando is . . . where exactly?'

Realizing I didn't know the answer to this, Macy jumped in again. 'Right now he's probably on set at the Jack Kane movie they're shooting in Central Park.'

The cop clicked her tongue but said nothing.

'It's true. He and Tania got special passes to go on set. They met Jack Kane, they spent one-on-one time with Natalia Linton. Tell her, Tania – it's the absolute truth!'

This was it – the moment our cop decided there was probably no case here and she was dealing with a couple of celeb-crazed fantasists. 'So what I suggest you do now,' she said, directing her attention back to me and making it clear that the police would take no action, 'is take the subway to Central Park, find your boyfriend and make sure you two stick together for the rest of your trip. Don't walk the streets alone, OK?'

I nodded.

'You're not going to even look for this stalker guy?' Macy demanded.

'I'm going to file the theft of the phone and the bag. I'm going to give you a reference to take to your insurers.'

'Cool. Thanks.' I jumped in before Macy could protest. 'Sorry we wasted your time,' I told the cop.

'You didn't,' she replied, in a tone that clearly meant 'you did'. Then she created a file and typed the bare details, gave me a printout containing a crime number. 'Say hi to Jack Kane from me,' she kidded as Macy and I left the building.

We didn't follow the cop's advice to take the subway back to the park. Instead we walked, me constantly checking my phone to pick up a call from Orlando, Macy quizzing me about my subway phobia.

'You get claustrophobic, right?'

'Kind of. I hate the whole idea of being underground.'

'The same way a lot of people freak out over heights. With my mom it was spiders, moths and driving her car. Stupid, huh? It got so she wouldn't exceed twenty miles an hour. She broke out in a sweat every time she had to overtake another vehicle, even a bicycle. It drove me nuts.'

'I'm sorry about your mom,' I said quietly.

'Losing her was tough,' she admitted. 'Breast cancer. But promise me you don't think this is weird – we're still in contact.'

'Don't Walk.' The red hand held us up as we tried to cross East 72nd Street. Steam rose from an air vent and we heard a train rattle beneath our feet. 'In contact, how?' I asked warily.

'You've heard of spiritualism, right?' Macy took out a packet of gum and offered me some. 'You know you can visit a medium and they put you in touch with the spirit world?'

'Walk', the yellow light ordered. We stepped over a frozen puddle and crossed the street.

'These people are psychic – you probably know. They pick up messages from members of your family who have passed. I know how crazy that sounds. Before this happened to Mom no way did I believe it.'

'But now you do?'

'Totally,' she said, glancing at me to judge my reaction. 'Actually I talk to Mom all the time.'

'That's not weird,' I assured her. 'As a matter of fact, I'm into that psychic stuff myself.'

'So who passed? Who do you talk to on the other side?' Macy sounded eager to know.

'I don't talk to anyone. They talk to me.'

'You're an actual medium? Wow, tell me more.'

I hesitated. 'I don't usually admit this to people.'

'OK, cool. If you don't want to talk – no problem.' She stepped out under a weak winter's sun, bold and bright. Her red hair and silver face studs marked her out from the monochrome crowd.

'But I think you'll get it.' I decided to take a risk. 'The spirits I'm in contact with – they're angels.'

She had another 'wow' moment, which almost led her into a collision with another pedestrian. 'Angels, as in wings and halos?'

'Not exactly, but the good ones – they appear in a weird silver light. Usually I have one special good angel to protect me,' I explained.

'From what?' She picked up another hesitation.

'There's also an army of dark angels,' I explained. 'They're tortured souls who fell from heaven and can never get back. Now they're totally evil.'

'And you can see and hear them, as if they're here in the flesh?'

I nodded. 'I feel them all around but I never know what shape they'll take. They're clever that way. They know I have this special connection with their world, that I'll fight them whenever they try to win more souls on to their side.'

'They do that?' Macy whispered with a shudder.

'They tried it with two friends of mine. They feed off young love and will try to drag you on to the dark side by showing up in your world as that perfect someone you'll fall in love with. They flatter you and get inside your head, make you fall out of love with the guy you're already with. Then they seduce you.'

Macy gasped. 'Are you serious?'

'Yeah. But if you make love with a dark angel you're finished. After that he has your soul.'

'What about your body?'

'He doesn't care about your body. It dies.'

'Thanks, I'll remember that,' she sighed, half kidding. There was a pause and then she said, 'And I was worried you'd think I was weird!'

'Sorry if this bothers you. Maybe I shouldn't have . . .'

'No, don't be sorry.'

'Sometimes I wish it wasn't like this,' I admitted. For a moment I pictured how romantic and easy life would be for me and Orlando if all we had to think about were starry nights and midnight swimming in the lake.

'Tania, I think you're amazing – I'm blown away,' Macy said. 'But does it mean that you always have to look out for the next time?'

'Always.' I nodded.

'And I guess you can't take things at face value any more?'

'That's the worst thing – not knowing who you can trust.'

'Except Orlando, I guess. You know you can trust him.'

Macy had read my situation exactly right. 'Without him I wouldn't get through this.'

She nodded and forged her way through the crowds. 'So let's go find him,' she said.

We made it to the Lincoln Center by two p.m. The wide plaza was thronged with tourists and it took me a while to work out that Orlando wasn't there.

'Check your phone,' Macy told me.

I checked and at last there was a text. Great news. ☺. Natalia got me an actual internship in the make-up section. ☺☺. Come to park, bring your new buddy. Collect passes from Security. See you on set xox

'Show me,' Macy said when she saw me frown. After she'd read the message she practically cartwheeled across the plaza. 'A pass for me!' she crowed. 'Come on, Tania, let's go.'

I couldn't have stopped her even if I'd wanted to. I

had to run to keep up as we dodged traffic, ignored the crossings and made it in record time to the volleyball courts in Central Park, where there was the usual crowd hoping for a glimpse of Jack Kane.

As it happened, we arrived at the exact same moment the star's helicopter flew in. People forgot whatever manners they might have had and shoved forward to get a picture, leaving space for me and Macy to approach the security guards.

'My boyfriend said to collect two passes from you,' I told the nearest one – not the same guy as yesterday but a similar bulked-up bodyguard type with a shaven head and no neck.

'Look, Tania, look!' Macy was practically squealing with excitement as the chopper blades clunked to a halt and her hero stepped out.

The security guy shrugged. 'That's the first I heard,' he muttered. 'Hey, Mike – you got any passes?'

Mike shook his head and turned away.

'He's so gorgeous!' Macy breathed, following Jack's every move as he crossed the courts and headed for the row of trailers.

'But my boyfriend is already on set,' I begged. 'He told me there were passes.'

'Yeah, you have to let us through.' Macy joined the

argument by ducking under the security ribbon and pushing right up against big Mike.

It could have got ugly, until a familiar figure strode across the courts towards us. 'It's cool, guys,' Charlie said as he produced two precious pieces of card in their plastic covers. 'The girls are with me.'

'Good to see you, Tania.' Jack Kane's lookalike steered me and Macy past the film crew setting up for an exterior shot of the boathouse. We were headed straight for the trailers. 'Orlando's busy making a name for himself with my sister in our make-up department so he sent me to find you.'

Macy was doing what everyone did when they first saw Charlie – she was staring at him open-mouthed, even though today he had played down the Jack Kane similarity with a grey knitted hat pulled down on his forehead and a thick grey fleece jacket.

'Cool,' she breathed when Charlie left us outside Jack's trailer. 'Actually, he's cute in his own right!'

'With Jack Kane you get two for the price of one.' I grinned then looked round again for Orlando. I saw him at last, heading in our direction with Charlie's sister, Gwen.

'Tania, where were you?' he exclaimed.

'Where was *I*?'

'Yeah, I called you three times before I finally left you a text.'

'I was in the lecture room. Anyway, where were you?' I countered. 'Why did you switch off your phone?'

'I was busy working. There's a no-phones-on-set rule.' Orlando was high on adrenalin, obviously dying to tell me the details of his morning's work experience, which meant he didn't pick up the silent signals that I needed to speak with him alone. 'Gwen was explaining how they get continuity in the wardrobe and make-up departments. It's incredibly detailed and technical, really cool.'

Any other time I would have loved to share the excitement that shone in Orlando's grey eyes, but not right now. 'Macy and I went to the cops,' I muttered under my breath. 'I got mugged again.'

He came down to earth with a bump. The light went out of his eyes. 'How come? Are you OK?'

'It was the same guy.'

'Tania has a stalker!' Macy's voice was loud enough to attract the attention of Charlie Speke, who had gone into Natalia and Jack's trailer and come out again with the three kids. 'We told the cops she needed protection but they totally didn't listen.'

Orlando took me quietly to one side while Macy went

95

on telling Charlie and Gwen what had happened in the car park. 'This stalker guy – are you still thinking he might . . . the dark angel connection, you know?'

I nodded. 'But I don't want to talk about it here. Later.'

Orlando picked up our role switch and gave a wry grin. 'OK. So was Macy with you when it happened?'

'No, but I'm glad she showed up when she did. She stepped out of the elevator and scared the crap out of him.'

'Excellent.'

'Macy's cool.' I glanced her way and saw that she was fully into retelling the story of our underground adventure. 'I'm thinking maybe I'll invite her to Bitterroot to spend Christmas.'

Orlando raised his eyebrows.

'She has nowhere else to go,' I explained.

'. . . and the knife was this big!' Macy was exclaiming. 'The kind a deer hunter would carry to butcher his kill. He was one scary guy!'

Things moved on pretty quickly from there. It had started snowing so the kids – Adam, Phoebe and little Charlie – clamoured to build a snowman, which meant Charlie and Gwen had to help them. Gwen dragged Orlando in, and soon grown-ups and kids had their full attention on building the biggest snowman in New York.

'When he's finished, I'll go to the wardrobe section and find a hat and scarf for him,' Gwen promised.

'A pink hat!' Phoebe clamoured. 'Our snowman is a girl.'

'That would make her a snowlady,' Adam, the child-adult pointed out.

'Mom, we're making a snowlady!' Phoebe called to Natalia, who had emerged from the trailer to see what was going on.

'More snow,' she sighed, stretching out her palm to catch flakes. 'I just know they're going to keep the airports closed.' Seeing me standing with Macy, she joined us. 'We're scheduled to fly out of LaGuardia Monday.'

The snow fell and I introduced Macy to Natalia Linton, who was dressed today the way a screen goddess should dress, in a full-length cream wool coat with a white fur collar and big Russian hat to match. Beneath the hat her porcelain face was flawlessly made up.

For once Macy was so overawed that she was tongue-tied. She left the talking to me. 'Thanks for getting Orlando some work on set,' I told Natalia. 'You've no idea how much this means.'

'Orlando is a sweetheart,' she replied. 'I wanted to give him the chance to let his talent shine through.'

Glancing across at the busy snowlady builders, I saw Gwen take time out to scoop up a handful of snow, pack it into a ball and throw it at Orlando. She made a direct hit and pretty soon he'd launched his own missile back at Gwen. The snowball knocked off her suede hat, which Charlie picked up and threatened to put on his own head. Phoebe and little Charlie giggled while Adam stayed out of the fun and games, doggedly packing more snow on to the snowlady's body.

'Let's help Adam,' Natalia suggested to Macy and me.

But we didn't have the chance before the trailer door opened again and Jack Kane came out.

OK, Macy, you're in for a shock, I thought grimly. Instead of glamour, think grunge. For charm, try sleaze.

'Frickin' snow!' Jack grumbled, pulling his jacket across his chest as he looked up at the grey sky and the whirling flakes. 'This weather is going to give Larry a coronary.' He almost slipped on the icy step then regained his balance.

'Larry King – he's directing this movie,' Natalia explained. 'They didn't forecast more snow; it'll throw the schedule.'

After his small skid on the step, Jack didn't stagger or blunder into anything, I noticed. He was clean-shaven and alert, so maybe he was sober. Major transformation.

Beside me Macy held her breath big time.

Natalia called him across. 'Jack, you remember Tania? She was here yesterday. And this is her friend Macy.'

'Hey, Tania, sure I remember you.' Jack gifted me his dimpled, movie-star smile. 'And that's your boyfriend rolling in the snow with my kids, right?'

Phoebe, Charlie and Gwen had grabbed Orlando by the legs and dragged him to the ground. Now the kids were rodeo-riding on his back.

Jack laughed good-naturedly. 'So, Macy, are you having a good day?'

'Totally!' she said breathily. 'I love every movie you've been in. I'm a total fan.'

'Don't let my wife hear you say that,' he warned with that special smile that oozed confidence. 'She tells me my head is way too big already.'

'I'm right, it is,' Natalia teased, with none of the tension in her voice that I'd picked up yesterday. 'Your ego is out of control.'

'So are we going to work today?' Jack called to his body double. 'Charlie, go ask Larry if he needs me.'

'Dude, you only just arrived,' Charlie pointed out. But what Jack wanted, Charlie did, so he took Adam along with him to find Larry King.

Meanwhile, Phoebe came running up to her daddy.

'Help us make our snowlady!' she begged and tugged at his hand. 'Please, Daddy, please!'

Jack pretended to resist, pulling back then suddenly letting go. She tumbled backwards into the snow, but before the laughter turned to tears, he quickly scooped her up and swung her on to his shoulders then cantered in a circle around the unfinished snow person. 'I'm Rudolph!' he cried. 'Charlie, look at Phoebe – she's driving Santa's sleigh!'

'Say "Giddy-up, Rudolph!"' Natalia called from the sidelines. She gave a contented sigh then chatted comfortably with Macy.

For a while it seemed everyone was happy except me, and maybe Adam. I spotted him by the side of the frozen lake, making his way back to the trailer without Charlie. From a distance – heavy snow falling, a small, serious boy paying no attention to his surroundings – he looked like he'd never entered into a snowball fight or ridden on his dad's shoulders in his life.

Feeling a sharp pang of sympathy, I went to meet him. 'Hey, Adam. What did Mr King say?'

Adam stopped and looked up at me with the enormous hazel eyes he'd inherited from his dad. His black hair was long and curly under a knitted hat with ear flaps and a zigzag pattern, his skinny little body all wrapped up in matching scarf, bright-blue ski jacket and gloves. 'He says we're through.'

'So no more filming today?'

He shook his head. 'Charlie said for me to tell Daddy.'

'Cool.' Offering my hand, I walked with him and tried to get him to talk. 'Do you like the snow, Adam?'

'Yes.'

'Me too. You can hear it crunch when you walk. What's the best thing about the snow for you?'

'I like that it makes the world white.'

'Yeah, that's beautiful.' Walking with Adam, feeling his little gloved hand in mine felt good. We took our time, stopped at the edge of the lake. 'See how the water freezes over. Isn't that pretty?'

I step out of the moment but this time not in a bad way. There's no painful split inside my brain, no dizziness – only a sensation that I'm rising with Adam over the frozen lake, still holding hands and looking down at the boathouse, surrounded by gently falling flakes of snow.

'Be happy,' a child's voice whispers. 'Keep a hold of my hand.'

I rise into the air beside my child companion, whose figure is surrounded by a soft glow. My body tingles then melts. I leave it behind and become pure spirit.

'Think of me when your dark angel attacks,' the child tells me. 'When evil comes, I will be here. Where there is darkness and chaos, look for the light.'

6

I lay in bed that night looking back to the starry night painting in MoMA, when Orlando and I had our dream moment.

I should have known at the time – nothing ever stays that good.

From which you can tell we'd had another fight.

'Let's take the subway,' he'd said. 'It's the best way to get round the city in the snow. Come on, I'm with you. It'll be cool.'

'You know I can't do that.'

Him: (sulking, with the trace of a sneer) Can't do, won't do? So we pay for a cab.

Me: (apprehensive, jittery) No, let's walk.

Jack and his family had flown off in their helicopter. Charlie and Gwen had taken Macy to a diner off Broadway and we were heading for Hubert Street.

'This is crazy,' Orlando had grumbled. He'd walked a little way ahead of me, ignoring the bright Christmas glow pouring out of shop doorways and fake stars twinkling in windows.

'What's wrong?' I'd asked when we finally made it to our hotel.

'Nothing.'

Me: So why are you acting this way? Would you rather be with Gwen? (Major mistake – I knew that as soon as I opened my mouth.)

Him: Tania, you have to stop doing that!

Me: Doing what?

Him: Getting your claws into every girl I spend time with. You do it every time.

Me: I do not! I meant Gwen and Charlie, not just Gwen.

Our voices were raised as we walked down the hallway towards the elevator. We didn't stop yelling all the way up to our room.

Orlando slammed the door behind us. 'I'm working with Gwen, OK! Work, as in getting to know the right people, learning the right moves, serving an internship, building a career.'

'Rolling in the snow is work?'

'Do I do this to you?' he yelled. 'Do I turn round and say don't talk to Charlie?'

'That's different.'

'How is it different, Tania? The way I see it, I have a hundred more reasons to be jealous of Charlie than you do of Gwen.' Orlando clips his words, gets the grammar right when he's angry.

'Charlie saved me from the stalker,' I pointed out. 'You didn't.'

'So I have to be there to protect you twenty-four-seven? I never get to have a life of my own?'

We stood face to face in our small room, knowing we were heading for a relationship car crash yet neither of us seeming to know where the brakes were. 'You do have a life of your own,' I cried. 'You're in Dallas, aren't you?'

'Well, thanks for letting me go to college,' he sneered. 'If you had it your way I'd be in Europe, dragging around in your footsteps.'

'No, that's not fair. It was me who wanted to go to Europe and do my own thing. You're the one who put pressure on me to give it all up and come to Dallas with you.'

Orlando stared angrily for a long time. In my head I heard the screech of tyres, the crash of metal, the splinter of glass. I felt a sob rise into my throat.

Stepping back from the wreckage, he let out a long

sigh. 'Why does it have to be so complicated with you, Tania? How come we're always dealing with angels and spirits and dead people?'

He left me tangled in twisted emotions, cut up by fear.

'Why can't we be ordinary?' he whispered.

Sunday was the last day of my course. It was nine thirty when Orlando (non-communicative, no touching or kissing) left me on Lincoln Plaza and went off for another morning as an intern on the *Siege 2* set. I'd already had a text from Charlie inviting Macy and me to join them in the afternoon.

Orlando still hadn't forgiven me and I still hadn't said sorry. Sorry for being insecure over every gorgeous girl who looks at you in a certain way, sorry we aren't ordinary.

When he and I fight it's like self-harm. I lacerate my own heart.

'See you,' he mumbled as he strode away. He has a way of walking – there's a small bounce in his step, a forward hunch that's so familiar to me. But today he looked like a stranger disappearing down the wide steps heaped with snow, across the traffic-jammed street, swallowed by the towering skyscrapers, lost in clouds of steam rising through ventilation shafts.

The second she saw me, in the entrance to the film school, Macy understood something was wrong.

'Did you see your stalker again?' she asked anxiously.

'No, I guess he lost interest. He found himself another victim.'

'So what happened?' Together we went up in the elevator and headed along the corridor to our classroom.

'I had a fight with my boyfriend is all.'

'Oh my God, that's why you look like death! You really do, Tania.'

'Thanks.' I knew I did – I'd looked in the mirror in the elevator and seen my pale face with dark shadows under swollen, red-rimmed eyes.

'So, forget this morning's classes. Go find him.'

'And say sorry?' I muttered.

Macy cornered me by the drinks machine in the lobby. 'If that's what it takes. Sorry's a small word.'

'I know, but I can't just walk out of here and follow him on to the movie set,' I sighed. 'We don't have passes until this afternoon.'

'OK, block out the problem until you see him again – put it to the back of your mind. Take deep breaths.'

Trying but failing to follow her advice, I went into the classroom and spent the entire morning rerunning the fight with Orlando, thinking of all the things I should and shouldn't have said, remembering the exhausted look on his face when he'd asked me why we had to be so complicated. Then I punished myself by picturing how happy he'd looked the day before, rolling in the snow with Gwen and the kids.

Whatever Adrian Ross told us about recent developments in indie cinema in post-Communist countries of Eastern Europe went totally over my head.

Our tutor ended the morning and wrapped up the course with a list of useful websites. They hardly registered with me until Macy dug me in the ribs. 'OK, torture's over – time to get out there and grovel.'

'This wasn't totally my fault.' I reacted with my first hint of defiance. 'Right after you went off with Gwen and Charlie, Orlando did his speciality detachment thing, which is what led to the fight in the first place.'

Macy nodded. 'I hate it when guys do that.'

'Like they don't even know you exist.'

'And they won't communicate. You try every which way but you can't get through.'

We were so deep in conversation that I hardly noticed the route we took across the Plaza and up Broadway towards the nearest entrance to Central Park. 'Give it to me straight, Macy – you saw how Orlando was with Gwen yesterday. What did you think?'

'Do you mean, was he coming on to her?'

'Or the other way around?'

Macy wrinkled her nose as she thought it through. 'Gwen's a couple of years older than Orlando,' she pointed out. 'And every day she meets seriously hunky guys through the work she does. I'm not saying Orlando's not a hunk – don't get me wrong.'

'So you think I imagined it?'

'Gwen definitely didn't mention him over supper.'

'I imagined it,' I repeated, this time with a thudding, sinking, sickening sensation that I'd made a total fool of myself.

We'd reached the security barrier inside the park and the usual band of fans. I recognized big Mike on duty in his high-visibility jacket. Macy paused and gave my arm a reassuring squeeze. 'Yeah, Tania. You have to cut Orlando a little slack while we're on set, then as soon as you find the chance to get him on one side – girl, you grovel!'

Today, on the afternoon of the last day of filming in Manhattan, Larry King was working with Jack on an interior sequence inside the boathouse. Orlando told me that Jack was sober. He greeted Macy and me at the door to the make-up trailer where Gwen was working her magic on Angela Taraska, the newcomer who was getting lots of press coverage for her off-screen antics with Jack. She had the typical starlet looks – blonde hair, wide-apart blue eyes, small nose, lush mouth – that could put her on the cover of every gossip magazine across America and the whole of the western world.

'Maybe that first day with Jack and the whisky bottle was a one-off,' Orlando suggested, paying close attention to Gwen's palette of shaders and blushers.

'Let's hope.' I stood to one side as Angela, ready for the camera, stood up from her chair and squeezed past us. 'Can we talk?' I muttered to him.

'I'm shadowing Gwen,' he explained. 'Can't it wait?'

Gwen overheard our whispered conversation and straight away let Orlando off the hook. 'Take a break,' she told him. 'I'm finished here for the afternoon. You'll find me on set when you and Tania are through talking.'

So we left the trailer and walked by the frozen lake, treading carefully – I mean literally and metaphorically here.

I began. 'How was your morning?'

'Cool. How was yours?'

'Not so good. I couldn't focus on the course because I was too busy running action replays of last night.'

'Let's not go over it.'

'I feel bad.'

'Forget it.'

'No, you're right. I don't know why I do this to myself. And to you.'

'So you admit it? Gwen is giving me her time; it's a professional deal, end of story.'

'I know it is. I'm sorry.' Our feet crunched on the packed snow. Across the tree-lined park, the skyline of tall tower blocks glinted under a weak sun. I decided to try and lighten the mood between us. 'You can thank Macy for this. She made it clear that it was time for me to grovel.'

Orlando stopped and stared out across the reservoir. 'You talked with Macy about us?'

'Yeah. She knew something was wrong and she dragged it out of me.' Wait – why was I even trying to justify this? Girls talk to their buddies about emotional issues – what's wrong with that?

'You go into our private stuff with someone you only just met?'

'I didn't "go into our private stuff"! I just told her what was bugging me. She said for me to say sorry. What's the big deal?'

He shook his head, turned and walked back

towards the trailers. 'You told her I was cheating on you,' he muttered.

'I did not. Orlando, wait!'

But he didn't look back. He just kept on walking.

Jack was sober and Natalia was happy.

'The airport reopened all their runways at midday,' she told Macy and me. We were drinking hot tea in her trailer and Orlando was on set with Gwen and Charlie. 'Tomorrow we fly out to Aspen.'

'Aspen, as in the ski resort?' Macy sighed enviously.

'Yes. We drive from there to a little town called Mayfield. We shoot for five days on the ski slopes then finally we get to spend Christmas in the Bahamas.'

Macy loved hearing how the glamorous life of her idol stacked up. 'Does Jack get to ski, or does Charlie do the dangerous stuff?'

Natalia laughed. 'They won't let Jack anywhere near a pair of skis, or even a cable car. Their insurance doesn't cover it. But Adam and Phoebe will definitely get to play on the nursery slopes without a mob of photographers spoiling it for them.'

'Hey, Tania, how close is your family's home to the place Natalia's talking about?' Macy asked.

'We're an hour away.' A drive from Bitterroot took you

through the National Forest, to the foot of Carlsbad and the small, lesser-known resort of Mayfield.

'That's so cool.' Natalia beamed from her silk-cushioned chair. Her beautiful dark copper-coloured hair was carelessly pinned back, with wavy strands escaping in tendrils. 'An hour's drive is nothing, Tania. It means you and Orlando will be able to join us on the new set. You can still be part of the team.'

'No way.' Macy was blown away. 'Lucky, lucky.'

'So come with us.' The sudden invite to my new friend took even me by surprise, though I already had it in the back of my mind. 'Spend Christmas in Bitterroot with me and my family.'

At first it was as if she hadn't heard me right, then she choked up and there were tears in her eyes. 'You really mean it?'

'Of course Tania means it,' Natalia assured her kindly. 'That's what people do – they look out for their buddies. So it's a done deal. You all three visit me and the kids in Mayfield. Orlando gets to do more work on make-up and I'll ask Larry to find you two girls some experience on the technical side – editing the day's rushes, whatever. How does that sound?'

'How does it sound?' Macy sighed. 'Pinch me. I feel like I've just died and gone to heaven!'

Jack was sober, but only until shooting finished for the day.

Then there was a small wrap party in a private room at the back of the boathouse and he fell spectacularly off the wagon.

'I blame the other famous Jack – Jack Daniels,' Charlie grumbled as he and I stood watching the megastar maul Angela Taraska. 'Whisky is his poison of choice. No Class A drugs – just pure, hard-core alcohol.'

We saw Angela simper and sigh. She didn't make a whole lot of effort to extricate herself from Jack's paws.

'You wouldn't believe how hard Natalia works to locate the bottles that he stashes away. Problem is, there's always a sound guy or a cameraman's assistant who'll buy a new one for him.'

'And someone with a camera to take the picture.' I noticed Natalia in the background instructing a security guy to delete images from a guest's phone then eject said guest. The pictures of Jack staring drunkenly down his co-star's cleavage would have been snapped up by the gutter press. 'It's her and the kids I feel sorry for,' I sighed.

Charlie nodded then went to help the security guy forcibly separate the sneaky guest from his cell phone, taking out the SIM card and destroying it in a candle flame on one of the tables . Scanning the dimly lit room – the improvised bar in the corner, the crush of people on a small dance floor, the big sound system by the door – I picked out Orlando deep in conversation with Gwen (no surprise there) and then Jack suddenly lurching away from Angela, across the room in my direction. I called for Charlie, who headed my way. But Jack got close enough for me to see that his eyes were unfocused and that the pores of his skin seemed to ooze alcohol before Macy suddenly stepped in between us. Charlie was too late to stop her.

It's dark. The air is stale. I inhale dust, I hear men cry out. Way above our heads a rescue drill grinds its way through the rock. There are corpses all around, and sightless, nameless, writhing creatures creeping out of the earth, bursting through solid granite to claim the dead men. There are bones stripped of flesh in every recess, bare skulls with black eye sockets and grinning jaws. I cower in the darkness.

Jack saw Macy and forgot all about me. He grabbed her round the waist and leered/danced/lurched/staggered with her until they'd done a full circuit of the floor and come back to where I stood. When he let her go, he almost fell full length at my feet. It was Charlie who broke his fall.

'Du-duh! So you see the real Jack Kane,' I muttered to

Macy, who could now judge for herself the raw, unedited version. I was still shaking from my vision of an underground hell and so felt less sorry for her shattered illusion than I might have done at some other time. 'Not pretty, huh?'

She brushed the air with the back of her hand. 'Give the guy a break. There's a stack of pressure on him to get this movie made. He's entitled to let his hair down once in a while.'

Dream on, I thought. But I didn't say anything, just watched Charlie try to straighten Jack out.

'Jack told me I was cute,' Macy sighed. 'He said he liked my hair – said it made me look—'

'Italian?' I sniped.

'Hot,' she said. 'Jack Kane said I looked hot!'

And I realized that it would take more than one drunken circuit of the dance floor to cure Macy's terminal case of hero worship. Meanwhile, I tried my hardest not to look in the direction of Gwen and Orlando.

As the evening went on, the music grew louder. At around ten thirty, when I was chatting with Charlie by the bar, I noticed Natalia slip away from the party.

'Come on, let's make sure she gets out of here safely,' Charlie told me.

I followed him out of the boathouse in time to see Jack's wife climb into a car and get driven away. The driver took her north out of the park on a kind of decoy route and, so far as Charlie and I could see, there were no paparazzi on her tail.

'It's good to get some air.' He took a deep breath and looked up at a clear, starlit sky. 'We made it through to the end of the week,' he murmured, as if he'd reached the final stage of a tough journey.

'As in, Jack is still in one piece and Larry got the footage he needed?'

'We got through the New York section. I won't say it was easy.'

'I hope they pay you plenty.' Under the stars I realized how close I felt to Charlie. It had been this way ever since he rescued me in the park. Besides, he single-handedly shouldered the burden of keeping the Jack Kane–Natalia Linton show on the road. 'I mean, they see you as more than just a body double.'

He gave me the trademark, knockout grin. 'You're sweet, Tania. I really hope you've got something out of all this.' He jerked his head back towards the boathouse and the sounds of partying. Then he gazed up again at the stars. 'Don't you just love the night sky? I look at the stars and I get a new perspective. Whatever we're dealing with here on planet earth, it's good to remember we're all just micro-dots, tiny specks of dust.'

I felt sad as I took in the crescent moon, a million stars. I thought of Vincent and his whirling, crazy vision. I thought of Orlando and me.

'You're going to be in Mayfield,' Charlie mentioned quietly. He waited with me in comfortable silence, in the quiet heart of the world's greatest city. 'So this isn't goodbye,' he added.

An hour later, Jack fell down and broke his crown. That is, he dropped to the floor dead drunk and they carried him out to his helicopter.

The party went on without him. For a while I talked art-house films with Larry King's assistant director, the woman named Lucy Young, then I danced with Charlie before handing him over to Macy, who, now that Jack had left a big vacuum in her life, seemed to target Charlie like a scud missile.

'I love this track!' she cried. 'It's my favourite. Dance with me, Charlie. Tania doesn't want to party any more. Come on, dance!'

My gaze followed them for a bit – him listening as she bawled above the sound of the music, smiling, keeping a steady hand round her waist. Macy was having the best time, laughing and dancing, coming on to Charlie as if he was the great man himself. I recognized from the way she moved in close and used her body that she didn't have to work hard – seduction came naturally to her.

And all this time you're wondering, what about Orlando and Gwen? No surprise – I hadn't actually had the willpower not to look. In fact I'd hardly been able to tear my eyes away all night. And every time I glanced, they'd be locked in conversation – no dancing, no physical contact, nothing that I could legitimately charge him with, except that Orlando had stayed away, had not said a word to me all evening and I felt that he was deliberately giving me a hard time. Yes, he was totally punishing me.

The party finished for me at one thirty with a single picture imprinted on my brain – Gwen with her soft, fair curls, dressed in tight jeans and a close-fitting silver sequin top, using her hands to demonstrate what she was talking about, with Orlando pushed too near to her by dancers spilling over from the dance area, catching her hand to stop her from knocking another guy's glass, listening and nodding, not letting go of her hand.

I left the boathouse straight away. Either that or make a big scene, storm across to confront Orlando and kill any chance that he and I would emerge from New York unscathed.

I was in the park alone, running without any clear idea of what I was doing or where I was going, just running.

I'd come to the area they call Shakespeare Garden and only then realized that I was heading in the wrong direction if I wanted to get back to our TriBeCa hotel. Jealousy, the green-eyed god had possessed me, confused me, sent me crazy.

I turned round, set off walking back across the deserted Ramble and past the boathouse, where party music still pounded out its heavy beat, then down the east side of the lake until I reached a huge bronze statue of an angel surrounded by cherubs, set in a frozen pond. She stared down with blind eyes, wings outspread – the Angel of the Waters.

She stands for cleanliness. Her cherubs are called Purity, Health, Peace and Temperance. She provides an ideal place for a night stalker to lurk.

He sprang out in his hunter's hat from behind her billowing bronze skirt. He'd prowled through the park after me, kept to the shadows, never made a sound. And now he confronted me, again with a knife and with a cruel smile. He didn't speak. He raised the knife and came towards me.

Terror shot through me as I turned and ran. There was a stone arcade ahead, with wide steps to either side. It felt as though my attacker was herding and pushing me wide of the arcade towards Bow Bridge, so I resisted and ran straight for the sheltering arches, stopping to catch my breath only when I believed I was out of sight. Leaning back against the cold stone and closing my eyes, I waited.

Ten, fifteen, twenty seconds passed. I heard nothing – no footsteps down the tiled arcade, no heavy breathing. After half a minute I ventured out from behind the pillar. Wham! He was there in front of me, eyes gleaming, close enough to touch. I gasped and fled down the row of arches. Again he seemed happy to let me go until I came out the other end of the arcade. Wham again! My stalker was there to meet me. He was behind me, to either side, a dozen versions of him materializing and vanishing at will.

He wasn't real. He sprang from the darkest corners of my psychic sensibility, my nightmare manifestation of a dark angel. There was no point running another step. I dropped to my knees.

The ground opens up beneath me. I'm Alice falling down the rabbit hole, tumbling out of this world. There are tree roots like tentacles trying to grasp me, underground tunnels leading nowhere, angels following me, blocking out the light.

I fall for ever. Deep under the earth the dead inhabit crumbling caves, endless tunnels. They cannot be counted. Bones pile upon bones, they crumble to yellow dust.

And there are terrible, agonized creatures there with gaping, slavering jaws, flesh burned black and eyes that glint like dying coals. They writhe and fall into the phosphorescent fires of hell.

Among the hopeless dead are groaning, suffocating ghosts – men naked to the waist and carrying pickaxes, who were caught in a tidal wave of slurry when tunnels they were building collapsed. Their eyes are wide with fear. I am with them in the dark, struggling for breath.

I slumped on to the snowy ground, fall unconscious. When I came round, a guy in a peaked cap with a star badge on his jacket raised me and supported me towards the nearest bench.

'Relax. I'm Central Park Police,' he told me.

7

I guess he saved my life. Without him passing by on his regular night patrol, I might have died from hypothermia.

He was detached and professional, assured me I was hallucinating when phrases like 'dark angel' and 'spirit world' fell from my lips. He said it made no sense that I was being chased by multiple ghosts but that he would look out for the guy I tried to describe: short, stocky, mixed-race, wearing a black jacket and a hunter's cap.

He asked me where I'd been and why I left the party alone.

'Do you need to get checked out by a doctor?' he asked when he considered I'd come round enough to talk sense to him.

'No, I'm not injured.'

'The guy didn't touch you?'

'No.'

'He stalked you but didn't follow through with any physical assault?' The park cop was starting to wonder how much I'd had to drink. His tone grew more judgemental. 'I'm thinking you don't want to put this on file at the precinct?'

'No, I already tried that.' Standing up, I felt dizzy and disconnected from my surroundings and it was obvious I wasn't going anywhere under my own steam, so my cop decided to escort me out of the park. He got the address of my hotel and gave it to the cab driver who he flagged down on Columbus Circle. 'Don't try this again,' he warned as I sank on to the back seat. 'No one's going to believe your story, OK?'

'What's the deal?' The skinny, wizened cab driver broke the boredom of his night shift by leaning out of his window to engage with the cop.

'Kid says she had a stalker who turned out to be a ghost or a dark angel or something.'

'Groovy,' the cab driver muttered cynically. Judging by his vocabulary and thin grey ponytail, he belonged to the LSD, flower-power generation. 'A chick who talks to angels.'

'Don't encourage her,' the cop grumbled as the cab pulled out from the kerb.

* * *

124

Down on Hubert Street, away from the Christmas lights, neon signs and giant digital screens advertising vodka, cars and lip gloss, I paid the driver and went into my hotel, not even daring to hope that Orlando would have arrived ahead of me. For a start, I had no idea how long I'd been lying unconscious, and had lost track of the time. Secondly, I hadn't received any texts asking me where I was, which meant he was still too busy partying with Gwen.

Sure enough, the room was empty when I turned on the light. I sat on the bed and spent hours listening for movement in the corridor, keeping vigil for Orlando until he chose to come back to me.

I wished we'd never come to New York.

At five thirty a.m. he opened the door and relief flooded through me.

'Hey, you're awake,' he said.

'Where were you?' As usual, relief turned to accusation in a nanosecond.

'At the party. Why did you leave without telling me?'

'I was tired. I wanted to sleep.' Watching him kick off his boots and jerk his T-shirt over his head, I realized he was back but was still a million miles away.

'I had a cool time,' he insisted. 'Those movie guys know how to party.' For the first time since he'd come into the room he gave me eye contact.

'Don't look at me that way,' I sighed. The glance contained a challenge then turned into a stare that said he really didn't want to talk about whatever was on my mind.

'You shouldn't have left early. You missed Macy making out with Charlie.'

'No, I saw that.' And you making out with Gwen. My silent accusation widened the gap between us.

'They left the party together.'

'Cool. I'm happy for her.' Exhausted, crying inside, I lay back on the bed.

'Then the park cops came to check up on us, which killed the atmosphere stone dead. They were looking for underage drinkers, said they'd found a girl out in the snow . . .'

'That would be me.'

'Hah. I didn't know you'd been drinking.' He sat on the opposite side of the bed, his back turned.

'I hadn't. Anyway, how could you possibly know?'

Ignoring my jibe, Orlando swung his legs on to the bed and lay down with me. Still there was that million-mile gap. 'If you weren't smashed, what in Christ's name were you doing out there in the snow?'

I turned away and curled up on my side. Our roles of

a few minutes ago were reversed. 'Leave me alone. I don't want to discuss it.'

'No, come on, Tania – be straight with me. It was dead people talking to you again, wasn't it?'

'I said, leave me alone. You're the one who's had too much to drink.'

'I'm right. You had another vision.'

'And what if I did?' I retaliated, frozen out by Orlando and unable to share the terror I'd felt by the Angel of the Waters, underneath the arches by Bow Bridge.

'I truly don't understand what it is with you. Why can't you walk away from all that crap?'

I sat up with a jolt of anger. 'What is it with *you*?' I challenged. 'It's not me who's changed. I'm not doing anything different.'

Head back on the pillow, Orlando closed his eyes wearily. 'Exactly.'

'And you think I don't long to walk away from the so-called crap, to live the kind of easy, ordinary life you want us to share?'

He opened his eyes but said nothing – barrier still up, locking me out.

'Orlando, you know how my dark angel operates.'

'Not again,' he groaned.

'Yes, again. He's always around, even when I don't

recognize him. Wherever I go, even in the city and away from the mountains back home, he's here with me. I'm a main target, remember.'

The blank, barrier-up look went on and on.

'You know this. You've seen him yourself – on Black Rock, then again by Turner Lake.'

Orlando stared at me for the longest time. 'Really, Tania, I'm thinking about it and trying to work it out. But if I'm honest with you – back there on the mountain, by the lake, I don't even *know* what I saw any more.'

Thank God the snow had eased enough for the airports to stay open. I wanted to be on that plane, away from New York, soaring above the skyscrapers into the clouds, trying to forget what Orlando had said – the way his betrayal had knocked me sideways like a physical blow, how lonely it felt.

But first I had to meet up with Macy to help her buy a plane ticket to Bitterroot.

'What's your flight number and departure time?' she asked me when I showed up alone outside her hotel.

I gave her the information. She bought the ticket online for a top-dollar, last-minute price. 'This is me blowing my inheritance,' she said with a grin. 'Hey, where's Orlando this morning?' She completed the transaction before she noticed that he was missing.

'He went to the park to say goodbye to . . . to some of the crew.' I don't need to tell you that we'd parted at the gate without a kiss.

'So do we join him there?' she asked eagerly.

'No. He said for us to meet him at JFK.'

Macy stared at me for a long time. '"Sorry" didn't work, huh?'

I shook my head.

'That's what I guessed at the party last night when I saw how he was acting.'

'With Gwen?'

'I thought – there's a guy who's working hard to make his girlfriend jealous. And you know what else I thought – and this is weird – Charlie isn't the only member of the Speke family to look exactly like a famous movie star.'

'How come?'

'I mean Gwen. She could be Lillian Gish's double – you know, the actress we saw on the first day of our course, the one the villains used to tie to the railway track and the hero had to save her. Gwen's eyes, mouth, that halo of golden hair – everything is identical.'

She was right, I realized. 'Well, thanks, that makes me feel a whole lot better,' I groaned, 'to know that my boyfriend has ditched me for a 1920s lookalike. Anyway,

I figured you were too busy with Charlie to even notice Orlando and Gwen.' Consulting my guidebook to find out where to pick up a bus for the airport, I saw that the terminus was nearby at Grand Central Station.

'Yeah, Charlie!' Macy sighed. 'You know, he's the sweetest guy, and so much fun. It feels like I've known him for ever, but how long has it actually been?'

'Under twenty-four hours.'

'Yeah, and yet I'd trust him with my life. I mean, you'd stand alongside Charlie in an earthquake or a hurricane any day. He's the guy who would save you from fire, flood, anything major you can think of.'

It was irrational, but as I listened to Macy bigging up Charlie, I started to feel jealous. After all, he was *my* rescuer, *my* caped crusader. 'You're sure it's not Jack you feel this way about?' I asked. 'You're not looking at Charlie and seeing Jack?'

'After last night, no way. Jack was way out of line.'

'You didn't think that way when he danced with you and called you hot.'

Macy tutted and flipped the argument aside. She raced on. 'I'm so happy Charlie will be there in Mayfield. I'll spend more time with him, get to know him better. Not that I expect a long-term relationship, don't get me wrong. I mean, as Jack's body double, Charlie travels

130

the world. After Mayfield they go to the Bahamas for Christmas. Jack owns a suite in Atlantis – that's near Nassau, where Michael Jackson had the penthouse. Then it's Europe for Jack's next movie, a spy thriller set in Geneva.'

'Stop!' I begged. 'Really – what happened? Yesterday it was Jack you were fixated on, not Charlie.'

Macy slowed down at last and gave my question some thought. 'It was. But then I took a reality check. Let's face it – even if you take away Jack's problems with alcohol and women, he's way out of my league.'

'That's true. Plus, he's married,' I reminded her. 'Unlike Charlie, I guess.'

'Oh yeah, Charlie's single. He just split from his last girlfriend. That was Angela – Angela Taraska. He knew her in LA before she hit the big time. Actually, it was Charlie who got her the audition for the major role in *Siege* 2. Without him, she wouldn't have made it.'

'Jeez, you learned at lot.'

'Yeah, but that's Charlie, you see. He helps people. I asked him, how did he feel when Angela got the part and started this affair with Jack – you know those two are an item, don't you? And poor Natalia, she just has to suck it up. It's in all the magazines; people talk about it all the time on Facebook.'

'Stop,' I said again. Macy's appetite for gossip made me uneasy. Besides, I felt the little seed of jealousy germinate and grow inside me.

On top of which I was bang in the middle of the biggest emotional crisis of my life so far – Orlando had slammed the door in my face and left me crying in the dark, abandoned me in the vast heavens where good and bad angels battled. I was lost among the stars and comets, hearing voices, watching out for those time-travelling destroyers of innocent souls, crouching in fear.

To cut out the drama and get back to basics, this last morning in New York was so not what I'd planned when Orlando and I shared our starry night moment.

'See!' Macy squealed, pulling out her phone and showing me a text message from Charlie. 'He says we should go meet them in the Loeb Boathouse. Orlando's there too.'

'With Gwen?' I asked. I couldn't help myself – the question slipped out.

'Hey, no need to go overboard. Gwen's cool.'

'It's not Gwen I'm worried about,' I said as I stuffed my guidebook into my bag and jumped with Macy into the cab she'd just hailed.

But it was, really. Macy was right: she was a Lillian Gish lookalike – small and dainty, with a heart-shaped face, rosebud mouth and fair curly hair. I recalled the way Orlando had kept hold of her hand and looked into her eyes. And I knew with a dull pressure round my heart that Gwen Speke was everything that I wasn't.

The film crew had moved out and the boathouse café was open for business as usual, so Macy and I followed Charlie's instruction to meet him round the back.

He was standing in a narrow doorway texting someone, so he didn't see us arrive. Even off guard, in charcoal-grey fleece and thick, lighter-grey scarf wound carelessly round his neck, he looked like he'd stepped out of an ad for a designer perfume. His stance was easy and graceful and when he did look up, his hazel eyes were clear and bright under those strong, straight brows.

Macy rushed forward and in the way he embraced her I knew they'd moved on beyond the first flirty stage into serious physical contact. In other words, I wondered where they'd spent the night.

'Hey, Tania.' Charlie greeted me warmly, his arm round Macy's shoulder. She snuggled close, her arm around his waist. 'We missed you,' he said.

I shrugged and looked past him down the narrow corridor, feeling strung out and wretched.

'You left early.'

'Yeah, I needed to sleep.'

'But it looks like you didn't,' he observed. 'Did I get this right – are you the girl the park cops picked up?'

'But I wasn't drunk,' I protested. Then I stopped myself before I got into details about my dark angel mugger.

Luckily Macy grew impatient and started to tug Charlie out of the cold. We went down the corridor into a small room where Larry King was holding a quick post-rushes meeting with Jack's co-stars, Rocky and Angela. Also there were Rocky's girlfriend, Lisette, Lucy Young and of course Gwen and Orlando.

Lucy held a finger to her mouth when she saw us enter to warn us that Larry was about to speak.

'I really needed Jack to be here this morning. We may have to reshoot some of the boathouse interiors and I need to look at his schedule for the second half of January. Now I hear that he'll be in Europe.'

'I texted Natalia,' Charlie informed him. 'Jack can't make it, but she's on her way.'

Larry nodded. 'OK, so, Charlie, maybe we can put you in some of the sequences and keep Jack's input to a minimum. But I guess it depends on whether Natalia will agree to that on Jack's behalf.' He and Charlie went on to discuss specifics of the star's contract while Macy sat down at a table with Orlando and Gwen, who gestured for me to join them.

'They talk about Jack like he's all washed up,' Macy sighed.

I agreed. 'He doesn't even recognize how much control he's handed over to Natalia and Charlie.'

'One day he's going to wake up and find they don't need him any more. Charlie will be doing it all for him.'

'Sshh,' Lucy warned as Macy raised her voice high enough to make Larry glance her way.

'Tania, I'm so excited you'll be in Mayfield with us,' Gwen said in a low whisper as we sat beside her and she squeezed my hand. 'How cool is that.'

'Me too!' Macy bubbled with positive energy as she told Gwen about her invitation to spend Christmas in Bitterroot. 'I'll be there. Plus Charlie's going to fix it with Lucy so that Tania and I get to spend time in the editing suite. We're so lucky to get this break. I can't believe it!'

I'd sat opposite Orlando in the only vacant chair, waiting on tenterhooks for him to acknowledge me with at least a smile. It seemed ages before he even looked at me. Then when he did, he was wearing the cut-off, distracted look that I was starting to dread. He didn't pay attention to Macy either, only tuning in when Gwen had something to say.

'We're booked into the biggest ski lodge in Mayfield,' she told us. 'Jack and Natalia and the whole cast – we take over the entire Carlsbad Lodge. Do you know it?'

'Sure – it's top of the range.' Orlando jumped in with an answer.

'Naturally. This is Jack and Natalia we're talking about, right?' Gwen smiled. She locked him into her bright gaze.

'It sits right under Carlsbad Peak. There's a dirt road up to an old silver mine. I could drive you there if you'd like to see it.'

I groaned inwardly. If he was doing this to punish me, it was working. But if it wasn't deliberate, I was in even deeper trouble because it meant I wasn't on Orlando's radar any more. I was history.

I saw him fix his attention on her, lapping up every word she said about the schedule for Mayfield, keeping eye contact and laughing at her small jokes, going to fetch her a Coke from the machine, sitting down again and twisting his chair away from me to face her more directly and shut me out.

I saw his back, the way his hair curled on to his collar, his hand resting on the table, fingers drumming lightly.

I saw her face, almost free of make-up, with a touch of mascara to curl her long lashes upwards from her light-brown eyes – the same hazel colour as Charlie's, while all her other features were a contrast to his. Her eyebrows were light and arched, her face a perfect heart, with a small chin and a cupid's-bow mouth.

She looked at me, blinked, smiled and turned her gaze back to Orlando.

As soon as I could slip away, I texted Grace in Bitterroot and told her what had happened. I'm losing him. He's the love of my life, my soul mate. What do I do?

She told me not to give in. Orlando loves you, she reminded me. Who is this Gwen woman anyway?

She's beautiful. He's hooked.

So fight, Grace texted.

She gave me the strength to go back in there.

While I'd been outside, Natalia had been spirited in through another back door. Adam was with her, but not the two younger kids, and while Natalia talked to the director, Charlie had taken on the usual role of surrogate dad.

'Hey, Adam, come over here. Stand on this table and wait while I clear the window. Now look out. Your snowman is still out there by the lake, see?'

'Snowlady,' Adam corrected as Charlie hoisted him up. He showed no interest in the half-melted figure.

137

Instead, he reached out and traced shapes in the misted part of the pane.

Here was this five-year-old kid standing on a table in a room full of adults, trying to make sense of the world by drawing snowflakes and then a sun hidden behind a cloud. He looked to me like the loneliest little boy in the world so I went up to him. 'Hey, Adam.'

He turned and smiled.

We leave the room. We look for the light. We rise above the world, through soft snow that has started to fall, through grey clouds, holding tight to each others' hands. We raise our faces to the warm sun.

'When evil comes, I will be here,' my good angel reminds me.

I smiled back at Adam. Was he really my good angel amidst all the darkness? Would this small child have the power to protect me from my dark angel's wrath?

Charlie came and swung Adam from the table on to his shoulders. 'Mommy wants me to take you shopping,' he told him. 'We can go to the biggest toy store in the city. You get to choose whatever you like.'

'I want to go home,' Adam insisted. He looked uncomfortable on Charlie's shoulders, being whisked from one situation into another.

'Later, buddy. First we shop. Then this afternoon you

fly out with Mommy and your sister and brother.'

'What about Daddy? Is he coming too?'

'Maybe. Maybe not.' Giving Macy a quick kiss on the lips, Charlie carried Adam towards the door.

'See you in Mayfield,' Macy called after him, not quite concealing a sudden panic that she'd miscalculated and the night she'd spent with Charlie might mean nothing to him. You could see it in her eyes, hear it in her high-pitched voice.

'See you,' he called casually, doing nothing to calm her fear. He paused in the doorway and turned. 'Tania, you'll be there too – right?'

'Sure she'll be there,' Natalia answered for me, her business with Larry King finished. She was pulling on her black, fur-trimmed leather gloves and zipping up a soft crimson jacket. As she waved goodbye to Adam, she took my arm and walked me down the corridor, inviting me to sit with her in the back of the car waiting at the door.

'Stay and talk,' she invited. 'I know you have a plane to catch, but I'll get you to the airport on time and fast-track you through security, no problem.'

'What about Orlando and Macy? What about our bags?'

'Charlie will take care of all that. Shall we drive?'

I nodded and felt the car ease away, driving slowly out of the park, under an archway of trees draped with

Christmas lights and across Fifth Avenue on to Madison.

'Tania, I need to talk to you about Adam,' Natalia began.

We were sealed off from the cold grey world inside a limousine, looking out at wealthy shoppers going in and out of twinkly designer stores under the all-seeing lenses of security cameras.

Adam – my one pinpoint of light in the dark cosmos.

Keep a hold of my hand. When evil comes, I will be here.

'Adam likes you,' Natalia went on. 'He talks about you all the time, says how pretty you are and how you know the right things to say. That's a rare connection for him and it makes me think it would be cool for you two to have more time together,' she confided. 'As a general rule, Adam doesn't take to strangers. I guess that's because of the life we lead.'

'You travel a lot,' I agreed.

'And our kids are pretty closeted. They have to be, given all the security issues. And then we have the paparazzi to deal with.' Natalia fell silent as the driver continued to cruise the streets east of Central Park. It was only as we passed the wide arched doors of St James' Church that I glanced at her and saw her fighting back tears. 'Take no notice,' she sniffed, reaching into her bag for tissues. 'I hate it when I do this.'

'It's OK, I understand.'

'I have no right to complain. The whole female population of the planet would kill to be in my shoes – right?'

'I guess. But they don't see the pressures of living the way you do.'

'They don't see the real Jack either.' Natalie's mini meltdown led her to opening up some more. 'You know what I'm talking about?'

The grabbing the bottle and the groping, the falling-down drunk and the chasing after his female co-stars.

'I tried to get Charlie to warn Angela,' she confessed. 'But then I realized the girl doesn't care how she reaches the top or who she has to get horizontal with. As far as she's concerned, Jack is just one more asshole along the way.'

Ouch. This was her own husband Natalia was talking about.

'I'm sorry. I shocked you,' she said.

'No. I do understand, honestly.'

'So thank you, Tania. You brought a breath of fresh air into our lives – I mean, for the kids and me, and we really do look forward to getting together again. And meanwhile, you and Orlando fly home to Bitterroot to spend Christmas with your families.'

And because Natalia had come clean with me, I shared with her in the back of the silent, gliding limo. 'Orlando's changed. He's drifted away from me over the last few days.' It was my turn to reach for a tissue.

'Do you know why? Is it Gwen?' Natalia's intuition kicked in and she immediately hit the target.

'You noticed?'

She nodded. 'She was pretty much in your face at the party, wasn't she? You want me to tell her to back off?'

'Yes. No. It wouldn't help. Orlando is the one who has to choose.'

'I hear you. But I could get her taken off the movie. We could find a replacement. You want me to do that?'

'Don't tempt me.' It was my turn to suck it up. 'But again, no thanks.'

'You're not ruthless enough, huh? Or is it that Orlando would blame you if Gwen lost her job and it would make things worse?'

'It's that.'

'So anyway, let me talk to Charlie. He'll know what to say to Gwen without being too obvious. But you don't know anything about this. We haven't had this conversation, OK?'

Her insistence wore me down. This time I didn't say no.

The clouds were heavy but the snow held off as we cruised on to Park Avenue. As the car stopped outside Natalia's hotel she gave me a personal invitation to join her and the kids the next evening. 'The Carlsbad Lodge at six thirty.' Then, before she stepped out of the car, she tapped on the glass partition to speak to her driver. 'Drive Tania to the airport. Get her upgraded and fast tracked through security. Her flight leaves at two forty-five.'

I sat in a window seat looking down on Manhattan – on the grey Hudson and the East River, on the miniature tower blocks below us. Orlando sat beside me in our upgraded seats while Macy settled in a couple of rows behind.

As the plane rose bumpily through the clouds, thick white vapour streamed by the window, cutting out my view of the ground. Wing flaps clunked, jet engines churned, the fasten-seat-belts signs stayed on until we reached our cruising height and the flight attendants rolled their trolleys along the aisle.

'Drinks, beverages, snacks.'

Orlando shook his head, hardly glancing up from a book Gwen had given him at the airport. She, not Charlie, had been the one to drive him and Macy to JFK but she'd already said goodbye by the time

Natalia's driver had dropped me off.

I asked for water and tried to steady my nerves. 'It feels so good to be going home,' I murmured.

He didn't respond, wouldn't share in my relief to be leaving my dark angel behind. So I prayed to myself that it was over. There would be no more stalker, no visions of underground hell, no repetition of what had gone before.

And I worked out ways to convince myself.

First up, what was so unusual about being mugged in the city? It happened every day – no way was I special. All the stuff about carousel horses coming to life and subway workers being crushed by rockfalls was pure imagination, like Orlando said. In other words, for the first time in my life I flatly denied my own psychic gift.

Secondly, even if – worst-case scenario – we were talking dark angels, where was the towering Zoran figure in this new situation; the charismatic leader rallying his troops? Where were the beautiful seducers like Jarrold and Daniel to ensnare me and draw me to the dark side?

In New York there was only the cult of Jack Kane and look how flimsy that had turned out. The guy had no power, was only clinging on to his star billing thanks to the people he had around him. He presented no threat at all.

And now we were going home to the mountains, Orlando and I. We would soon be walking by Turner Lake, rekindling the emotions I longed to feel again.

'Don't you love the way the clouds look from up above?' I murmured. They were golden and bright, a soft cushion of light.

His head didn't turn; his eyes stayed fixed on the page.

We flew on. I watched the sunlight on the clouds, heard a small voice telling me to hold tight to the hand he offered.

8

The moment they knew I was home, Grace and Holly rushed to my house.

'The sisterhood is back together!' Holly crowed, hugging me and demanding to know every detail of my trip.

Grace as usual kept down the decibels but her welcome-back smile let me know she was pleased to see me. 'How are things?' she asked quietly.

'With Orlando? Later,' I replied. Right now Holly was firing out questions about the shopping, the restaurants, the cinemas and theatres, the whole Christmas vibe of New York. And once in a while she remembered to include Macy, who was sitting quietly for once. 'You two met at the film studies course, right?'

'Actually, in Central Park,' Macy told her. 'We were together in the crush waiting for Jack's helicopter to arrive.'

'Yeah, I heard about the Jack Kane connection.' Holly admitted to teeth-gnashing envy. 'What I'd give to have been there,' she sighed.

'It was out of this world,' Macy admitted. Next to larger-than-life Holly on the sofa, she seemed smaller and quieter. She'd taken out her nose and eyebrow studs and some of her ear decoration too, though her cropped red hair still sang loud. 'I've loved Jack ever since I was a little kid, went to all his movies, had posters on my wall. He's been my idol.'

I noticed she missed out the part about the world's top movie star falling down drunk at the wrap party and all the other smutty details.

'And now you're there in the heart of things, mixing with the slebs.' Sighing extravagantly, Holly sprang up and grabbed me with both hands. She swung me on to my feet then backed me up against the tall Christmas tree by the window. 'You totally have to get Jack's autograph for me, and Natalia Linton's too. When do you go to Mayfield?'

'Tonight. We're all invited – me, Macy and Orlando.' The additional invite had come through from Charlie on Macy's phone; Get O to drive u and T to Mayfield for 6pm, he'd texted early this morning.

'Cool. So any one of you can get me the autographs,

OK. Or hey, how about this?' Holly's eyes lit up with what she thought was a great idea. 'What do you say Grace and I tag along too? Then I can meet Jack in person and get him to sign his name in person.'

'No way.' Macy was grinning but her negative carried a lot of force. 'I don't think that would work.'

'It wouldn't,' I agreed. 'Security is tight, especially around the kids.'

Stepping back, Holly brushed against the silver baubles on the tree. 'And you, Tania – you're telling me this and you're my best buddy,' she accused, hanging her head in OTT disappointment.

'So – Orlando?' Grace stepped in with a change of topic. She dragged my attention where I still didn't want it to go.

'We're not good,' I admitted. 'But I'm hoping now we're back home things will get better.' The words were bland but the feelings behind them were chaotic. I was pained by the memory of how we'd driven home from the airport in silence, how he'd landed the briefest of cold kisses on my cheek when he dropped me and Macy off on Becker Hill. Then when I'd called him this morning his phone had gone on to voicemail. All of these things settled heavily on me and seemed to bruise my heart.

I remembered how I'd lain awake all night, reliving recent days with the name Gwen constantly on my lips and the picture of the two of them together at the party at the forefront of my mind – her heart-shaped face and golden curls, his smitten, lovelorn look. 'How can he do this to me?' I'd asked myself from that lonely place.

And I'd got out of bed and gone to the window, searched for hope among the stars.

'How can it be not good between you and Orlando?' Holly gasped. 'You two have been so through much together – you're rock solid.'

'I guess that's the problem. Orlando thinks I've dragged him through too many dramas and crises. Now he wants us to be – how did he put it? – "ordinary".'

'But you don't bring it on deliberately – it's the way your brain is wired.' Gentle Grace put my case. 'You can't help being psychic. Orlando knows that.'

'I thought he did. But in New York it was different.'

'You had more . . . episodes?' Afraid to mention the dark angel word, Grace hesitated and glanced in Macy's direction.

'It's cool – Macy knows,' I said. 'She believes in messages from the spirit world.'

'Totally,' Macy confirmed. 'I'm in contact with my mom, but my psychic ability is nothing like as highly developed as Tania's. She obviously has a special gift. I'm jealous.'

'So how was it different in New York?' Holly followed the serious turn in the conversation, drawing me back to the sofa and sitting me down.

'I can't tell you exactly, but somehow Orlando wasn't there for me.'

'Right from the start – as soon as you got there?' Grace asked.

'No, in the beginning we were good.' Starry-night good.

'So when did it change?'

'When we got separated in Central Park and I was mugged. It's OK, I wasn't injured,' I said quickly as Holly and Grace gasped. 'I didn't even report it to the cops at first. But I had that feeling – you know, the nightmare stuff where everything shifts and I'm in the middle of something really weird? And at first Orlando was – well, he was Orlando. He understood. He fixed things for me.'

'Then next day the same guy stalked her in a car park.' Macy cut in hurriedly. 'This time I was there with her so I took her to the cops.'

'Yet when I tried to talk to Orlando, he blocked me. He really didn't want to know.'

'That's so not like him!' Holly protested.

'No, but that's how it stayed for the rest of our time in the city.' I faltered, then decided to come out with the whole truth. 'It turns out, the stalker wasn't who he seemed; he was sent from the dark side.'

Quickly my words took effect. Grace had been there, and so had Holly. They both had direct and terrifying experience of the dark angels' power. 'Did he hurt you? Are you OK?' they asked breathlessly.

'Physically, yeah. Emotionally, no; I'm a mess.'

'So why is Orlando acting this way?' Holly was up from her seat again and pacing the room. 'He should be with you, taking care of you.'

'He has other things on his mind.'

'Gwen.' Grace guessed from our recent exchange of texts.

'No! I'm not hearing this right. Orlando can't have left you to be with another girl.' At first Holly refused to believe it. Then she dragged everything out of me – exactly who Gwen was and how she first got Orlando's attention, every detail of the way she looked and acted. 'And has anything, you know – actually happened?' she asked at the end of the interrogation.

'No.' Macy jumped in before me.

All eyes turned to her, the girl with the blazing hair and thickly mascaraed lashes. 'How come you know the answer?' Holly asked.

Macy blushed and shifted awkwardly in her chair. 'Charlie told me,' she mumbled. 'I talked with him earlier.'

'Who's Charlie? What did he say?' Holly demanded.

Long story, Macy said, but it turned out Natalia had explained to Charlie the problem I was having with his sister, as she'd promised me she would. Charlie had talked to Gwen, told her to back off from Orlando. She'd sworn that nothing was going on between them. Charlie had said back off anyway if she wanted to keep her job – all this within the space of twenty-four hours.

'But really, nothing happened between Gwen and Orlando,' Macy insisted.

'Are you sure?' Grace pressed.

'One hundred per cent. Grace swore on her life.'

'Which makes me look totally pathetic and stupid,' I mumbled after a long, uneasy pause. I hung my head, blocking out three concerned faces, glimpsing out of the corner of my eye the shimmering decorations on the tree and the tiny angel with silver gossamer wings perched precariously on the top.

'Skiing is good in Mayfield,' Dad told me over lunch.

Mom wasn't there; she was in Beijing for three days –

her last job before her Christmas break. It was only a couple of months since she'd been treated for blood clots in the brain, yet here she was back at work full-time, busy finding office premises for multinational companies.

'Plenty snow,' he said in his American–Romanian way – deep, deep voice, articles and prepositions pared back to the minimum.

'Cool,' I said, pushing my food around the plate.

'So smile. Feel happy.'

'We won't be skiing,' I pointed out. 'We'll only be visiting. Natalia has asked me to babysit Adam. Macy and I will get to edit the rushes.'

'Big star friends. You see filming. All good.'

Standing up from the kitchen table, I told him I'd better look for Macy. 'She went out for a walk, but that was over an hour ago.'

Dad looked up at me, fork in hand. 'Cool hair,' he commented.

'You mean Macy? Yeah, cool.' It was odd for Dad to focus on the superficial. Usually he'd go deeper than that, but with Macy it was hair.

'Lonely since Mom died?' He'd heard her story late last night – the cancer diagnosis, the failed treatments. Macy had given him the facts in a brisk, non-self-pitying way and he'd empathized, told her she was welcome to stay in

Bitterroot for as long as she liked. 'But lucky she has money,' he added – still focused on the superficial, notice.

'Yeah, if you can call it in any way lucky to have no dad and then lose your mom before you reach twenty.'

'I hear you.' Like me, Dad was stirring his food round his plate. 'You have soft heart, Tania.'

'You too.' I squeezed his shoulder as I passed by, grabbed my jacket from its hook and headed off to find our guest.

Orlando picked up Macy and me at five p.m. and drove us to the Carlsbad Lodge in his dad's grey truck. She sat up front with him; I was in the back. She chatted about the scenery. I stayed silent.

'I can't wait to see Charlie,' she burbled. 'Tomorrow he's promised to show me the old silver mine and some of the other locations they've chosen for the siege scenes. Tonight he'll take me to cocktail hour, introduce me to his buddies. It's going to be a cool evening.'

It was a long hour's drive, that's all I can say.

Meanwhile, here's my mini-travelogue about Mayfield: like its famous neighbour Aspen, the town grew up during the Colorado silver boom way back in the 1870s. Those tough old miners fought off the Ute Indians and stuck around right through the eighties and into the nineties. They set up a lumber company, built a bank, a theatre and a hospital. The lucky ones grew rich and constructed lavish houses in the foothills of the Carlsbad Range. But by 1895 it was all over. Boom and bust.

So what did they do with those big old buildings? Well, what did they have plenty of in Mayfield when the silver ran out? They had snow and not much else. What can you do with snow? You can ski on it. You can get through the entire twentieth century by attracting wealthy celebs who long for time out of the rat race – actors, silicone valley billionaires, supermodels, rock stars. They buy up the old lodges as second homes. You open up high-end restaurants and designer boutiques – Prada, Gucci, Louis Vuitton. You ooze class and keep out ordinary joes. That's the whole story of Mayfield.

Oh, except that it sits on White Rapids Creek, a tributary of the Colorado River, and is surrounded by mountains and wilderness areas, and in December the temperature never rises above freezing point.

End of history lesson. End of sixty minutes listening to Macy chitchat about everything from the amazing colour of Charlie's eyes (hazel but when you got close you saw that they were flecked with green) to the cost of Chanel perfumes at JFK duty-free.

Eventually the Carlsbad Lodge came in sight, sitting at

the base of the mountain backed by a semicircle of tall redwoods. It was a four-storey building, probably started in silver mining days and extended in the same lodge style over the next hundred years. I counted at least twenty gables on the snow-covered roof, each one twinkling with strings of festive lights, while the path to the main entrance was lined with five-metre-high snow-laden trees, also twinkling and shimmering in the early evening dusk. Think Disney World at Christmas to get the impression I'm aiming for.

Orlando had hardly pulled into the main parking lot before Macy leaped out of the car and ran off to look for Charlie. I saw her disappear between the Christmas tree sentries through sliding glass doors dressed in a red micro skirt and black tights, with heeled ankle boots decorated with silver studs and chains that jingled as she ran.

'Jeez.' Orlando gave a sigh.

'I know. She can be a little too much.'

'You invited her,' he reminded me, getting out of the car and slamming the door.

I followed him out of the truck, stopped him in the parking lot as he headed towards the hotel. I'd put up with a lot from him over the past few days, I realized. I'd fallen into serious self-doubt, but his last small piece of bad behaviour against Macy was what tipped me over the edge.

'Orlando, what got into you?' I demanded, my breath turning to mist in the sub-zero temperature.

'Nothing.' He tried to push by but I blocked his way.

'Talk to me,' I cried. 'Why are you so mean to everyone? What happened?'

'Nothing,' he said again.

'It's like you're a different person. You're not the gentle, lovely, loyal guy I know, the one who told me he loved me and would always be with me, no matter what.'

It was as if I'd hit him, the way he recoiled. He took two steps back, his features contorted into a dark frown. Then he shook his head. 'I'm the same,' he muttered. 'All I'm saying is, it's time for us to move on.'

'"Us"?' I echoed. 'Right now I'm starting to feel like there is no "us". You've turned your back on me and walked away.'

'No.' He looked into my eyes and drew a deep breath.

'Yes!' At last I had his full attention. 'You say you love me and you know I love you, will always love you no matter what. But if this really is too much for you,' I said, waving my hand towards the night sky to show that I was talking about cosmic conflict, 'I will understand. I won't blame you if you're honest with me and tell me that's why you have to back off.'

My words sank in. I saw a mixture of emotions flicker across his beautiful face – guilt maybe, confusion for sure, and all kinds of pain. Tears filled his eyes. 'I'm sorry,' he murmured, reaching out and taking my hand.

'No, don't be. It was always going to reach the point where it was too much to expect – that you'd be there with me every time this nightmare came back. Don't feel bad.' Now I was crying. 'I'll try to get through this alone. But, Orlando, when it's all over, when I finally get my dark angel to quit and I have my life back, I just hope and pray you're still there waiting for me.'

He gazed at me for what felt like for ever, his eyes clouded and unsure. 'You don't know how sorry,' he said. Then he let go of my hand and, without once looking back, he strode across the parking lot into the hotel.

The first thing Natalia did when I visited her in her premier suite was to show me a video of the kids skiing.

It was growing dark and we were in a penthouse room with the best view of the Carlsbad range – snow-covered mountains glowing with a pale-violet light as the sun finally vanished. Macy and Orlando had already gone with Charlie for a tour of the hotel facilities – spa, pool, gym – before cocktail hour in the private bar on the ground floor of the sprawling, chalet-style building.

'There's Adam.' Natalia pointed out a tiny figure in a bright-blue jacket, wobbling down a nursery slope, then Phoebe falling over and being put back on her feet by Charlie. 'So cute,' she sighed. 'We actually kept the press at bay for two whole hours so the kids could have fun.'

'It looks cool.' Actually, it did. I enjoyed watching Adam get his balance and gather speed. He grinned, then whirled his arms and yelled as he ploughed into soft snow and came to a sudden stop. But since my mind was still on the recent talk with Orlando, I must have come across to Natalia as less than enthusiastic.

'Are you OK?' She pressed Pause, just at the moment when the screen showed Adam's smiling face in close up, looking directly at camera. 'How are things with Orlando?'

'Better, I guess.' He'd said sorry, but what exactly did that mean? Sorry for the way he'd been acting, or sorry for what he was about to do to me? I felt the same old sword hanging over me; dreaded the cut of its blade.

'So you don't want to be sitting here watching Adam and Phoebe taking skiing lessons,' Natalia realized. She pressed the Off button. 'Right now you'd rather be with him.'

She checked herself in the mirror – dress-down movie-star style today included designer jeans and Louboutins, skinny black top and hair swept up but with tendrils escaping, chunky green stone necklace to match her eyes – and led the way into the elevator to take us down to the bar. 'Don't worry, Tania – Gwen won't be here,' she promised.

It turned out she was right. Classy cocktail hour at the Carlsbad featured a guy at a piano playing nineteen-forties swing, lots of colourful drinks served by incredibly good-looking bar staff, acres of black granite bar tops and a bunch of A-list actors having a good time.

Though there was no sign of Gwen, Rocky Seaton was there with his long-term girlfriend, Lisette (note: dark hair, well-defined, sculptured features). So was Angela Taraska, working the room in a low-cut scarlet dress and sky-high heels.

At the time I showed up with Natalia, Angela was cosying up to Larry King, who looked like he was enjoying the Taraska experience as a perk of the job. But soon after we arrived, Angela split from Larry and zoned in on Jack.

Jack was at the far end of the bar, sitting on a stool, hunched over an empty glass. From a distance it looked as if he'd started the party early.

I watched Angela sit beside him and give a lip-gloss smile as she leaned in with her head tilted at a flirty angle.

She asked him a question, listened to the answer then wiped the grin. Quickly she slid off her stool, fixed the smile back on and made a beeline back to Larry – aim again and fire.

'Did you see that!' Macy had sneaked up behind me. 'What an idiot.'

'Why, what did she do?' I imagined an exchange of words – Angela coming on to Jack as usual, Jack slurring his speech, cussing, cutting her down. Angela in retreat.

Macy laughed. 'She thought Charlie was Jack. How dumb can you get?'

I looked again at the figure sitting at the bar. There was a handsome bartender nearby – around twenty, fair-haired, Nordic fitness freak – who filled the empty glass with something that definitely wasn't whisky. The purchaser lifted it to his lips with a steady hand.

'Charlie!' Macy called to him across the room and he waved back. He set off towards us without stumbling or swaying, stopping only to have a short conversation with Lucy Young, then with Rocky and Lisette.

'Charlie knows everyone here,' Macy sighed impatiently. 'They all want a piece of him.'

'So where's Jack?' I asked. By this time Natalia had moved off to chat with a bald-headed guy I recognized as a member of the technical crew.

Macy shrugged. 'In the air, somewhere between LaGuardia and Aspen. He missed his plane so they hired a private jet to fetch him.'

Watching Charlie network, I made a quick mental note that the great Jack Kane was rapidly becoming superfluous, not only professionally but socially too. The piano player launched into a new number, and meanwhile I scanned the dimly lit room. 'Have you seen Orlando?' I asked.

'Not in a while.'

'But he did come down to the bar with you and Charlie?'

She nodded. 'He seemed quiet though. Said he wasn't in the mood to party so I guess he left.'

'Where would he go?' Apart from anything else, he was our driver back to Bitterroot so he couldn't stray far.

'He'll be back,' Macy assured me. As Charlie finished talking with Rocky, Macy broke away to claim him, but glancing round at me she seemed to have second thoughts and hurried back. 'Sorry, Tania, I wasn't totally honest with you about Orlando.'

'You do know where he is?'

'Yeah, he didn't just leave the party for no reason. He got a text from Gwen.'

'Saying what?'

'This time I really don't know. But whatever it was, he was out of here in a hurry. Don't tell him I told you, OK?'

Macy left me with the blade swinging down and cutting into my flesh. Multiple stab wounds to the heart.

Blindly I left the room and ran through the quiet hotel lobby, knocking down a sign that said 'Private Party – No Entry', rushing out into the cold, dark night.

Alone under the stars I struggled for a new perspective. I was small; the universe was immense. However bad I was feeling, what happened here and now made no impact on the fact that the world turned and orbited the sun, the moon waxed and waned, stars exploded in a cloud of gas and fell from the sky.

I welcomed the darkness and the blasts of icy air as I walked down the drive and through the gates away from the hotel towards the ski-lift terminal – a vaulted structure on giant steel stilts with a viewing platform overlooking steep, undulating slopes. Cables radiated from the far end of the terminal, each stretching high on to the mountain, supported by steel pillars – the only man-made features in a white, empty landscape.

I sat on a frost-covered bench beneath the raised platform, fighting the urge to cry, not noticing the two figures – a guy and a girl – that walked down the mountain until one of them strode towards me and shone a flashlight in my face. It was his loose, loping walk that I recognized.

'Tania, you went too far.' Orlando directed the beam into my eyes and seized my hand. He dragged me to my feet. Gwen hung back and came to a stop about five metres away. 'How does it feel? Come on, tell me – does it feel good to get Gwen thrown off the movie? Do you think you won some kind of battle?'

More pain for my battered heart. 'I didn't do it,' I gasped. 'I swear it wasn't my idea.'

'You're a liar!' he sneered. 'Who else has a reason? It was you – you made this happen. Come here, Gwen. Tell Tania what your brother said to you. Let her see what she's done!'

'Don't!' I pleaded, trying to twist myself free of his grasp. The force of his anger left me reeling. I felt sick with shock.

'Orlando, don't hurt her.' Gwen came forward and took his free hand. She was shivering in the moonlight, her face ghostly pale. 'Leave her alone, please!'

'OK so I'll tell you,' he went on, still gripping my wrist. 'Charlie admitted he was under pressure. He said he was carrying out orders and he was sorry Gwen lost her job but he was sure Natalia would soon get her some work on another movie. But right here and now she had to step back and give you some space. You, Tania! You're the reason.'

'I didn't ask anyone to do that, I swear.'

'I'm sure she didn't, Orlando.' Again Gwen pleaded for him to let me go. 'It was Natalia's idea to protect Tania. I know she really values you both. It was her way of fixing things between you.'

'They didn't need fixing!' Beside himself with anger, Orlando finally released me and flung me sideways so that I fell to my knees in the snow. 'And if they did, that's between Tania and me – no one else.'

It was Gwen who helped me to my feet. 'I understand,' she told me under her breath. 'I can see how you might have got the wrong idea about me and Orlando.'

I stepped back, saw her pretty, delicate face in the moonlight and was about to believe her but then I suddenly glimpsed something dark and cold in her eyes that stopped my breath.

'Yeah, well, I can't,' Orlando stormed. One by one the ties that bound our two hearts were stretched to breaking point. 'I blame you for this, Tania, and only you. You went too far. It's too much.'

'Orlando, come back,' Gwen pleaded, as, with a gesture of disgust, he strode down the slope towards the hotel. 'Tania, I'm so sorry . . .'

I stared at her and again the softly spoken words didn't fit with the cruel glint in her eyes.

'I didn't mean for this to happen,' she said, turning to run after Orlando.

I was alone again, with the same feeling you would get if you were stranded on a narrow ledge overlooking a frozen crevasse. Fear paralyses you, almost stops your heart as the ice creaks, the ledge crumbles and at your feet the glacier starts to shift. My whole world was splitting and sliding, my starry-night dream was broken. I would never get the old Orlando back.

9

I don't know how long I stayed on the steel bench beneath the ski station, only that I was shivering with cold and shock when Charlie eventually came to fetch me.

'Gwen told me you were out here,' he began. 'I figured you might need a shoulder to cry on.'

I let out a heavy sigh. 'My life is all out of control,' I groaned.

Immediately he tuned in to my mood. 'I know the feeling. It's like you're being carried along on a huge avalanche and you have no power to stop it. You're just one little tiny figure alone on the mountain.'

'Exactly.' Our synchronicity dragged a fleeting smile out of me. 'You're smart, Charlie.'

He smiled back. 'No, really. I can see you're going through a tough time, that's all.'

'How can I get Orlando to understand me the way you do?' I asked. 'I almost did, down there in the parking lot. For a few seconds I broke down the barrier that went up between us when we were in New York, but that was before he found out what happened to your sister.'

'And now?'

'Now he blames me and we're being torn apart. It hurts so much.'

'I truly am sorry,' Charlie said, sitting close beside me. 'I hate to see you like this.'

Aching for comfort, for a way out of my cold, deserted loneliness, I let him put an arm round my shoulder.

'Here, take a drink,' he said, pulling a bottle from his pocket. 'It's strong, so just a small one.'

Without pausing to think, I took a swig from the bottle. The alcohol burned as it hit the back of my throat.

Charlie grinned. 'I'm like a St Bernard dog. They're the ones who come into the mountains looking for avalanche victims with a miniature barrel of brandy strapped to their collars. Did it hit the spot?'

'Whoa! What's in that bottle?'

'Don't ask. But it's good, huh?' He took it and tilted his head to take a drink. 'At least it makes you feel warm, even if it's only an illusion. Here, Tania, take this.'

Without waiting for me to protest, he slid out of his jacket and placed it round my shoulders. I shuddered as I felt his body heat still in the jacket and the gentleness of his fingertips as they brushed my neck.

'Now it's you who'll freeze to death,' I mumbled.

'Not me – I'm the tough-guy stunt double, remember.'

His jacket felt and smelled good in the crisp night air. I accepted the bottle and took another drink. 'Remember when you told me we were just specks of dust?'

'Outside the boathouse? The sky was like this; the moon was a thin slice of melon. We said how we loved star-gazing.'

'I was sitting here thinking the same thing all over again – we're tiny and so are our problems. But then they all blew up in my face and grew huge again. I just found out how much Orlando hates me.'

'Hate's a strong word.'

'It's true – he does.'

'He must be out of his mind.' Drawing me to my feet, Charlie made me slip my arms into his jacket then took my hand to lead me off the mountain.

'Whoa!' I said again. By now my head was swimming. I had to rest against him as we walked to the hotel. More than swimming, actually. It was as if the top of my head had come off and released my dark thoughts

169

and my inhibitions all at once. They flitted like bats around a church steeple then flew off into the ether.

'Orlando doesn't realize how lucky he is.' Steering me away from the main entrance, Charlie led me down a side path between two high banks of cleared snow towards a side door into an annexe to the main hotel. 'Sorry, I didn't mean to make that sound so cheesy.'

'No, it's OK. Thank you,' I told him. 'You're always good to me, Charlie. It means a lot.'

We were through the door, walking hand in hand down a warm, carpeted corridor into a room where the moon and stars shone through the window and where there was a cream leather sofa, a table with a TV and a bed with a crimson satin throw.

'Where are we?' I wanted to know. I wasn't feeling scared, just curious.

'This is my room. Come over here, sit down.' He drew me to the sofa and took off the jacket.

'Hey, what about Macy?' I realized suddenly. 'She won't like us being alone like this.'

'So?' He stayed close, snuggling me against him.

'You don't care?'

He smiled. 'What exactly did she tell you?'

'Everything.'

'What toothpaste I use? What I eat for breakfast?'

'Pretty much.' I grew fascinated by the colours in Charlie's eyes. Macy was right – they were hazel mixed with a darker chestnut brown and flecks of green. I liked the smoothness of his skin, the angles of his cheekbones and jaw.

'She told you we're an item?'

'Totally.' I floated. All thoughts, good and bad, had flitted out of the hole in the top of my head. Everything around me looked warm and inviting – the soft red cushions behind my back, the yellow glow of the bedside lamp.

'Let me spell it out in plain English,' Charlie murmured. 'It's not me Macy is in love with, it's Jack.'

'That thought did occur to me,' I whispered back. Don't smile like that, I thought. Don't make that dimple. And don't stroke my cheek with the pad of your thumb – that feels way too nice.

'Me – Charlie Speke – I'm nobody, remember. I come way down Macy's list.'

'She's always worshipped Jack; she doesn't deny it.'

'Right. I'm a lame stand-in.'

'And how about you? Do you care about Macy?'

No reply at first, but he did it again – he gave me the killer smile. 'Watch out for Macy,' he told me. 'Don't buy into everything she tells you.' Then he drew me

171

even closer. His features blurred; I melted into those magical eyes.

When he kissed me and held me in his arms, for a moment I wasn't the lonely figure lost in the snow.

His lips were on mine, he gathered me up and carried me to the bed. My arms were still around his neck as we fell back on to the crimson cover.

'Wait,' I said. 'I want to explain.'

He kissed my neck, started to unbutton my shirt. 'Don't talk.'

'It's about why Orlando and I fought in the first place,' I said. I had some fuzzy idea that if I told Charlie about my connection to the spirit world and how that complicated my situation with Orlando, how it meant I was always on the run trying to avoid the forces of darkness, then Charlie would understand this the way he understood everything else about me. He might even be there at my side the next time my dark angel chose to strike.

'I don't care.' He pressed me down on the bed, and as he went on kissing me, I started to want him back.

Then suddenly, without any warning, I panicked. 'No, wait. This isn't me. I'm not this kind of girl.' Now I was the cheesy one whose words were letting her down. And they didn't convey how close I actually was to becoming the kind of girl I meant. Lucky for me, somewhere deep in my brain, as my body longed to respond to Charlie's touch, my old sense of right and wrong kicked in.

'Don't fight it,' he whispered. Lips everywhere – on my face, my neck.

I fought against my own longing. 'Charlie, stop.' Somewhere I found the strength to push him away. 'What are we doing?'

He rolled and I sprang breathlessly from the bed, dragging the satin throw with me.

'I'm sorry. I can't do this.'

He lay for a while, staring up at the ceiling. Then he took a deep breath and stood up, walked to the window and stared out at the night sky. 'Don't be sorry,' he said calmly and without looking at me.

'We can still be friends, can't we?'

'I'm the one who's sorry – in ways you can't understand.' Now he turned towards me and slipped back in his old role of caring caped crusader. 'Sorry that I read it wrong, Tania – I thought there was a connection.'

'There is,' I said quickly, only just stopping myself from falling into the corny 'I really like you' routine.

'And I apologize for choosing that moment,' he continued. 'You were vulnerable. I shouldn't have put you under pressure.'

'You didn't. It's OK. Let's forget it.'

Slowly Charlie smiled.

'Don't,' I pleaded.'

'Don't what?'

'Don't smile at me.'

'OK, I won't.' He made a serious face. 'Better?'

I took a deep breath then let out an embarrassed laugh. I had to get out of this room before I did or said anything else stupid so I clutched my shirt across my chest and headed for the door.

'So we're OK?' he checked. 'You won't let this come between us. You'll be on set tomorrow as planned?'

'I'll be there,' I promised. I was out in the corridor, getting lost in a dimly lit, carpeted maze, following the sounds of a party – swing tunes on the piano, people laughing, doors opening and closing.

'So I won't be back tonight,' I told Dad half an hour later, when I'd got over the episode with Charlie and called home.

Orlando's truck was gone from the parking lot. I'd seen neither him nor Gwen since the gut-wrenching argument by the ski-lift terminal.

'Where will you stay?' he asked.

'Here at the lodge. It's no problem – they gave me

a room. Charlie fixed everything.'

'Who is Charlie?'

I explained and told him not to worry.

'I worry,' he argued. 'But not about this Charlie guy.'

'About me and Orlando?'

'Where did he go? Did he give reason?'

'We had a fight. Now he's not answering his phone. That's all I can tell you.'

There was a long silence during which I could almost hear Dad's brain clicking into overdrive. 'Don't leave hotel,' he said finally. 'Stay safe.'

'I will,' I promised. 'Oh, and Macy's here too. Don't worry, we're both cool.'

'Call me tomorrow morning, early.'

'OK, Dad, someone's knocking at my door. Got to go.' I came off the phone to find Macy standing in the corridor. Her eyes were red and mascara was streaked down her cheeks. 'Don't tell me – you and Charlie—'

'Can you believe it – he finished with me!' she wailed, stumbling into my room and flopping on to the bed. 'I don't get it. One minute we're dancing and having fun, next thing I know he disappears. Eventually I go to his room looking for him. The throw is pulled from the bed, the window's open and the moonlight's flooding in but he's not there. I go back to the party. Jack's shown up and everyone's sucking up to him, offering to buy him drinks. I'm about to ask if he's seen Charlie lately when Angela grabs hold of him, and I *mean* "grab". She sticks an elbow in my ribs and tells me to back the hell off – I'm not even interested in Jack any more, if only she knew. I'm in a corner calling her names and licking my wounds when finally Charlie arrives.'

The express train of Macy's voice slowed down at last and she let her head drop forward. A sob rose in her throat.

'What did he say?' My own voice trembled from her mention of the bedcover. How much had Charlie told Macy about my visit to his room?

'Nothing. Zero, zilch. He acts like I'm not there.'

'So what did you do?' I hardly had to ask. I could just imagine Macy striding across the bar in her red micro skirt and jingling ankle boots, her hair all aflame, ready to resume.

'I wait until he's finished talking with Natalia then I ask him to dance. That's all.' Rubbing her eyes with the heel of her hand, she only managed to smudge more mascara down her cheeks. 'He doesn't say anything – it's all in the look.'

'Nothing? Not a word.'

'The look says "Do I even know you?" Then he turns

his back and orders another drink.' The memory was too much – Macy's voice broke and her body shook with sobs.

'That doesn't sound like something he'd do.' Even though I'd recently experienced a new facet of Charlie's character, I hadn't expected him to cut her dead. I'd thought at least he would let her down more gently. Then again, no way would I have predicted the move he'd just made on me.

'What did I do wrong?'

'Nothing. Charlie always knew it wasn't going anywhere, but you didn't realize that, I guess. I'm sorry.'

Sniffing loudly, Macy scrubbed at her face with a tissue she took from her purse. 'Thanks, Tania. And I'm sorry too. Here's me falling apart over Charlie when the focus should be all on you, after what you've been through. Orlando and Gwen – did they show up yet?'

'Yeah,' I admitted. 'But let's just say we still don't have a ride back to Bitterroot.'

'We don't?'

'No, the truck's missing from the car park. Orlando found out that Gwen doesn't have a job here any more so I guess he drove her back to Aspen, to the airport.'

'And how are you doing?'

'Don't even ask.' The effects of the alcohol Charlie had

given me had long ago worn off, leaving me feeling sour-mouthed, flat and empty.

'Are you angry with him?'

'No. I'm just kind of numb. All I want to do is see him, talk through this, work out where we go next.'

'Good luck with that.' Macy kicked off her boots then picked them up as she headed for the door. 'Pity you can't do some magic here – commune with your spirits and get them to do nasty things to Gwen.'

I smiled weakly. 'Yeah, unfortunately it doesn't work like that.'

'You know – do a deal with your dark angel mugger, get him to scare Gwen off big time. Couldn't he shape-shift into some kind of monster and gobble her up?'

'Which would really make Orlando love me lots!' I knew Macy was doing her best to lighten the mood but actually it was having the opposite effect and I was toppling from that icy ledge into a pit of despair. 'I think I'll stick with my original plan of waiting for him to show up and talking it through.'

'You need to sleep,' she advised. 'Tomorrow it'll look different – better maybe.'

I thanked her, feeling relieved when the door finally closed behind her and I could take off my clothes and curl up under the sheets.

By now my head was aching and my stomach churned – again, thanks to Charlie and the St Bernard moment by the ski lift.

It passed through my mind that alcohol had been at the core of his plan to get me into bed. What did this remind me of? I tossed and turned until it came to me: drink had played a major role in Zoran Brancusi's Heavenly Bodies celebrations at Black Eagle Lodge. The morning after his party, Holly and I had felt this same way – hungover and dazed, with huge gaps in our understanding about what had happened the night before. Likewise the birthday party for Antony Amos at New Dawn, when Channing and the rest had performed their shape-shifting tricks.

Stop. What was I doing comparing Charlie to dark angel seducers like Daniel on Black Rock and Jarrold at New Dawn? This just showed you what happened when you had too much contact with the dark side – you begin to suspect even the best people.

I sat up and put on the light to clear my head. On the bedside table my cell phone told me I had a new message from Charlie: How r u doing? Did Orlando make contact? Sorry I lost control earlier. Do u forgive me?

I texted to tell him no then yes, turned off the light, tried to sleep.

I stand on a ledge. Below me is a deep crevasse. Above my head, angels are at war, eclipsing the sun. A million light years away stars explode and die.

I am alone on a high snowy peak. My ledge gives way under my feet; I fall for what feels like for ever between ice cliffs, away from the light. I am in darkness at the bottom of the crevasse, crawling on hands and knees towards a dim blue light. A tunnel opens out into an underground ice cave, glowing like blue glass. Icicles hang from the roof, sharp as knives. Ice sheets crack and groan, the cavern floor splits then gives way and I fall again.

I am sliding towards the dark centre of the earth, reaching out. There is nothing to hold on to.

Ice gives way to rock. I hear pickaxes, the rumble of carts along steel tracks, the distant call of men's voices. When I try to cry out, no sound comes from my mouth.

Miners swing their pickaxes and hack into the rock, their faces lined with fatigue, caked with dirt and sweat. They crouch and crawl along, coughing dust from their lungs, praying that pit props will hold, that the weight of the mountain above will not crush them.

I too crawl and cough. I pray.

Hell is all around.

A creature blocks my way. He is on all fours, with a man's head and torso, but the limbs and lower body are massive and *bear-like. His brown eyes shine bright in the darkness. When he opens his mouth and snarls, I see sharp canine teeth strong and long enough to tear me apart.*

The mouth opens then snaps shut. He creeps towards me.

I am choked by dust. It is in my nostrils, my mouth, my throat. Rocks fall but the beast keeps coming. His foul breath is on me; a boulder blocks my retreat.

There is nowhere for me to run.

I woke up in terror, unable to catch my breath. I turned on the light to make sure that the creature was not in the room. I still felt his breath, saw his piercing eyes.

For me there is no border between sleep and wakefulness. The dark forces can step from nightmare into reality and however hard I run I can't shake them off. They are dragging me to the dark depths of hell.

Larry King looked worried. He had five short days in Mayfield to shoot the final scenes for his *Siege* sequel and day one had got off to a bad start.

'What do you mean, Jack's still in bed?' he demanded when a runner gave him the news. 'Lucy, Tania, Macy – anybody – go tell him to get his ass out here!'

Macy and I were shivering on the mountain along with fifty members of the crew plus extras, including a couple of the good-looking bartenders from the night before. Rocky was in costume, ready for action. Even Angela the Vamp had hauled herself out of somebody's bed, made it to the make-up trailer by six a.m. and was standing by.

'Tania, go knock on his door,' the assistant director ordered. 'Find Natalia. Tell her Jack is costing us money.'

I didn't want to go back to the hotel. What if Orlando put in an appearance here on the set and I missed him?

'Don't worry, I'll text you if he shows up,' Macy read my mind.

So I walked quickly down the slope, past the ski-lift terminal where I'd last seen Orlando, between the rows of trees lit up for Christmas and on into the main hotel lobby with its tall tree glittering with silver baubles, bearskin rugs on the floors and glassy-eyed elk heads staring down from the walls. Luckily this is where I ran into Natalia with Adam and Phoebe, all dressed up for a morning's ski instruction.

'Wait here with Tania,' she told them after I'd passed on Larry's message, and she disappeared into the elevator.

'Daddy's sick,' Phoebe told me sadly. She was all in red, with white furry trim and big white mittens. 'He was angry with Mommy and said bad words.'

Adam looked straight ahead without saying anything.

'Maybe he's better now,' I told Phoebe quietly. As it

happened, I was still feeling queasy myself, putting it down to a combination of alcohol and anxiety about Orlando, who still wasn't answering his phone. *Please come back!* were the three words constantly repeating themselves and drilling holes in my brain.

Luckily it wasn't long before the elevator door opened and Jack stepped out. I could tell it was Jack, not Charlie, by the shaking hands and a complexion the colour and texture of uncooked pastry.

'What time is it?' he growled at me as he walked unsteadily towards us.

I looked at my watch. 'Eight thirty.'

'Jesus Christ,' he groaned, running a hand through his unwashed hair. He hadn't shaved either and was as far away from his suave and sophisticated movie persona as it's possible to imagine. 'I asked for a seven a.m. wake-up call. Where the hell is Charlie? Has anybody seen him?'

'On one of the chairlifts,' I told him. 'He's rehearsing a stunt for a scene later today.'

Jack tried to shake off the alcoholic fug inside his head by striding out into the fresh air. Adam, Phoebe and I followed slowly.

'This is all down to Charlie,' he complained. 'Part of his job is to fix my schedule and get me in the right place at the right time and I pay him plenty to do it.'

'Even Charlie's not perfect, I guess.'

My comment struck a chord with Jack – so much so that he turned on me and laughed. 'Oh yeah, Mister Charlie Speke – everybody's favourite guy, including my wife's.'

Wincing, I began to walk off with the kids but Jack didn't let us go.

'In the beginning – you know, like they say in the Bible – in the beginning there was no Charlie. It was just me and lights, camera, action. I did it all by myself, clawed my way to the top of this lousy business without him. When I first met Charlie, he was an out-of-work catwalk model, a nobody.'

'He admits it,' I said, hoping to calm Jack down. Phoebe clamoured to be carried so I picked her up. 'He's the first to say that he owes you everything.'

Jack came close, breathing stale whisky over me and his daughter while Adam stood as close to me as he could get. 'Let me tell you something, Sharon, Marcia – what the hell's your name?'

'Tania.' I tried not to back away, to hold my ground.

'Let me tell you something, Tania – with Charlie, what you see is not what you get. You all think he's the good guy, don't you?'

I nodded, holding tight to Phoebe, whose little arms

were clasped tight round my neck.

'The guy who stands in for me in action sequences, who's there to pick up the pieces when I fall apart.'

'That's what Charlie does – he helps people. He's been there for me a couple of times,' I told him, editing out my previous night's experience on the red satin bed throw.

Jack snorted with laughter. 'Sweet! Didn't it occur to you that Charlie is part of the problem here?'

'How?' I wanted to know. For a severe alcoholic, Jack was talking coherently for once and following a strong, anger-fuelled train of thought.

'Suppose I was a drug addict,' he went on. 'An addict has to have a supplier – you get what I'm saying? Likewise with a whisky drinker with a wife and a whole team of people dedicated to keeping him off the booze – it only needs one member of the crew to break the don't-give-Jack whisky rule.'

'Charlie wouldn't do that,' I protested.

Again Jack laughed. 'That's what I mean – Charlie fools everybody. And you want to know why he buys me the frickin' whisky whenever I ask him? Well, it's obvious – the more Jack drinks, the more work Charlie gets. Jack ruins a scene and Charlie steps in. Jack's too drunk to show up to a movie premiere, frickin' Charlie's right up there on the red carpet with Natalia. Speaking of which . . .'

He caught sight of someone approaching from behind and I turned to see Natalia hurrying out of the hotel towards us.

'I called Rocky,' she explained to Jack. 'Charlie's working on an action sequence right now so Rocky will come and take you to where you need to be.'

'Charlie, Charlie,' Jack sighed, crouching down to Adam's level. 'Everything's about your Uncle Charlie, right?'

Adam screwed his eyes into narrow slits and bunched up his mouth.

'Hey, I'm kidding!' Jack laughed. 'Go skiing with your sister. Have fun.'

Natalia looked as if she was going to lay into him then bit her lip. 'Let's go,' she told Adam and Phoebe as Rocky strode down the hill.

'Dude, we need you,' Rocky called. 'If we don't get you on set within the hour, Larry swears he'll kick you off this movie for good.'

I didn't go back on set. Instead, I went to my room and took time out to think about what Jack had just said.

True, Charlie wasn't perfect – I knew that all too

clearly now. But I found it hard to believe that he was Jack's drinks mule. Jack's paranoid, I thought. Never believe an alcoholic.

Then again, I could see Charlie's motivation for acting the way Jack said he did. Be needed, be the rock that everyone could rely on – it was a good route to the number one spot.

It was no good – I couldn't work it out. But following my gut feeling, it was still Charlie's word that I trusted. After all, as far as I was concerned, until last night he hadn't put a foot wrong.

As I sat on my bed, I happened to glance out of my window and catch sight of Adam and Phoebe on the mountain. Natalia was standing at the top of the nursery slope. I saw Phoebe in her bright-red ski suit set off, travel a few metres then fall over. Then Adam started his downhill journey. He gathered speed, overtook his little sister then shifted his weight and curved off track. He disappeared over a low ridge in a spray of sparkling snow.

I blink. I am in a white wilderness under a pure blue sky. Sun's rays sparkle on the pure, untrodden snow.

'I am here,' a woman whispers. Her voice takes me back to a room with pink walls, butterfly stencils, the scent of soap. A baby's mobile toy tinkles above my head. I lie asleep as the

sun shines through the slats of the blind, wrapped in silence. I hear the whistling wings of a dove. She is white, pink and grey as she alights on a sunlit branch. More doves fly in a wide arc across a blue sky. 'I am here,' she whispers. 'Don't be afraid.'

I am alone in the snow but I am not afraid, hearing the voices of my good angels. My angels of light are with me – Maia and Zenaida, shifting from woman to bird and now into the shape of an innocent child. They lift me from the snowy slope. I am weightless, I shine like them.

And now another voice – the child's. 'You are in danger,' he says. 'Be sure of one thing – the dark forces are gathering.'

'I know it,' I whisper. I see devils rising from the centre of the earth with human faces and bear-like limbs. They explode on to the surface, jaws snapping, claws swiping the air. They gather in the frozen wastes to fight to the death with my angels of light.

'Be ready,' the child warns. 'Anger and bitterness sit in your dark angel's heart. You are his chief enemy.'

Maia and Zenaida support me as a pure light shines on to the snow beneath us. It sparkles. At its centre a child stands with arms raised. His face is full of hope. For the first time I whisper his name: 'Adam.'

Natalia swept on her skis down from the top of the slope and over the ridge. She brought her eldest son back into view – a blue-clad boy carrying skis, trudging through soft snow, leaning forward as he bore the weight of his parents' bitter battles on his small shoulders.

'Orlando, please come back.' I muttered my mantra out loud as I walked slowly up the mountain. I was at an all-time low, asking myself what love was worth in the enormous chaos of the world we live in.

What does it really mean when someone tells you they love you? Is it any more than a trap – something that shackles two people and keeps them in prison until the next temptation comes along, until lust forces open the door of the cage and lets one of you out? Cynical me says, 'Forget Vincent's stars and the dream of loving for ever until death do you part.'

I hadn't walked far before I glimpsed Orlando and Gwen sitting together in a chairlift, inside the terminal where we'd argued the night before. The cab swayed as Orlando stepped down from the platform. I watched in mounting dread as he made it to ground level then stumbled across my path.

I gasped his name, put out my arm to stop him from falling. 'You didn't drive to Aspen? For God's sake, where have you been all night?'

He sank to his knees.

'What's wrong, Orlando? Are you sick?' I was

scared by the paleness of his face, the lack of focus in his eyes.

He looked up at me in total confusion.

'It's me – Tania. Have you been out on the mountain all this time? What is it? Speak to me.'

But he didn't get up, just knelt in the snow as if all his strength was gone and it was all he could do to keep on breathing.

'Here, take my hand,' I told him.

His eyes closed then flickered back open. He was trembling and groaning as if every movement hurt.

'You're sick. You need to see a doctor.' Maybe pneumonia or hypothermia. Desperately I tried to fix a label on it so that I could delay thinking the worst. Again I offered him my hand.

Then Gwen came down the steel steps. Orlando heard her footsteps. He leaned forward to brace his arms against the ground and gain enough leverage to haul himself upright. He was on his feet by the time Gwen reached his side.

'What's wrong with him?' I begged.

She stared indifferently at me – that same cold, dark stare I'd seen last night, so different to the gentle, generous impression she gave when we first met her in the make-up trailer in Central Park.

'Orlando, it's time to leave,' she told him quietly but firmly.

He took a deep, shuddering breath then tried to follow her down the slope. But he could only make a few faltering steps before his knees buckled and he fell again.

'Let him be,' Gwen ordered as I rushed to help. She concentrated hard on Orlando as if she was conveying a message via telepathy, or as if she was a hypnotist and he was her subject.

My eyes widened and I felt my stomach flip in panic. Still I couldn't bear to put what was happening into words.

'Good!' Gwen coaxed as Orlando stiffly raised himself. 'You see, it's easy when you listen to me.'

I close my eyes, the mountain range tilts, two worlds collide inside my brain. First one black creature creeps out of the entrance to a cave, then two, three, four – until they're too many to count – bears on hind legs with shaggy limbs and human faces.

Then a loud roar and a beast three times the size of the bears bursts from the cave. His coat is matted with ice; he is more human than bear, with a savage, snarling face. He crouches then leaps towards me, towers above me, ready to seize me and squeeze my final breath from me.

The blindfold fell from my eyes at last. I saw Gwen

and recognized what she was.

'Come with me,' she told Orlando.

'Don't go!' I begged, tearing at his jacket. 'You see what she's doing, who she is!'

He turned his vacant gaze on me.

'She's a dark angel. You're in her power.'

He heard without understanding. He followed her siren voice.

'That's good, Orlando. You're leaving your old life, stepping with me into a glorious, shining future.'

I ran after them. She turned her gorgon stare on me and stopped me dead. I was like stone.

I opened my mouth to cry out for help. No sound came.

Black snakes slither from a white crevasse. They writhe out of the frozen depths and wind themselves around me.

I stood paralysed. My whole body felt crushed and bruised.

Gwen led Orlando back to the chairlift terminal. With all the willpower I possessed I fought my inertia and ran up the steps after them, my feet ringing on the metal treads. They went in together, stepped into a gondola. The machinery started to whir.

Inside I was screaming for him not to go, to stay with me, but no sound emerged.

The lift jerked and jolted forward. It rose up the mountain. Sunlight blinded me. My face felt scorched. Still I couldn't move even to shield my eyes until the lift carrying Orlando and Gwen reached the shadow cast by Carlsbad. I saw it rise higher, grow smaller.

'He's mine,' Gwen's voice whispered. Seductress, leading him through hell's gates.

She deals in death. She stands at the right hand of my dark angel.

'*Be brave,*' *Adam's voice says. He comes to me on the cold wind gusting down the white slopes. 'Keep a hold of my hand and believe in me. When the mountain cracks and the avalanche sweeps down into the valley I will be there. Look for me in the sky above Carlsbad, in all the wild places. Do not be afraid.*'

'*I believe in you,*' *I whisper. One evil spirit rises from hell and a good angel is released from heaven. Bright day and dark night are evenly matched in the eternal battle for our souls.*

10

They say you can die of a broken heart.

But I was still alive to feel the pain of losing Orlando.

I saw Gwen take Orlando up the mountain. My heart broke, my dreams lay shattered at my feet. By some miracle I went on breathing.

At lunchtime Macy came to find me in my hotel room. 'You have visitors,' she said. 'They're in the lobby outside reception, looking for you.'

It was as if she was speaking to me through a heavy veil that had settled like a shroud. 'Who is it?'

'Grace and Holly. The girl on the desk is trying to tell them the whole hotel is closed to the public. They need security passes even to come through the door.'

I roused myself enough to go down and see them. By the time I got there, another member of staff had arrived to back up the receptionist. I recognized the good-looking

Nordic bartender whose name badge read Owen.

'Hey, Tania – explain who we are!' Holly exclaimed as I came into the lobby. You could practically see the sparks coming off her. 'Tell them they can't stop us visiting you.'

'This is private property,' Owen said for probably the tenth time. 'The hotel, the grounds, all the ski slopes you see up there – they belong to Xcel.'

'Oh yeah, they also own the air we breathe?' Holly in full flight is unstoppable.

'Who exactly is Xcel?' Grace asked the receptionist, who looked like she'd just stepped out of a beauty salon – dark hair impeccably straightened, nails professionally manicured. Her badge read Amber.

'They're the management company who run this resort,' Amber explained smoothly. 'They rented out the whole place to Starlite for the duration of the shoot. Starlite is the production team behind the Jack Kane movie.'

'So they put in a clause saying absolutely no visitors?' Holly challenged. 'They turn this place into a fortress?'

'You got it,' Owen said, directing his next remark at me and Macy. 'Hey, guys, tell these people they can't be here. They have to leave.'

'You have to leave,' I echoed with a sigh. 'I already warned you about the security up here.'

'OK, so your dad called me.' Grace took no notice. 'He said something bad had happened with Orlando.'

My face told her it was true.

'So Grace called me and we jumped in my car and drove over,' Holly added. 'Looks like it's a good thing we did.'

'Come for a drive with us,' Grace suggested as Owen used his phone to call for reinforcements. We linked arms and walked towards the parking lot, with Holly and Macy following close behind.

'Call off the gorilla!' Holly yelled at Amber over her shoulder. 'We're out of here.'

Holly drove up a single-track road marked by thin orange poles. It led past the old silver-mine workings to the summit and she muttered as she went that Xcel would take over the entire mountain range if they thought there was a profit in it. A snowplough had been through but the surface of the road and the hairpin bends were still treacherous. Below us, the chairlift cables radiated from the terminal by the hotel, linked by steel towers that strode up the mountain, ending in smaller terminals dotted across the jagged north face. Ahead was the conical peak of the county's highest mountain.

'So how?' Grace sat with me in the back seat, with

Macy up front alongside Holly. 'How and exactly why did Orlando leave you stranded without a ride home?'

'That was the problem. We had no clue why he did it,' Macy said, in a hurry to answer for me as usual. 'He didn't say a word – not even a phone call or a text. His truck was gone. That's all we knew.'

'Tania?' Grace prompted.

'Macy's right. But I told Dad we each had a room, so not to worry.'

'He worried,' Holly muttered, gripping the wheel as the back wheels spun and skidded. 'And, Tania, your dad is Mister Cool, so when he stresses, we know there's a problem.'

'And this morning – did you see Orlando?' Grace always stays focused and calm, cutting to the quick.

'I did, and let's just say it was close to being the worst moment of my life.'

'That bad, huh? Why, what did he say?' Holly reached the end of the track and parked on an overlook. We were way above the ski slopes, surrounded by a thin white mist that crept down from the summit.

'Nothing. That was what was so awful. He was with Gwen and I don't even know if he recognized me.'

'You're kidding – of course he knew you.' Though Holly sounded confident, it was obvious from the quick glance she gave me that she was ready to freak out.

'No, really. He looked at me in a total daze.'

'So he was hungover.'

'No,' I insisted. 'It was like there was no one there. He just did whatever Gwen told him.'

Grace listened carefully, staring out of the window at the creeping mist. 'What you're saying is that Orlando's under Gwen's control, the same way I was with Ezra?'

I nodded. 'And Holly with Channing. You were like zombies with empty spaces where your brains should be.'

We shivered as the mist seemed to seep into the car.

'I can't get rid of those memories,' Grace confessed. 'I still have nightmares – the feeling of being trapped. I mean, I truly thought Ezra was some kind of god. I worshipped him, would have done anything he wanted, even thrown myself down the mountain for him. And I'm sure I spouted lots of weird stuff when I was under his control.'

'Yeah – about daring to step outside the narrow limits most of us live our lives by, to let your mind expand and embrace the spiritual world. You said of all that,' Holly reminded her.

'You too, Holly. After you went walking in the wilderness with Channing and almost froze to death, you were exactly the same. Totally spaced out. We thought we'd lost you for ever.'

'God, it sounds like you were both brainwashed!' Macy gasped.

'That's how they work,' I explained. 'Dark angels – they make you fall in love with them and then they control you for all time.'

'And let me get this straight – they're spirits; they have no physical presence?'

'They can shape-shift and take human form, but no, they're not human.' They're carved masks hanging on a wall that come to life when you pass. They're beasts of the forest painted on a chapel wall, wolves and bears, dogs with slavering jaws. 'They're the most powerful force for evil you can get.'

'So what are we waiting for?' Holly asked as she switched the engine on. 'We have to drive back to the lodge and get Orlando out of here before it's too late.'

'Owen tells me you had a problem with hotel security,' Charlie said at the entrance to the Carlsbad Lodge parking lot. He was still dressed in the red jacket and Oakley shades he'd worn to rehearse an action sequence on the ski lift. When he'd seen Holly's car come down off the mountain he emerged from the lodge and waited by the barrier with Owen the Viking barman. He totally ignored Macy, I noticed.

Both Holly and Grace made the usual mistake and underwent five seconds of shock and awe that they were face to face with a megastar.

'No,' he corrected. 'Tell them, Tania.'

'This is Charlie Speke. He's Jack's stunt double.'

'So yeah, actually we do have a problem.' Holly recovered first and leaned out of the driver's window. 'I'm Holly Randle. That's Grace Montrose in the back. We drove over from Bitterroot to see Tania but they wouldn't let us through the door.'

'No big deal – security issue solved!' Charlie announced as he produced two name tags with an official Xcel logo printed along the top. Mr Fix-it filled in the spaces with the two names Holly had just given him. 'You all want to come and have lunch?'

I wasn't sure, so I turned to the others.

'Lunch is in the bar where Owen works,' Charlie added. 'Everyone will be there.'

'Including Orlando and Gwen?' Grace checked.

'There's been a problem with Gwen's position as make-up artist so I can't swear to that.' He turned to the barman. 'Owen, did you see a tall, dark-haired guy, aged about eighteen, and my kid sister – a small girl with curly fair hair?'

Owen nodded. 'They ordered chicken Caesar salad.'

'Cool – we'll have lunch with them,' Holly decided.

But she wasn't the first out of the car – it was Macy, dressed for the weather in cute fur-lined suede boots, skinny jeans and a big cream sweater with a black zigzag pattern. And it wasn't Charlie she made a bee line for – it was Owen with the long blond hair, blue eyes and serious muscles.

'Babe, if you're the one serving the drinks, I'm there ahead of you,' she said with fluttering eyelashes and comedy femme fatale voice that made Owen grin. She sashayed across the parking lot, making the most of her compact, curvy body to keep her new friend's attention glued to her slim waist and toned butt. Watch out, Charlie – this is payback time!

We followed, and I found myself strung out with nervous anxiety that I was about to see Orlando and Gwen together again.

'Macy doesn't waste any time,' Charlie commented as he held open the door.

I managed to smile and explain to Grace the situation between him and Macy. 'Until last night she hung on every word Charlie said. She stuck to him like glue. It was true love.'

'Wow, it's hard to keep up,' Grace observed, walking ahead while I hung back to look at Charlie to see if there was even a tinge of regret about Macy.

He held my gaze. 'I spoke to Gwen earlier,' he said, quietly changing the subject. 'I'm having second thoughts; maybe it's better if you two don't take lunch together.'

This irritated me. Don't push me around, I thought. 'I wasn't thinking about eating,' I told Charlie abruptly. Then straight away I regretted it. 'Thanks for getting badges for Holly and Grace. They drove over from Bitterroot to make sure I was OK.'

'They heard about the situation with Orlando? Listen, this isn't easy for Gwen either.'

'I don't want to talk about it.'

But Charlie was determined. He stopped me in the entrance to Owen's bar. 'I know my sister. She's not the type who sets out deliberately to wreck relationships.'

'She did a pretty good job here,' I pointed out, anxiously scanning the busy room.

Charlie shook his head. 'Gwen told me Orlando made the first move.'

'Really, I can't listen to this.' I felt sick. And anyway,

how did you even start to tell someone that their sister came from the dark side, that she'd been possessed by a devil and wasn't human any more? I broke away and tried to catch up with Grace and Holly, who had located Orlando and Gwen drinking coffee in a quiet corner of the bar.

Orlando saw them and instead of ignoring them as I expected, he smiled then stood up to beckon them across. It seemed his old energy was back. 'How do you do it?' He pointed to the pass Holly wore around her neck. 'Those things are like gold dust.'

'Hey, how are you doing?' Holly sat down at their table, leaving room for me and Grace.

'Good,' he told her, smiling at Grace and giving me an awkward, apologetic shrug. Back to normal, except that nothing was or ever could be normal until I'd got him away from his dark angel. 'By the way, this is Gwen. She's been working for Starlite in make-up. Gwen, meet Holly and Grace, friends of mine from Bitterroot.'

I stared at him, then at Gwen. What was going on here? Where was the empty zombie look, the seismic disconnect of first thing this morning? I mean, we could have been a normal bunch of buddies catching up over a coffee.

Grace and Holly were obviously wondering the same

thing. Where was the dark angel influence I'd warned them about?

While Grace took her time to study Gwen's calm, delicate features, Holly forged ahead. 'So, Orlando, we were worried about you.'

He spread his palms, gave another casual, self-effacing shrug.

'You're OK?'

Before Orlando could answer, Gwen got up from the table. 'I'll leave you guys to talk,' she said quietly before melting diplomatically into the background.

'Is this about me and Gwen?' He asked Holly the direct question. There was still no sign of his nightmare on the mountain when he'd followed his new lover's siren voice. No – he was sitting with legs wide apart, leaning back in his chair, inviting Holly and Grace to ask him any question they wanted.

'It's more about you and Tania,' Holly said. 'Orlando, what the hell happened in New York?'

He shook his head and rocked his chair forward, his hair falling across his forehead. 'Nothing happened. Tania and I just reached the end of the road.'

'As simple as that?' Holly's mother-tiger instinct kicked in and she sprang to defend me against the lame phrases he was beginning to spout. End of the road. Going separate ways. Moving on. 'Do you know what this is doing to Tania? Have you any idea how much you've hurt her?'

For the first time Orlando grew defensive. 'I told her I couldn't be there for her. I warned her she'd have to let go of the dark angel stuff.'

'Like she has a choice!' Holly snorted. 'Tania doesn't choose to hear what she hears, see what she sees. Think about it, for Christ's sake.'

'I'm thinking, and what I know is, she'd rather use her psychic powers than work at her relationship with me.'

Now this was weird. You always imagine you'd love to have a friend like Holly to fight your corner – ballsy and totally on your side – but when it actually happens you get a surreal feeling that you're not there, you don't exist.

Grace could sense that this was happening to me. 'Tania is sitting here,' she reminded them coolly. 'And anyway, Holly, we're not interested in poking around in what happened in New York. Orlando, we just want to check you and Tania are both OK.'

'Do I look OK?'

Grace studied his untroubled expression. 'Yeah, but I guess that's the problem,' she said slowly. 'Somehow you look too OK, considering you just split from your long-term girlfriend.'

Orlando shrugged and stood up. 'Then I guess I can't win.' He set off to find Gwen but stopped to share one last thought. 'Forget about me and focus on Tania,' he advised Grace and Holly. 'She just tried and failed to get Gwen thrown off this movie. If you ask me, she's the one who needs your help.'

'His eyes are clear and focused.' Holly began the checklist of reasons not to believe that Orlando was in danger. 'All his reactions – coordination, balance, they worked perfectly.'

'No memory gaps,' Grace added. 'No mention of weird spiritual stuff.'

'So I imagined it,' I muttered. We'd stayed at the table after Orlando had left. Over by the bar Macy was still busy working her magic on Owen while a lot of the production crew were finishing their lunch and leaving for the afternoon's filming.

'We're not saying we don't believe you,' Grace assured me. 'But we do have to check out all the possible reasons for the way Orlando acted last night.'

'And again this morning.' I told them how he'd collapsed in front of me, how Gwen had taken total control. 'And don't tell me he was hungover,' I pleaded.

There was an awkward silence while Holly and Grace

exchanged worried looks. 'Really, he wasn't!'

'So now he's back to normal,' Holly pointed out. 'That didn't happen to either me or Grace. And remember Oliver – the kid on Black Rock? Once the dark angels got their claws into him, he was totally zombified.'

I nodded. I was the one who'd found Oliver's body amongst the burned roots of a redwood tree. The fire service had carried the corpse down from Black Rock and informed his mother. Zoran Brancusi had denied any knowledge of how he'd died. But I'd been there and I knew.

'I guess they got smarter,' Grace said with a hint of uncertainty. 'Gwen moves in on Orlando and starts her mind-control games, makes him walk away from the only girl he's ever loved but at the same time she doesn't turn him into a total weirdo, so it's not obvious to outsiders what's happening. See what I mean – they fine-tuned their technique.'

'So what's their next move?' Holly wondered.

'You know what it is!' I cried, breaking through Grace's calm logic. 'Gwen got through the seduction part with Orlando. She worked her spell. Now he's turned his back not just on me but on all of his old life – his mom and dad, his high school friends, his college buddies.'

'You don't think he'll come home?' Holly checked.

'Not in a million years.'

Grace agreed. 'If you're right, the next move is some kind of initiation ceremony for Orlando – a celebration.'

'Which is when he actually steps across to the dark side,' I confirmed. 'They win. We lose.' It sounded so scary put into words that I began to shake.

'But it hasn't happened yet.' Holly was the one to think ahead. 'We still have time.'

'How? What do we do?' The trembling got worse. I hyperventilated and felt my hands and arms begin to tingle.

'We try to find out a few things. For starters, who exactly is Gwen? What can we find out about her?'

'Holly's right,' Grace agreed. 'We learn all we can. That's how it works. Once we know more facts about the dark angels we can start to take back some of their power.' She held my trembling, tingling hand until the wave of fear had passed. 'What about your good angel? Has she shown up yet?'

'He, not she.'

'Who is he? What does he say?'

'He tells me to hold his hand and be brave.' I shook my head and sighed. I missed the strength of Maia and Zenaida, who had been there for me before, heading up the army of good angels who did cosmic battle against the forces of darkness. 'He's really young. I'm scared he's not strong enough.'

'But you have to trust him,' Grace told me.

It touched me and made me smile – her total faith in Adam, my good angel. 'Thanks,' I told her.

'And remember, Gwen won't be acting alone,' Holly reminded us. 'There are others. We have to work out who they are.'

'If I knew I would tell you,' I sighed. 'There was my mugger in New York – he was one for sure. But now look around you here on Carlsbad. We know there's Gwen but she can't be the leader.'

'Why not?' Grace asked.

Thanks to her and Holly, I started to take deep breaths and slowly got back to trusting my instinct. 'I don't know. She just isn't.'

'We're looking for a cult figure like Zoran,' Holly decided. The room was empty now except for Macy still at the bar with Owen. 'How about Jack Kane?'

'That just doesn't seem right either,' I argued. And I shattered some illusions by telling them about the dirty underbelly of megastardom – the booze, the girls, the self-destruction.

'His wife?' Grace suggested. 'Could Natalia be the one?'

'Again – no.'

'Why not?'

'You'd have to meet her to know why not; she's an amazing person. She stepped in and helped me and Orlando when we were in New York. As soon as she heard we were studying film and costume, she got us on to the set as interns. Plus, she's a great mother to her three kids.'

'You admire her,' Grace said softly, curiously.

'I do. Doesn't everybody?'

'Everybody?' she pressed.

'Apart from the guy who married her. But then Jack doesn't admire anyone except himself.'

'So Natalia has charisma.' Holly saw where Grace was leading. 'Which means we need to check her out. Plus the director of this movie . . .'

'Larry King,' I reminded her.

'Plus Jack's co-stars and the technical crew – anyone from Starlite who's connected to *Siege* 2.'

'Add Charlie to the list,' Grace insisted. She'd spotted him coming into the bar and talking to Owen and Macy. 'He's Gwen's brother, remember. If she's on the dark side, Charlie's a definite possibility.'

My first reaction was, 'No way! Charlie is the one who helped me in Central Park. He's everyone's hero.' Then the false move he'd made last night hit me again – the slug of alcohol from his flask, the bed with the satin throw, moonlight streaming in.

'Yeah, definitely Charlie.' Holly picked up my hesitation and brought him into the frame.

Across the room, Macy leaned across the bar to give Owen a peck on the cheek plus an eyeful of cleavage. Charlie didn't react. He simply passed on a short message to Owen then walked away, past the table where Holly, Grace and I sat.

'If you see Jack any time soon,' he said to me, 'tell him Larry's made some late changes to his script. He might need to read through before he goes on set.'

'Cool.' I was still knocked off balance by our new suspicions about him. Light to dark, good to evil – it was a major shift and it hadn't fully sunk in. But I hid my confusion by picking up the cup of coffee that Gwen had left on the table.

'Why do I feel my ears burning?' Charlie asked with his drop-dead gorgeous grin. He couldn't do anything about his smile – it was just part of him.

'What makes you think we were talking about you?' Holly challenged without missing a beat. Boy, she was good. 'Either you're so vain – as in you totally know you're the hottest topic of conversation for every girl you meet – or maybe it's based on actual evidence.'

Charlie's smile broadened, the dimple deepened. 'Tania, tell them I have supersonic hearing. While I was standing at the bar I picked up every word you three girls said.'

For half a second even Holly was thrown. Then she laughed and asked him to warn us about any other superpowers he might be hiding from us.

'Later,' he promised, finally leaving the bar.

'Oh my God!' Holly cringed. 'He didn't hear . . . he couldn't . . . could he?'

Through the window I saw Charlie leave the building and cross paths with Jack and Adam, who were coming off the nursery slopes. Jack carried his son's skis, hat and gloves and was looking relaxed for once, but when Charlie spoke – presumably to pass on Larry's message about the script – his mood quickly changed. Thrusting the skis on to Charlie, he left him to take care of Adam and stormed into the hotel alone.

He headed straight for the bar, bringing with him a blast of cold air mixed with the whiff of testosterone and stale breath. 'Get me a whisky,' he told Owen. 'Make it a double.'

Macy put a hand on his arm. She said something that made him push her away so hard that she toppled against a stool then dropped to the floor.

I went to help her up.

'Whisky,' Jack snarled at Owen, who slowly reached for the bottle on a shelf behind him and poured the drink into a glass.

'Wait,' I protested. 'Jack, what are you doing here?'

He didn't turn his head but his eyes slid sideways to catch sight of me still trying to help Macy to her feet. 'I'm minding my own frickin' business,' he said savagely. 'Tell your buddy she should do the same.'

'What did you say to him?' I hissed at Macy, making sure I stood between her and Jack.

'I passed on Charlie's info about the rewrites.' The knockback only seemed to make her more determined to get the message into Jack's thick head. 'Hold back on the whisky, Owen. Holly, Grace – go fetch Charlie. Tell him we have a situation.'

'"Go fetch Charlie"!' Jack mimicked. He leaned across the bar for the glass but Owen was there before him, swiping the whisky out of his reach. The liquid in the glass sloshed and spilled on to the polished granite surface. 'What exactly is it with Charlie? Is he my stunt double or my full-time jailer?'

'Did you two just have a fight?' I asked, wondering what had pressed Jack's buttons.

Jack's answer was a stream of abusive adjectives

213

followed by 'Charlie frickin' Speke'. Then he launched an attack on Owen for grabbing the glass and spilling the whisky, on me and Macy for breathing, on the whole world for existing.

'So Larry needs you on set,' I said, trying not to blink and grimace as spittle sprayed from Jack's mouth.

'They're filming a scene outside the entrance to the old silver mine,' Macy told us. 'It's at the end of the dirt road, just down from the overlook. Holly could drive us up there.'

As she went off to ask Holly the favour, Jack ran out of venom and slumped forward on to the bar. He breathed heavily and there was sweat trickling down his face.

'You OK?' I asked, noticing that Owen had retreated through the swing doors into the kitchen behind the bar.

He leaned forward to rest his head on his arms, letting the air out like a deflating balloon. 'My life is a mess,' he groaned. 'My kids hate me and my wife has decided to file for divorce.'

I gasped, unable to find any words beyond, 'Jeez, I'm sorry.' Not really equal to the occasion, I admit.

'Yeah.' Jack looked up with tears in his eyes. 'She files for divorce and she doesn't even tell me in person. She gets my frickin' alter ego, her messenger boy, to deliver the news instead.'

'Just now, when you came off the nursery slopes with Adam?'

'Yeah, right there,' he sighed. 'Charlie announces Natalia and I are through. This is the day I lose my kids, my wife, everything.'

11

Now Jack Kane and I had plenty in common.

I'd lost my starry-night lover; he'd lost his beautiful wife and family.

People fall apart in different ways but the actual moment when the heart breaks must be the same for everyone. Pain is universal. Suffering is something we can all relate to.

Macy fixed the ride up the mountain with Holly and Grace and between us by some miracle we managed to get Jack on set in time for Lucy Young to hand him the rewritten screenplay to study before Larry called for action.

'Charlie told us you couldn't make it,' she confided. 'Larry was ready for him to stand in for everything except the dialogue.'

'I'm here, aren't I?' Jack grunted, and snatched the

flimsy script from the assistant director. 'So Charlie can go to hell.'

'I'll go tell the guys in make-up,' Lucy promised, hurrying off towards a trailer parked on the overlook.

'You're sure you can do this?' I checked with Jack. Up here on Carlsbad an icy wind whipped up a top layer of loose snow that swirled around our feet. It was so cold that our faces, fingertips and toes soon felt frozen solid. I thought of the shock news Charlie had given him and of the effect it would have on his already wrecked nervous system.

'Yeah, if you give me that drink,' he joked, kidding around by extending his hand and making it tremble big time.

'Sure, that'd solve everything.'

Grunting, he shot me a glance then cleared his throat. He began to read through his script, ignoring Angela the Vamp when she emerged from the trailer in the latest skiwear, ready to shoot a sequence of her emerging from the entrance to the old mine carrying a gun, looking over her shoulder then running towards a cable car, climbing in and setting off down the mountain.

As she got into position, I took in the mine entrance – a rough arch hacked into the rock, supported by ancient timbers – and for a second, pale monsters from my underground nightmare roared out of the darkness, wailed and flew up into the bright sky then melted away.

'Scene twenty-five. Exterior. Entrance to silver mine. Angela's character just shot me,' Jack explained. 'There in the interior of the old mine. We're partners in a big gold heist back in the city. Rocky plays the undercover cop who finally catches up with us. We have to ski across country then hole up in the mine, hoping he won't find us. We're under siege for three days then bad weather forces Rocky and his men off the mountain. This is the part where Angela double-crosses me. She stashes the gold deep in the mine, shoots me and leaves me for dead.'

'Nice,' I muttered. It was no stretch for Angela Taraska to play a character who would shoot a guy for money.

'Before she fires her gun, I say to her, "Don't kill me." She says to me, "Give me a good reason why not." I now say, "Because in this state they still have the death penalty. You think I'm worth the risk?" She shoots me anyway.' Laughing at the idiotic script, Jack tossed it in the air.

I watched its pages separate then flutter down on to the snow, looking up only when Lucy called for Jack to come to the trailer while Larry King asked Angela for take two.

* * *

218

Later I spotted Natalia on set with Charlie and the kids and wondered how come she was acting as if she hadn't just called time on her marriage. 'Acting' is the operative word here, I guess.

'Hey, Tania!' Natalia waved me across to where she stood. She seemed very together – beautiful as ever in her dark-red coat, wearing big Ray-Bans and her hair loose over her shoulders 'I was worried about you. Are you doing OK?'

I sighed and shook my head. 'I talked to Orlando but I couldn't get through to him. It feels like he's definitely made up his mind to stay with Gwen.' Keep it short, I thought. Don't go into dark angel detail. I smiled weakly at Phoebe perched on Charlie's shoulders, then at Adam, who stood slightly apart from the group.

'I truly am sorry,' Natalia told me. 'We did our best to break them up before the relationship really got into gear but it doesn't seem to have worked. For one thing, it turns out Larry insisted that Gwen keep her job.'

'Yeah, I was wondering about that.' Listening to her smooth explanations, I studied her pale, sensitive face for any sign of what was happening between her and Jack.

'So she's still around and I guess it's time for you to move on,' Natalia suggested, and she seemed impatient when I didn't respond. 'No – not ready yet?'

Again I shook my head. I could have come clean then and declared that I'd never be ready to move on and abandon Orlando, that I ached for him every moment of the day and I was desperately working out my own way to drag him back from the dark side. 'I'll never, never give in,' was what I would have said if I'd let Natalia see what was in my bruised and battered heart.

What prevented me was partly the idea that she'd switched focus since our last meeting. It was hard to pin down – just that she seemed more detached, less interested in my problems. Call it a loss of empathy. And the other reason I held back was that Gwen's brother was there, sharing our conversation.

Charlie swung Phoebe down from his shoulders, took the baby from Natalia and promised to take care of him while she went to the trailer to give Jack his five-minute call.

'It's like having a fourth child,' she sighed as she left us. 'I have to organize Jack's day from the time he gets out of bed to the minute his head hits the pillow at night.'

But for how much longer, I wondered. Who would child-mind Jack Kane when the divorce came through?

'I'm amazed he even showed up,' Charlie commented. 'I tell you, if we get through to Saturday, it's a miracle.'

'Sshh, don't let the kids hear you,' I warned. I noticed

Adam drift further away, trudging through the snow towards the camera crew, ten metres from the entrance to the old mine.

'So how much does Adam know about what his parents are going through – the divorce and everything?'

I'd planned for this to bring Charlie up short and it worked.

'Jack told me,' I went on steadily. 'You'd just dropped the bombshell in his lap, down there outside the hotel. So yeah, you're right – it is amazing that he showed up at all and he's not drowning his sorrows in the hotel bar. Mind you, he did try that, but Macy stopped Owen from giving him the drink.'

Charlie frowned. 'It looks like you girls got more involved in Natalia and Jack's problems than I knew.'

'More than I like,' I admitted. I was keeping one careful eye on Adam, who had skirted round the film crew and seemed curious to find out what was inside the entrance to the mine. 'Watch out for monsters!' I wanted to yell. To everyone else it would have sounded like a game that kids played, but he and I knew different.

'You're right, it's not a good place to be,' Charlie warned. 'When people like Natalia and Jack go through a divorce it can get messy.'

He meant rich people, attention-hungry celebs. I agreed with this at least. 'I'm sad for them. I wonder where they go from here.'

'They stick to the plan of going to the Bahamas for Christmas,' he explained. 'It's important the news doesn't break until the new year. They want to keep it out of the gossip columns, off the blogosphere. You hear me?'

'The secret's safe with me,' I promised. I looked again for Adam beyond the cameras, the sound equipment and the bunch of technical crew members gathered around Larry and Lucy and felt a jolt of alarm when I couldn't pick out his small blue figure.

There was no time to follow this up before Jack emerged from the trailer followed by Natalia, Gwen and Orlando.

Gwen and Orlando. The way the names had begun to couple up so naturally gave me a big wrench and that sick feeling in the pit of my stomach.

Jack strode towards the director and presented himself for duty with a mock salute.

'Scene twenty-six. Exterior. We shoot this sequence at the entrance to the mine,' Larry explained. He looked up at the clouds gathering over the mountains, asked for lighting levels to be checked then went on to talk Jack through the scene. 'You've been shot in the right shoulder.

222

You know you have to make it down the mountain before nightfall, so you come out of the mine in time to see Angela escape in the chairlift. You're losing a lot of blood.'

'Blood!' Jack declared, slipping his right arm out of his black ski jacket to show Gwen's handiwork. His shoulder and arm were stained crimson.

'There's no dialogue – this is all action. Scene twenty-four, which we shoot later this afternoon, is where we rewrote the script, right?' From experience, Larry felt he had to speak to Jack as if he was a kid. 'Here, in this scene, you start to run towards the ski station; we track you, see you stumble and sink to your knees. Cut.'

'Blood in the snow.' Jack's sardonic voice cut across Larry's directions. 'What's my mindset here, Larry? What's my motivation and who the hell cares?'

'Let's just shoot,' the director decided, while the crew took up their positions and Lucy led Jack to the mine entrance.

I had an urge to follow them and find Adam before the call for action but my feet were rooted to the spot. I stared at the dark tunnel into the mountain and experienced that hypnotic, paralysing moment before reality crashes into unreality.

Worlds collide.

Darkness sucks me in. I'm drawn into a vortex, swept off

my feet, gasping, clutching at stale air. The roof of the mine drips with slime, there is black water in the tunnel, the wooden props splinter and crack.

I lose my footing and am carried by rushing water, deeper into the mine until at last the tunnel opens into a cavern and my body slams against a wall of rock.

A candle lights the cave. Seams of precious silver glint above my head. Rusting pickaxes and shovels are abandoned on a ledge.

'Don't leave me,' an injured man pleads. 'Take me with you. Get me out of here.'

Boots crunch over rock, the sound fades. His companions abandon him.

More props collapse, the roof caves in. Boulders fall. A choking dust fills the cave as the candle flickers and almost dies.

A hand grasps at my arm, the agonized face of the trapped miner emerges from the cloud of black dust. 'Don't leave me!'

We're not alone in the cave. A bundle of rags turns out to be a rotting corpse, the face stripped of flesh, eyes already gone, dark sockets gaping. There are more skulls kicked into a corner, bones and a pair of leather boots with worn soles, without laces.

I free myself from the dying man's grasp. I try to breathe, to follow the fleeing footsteps. Rocks fall all around me.

The man chokes and coughs, there is a rasp and rattle in his throat. He doesn't speak again.

I'm crouched forward; my hands and knees bleed. But still I'm determined to live.

'Be brave.' A new voice brings fresh hope. Out of darkness and chaos comes light.

I look up. The candle grows brighter to form a halo round the child's face. His brown eyes are tender; they pity me.

'Don't leave me,' I beg. I echo the dead miner's words, feel my heart race.

Adam my angel of light stays with me. He protects me from the falling rock, shows me a safe place. 'You're not alone,' he promises as he leads me to safety. He has the full mouth and the dark, curled hair of a choirboy, with a glowing halo around his head.

'As long as you search for the truth, I'll be with you.'

'I've been here before,' I groan. I'm weary to the bone, too tired for the struggle. I'd fought fire and water. Twice I discovered the truth and brought my friends back from the brink. But still my dark angel hounds me. He snaps at my heels. He won't rest until he's destroyed me. 'When will it end?'

'This is the third and final battle,' Adam promises, and to me this is wonderful news – something that I am slow to take on board. 'Three times, and only three, the dark forces may try to destroy you.'

'You're sure?' I whisper. 'If I come through this, they'll have to leave me alone?'

Adam's face is solemn as he nods his head. 'This is their last attempt.'

'After that?'

'There is truth, there is light.' The angelic boy gazes at me with love and compassion. 'In the end, you will be free.'

The revelation astonishes me. It brings a blast of energy through my aching, exhausted body. I find the strength to go on.

When I open my eyes and look up, it was Orlando who bent over me. In that short moment it was as if a dam had burst at the entrance to my heart, and hope flooded in.

'Tania passed out,' he yelled, easing one arm under me and raising me from the snow.

Orlando held me. That was all I knew.

'Grace, fetch help. Find a medic.' He supported me and held me against his chest, hugging me for warmth.

Then other people showed up – Holly raced to my side and helped Orlando raise me to my feet. 'Can you stand? Come on, Tania – look at me. Focus. Try to walk.'

A first-aider felt my rapid pulse, thought that I was probably having a panic attack. 'Breathe slow and deep,' she instructed. 'Keep your eyes open.'

I don't know how much time passed before Gwen arrived with blankets and Orlando released me from his arms. He stepped aside.

Come back. Hold me again. Never let me go.

He stepped back and the hope in my heart drained away.

'Breathe,' the first-aider insisted. 'Big, deep breaths, in through your nose, out through your mouth.

My arms and hands tingled, my legs buckled again.

'We need a stretcher,' someone said. It was the last thing I heard before I fainted a second time.

I woke up in Natalia and Jack's penthouse suite, in the lounge area with a balcony overlooking the mountain. It must have been late afternoon because light was fading from the sky.

At first I thought there was nobody in the room, and from my position lying full length on the cowhide sofa I stared around at the deer and elk heads adorning the wooden-panelled walls. The dead animals stared back at me and gave me the creeps.

'Definitely a panic attack,' a woman's voice was saying.

I craned my neck to see two people in the room next door: Natalia and another woman – possibly the first-aider who'd checked my pulse. I was longing for

Orlando to be there too.

'She should be fine,' The first-aider told Natalia as she was shown out.

'We'll keep her warm and make her rest,' Natalia promised.

I heard the click of the outer door and felt rather than saw Natalia come back into the room.

'You're awake,' she said softly as she came into view.

'Where's Orlando?' I asked in a woozy voice. 'Did he come with us?'

'No, he and Gwen stayed on Carlsbad to shoot the scene. Larry said he needed more blood.'

I groaned.

'Can you sit up?' Natalia asked, helping me to swing my legs from the sofa on to the floor. 'No, don't try to stand, not yet.'

'Sorry,' I mumbled. My head still swam and my legs felt weak. 'Me wimping out – that's just what you don't need.'

'No problem.' She sat beside me and together we watched the sky turn violet then red as the sun sank behind the mountains. There was a last rim of gold, a flare of amazing colour before everything – the snowy peaks, the ski slopes, the tall Christmas trees lining the hotel driveway – turned grey.

'You have two interesting friends,' Natalia commented, apparently happy to sit and pass time.

'Holly and Grace?'

'Yeah. Plus Macy – make that three.'

'"Interesting"? That doesn't sound good.'

'Girls like Macy and Holly don't come off an assembly line. They're pretty unique. And I guess I'm surprised you're close with them. I think Grace is more your style.'

'I've known Grace for ever.'

'Does she have a boyfriend?'

'Yeah – Jude.'

'Is it the real deal? Are they loved up?'

'Totally.'

'What about Holly?'

'She's in a relationship with Aaron. We all hang out together – Grace and Jude, Holly and Aaron, me and . . . .'

'Orlando?' Natalia gave me a sympathetic smile. 'We have to recognize that things change,' she sighed. 'And don't I know it.'

'Sorry, I didn't think.'

'It's cool; I'm happy to talk about Jack and me. You're smart so you probably realize we've been washed up for a long time. The really painful part came about twelve months back, when I finally understood he wasn't going to stop drinking. That was after his third spell in rehab.

Until then I kept on hoping he'd change. But guess what – he managed to keep away from alcohol for a whole twenty-four hours, then he binged for two days and nights. That was it – the end.'

'And you have three kids together.' Stating the obvious is an annoying personality trait and I hate it when people do it to me, but the clumsy words fell out of my mouth.

'Yeah, the kids.' Still watching the colours fade from the mountains, Natalia lapsed into a painful, lonely train of thought, until a sudden commotion in the corridor broke the silence.

'We need to see her!' a familiar voice insisted, seemingly followed by pushing and shoving.

'That sounds like Holly,' I murmured. With a big effort I got to my feet and started towards the door.

'We're not leaving until we see her. Let go of me, you big, frickin' baboon!'

Quickly Natalia overtook me. She flung open the door to find Holly wrestling with a guy in a black polo shirt with a white security badge pinned to his chest. Behind her, a second guy kept a careful watch on Grace, but he wasn't quick enough to stop her from stepping around Holly and slipping past Natalia into the suite.

'Tania!' Grace gasped when she saw me totter towards

her. She lowered me into the nearest chair then squatted beside me. 'Are you OK?'

'This is a hotel, not a fortress!' Holly kept up the ruckus in the corridor while Natalia told the security guys to back off. The more she tried to intervene, the louder and more physical Holly became. 'We're not leaving – get it?'

Grace used the time to whisper a message. 'Listen, Tania, they're ready to throw us out. We want you to come with us.'

I shook my head until I thought my brain would come loose. 'It's Orlando – I won't go!'

'OK, but once we leave, you'll be totally alone. Can you deal with that?'

'You lay one finger on me and I'll sue the hell out of you!' Holly yelled at the bigger of the two men. Meanwhile, Natalia had disappeared down the corridor, presumably to fetch back-up.

'What choice do I have? I can't leave him.'

'So Holly and I will drive back home. We'll get help and come back. Shall we tell Orlando's parents?'

Again I shook my head. 'It sounds too crazy to people who don't know. They'd only do what you folks did – they'd drive out here in a blind panic and wouldn't even get past the gates.'

Out in the corridor, the two heavies had succeeded in backing Holly against the wall. She was still yelling, but it was two against one, with more people approaching.

'We'll be back,' Grace promised. 'Tomorrow at two p.m. – meet us at the overlook. Can you do that?'

This time I nodded.

'Don't tell anyone. Take the ski lift to the top of the mountain. We'll see you there.'

This was all she had time to say before Natalia reappeared with Amber, the hotel receptionist, closely followed by Macy and Owen. Owen backed up the security guards while Amber came in to inform Grace that unless she got Holly to calm down and leave the hotel, she would call 911.

Grace stood up, cool as anything. 'No need. We're out of here,' she told Amber. 'We've done what we came to do, which was to make sure Tania's doing OK.'

Amber kept up her slick, professional front. 'I understand. It's natural for you to be worried about your friend, but Miss Linton is taking good care of her.'

'We needed to see that for ourselves.'

'Again, I hear you. But our security guys have a job to do. If you take a look at your temporary passes you'll see that they ran out of time.'

'. . . One frickin' finger!' Holly warned Owen.

'OK, Holly, let's go,' Grace insisted, smiling at me as she took control.

It's obvious but worth saying anyway – Grace is exactly the friend you need in a crisis. People think she's soft and gentle, golden and sunny, but underneath she's smarter and sharper than anyone I know.

She stepped out into the corridor and instantly took the heat out of the situation, giving me a small, reassuring wave as she took Holly's arm and walked her out of sight.

'Whoa!' Macy laughed. 'What a day, right?'

Drawing a deep breath, I tried not to think about Grace and Holly driving back to Bitterroot without me. Instead, I focused on our meeting again in less than twenty-four hours.

'No way will they get passes.' The confrontation hadn't dented Macy's joie de vivre. In fact, she was smiling and giggling her way through the drama. 'Did you see Owen? The guy had martial arts training, don't you think? If your buddy had made a wrong move, he'd have laid her flat.'

Natalia frowned. 'Macy, it's not funny.'

'No one got hurt, did they? Plus, Tania's OK now – it was just a panic attack. Happy ending.'

'I guess.' Natalia sighed then looked at her watch. 'Tania, you're welcome to stay here as long as you like, only I have an appointment with the Starlite chief exec.'

'No, I'm OK. I'll go back to my room.'

'I'll make sure she gets there,' Macy volunteered.

'I have just enough time to change my clothes and go meet Ryan James at a private reception. His helicopter's due to land at seven.'

'No problem,' Macy insisted. Then, seizing me by the arm as if I was a senior citizen who needed help to cross the street, she steered me into the corridor.

'Call me if you need anything,' Natalia insisted as she closed her door.

Macy and I walked what felt like miles of carpet. Rather, I walked, she chattered, bubbled and fizzed. 'Ryan James is the executive producer on the *Siege* movies,' she explained. 'He financed the whole deal – in fact, he *is* Mister Starlite!'

'Take it easy,' I pleaded, stopping to draw breath before I pressed the elevator button to take us down to my room on the third floor. The door opened and for a moment I was back in the underground car park in New York. My mugger was stepping out of the lift with his bullet-head concealed beneath a fur-lined hunter's cap. He was here at Carlsbad Lodge, carrying a knife.

Then my muddled brain clicked back into reality

mode and Macy and I stepped into the elevator.

Between floors, Macy rambled on. 'Owen's met Ryan on a couple of previous occasions. Actually, Owen knows a lot of important people. He's an up-and-coming actor – this bar job is only temporary. Isn't that cool, Tania?'

'If it's true,' I cautioned. Not for the first time I thought that fifty per cent of what Macy told me could be wishful thinking. Take her overnight stay with Charlie as an example – in Macy's mind sleeping with Jack's stunt double meant they were practically engaged.

'Of course it's true. I'm only dating the next hot Hollywood superstar!'

'You and Owen are dating?' I asked as we stepped out of the lift.

'Yeah, he's invited me to the final wrap party on Saturday night. It's going to be cool. Everyone will be there. There'll be live music, themed costumes – everything!'

Oh, crap! My legs almost buckled when she said the word 'party'. It was the first I'd heard of it but it straight away made total sense. A celebration to mark the end of filming was exactly the occasion the dark angels needed – time for dressing up in costume, playing music, creating a ritual and finally inviting Orlando across to the dark side.

Now I definitely needed to be alone, to clear my head. 'OK, Macy – my room's number 310, just down the corridor. You can leave me here.'

'Sure?' she asked, checking her reflection in the mirror-wall at the back of the lift – big-volume, flame-red hair, ear and nose studs, strappy black top with a zipper running diagonally across her chest from shoulder to waist.

'Yes – get back in the elevator before the door closes.'

'If you're OK now . . .'

'I am. Go find Owen – go!'

She stepped in as the door slid shut.

A final wrap party on Saturday, a movie mogul arriving in a helicopter – there was a lot to think about as I made my way to my room, swiped my plastic key and staggered the last few metres to my bed. The sheets were already turned back and there was a silver-wrapped chocolate mint lying on the pillow.

My head swam. I thought of the supercharged Formula 1 pace of Macy's love life with all its swerves, skids and manoeuvres, and it scared me. Now Owen, not Jack and definitely not Charlie, was the one who could do no wrong. I remembered the manic look in her eye, compared it with Orlando and Gwen then felt my heart skip a beat.

Lying on my back, I reached to switch on the bedside light. Get to the truth for a third time and find freedom, my good angel had told me, back in the old silver mine. No more death and suffering – this time for ever.

But truth shifted and floated; it swam inside my head and couldn't be grasped.

Who was my real enemy, the dark angel I must name and defeat? Had I met him yet, back in Manhattan or here on Carlsbad? So far I had no way of telling.

All I knew as I lay on those cool, crisp hotel sheets in the pool of gentle light cast by the lamp was that I had until Saturday night to save Orlando.

12

It turned out Ryan James wasn't the quiet, fly-on-the-wall, grey-suited type of investor – he was the total opposite.

I ran into him at breakfast the next morning and no one had to tell me who he was.

There in the restaurant was this guy in his forties with a mane of blond hair. It was swept back from his small-featured, tanned face and curled over the collar of his white cotton shirt, worn with jeans and a belt with an ornate silver buckle – the type cowboys like to wear. He looked like he had at least one personal trainer, plus hair stylist, manicurist and masseuse on his permanent staff.

The money man's presence at the breakfast bar acted like a magnet and all of Starlite and Xcel's employees were the iron filings.

'Let me get that for you, Mr James,' said the girl serving

bacon. She took the warmest plate from the bottom of the pile, scooped up six rashers and asked him would he like his eggs over easy.

'Sir, would you prefer wheat toast?' asked the man behind the toaster.

'Fresh fruit, Mr James?

'Coffee with that, sir? With cream or without?'

Ryan smiled at each and every one, shook hands with a member of the sound crew, even remembered that his name was Robert Brownlow, gave him a pat on the back and moved on.

'Hey, Larry!' he called to the director, who had made sure to get down to breakfast before his boss. 'Be a good guy – scootch over and squeeze in an extra seat for me at your table.'

Larry King jumped up like he'd been scalded, rearranged the furniture and stayed standing, ready to shake the hand of the guy who was financing what he hoped would be a whole string of *Siege* movies if only Jack Kane would clean up his act and stay alive for five more years.

'How're you doing, Larry?' Ryan skipped the formal handshake and slapped him on the back instead.

Sitting at a nearby table with Macy, I noticed that Mr James's forehead was as uncreased as his freshly ironed shirt. Closer inspection told me that his lips had most likely been pumped up with collagen and that the mane of hair owed a lot to a professional colourist.

'What do you think?' Macy whispered, loud enough for our whole table to pick up. 'Has he had work?'

Eaters at our table gasped then clanked their cutlery and shuffled their chairs in case Macy came up with another comment which could get them fired.

'I'm not even looking,' I lied, and told her I was too busy waiting for Orlando to show up.

Ryan meanwhile was asking after his most bankable star. 'So, Larry, how's Jack? Is he screwing his leading lady like they say in all the gossip magazines?'

'Never believe what you read,' the director told him with an uncomfortable laugh and a glance towards the corner of the room where Natalia was dividing blueberry pancakes between Charlie, Phoebe and Adam.

'Did I say I believed them, Larry? I'm just interested in the column inches our boy generates. The only thing I really care about is – is he showing up for work?'

The director trotted out the answer that Ryan wanted to hear. 'Yeah, we're on top of the schedule. We have a great cast. Rocky is superb in this movie.'

'Pity we have to kill him off,' the great man smirked. 'Likewise Angela – she meets a sticky end on a ski-lift ride if I remember the screenplay correctly.'

Larry dared to disagree. 'No big deal. There are a hundred Angelas out there, all waiting to step into her Manolos.'

'Ah, Natalia!' Ryan took his nose out of his bacon and eggs long enough to spot another bankable star and call her to his table. 'Beautiful as always. How do you do it? Up partying until three, and here you are, fresh as an eighteen-year-old.'

'Hey, Ryan.' Accepting the compliment and the chair he'd vacated, Natalia seemed happy to be there, offering both porcelain cheeks to be kissed by those collagen lips.

'Which is more than can be said for Jack,' Ryan went on, trying to knot his brows into a recognizable frown. 'This poor girl's husband didn't make it past ten thirty.'

Larry came in with a quick explanation. 'He knew what time we started shooting this morning. I asked Charlie to get him to bed early.'

'Charlie Speke.' Ryan prided himself on knowing every detail of budget, script, locations and cast, even down to the star's body double. 'It's good to have him on the team, huh?'

'We definitely couldn't do these movies without him,' Larry agreed. 'What this industry needs isn't more CGI and 3D special effects – it's more clones like Charlie.'

'You hear that, Charlie?' Ryan spotted what he thought was his secret weapon getting coffee from the bar. He ordered Lucy Young to move off the table to make room. 'You play your cards right and you could stop being a stand-in and start being a major player.'

'Oh!' Natalia was the first to spot Ryan's gaffe. After all, she was still married to Jack and it was definitely Jack who was sitting down next to her. The trembling hand gave him away. 'You're so funny!' she giggled at Ryan.

'And I'm busting my sides,' Jack grunted. He was bleary-eyed and unshaven – a movie star long past his sell-by date. Going on to talk to Larry about the day's schedule, he turned his back on Ryan, who in turn chatted with Natalia about a new Starlite project he was working to get off the ground.

'With a major role for you,' he promised her.

A gorgeous smile lit up Natalia's face – the sort of smile a camera wants to get close to and linger on.

I gazed at her from the next table, fascinated by her ability to paper over the cracks in her marriage, and was only distracted by Macy springing up from her seat and running to greet Owen with an enthusiastic kiss and hug. He was off duty, dressed in a black T and jeans, and with his Scandinavian looks he made a big impact. I couldn't make up my mind whether or not he was glad about the kiss. In any case, he was followed into the restaurant by Gwen and Orlando, who saw me, spoke quietly to one another then quickly turned and left.

'Ouch!' Macy mouthed to me from across the room. 'Are you OK?'

I nodded, though I wasn't, of course.

'Talk about twisting the knife!' she whispered as she and Owen came to sit at my table.

I had to get up and out of there. Choking back tears, I ran out into the hotel lobby, where Amber on reception was busy handing out room keys to members of Ryan James's staff. It looked like the helicopter pilot, a couple of personal assistants who could have stepped straight off the Miss World podium, and a whole bunch of well-built guys who must be his bodyguards.

'Jay Weller? You're in room number 311.' Amber handed a key card to the first man in line.

The bodyguard took his key and walked towards me. I looked once and then twice; felt my heart bump and beat unevenly. Weller was mixed-race, short and heavy set. He passed by almost close enough for me to touch.

I smell death. Fear rises like a black tide and drowns me.

Ryan's bodyguard didn't glance my way. He examined his plastic key, mouthed the numbers '311', and pressed the elevator button.

243

Fear rises. I run to hide behind the Angel of the Waters statue but the guy with the knife waits for me; he's right behind me as I flee towards the arches beneath Bow Bridge. He stops to watch me as I run along the tiled colonnade. Any time he likes, he can reappear and plunge the long blade into my heart.

It was definitely my New York mugger and now he had a name – Jay Weller. He was here in the Carlsbad Lodge, in the room next to mine. He pressed the button and stepped into the elevator. I saw the back of his shaven head, the short, thick neck and the broad shoulders.

Struggling for breath, I leaned against Amber's desk. She gave me a puzzled glance as she handed out the next room key to a much taller guy with striking blond hair similar to Owen's – thick and almost shoulder length.

'There you go, Mr Nixon – room number 315,' Amber informed Ryan's second bodyguard.

He turned and I saw him clearly – the broad, strong face and square jaw, the clear grey eyes that looked straight through me.

I am by a lake in late summer. There are swimmers in wetsuits plunging into the water. Sunlight catches the rising spray. Lake Turner is alive with thrashing limbs.

Beneath the lake lies a flooded town with streets and empty houses, a church with a steeple, rows of underwater graves.

Uprooted trees lie on the bed of the lake, their bare limbs trapping corpses that have drifted free of their rotting coffins. Souls call out to me, hands stretch and catch at me, they drag me down.

A boy swimmer drowns. It is his time to die. He rests with the skulls in the West Point graveyard. Another swimmer plunges to find the first boy but rises to the surface empty-handed. Water streams from his handsome features. A broad, strong, big-jawed face, with the head thrust back and blond hair trailing in the water. He is a member of the New Dawn Community on the western shore of Turner Lake. His name is Jarrold Nixon.

Ryan's second bodyguard also walked by without acknowledging me, but I knew beyond doubt who he was.

Wolf man Jarrold crawls through the thorn bushes towards his lair. I follow. His amber eyes entice me in. He rears on to his hind legs and roars. With one swift move he has me between his jaws.

Now I was beyond doubt – dark forces from Central Park and Turner Lake were gathering on Carlsbad. The past was becoming present and there was no escape.

A third man took his key and heard Amber announce his room number – 313. He followed Weller and Jarrold towards the elevator.

I see only his eyes and the bird mask he wears, the black feathered cloak. He hovers over me.

I see his physical perfection, hear his charming, educated voice telling me that his name is Daniel.

There is smoke in the air. Black Rock is alight. The forest burns. Wild horses gallop around an arena and break through the fence. My dark angel appears surrounded by smoke and flames. A horse rears, he falls under her hooves, his skull smashed. Blood stains the rock.

'Daniel,' I whispered as the third man entered the lift. He was resurrected – the underworld god of Zoran Brancusi's Heavenly Bodies party, always beautiful and damned.

'Saturday's party isn't themed around Christmas the way you might expect,' Macy explained as we sat in the chairlift on our way to the silver mine.

It was a two-person gondola and she sat opposite me. Every time the wind blew and the gondola swayed, I closed my eyes and gripped the safety rail.

'Ryan has decided a Christmas theme is way too obvious so he's sent for costumes from the Starlite back list. His guys are going to fly them in all the way from a warehouse in New Mexico. How much fun is that?'

Letting her chat on, I stared down at the snow. It was

over an hour since Daniel, Weller and Jarrold had checked in but my heart was still pounding and my mouth was dry.

'Owen and I want to share a theme – do something different so we stand out from the crowd. He has to work behind the bar but all the Xcel staff will be in costume as well as the Starlite team. Really, I can't wait.'

As the gondola jerked and came to a halt near the old mine, Macy jumped out ahead of me. She was about to run to join the technical team setting up for the morning's filming when she had second thoughts and waited while I stepped down from the lift. 'Did something bad happen?' she asked as the empty chair jerked, rocked then set off again.

I nodded, but this wasn't the time to explain about the bodyguards. My heart was beating too fast and it was all I could do to keep the lid on the panic that kept on rising.

'Sorry, I should have asked sooner,' Macy sighed. 'I could see you weren't doing well at breakfast.'

'It's cool. I'm still working out what to do to get Orlando out of here.'

'No, really – I'm sorry. I get an idea in my head and I run with it. Right now I can't seem to think of anything or anyone except Owen.'

'I noticed,' I said with a wry smile as she linked arms and walked me away from the movie set. 'But really, what do you actually know about him?'

'Nothing, and I don't give a damn. Stupid, huh?'

'Or brave.' What did I know? Only that the single thing that stops most of us from acting the way Macy did is the fear of rejection.

'My problem is, I don't know how to live my life any differently. I guess it's the way I'm wired.' There was a long pause as we walked up the mountain between some snow-laden redwoods, then Macy eased her arm out of mine and stopped to gaze down into a steep-sided, sparkling white valley. 'If you want to know the truth, my life is crappy right now,' she confessed. 'I don't have anyone – no long-term relationship, no family to lean on.'

'It won't always be like this,' I said. 'You'll find someone to love. Everyone does.'

'That's so true. I found Owen.'

I held back from pointing out that her twenty-four-hour relationship with the good-looking barman hardly ticked the long-term box. 'See, guys are attracted to you – you're smart and cute, and one thing you definitely do is stand out from the crowd.'

'Owen is a fascinating guy,' Macy insisted. 'He likes to

work out, that's obvious. But I did find out another side to him. He studies American history, he reads classic literature and guess what – he's been to acting college in New York. When he was thirteen years old he auditioned for a part in a Spielberg movie.'

'I hope he makes it,' I said, standing back from the ledge. I admit that I felt scared for her as she talked herself into believing in her latest boyfriend.

'He only took this bar job because he knew they were shooting a movie here. He figured he could get himself noticed. That was a smart move. He knows you have to be in the right place at the right time. It's the secret to success.'

'Macy, don't go any further,' I warned. A cold wind blew from behind and pushed her closer to the edge.

She laughed and spread her arms wide. 'Imagine if we could fly!'

'Step back.'

'Whoo! Like an eagle soaring over the mountains.'

The wind caught her and tipped her forward. I lunged, grabbed her arm and dragged her back. 'Let's go,' I insisted.

That morning Larry shot the final scenes between Jack and Angela. I shadowed Lucy in her role of assistant director, handing out rewritten scripts to the actors and crew.

'This is the last change we need to make,' Larry instructed. 'Jack, you stagger out of the mine with the gunshot wound to your left shoulder. No dialogue here – we took it out. But you see Angela ready to climb into the ski lift. She realizes you're still alive, aims her gun and fires. You take a second bullet. We get you in close up then fade.'

'Am I dead?' Jack asked, flipping through the next few pages of his script. 'Christ, no – I survive. I'm a man of steel.'

'Let's not waste time,' Larry snapped. 'Charlie, stand by. We need you for the next action sequence.'

You could have cut the tension with a knife as Jack went through the motions – stagger out of the mine with right arm clutching left shoulder, drop to knees as Angela fires gun, fall sideways into snow.

'Cut!' Larry called as the fake blood flowed.

And that was all that Jack needed to do: stagger, clutch, drop, fall. His work for the day was over.

'They got me out of bed at six thirty for this!' he muttered as a driver picked him up and drove him down the rough mountain track to the hotel.

After that, Charlie took over, swinging into action as

250

the cameras rolled. First he raised himself from the blood-soaked ground then staggered on towards the gondola, where Angela Taraska's body double aimed her by-now empty gun. Realizing she was out of bullets, Charlie grabbed the back of the gondola as it set off down the mountain. Angela's stand-in leaned out and bludgeoned Charlie's hands with the gun. He clung on, was raised from the ground and dangled from the lift, swinging himself up and into the gondola, where he and the Angela double fought to the finish.

I saw the gondola rock violently and held my breath as Charlie was almost thrown out. He was left dangling a second time, and again he swung himself back in. This time he overpowered his opponent, forced the gun out of her hand then shoved her clean out of the gondola. She screamed as she lost her grip. I watched her fall.

'Cut!' Larry yelled.

We broke for lunch and trooped down to the hotel restaurant, which was crowded with all the people I dreaded seeing. Top of my list were Orlando and Gwen, though Weller, Daniel and Jarrold came a close second. Ryan James's dark angel bodyguards were playing slot machines in a bay by the entrance.

Daniel turned and gave me the smile that I remembered

from Black Rock - easy and alluring. I recoiled as if I'd walked into a blast of scorching hot air.

Jarrold kept his back turned but looked ready to spring into action at any small signal from their boss, who was holding court at a table in the centre of the room. Ryan was dressed in grey sweats, straight from a workout in the gym, calling for his favourites to join him.

'Natalia, sit beside me here. You know about the party on Saturday, right? You get to dress up in any costume from the Oscar-winning movie *Carnival* – crinolined gowns, beautiful seventeenth-century hats and masks. Just ask and it's yours!'

I watched Natalia slip into her grateful, gracious mode. She smiled, tilted her head, rolled her eyes and batted her lashes at Ryan, ignoring a whispered remark from Jack when he sat down heavily at the same table.

'I said, why not go as yourself?' Jack repeated. 'Wear the red dress the paparazzi went crazy for at last year's Oscars – slashed to the thigh, maximum exposure.'

Ryan moved the muscles in his face that still worked enough to show disapproval. 'That's not fancy dress.'

'Sure it is,' Jack sneered. 'Everything my wife pours herself into for the cameras qualifies as fancy dress. You think she looks this good in private?'

'Ignore him,' Natalia told Ryan. 'That's just Jack's

weird sense of humour.'

'Yeah, go ahead and ignore me, Ryan.' Leaning back in his chair, Jack pulled his fingers, cracking the knuckles one by one. 'Everyone else does.'

The chair wobbled dangerously and he had to jerk forward and catch the edge of the table to stop himself from tipping backwards and sprawling across the floor. I was surprised how fast his reactions were when it mattered.

Jack grinned then leaned forward confidentially. 'I'll let you into a secret, Ryan. Natalia ignores me so successfully that she neglected to tell me she filed for divorce.'

People close enough to hear this remark took sudden, sharp intakes of breath. Ryan instinctively turned to his bodyguards. Natalia sat without any visible reaction.

'What?' Jack mocked. 'Come on, it's a no-brainer.'

'Not now,' Natalia protested quietly.

'Am I spoiling someone's lunch? Did I break the rules and say out loud what people have known for ever?' He scraped his chair back from the table and stood on it, spreading his arms to make a public declaration. 'Natalia and I have split. She filed for divorce. It's official!'

The scraping of the chair set my nerves on edge. I noticed Jarrold and Weller approach Jack while Daniel made sure that no one else came into the restaurant. Gwen, who had been hovering by the door with Orlando, asked to leave but Daniel blocked her exit.

'OK, guys!' Ryan waited for Jarrold and Weller to take up position on either side of Jack's chair. 'Everyone in this room is an employee of Starlite and you all signed a confidentiality clause in your contract. That means nothing gets out beyond these four walls. Nothing!'

'Yeah, like I said – ignore me,' Jack laughed, pushing against Jarrold as he jumped down from the chair. 'It must be last night's whisky doing the talking.'

Jarrold took a step back then blocked Jack's intended route out through the French doors into a festive courtyard decked with baubles, lights and a tableau depicting a Christmas sleigh pulled by fake reindeer. A nod from Ryan brought my Central Park thug forward, leaving Jack with no place to turn. The only thing left for him to do, other than punch his way out, was walk with the bodyguards towards the main exit, where Daniel held the door open to allow them through

'OK, the show's over,' Ryan insisted as the tension broke and a low babble of voices filled the silence. 'Remember, no leaks to the press, and nobody goes on Facebook or Twitter to inform their buddies.'

'And now we have work to do,' Larry announced.

'Lucy, I need Rocky and the extras back on the mountain, ready to start shooting in thirty minutes.'

'I'm out of here.' I whispered to Macy that I needed fresh air but I had to pass within five paces of where Gwen and Orlando stood, steeling myself to walk out of the restaurant under their hostile gaze, through the lobby and along the driveway towards the ski-lift terminal.

A strong wind blew, light snow was falling as I climbed the steel steps to the platform and waited for the next gondola to arrive. I looked at my watch. One forty-five p.m. That gave me fifteen minutes to make it to the overlook and my planned meeting with Grace and Holly.

13

The sudden switch of temperature made me shiver as I waited for the gondola. I'd come out of the warm hotel into minus ten degrees and now back into the artificial warmth of the glass and steel terminal, all the time looking over my shoulder to make sure that no one was following me.

In fact, I was so busy checking the empty slopes behind me that at first I didn't notice Rocky Seaton sitting on the bench by the window, quietly minding his own business. He was wearing a black knitted hat and a blue padded jacket with a thick paperback jammed into one pocket.

'Up here at ten thousand feet the wind cuts right through you,' he observed. 'I hope you're wearing layers.'

'Yes, thanks – I'm good.'

'Only, you look to me like you're freezing.'

'I'm cool.'

'In case you're wondering, the operator discovered a fault on the bullwheel,' Rocky explained as I looked in vain for a gondola. 'He switched off the motor and went to find an engineer.'

'That's not good,' I sighed. Another look at my watch told me I now had only five minutes to make it to Carlsbad overlook.

'Don't worry – they'll wait for you, whoever they are.' Rocky had considered things for a while then took a stab at the reason I was leaning out of the door watching anxiously for the engineer. 'Anyway, it pays to keep your boyfriend waiting occasionally.'

'I'm not meeting my boyfriend,' I protested, relieved to see two businesslike figures hurrying up the hill.

'No? Aren't you with the kid who got the internship when we were shooting in New York – the tall, dark guy?'

'Orlando. No, I'm not with him any more,' I mumbled as the chairlift operator led the engineer up the steps on to the platform and showed him the problem with the bullwheel.

'What happened? Did he get sucked in by the bright lights and glamour?' Rocky asked.

'You could say that.'

'Sorry, I'm being too personal.' He checked his own

watch then asked the engineer how long it would take to repair the fault, before taking up the conversation where we'd left off. 'It's Tania, isn't it? I just thought you looked like you needed someone to talk to.'

'No, I'm cool, thanks.'

Luckily all the engineer had to do was switch to back up while he replaced an electrical fuse. 'Ready to roll,' he reported, flicking the switch to restart the motor.

'But if ever you do need someone.' Rocky insisted on me stepping into the first gondola while he waited for the second. 'Remember I'm a pretty good listener.'

OK, so I'd be late. The gondola rose unsteadily up Carlsbad in the icy wind, moving slowly towards the first steel tower. But Holly and Grace would wait for me; they would understand. I looked down on the group gathered by the entrance to the old mine – technicians whose footprints had churned up the smooth surface of the snow and who were now crowded around cameras and sound equipment, plus a bunch of actors standing under a canvas shelter, taking direction from Lucy and Larry. I made out Charlie Speke heading with Adam towards the nursery slope then looked ahead to judge the distance up to the overlook. It was then that I felt the gondola jerk and come to a halt.

Crap – another fuse must have blown on the bullwheel and I was stranded high on the mountain. Wind rocked the car suspended from the taut steel cable and a sudden flurry of snow swept down from the summit. Fear seized me by the throat. I pictured the stretched wire straining, fraying and snapping. I saw myself plummet to an icy death.

I hear wings beating in a white wilderness. The world is ice bound and silent. I have come face to face with the first incarnation of my dark angel. Like an eagle with a sharp beak and cruel talons, his black wings spread wide.

Sheer cliffs of ice tower to either side. I am alone in a deep, frozen crevasse.

Stranded on the chairlift, I had plenty of time to remember Zoran's final attack.

'Be brave. Find out the truth.' Pale-gold light breaks through clouds. Adam's voice is carried on the wind. It emerges from the snow flurry and chimes in with the sweet voices of Maia and Zenaida, my small team of good angels. 'Catch the devil by the throat.' They chant their mantra. 'Be strong.'

'Thank you,' I murmur as their light warms my face.

Then the overhead cable moved again and I was carried towards the terminal on the summit of the mountain.

* * *

The first thing I expected to see when I stepped out of the gondola was Holly's car. It should have been in the parking bay backed by a rough fence, next to a sheer fifty-foot drop. But no. What I saw in its place was a familiar grey truck belonging to Orlando's dad – the car Orlando had driven from Bitterroot to Mayfield last Tuesday evening.

Orlando was here on the overlook. Had he already seen Holly and Grace and said something that had made them turn around and head for home? Squashing the questions that fluttered inside my head, I grew angry at the idea that Orlando might have tricked them and, worse still, that they might have believed him. So I strode towards the truck and wrenched at the door handle. It was locked. I swept snow from the windscreen and peered inside.

'Orlando!' He was sitting at the steering wheel, staring out with the empty, blank expression I dreaded. 'Open the door. What are you doing here?'

Still he didn't react so I thudded my fists against the driver's door until at last he unlocked it and allowed me into the cab. I climbed in, brushing snow from my jacket and shaking it from my hair. 'How long have you been sitting here?' I demanded.

Slowly he turned his head, his gaze unfocused and

with a frown knotting his brows. I thought I knew every millimetre of his face – the smooth texture of his skin, the exact angle of his cheekbones and jaw, the way his lashes curled. But now as I looked at him, I hardly recognized him. What was different? Not the shapes and the angles, not the grey of his eyes and the forward sweep of his dark hair. No, the difference was in the stillness of his features, the paleness, the emptiness, the lack of life in his eyes.

'Say something!' I pleaded. 'Explain why you're here.'

Still moving slowly, he turned away, leaning forward to switch on the engine, turning on the wipers to clear the screen. They laboured under the heavy weight of settled snow as Orlando began to reverse the truck off the overlook on to the single-track road off the mountain.

'Stop. Where are we going?'

He didn't reply until he'd completed the manoeuvre and we were pointing downhill. 'Sit back,' he muttered as he leaned forward to clutch the wheel and rev the engine. 'Don't talk.'

'Did Gwen send you?' I demanded. 'What's her plan here? Are you and I supposed to go through the whole thing again – me begging you to come home, you telling me I'm crazy, rejecting me, telling me it was all a mistake, that you never loved me? Is this where you finally break my heart? Don't bother. It's already broken.'

Part of what I said must have got through because Orlando took his foot off the accelerator and slumped forward.

I saw by the way his hands gripped the wheel that a struggle was taking place inside him and I reached out my own hand to try and reconnect.

'Come back to me,' I pleaded. 'Orlando, it's not too late. You must keep on fighting what Gwen is trying to do to you – please!'

He held the wheel so tight that his knuckles turned white. When he spoke, his voice was slow and slurred. 'Tania, I can't do this. She told me not to talk to you, said I can't be near you any more.'

'So why are you here?'

'She wanted me— No, you don't want to know,' he groaned, stamping on the pedal, making the tyres spin and whine on the icy surface. His defensive barrier was quickly back in place as we slid sideways and the back end of the truck lodged in a gulley. He swore and put his foot down hard, only succeeding in churning up the snow and digging us deeper into the ditch.

'She wanted you to do what – deal with me?'

He shook his head.

'Yeah, that's what she told you. She said, "Don't let

Tania come back down the mountain. Do whatever you have to do.'''

'I can't talk about it,' he said as he wrenched at the handle and flung open the door.

'What now?' I cried as he jumped out, grabbed a spade from the trunk and started to dig. I followed him, sinking knee deep into a drift. 'Getting stuck in the snow wasn't part of Gwen's plan, was it? She knew about the meeting with Holly and Grace – someone told her about it. You saw them, didn't you and persuaded them to turn around? What did you tell them?'

'Yeah, I saw the girls,' he admitted as he dug. 'It made me laugh out loud, the way they zapped in on their superhero rescue mission. But they were easy to fool. All I had to do was tell one big fat lie.'

'You lied?' I echoed faintly. Any hope I had that help was at hand was rapidly fading.

'I told them your mom got sick again and you went home to take care of her.'

'How could you say that?'

'Easy,' he mocked. 'I said, "Tania's mom is back in the hospital. Tania went to visit her." It worked like a dream.' Orlando laughed as he carried on digging us out. 'Where are Holly and Grace now? Do you see them?'

'They'll soon find out it's not true. They'll be back.'

'But not soon enough – not with thirty centimetres of snow forecast. It'll block the road out of Bitterroot. Anyway, what did the dumbasses hope to achieve, coming back here to see you?'

'Orlando!' I cried. 'Listen to yourself. These so-called dumbasses are our friends, not our enemies. They're on our side.'

He cleared the back wheels then thudded his spade into the heap of dug snow. 'We don't have a side any more, remember. There's you and there's me. You're in your own crazy little world, Tania, and finally I'm free. It took me a while but then I met Gwen and she knew how to put it into words for me – the doubts I always had about the whole dark angel thing, the way you manipulate me and make me feel guilty all the time. She made me realize I had to stop you doing that.'

'By driving me off the track and abandoning me? Is that what this is about?'

'Whatever it takes to be free,' he muttered.

'Please don't,' I begged, covering my ears to try to block out his stinging words.

'Gwen showed me how far you'd dragged me down, how close you were to destroying me.'

'No. You can't trust Gwen. She twists everything. It's what they do.'

Orlando seized the spade and threw it into the truck. '"They"?' he challenged.

'The dark angels. They're beautiful on the outside – that's how they seduce you and draw you into their world.' I was in the last-chance saloon and I knew it, so I put everything I could into trying to convince Orlando that he was in deadly danger. 'But listen to me. They play with your mind and trap you. They're twisted by their desire for revenge and they want you to join them in hell for ever.'

'Gwen said you would try this,' he said scornfully as he shoved me back into the truck. 'She warned me about the types of mind games crazy people like you use. But it won't work this time, Tania.'

I fell against the steering wheel and he leaned in to pull me upright. Instinct made me grab his arm. 'Stop,' I pleaded. 'Whatever it is Gwen has ordered you to do to me, you can choose to stop right now.'

He laughed in my face. 'Watch out, here comes Tania's paranoia! Now crazy girl lets her imagination off the leash. This is where she thinks I'm going to drive her over the edge of a cliff and finish it for good. Or would you rather I tie you up and dump you back on that overlook where you could take in the view and slowly freeze to death?' Slamming my

265

door, he walked round to the driver's side.

I let out a sob of fear and frustration that the guy I was arguing with was no longer the Orlando I knew. He was a total stranger. Then I tugged at the door handle and scrambled out of the truck, aiming to reach the chairlift terminal on foot. But I didn't get more than three steps through the soft snow before he caught up with me and blocked my way.

'You're not making this easy,' he sighed. 'All you have to do is sit in the car.'

'I'm not coming with you,' I said, pushing against him. By this time I could hardly make out the steel tower because of the blizzard driving in from the north, but I could hear the whir of the cable and the clink of metal as a gondola passed overhead.

'And I'm not letting you get on that chairlift.' Orlando refused point-blank to get out of my way. 'We take the truck.'

'I don't trust you,' I yelled. 'I don't want to go in the truck with you.'

Exasperated, he threw himself at me, wrapped both arms tight around my chest and hauled me off my feet. I kicked and struggled, knowing that even if Orlando failed in his mission and I made it back to the lodge, dark forces were gathering in the corridors of Carlsbad Lodge –

Jarrold hiding round a corner, Daniel laying in wait in a room close to mine, Weller stepping out of the elevator.

A gondola clicked along the cable and paused at the terminal just long enough for a figure in a blue jacket to step out. As it emerged out of the blizzard and strode towards us, Orlando let me go.

'So, Tania, you weren't being straight with me,' Rocky Seaton said. 'You came to meet your boyfriend after all.'

He'd spotted us through the falling snow – Orlando dragging me towards the car, me fighting him off – and I guess he thought we'd had a typical lovers' fight. In any case it wasn't the reason he'd come up the mountain.

'Something bad happened,' he told us, his face deadly serious. 'Adam Kane went missing.'

It was as if someone had shot me through the heart. It stopped beating and for a few moments I thought it would never kick back into life. 'No, that can't be right!'

'It is. Everything's crazy down there. They have everyone searching for the kid.'

'I saw him heading for the nursery slopes with Charlie. He was totally fine.'

'Charlie came back without him. He ran to the lodge to raise a search party.' Rocky gave us the facts calmly, walking Orlando and me back towards the ski lift. 'Natalia

267

is asking for you, Tania. She's half crazy but you were still the one she wanted.'

With my heart thumping against my ribs I stepped into the chairlift, hardly noticing when Orlando pulled back and told Rocky he would drive his truck down the mountain. 'Did Charlie say exactly what happened?' I asked Rocky, who climbed into the gondola with me.

'Adam took off down the slope while Charlie watched. He saw him veer off track and disappear over a ridge.'

'Did he follow?'

'Charlie says he went right after him – he was only about thirty seconds behind. When he took the ridge he found the next gorge was lined with redwoods. He tried to follow Adam's trail but it just seemed to end at the base of one of the trees. Then he found a pair of abandoned skis and started to yell the kid's name – nothing. So he ran to fetch help.'

'And that's where the search party is now – in the gorge?' I checked as our gondola reached the main terminal. I'd already seen that the entire film crew had come down from the old mine to join the search. Among them, Jack stood out at the head of the bunch striding across the nursery slopes towards the ridge where Adam had vanished.

'The theory is he lost control and crashed into the

tree. Then, instead of waiting for Charlie he set off on foot towards the hotel, but he didn't make it.'

'My God!' I groaned. Rocky and I had joined the stream of people descending on the gulley where Adam had disappeared. 'He's a tiny kid. It's snowing. What are his chances?'

'Don't even think about it,' Rocky advised as he took me to where Natalia was standing with Charlie, Gwen and half a dozen other helpers, all gathered around her.

Natalia saw me and broke free from the group. She stumbled towards me and almost collapsed into my arms. 'Is he with you?' she pleaded. 'Tell me you have him safe!'

I shook my head and tried to hold her up, tried to think straight in a world that was falling apart. Snow blew into our faces and wind whipped through the trees where the search was concentrated.' Did people stay behind to search the hotel?' I asked Charlie, who took Natalia from me and held her close.

He nodded. 'That's our best hope – that somehow he made it to the lodge. The problem is there are no tracks to follow. The snow and the wind take them out in seconds.'

I took a deep breath to steady myself, closed my eyes and when I opened them again I saw Jack stumbling through the snow. He came up behind Charlie and wrenched him away from Natalia. Then he spun him round and threw a low punch, hitting Charlie in the stomach. Charlie staggered back but kept his balance. Jack swung his fist again. He toppled forward into the snow without making contact. Charlie stood over him, drawing back his foot, ready to kick out at Jack.

The fight lasted maybe ten seconds before two guys from the Starlite technical crew stepped in to restrain Charlie and drag Jack up off the ground. By now I was holding Natalia again, trying to lead her towards the hotel until Gwen stepped in.

'It's OK, Tania, I've got this.' She put herself between me and a sobbing, shaking Natalia. Taking control, she gave me an intense, angry look that I fought against and then gave in to. I felt my willpower weaken and crumble under her dark angel strength.

So I stepped away and got drawn back into what was happening between Jack and Charlie.

'Fuck you!' Jack broke free from the cameramen and threw himself at Charlie, who stood his ground as Jack swore, grunted and swung wild punches. 'Look what you did. First you wreck my marriage and my career and now you lose my kid.'

Charlie didn't flinch under the accusation. His face was impassive as two more guys piled in on top of Jack and succeeded in dragging him away. It was me who went to pick Jack up from under the nearest tree while Charlie followed Gwen and Natalia towards the hotel.

'Listen, Jack – you want to find Adam. We all do. So forget about Charlie. Think about your son. They say he crashed his skis into a tree then tried to make his way out of the gorge instead of waiting for Charlie. Does that sound like something Adam would do?'

Jack was back on his feet, but instead of listening to me and helping to figure it out, the very name 'Charlie' sent him crashing out of control again. He swore and pushed me away then staggered off deeper into the stand of snow-laden trees. Which left me alone and desperately wondering where my good angel had gone.

I close my eyes and open them on my parallel universe. I'm in a white world which sparkles in the sunlight. The surface of the snow glitters.

Adam appears surrounded by his halo of light. I walk towards him without my brain actually telling my legs to move, and it's not really walking – more like floating. He's smiling, telling me he's not lost, holding out his hand.

I relax. I breathe again. My body tingles from head to toe.

'You will find me,' Adam says softly. He looks incredibly young – hardly more than an infant. 'The secret will be unlocked.'

'Thank you for being here,' I whisper, and as I look up into the clear blue sky a flock of grey doves soars high overhead and a woman's voice speaks though she remains invisible.

'Keep on searching,' Maia's slow, soft voice urges. 'Rise to this final challenge. Be open to our voices, look around you with the innocent eyes of a child. Do not forget to reach out and take our hands.'

'Where shall I look?' I murmur. I want to find more than Adam's disembodied, beautiful spirit – I need to find the boy himself.

'In the place that you fear the most,' Maia tells me. The doves swoop low. Sunlight catches their wings – the flashes of white, the soft greys and pinks of their feathers as they alight. 'Evil dwells in the dark,' she reminds me. 'Deep in the ground the dark angels gather – fallen angels, devils in disguise. They exist in terrible, infinite darkness – the darkness of the soul.'

'Under the ground,' I murmur, and my heart quakes at the sounds of rockfall, the desperate voices of trapped men and the unnameable monsters who twist, writhe and crawl towards the light. 'I have to search for Adam in the old mine?'

'Have courage,' Maia tells me as the golden vision of Adam starts to fade and the doves take flight. 'Be prepared for anything.'

I shake with terror at the prospect of entering the mine. 'Can't you come with me?' I beg.

We are always at your side. We are bound together by love.'

I know it in my heart but the fearful part of me casts a cold, deep shadow of doubt.

'Go,' Maia urges.

'And after I find Adam in the mine and take him back to Natalia, what then? How do I overcome my enemy?'

'Keep your heart open; be prepared,' she insists. She points to Adam's fading light. 'You must hurry,' she reminds me.

The white world still sparkles but a sinking sun casts long shadows. The doves have disappeared.

'Hurry!' Maia urges.

I close my eyes and open them on the real world.

Jack stumbled back towards me. He emerged from the redwoods, his lips stretched in what looked at first like a smile but which was really a sign of torment – gritted teeth, mouth sucking in air, black hair coated with snow. 'I can't find him!' he cried.

I ran to meet him. 'Come with me. We have to look inside the old mine.' Setting off without waiting to see if Jack would follow, I struggled through snowdrifts until I reached the chairlift terminal and only then paused for breath. Then I turned and saw that he'd staggered after me.

Reaching one of the steel stilts that supported the

weight of the platform above our heads, he leaned against it and tried to heave more air into his lungs.

'Are you OK? Can you keep going?' I asked.

Swearing and pushing me aside, he forced his legs to carry him higher up the mountain towards the entrance to the old silver mine. Now it was me struggling to keep up, feeling the burn of my thigh and calf muscles and the cold ache in my lungs. I'd fallen twenty or maybe thirty paces behind Jack when I saw him crouch and enter the dark tunnel then disappear from sight.

'Wait!' I yelled. Though my good angels had led me here, I was still scared that the roof would cave in if anyone disturbed the decades of neglect.

Jack took no notice. I reached the entrance and came up against a fug of stale air that carried the stench of the animals that had holed up here over many winters – mainly wolves and bears. Brushwood was scattered over the rough floor, mixed with dried animal droppings and lengths of old, rotten timber. I almost tripped over a coil of frayed rope, and then a large roll of rusty razor wire that had trapped an unwary wolf and held him fast until he starved to death and the flesh had rotted from his bones. I made out his ribcage, scattered vertebrae and yellow skull in the gloomy shadows, the long jaw, the curved canine teeth.

'Adam!' Jack was ahead of me, yelling his son's name. His voice reached me, muffled and desperate. Seconds later he'd turned around and was stumbling back in my direction.

I put my arm out to stop him in his tracks. 'Watch out for the razor wire.'

'Adam's not here,' he cried. 'The tunnel's blocked. You were wrong – he didn't come this way.'

'Wait here. Let me take a look.' I left him and ventured deeper into the mine, feeling my way. Twice I stumbled over loose boulders, knocking my shins. Once I banged my head against a sharp rock. 'Adam?' I called over and over, each time hoping for a faint reply. Then I came to the rockfall that Jack had described. I had to stop then and seriously consider my vision.

'Maybe I just wanted it to be true,' I muttered. Perhaps I longed for them to appear and tell me where to search, but it was only my mind playing a trick on me. The thought left me feeling confused and lost, opening the door to more dark doubts lurking in the underground gloom.

Then I heard Jack stumble towards me, felt him grab my arm and drag me towards the entrance. 'I shouldn't have listened to you.'

I resisted. 'No, I do believe Adam headed this way.

Maybe he found shelter here for a while and then moved off again.'

'So where is he now?' Jack stumbled against a boulder then caught his foot in the roll of razor wire. He stooped to tug at the wire with a gloved hand, swearing as one of the spikes pierced the glove before he managed to uncoil the wire across the shaft floor and step free, leaving me trapped behind it.

As he swore again and ran off, I felt my stomach twist and churn.

This is hell. Hell is total darkness – solid rock above my head and below my feet, in front and behind. There is no room to move.

I cry out but no one hears. There is no air left to breathe.

And this is how it will be if I let my dark angel defeat me. Trapped without oxygen, I will die in the dark and no one will ever find me. I will lie in this dark mine like the wolf caught in the wire.

I gasped and blundered on, trampling the wire and stamping on the wolf's skull as I went. I followed Jack out of the mine into the blizzard on the mountain.

The snow and the light blinded me. I blinked, then shielded my eyes from the flurry of white flakes, able to make out Jack about twenty metres ahead of me, running and falling, picking himself up, staggering on towards a small bunch of people – two adults and a child – huddled under the flimsy canvas awning erected by the film crew. I heard his voice croak out his son's name – once, twice, three times – then I saw him reach the shelter and sink on to his knees, gather the child in his arms and hold him.

'Tania, we're over here!' Grace called.

Confused, I waited for Holly to come up and meet me.

Jack was on his knees, hugging his son. Adam cried. Jack cried. We all hugged each other and let tears of relief flood through us.

Adam, my angel of light was safe.

'What did you think – that we'd believe Orlando's crappy message about your mom and drive the hell out of here?' Holly demanded as she dragged me under the awning.

14

I kept in mind what Maia had said and held it close to my heart: 'Prepare for anything to happen.'

The last thing I would have predicted was Holly and Grace staying on Carlsbad and being in the right place at the right time to rescue Adam.

But if you stop and think about it, no way would they have taken on board Orlando's b.s. message without checking it out.

'We drove down Carlsbad to where we could get a signal on our cell phones,' Grace explained from the safety and warmth of the Carlsbad Lodge bar. Owen was serving drinks as usual while Macy perched on a stool chatting with him whenever business grew slack. 'We had to drive almost into Mayfield Old Town. Holly called your dad from there and asked him was it true that your mom was sick again?'

'I'd already wagered a million bucks he'd say no,' Holly told me.

'Which you don't have,' Grace pointed out sweetly.

'So anyway, your dad said no, your mom was currently on a plane back from China. He wanted to jump in his car and drive up here to talk with you and Orlando, check you were both OK. But they already have thirty centimetres of snow in Bitterroot. They closed all the highways until the graders can clear them.'

'We swore to him we'd hang around here in case we were needed,' Grace went on. 'Actually, we had no choice. The snow got worse; we're trapped here. So Holly parked her car on the hotel parking lot and we set out on foot to find you.'

'That's when we ran into Adam.' Holly gave a broad smile. 'It turns out we saved the day. We're the heroes!'

I smiled back warmly, remembering how we'd hugged and cried, how Jack had promised Adam that he would never let anything bad happen to him ever again. Adam had kept his arms locked tight around his dad's neck as Jack had carried him down the mountain.

We'd reached the hotel in the heaviest snow of the winter so far. Total white-out.

Jack kept tight hold of Adam as Amber called from reception for the hotel medic and news of the rescue spread fast. Charlie ran in out of the snow and tried to share with Jack how relieved he was that everything had turned out OK, but it was obvious that Jack still blamed him. He'd blanked Charlie and carried Adam to the elevator.

I could only imagine the reunion between Natalia and her son as the lift door opened on the penthouse suite and she learned that he was safe.

'We're the heroes, so now they throw us out into the cold,' Grace warned as two security guards appeared at the door of the bar. 'We don't have passes, remember.'

But the men stayed where they were and gave way to Rocky Seaton, still wearing his blue jacket and black hat. 'I just heard what you girls did,' he beamed as he strode to join us.

'They're not going to throw us out?' Holly jerked her thumb towards the guys guarding the door.

'Let them try.' Rocky put on his best menacing-cop scowl then broke back into a grin. 'Actually, no. I just spoke to Jack. He's convinced you saved Adam's life – five more minutes out on the mountain, hypothermia would have set in and it would have been too late.'

'Is that what the doctor says?' I asked.

Rocky nodded. 'Jack wants to show his gratitude.'

'Adam's doing well?' I checked as we left the bar and

280

went up together in the elevator. It stopped before we reached the penthouse to let Charlie and Gwen step in.

'Adam will be totally fine, thanks to you,' Rocky assured us. The 'thanks to you' was delivered with one eye on Charlie, no doubt as a strong rebuke. 'What the hell were you doing, letting a five-year-old kid out of your sight in the worst snowstorm of the year?' Unspoken, but clearly understood.

Charlie didn't react, and neither did Gwen. They stood facing the door with their backs to us, but I could see their reflection in a full-length mirror – their faces stern, their eyes unblinking. Half expecting Gwen to zap me with her dark angel eyes, I quickly looked down.

'So did Orlando make it down the mountain in his old truck?' Holly asked Gwen straight out, no beating about the bush.

I shot her a startled, guilty look. So much had happened lately that this was the first time in thirty minutes I'd spared a thought for Orlando.

When Gwen didn't answer, Holly pushed harder. 'He was up on the overlook when we last saw him. It was already snowing pretty bad.'

The lift whined then jerked to a halt at penthouse level. The door slid open.

'I haven't seen Orlando since midday,' Gwen told us

quietly but firmly as we all stepped out. 'Right now I have no idea where he is.'

Adam was tucked up in bed. His favourite superhero DVD played on a big flat-screen TV on the facing wall. Phoebe played with trains on the floor while Charlie perched on Natalia's knee and tugged at the silver beads on her bracelet. Jack was sitting on the side of Adam's bed but as soon as Holly, Grace and I walked in, he stood up and came towards us.

For a while he couldn't find the right words. 'Thank you doesn't cover it,' he murmured, shaking us each by the hand. 'If there's anything – *anything* I can do . . .'

'You can sign the back of my shirt,' Holly quipped. 'I'll get it digitally copied on to a million Ts and make megabucks.' Then she grinned at Adam and asked him how he was doing.

'I'm good,' Adam answered shyly. He glanced at me and gave me the brightest, most special smile.

'Tania, you want a permanent position with Starlite?' Jack offered in a recklessly upbeat surge of gratitude. 'Natalia can fix it with Ryan James any time you like.'

'Thanks, but no thanks. I'm just glad Adam's OK.'

'The job is yours anyway.' Turning to Grace, he

asked her full name then promised her VIP tickets to the red-carpet premiere of *Siege 2*. 'You think I won't remember?' he challenged, tapping his head with his forefinger. 'It's stored in here: Grace Montrose, Holly Randle, Tania Ionescu – the three girls who saved my son's life.'

'This is in case he forgets.' Natalia interrupted to show us she was typing a memo into her laptop. She seemed calm after the gut-wrenching experiences of the early afternoon. 'Right now we're all on a high with relief. Tomorrow something else will take the place of today's big drama.'

'I won't forget,' Jack argued, trying not to react to Natalia's public put-down. 'Just like I won't forget who caused this whole thing in the first place.'

Natalia shook her head and lowered Charlie on to the floor to play with Phoebe's trains.

'I'm serious. Charlie Speke – that's the guy.'

'He's in the next room.' Natalia warned Jack to keep his voice down.

'I know it and I don't give a crap. I'm only speaking the truth. I've already told Charlie point-blank – I don't want him anywhere near my kids from now on.'

Watching Natalia's face, I suspected she wanted to argue the point but had decided against it in front of

Adam, Phoebe and Charlie. However, her silence spoke volumes.

'I don't care what you think,' he told her, his voice rising as his anger ignited. 'This isn't about you and your blind spot over a guy who's working to take over my life, Natalia. It's about what's safe for our kids.'

'We'll talk about it later,' she insisted, as Jack stormed out of Adam's bedroom. She gave me a resigned smile as we too said goodbye and left the recuperating patient.

'Thanks from the bottom of my heart,' Jack told us out in the lobby. He'd managed to regain control of his temper without a big explosion and now he seemed subdued. 'Natalia doesn't believe I can stay sober,' he confided. 'Even though I told her from now on, no more alcohol.'

'That's good,' I agreed after a couple of seconds' hesitation. I had no direct experience but from everything you read about the behaviour of AA members, there's a gap the width of the Grand Canyon between deciding to quit drinking and actually doing it.

'It's true,' Jack insisted. 'Today I had the biggest shock. It made me realize my kids are my whole world and that I need to get my life on track and be a good father. Nothing else matters.'

'That's really cool,' I murmured, with Holly and Grace

nodding beside me. They didn't know about the divorce yet and seemed pretty convinced that Jack could turn over a new leaf. Holly especially was still suffering from a serious case of hero worship as far as Jack Kane was concerned.

'No more partying,' he promised as the elevator door slid open. 'They say it can't happen, but I swear to you that this particular leopard has totally changed his spots.'

'So, where is Orlando?' Grace was the one who refocused us when we got back to my room. She peered through the French windows, beyond the balcony out on to a dark, snow-covered night scene – pretty as a Christmas card so long as you didn't have to be out in those sub-zero conditions. 'Do we believe Gwen – that she has no idea?'

'No way.' Holly was ready to bet her non-existent million bucks for a second time. 'You remember how she wouldn't make eye contact in the elevator? I'm guessing she knows exactly where he is.'

This gave me the opening I needed to update them. 'You're going to hate me for dragging you back into the dark angel stuff,' I warned. 'You're sure you want to hear it?'

Grace grimaced and drew back but Holly jumped

right in. 'Let me guess what you're going to say,' she insisted. 'The dark angels have developed another new way of working. This time they're not targeting any of us three. They know we're not about to fall victim and be seduced a second time around. Instead they've got their claws into Orlando.'

'Exactly that,' I confirmed.

'Oh, that's clever,' Grace said slowly. 'Tania, they're using the guy you love to destroy you.'

I felt my heart quake as Holly and Grace put into words my worst fears. 'They know I'll never leave him,' I admitted. 'I'm always going to be here for him.'

'Even if he tells you he doesn't love you any more,' Holly predicted, 'which he's already done?'

I nodded and felt tears well up. 'Sorry,' I mumbled as they slid down my cheeks.

'What are we saying?' Grace checked with Holly, closing the curtain and slowly pacing the narrow space between the bed and a chest of drawers. 'We can see that they'll use Orlando – it's obvious what they're doing there. But do we believe that they'll warp and twist his mind to the point when he'll actually try to *kill* Tania?'

I shuddered, trying to deny it to myself, but remembering Orlando's frenzied, reckless actions on the way down from the overlook.

'They could do that.' Holly insisted. 'They can do any kind of mind control, can't they? They sent Orlando up the mountain. What was that all about if it wasn't for him to snatch her and drive her over a cliff, ditch her miles from anywhere and leave her to freeze to death?'

'Oh, please,' I gasped. 'We're wasting time. All I know is, the dark angels are gathered here and we have to find Orlando and save him.'

Holly nodded. 'So we start in the obvious place,' she decided, opening the door on to the long, dimly lit corridor and looking both ways.

'Which is where?' Grace asked.

'In Gwen's room – wherever that is,' Holly said.

'She's currently up in the penthouse with Charlie,' Grace recalled. 'So if we're going to search her place, we'd better find out where she's staying, get in there, find what we're looking for and make it out again fast.'

Gwen Speke. Grace typed the name into the current guest list on the computer in reception while Holly and I drew Amber from her station in the main hotel lobby.

'We have a message from Natalia and Jack,' Holly told her. Of the three of us, she is far and away the most convincing liar. 'They're stressed about the weather and how soon they'll be able to fly their family out of here. They said, could you go up to their suite in person and help them log on to the Mayfield twenty-four-hour forecast?'

Amber wouldn't have deserted her post in reception for anyone else, but this was Jack Kane and Natalia Linton. Besides, it was a quiet Thursday evening and no guests could check in or out because of the snow.

'You're so damned good,' I muttered to Holly as Grace checked Gwen's room number.

'210,' Grace announced. 'That's the room directly below you, Tania.'

'Make sure you click off the guest list and go back to screensaver,' Holly reminded her as she stole a master key card from its numbered slot beneath the desk and headed for the lift.

We were up to the second floor and stepping out into an identikit corridor before we could draw breath – miles of dark red carpet, dim wall lights, door after door after door. Holly led the way, following the room numbers until we came to 210. She used the master key and within five seconds we were inside Gwen's room.

We're talking a room of a hundred and twenty square feet including a small bathroom off. In the main room there was a bed, a chair, a table. A floor-to-ceiling closet lined one wall.

'Check the bathroom,' Holly told Grace, while she slid open the closet door. Meanwhile, I sifted through the books and papers on Gwen's bedside table.

'He's obviously not hiding in here,' Grace reported as I found Gwen's bag and checked its contents.

'Unless the dark angels miniaturized him and locked him in this room safe,' Holly frowned, punching random numbers and failing to crack the code.

It didn't matter because inside the bag I found a wallet with several twenty-dollar notes and a couple of credit cards. I slid out one of the cards and read an embossed name: 'Carrie Hall'. A driving licence gave me the same information. With fumbling fingers I unzipped the bag's front pocket and drew out a passport, which I flipped through until I came to the name and photo. 'Carrie Hall' The picture showed Gwen staring stonily at the camera in an automatic photo booth.

'Look at this.' I showed Holly and Grace the passport. 'What does this look like to you?'

'It looks like Gwen isn't who she says she is,' Grace murmured. 'Maybe Charlie doesn't have a sister after all.'

'So let's get out of here before Gwen or Carrie or whoever she is comes back,' Holly decided.

I stored the precious piece of information in my memory and was about to follow them out of the room when I remembered that we hadn't checked the French windows leading out on to the narrow balcony. 'Wait!' I called and drew back the curtain.

A face stared in at me through the glass. I gasped then tried to make out who it was. 'Orlando?' I whispered, more in hope than belief.

The face was half hidden by a dark hood that came low over the eyes and a scarf pulled up over the mouth. The eyes were brown with huge pupils. It wasn't Orlando.

The guy on the balcony drew back his hood to reveal a shaven head. He raised a hand and pushed at the window. I shoved my shoulder against it to stop him coming in. 'It's Weller!' I cried.

My heart beat so loud I was sure it filled the room. Holly ran to throw her own weight against the window, but even together we couldn't stop the intruder from forcing his way into the room. He thrust the door open and sent us sprawling.

'Get up!' Grace yelled from the corridor. She dashed back into the room and pulled us to our feet while Weller stood guard by the window. We scrambled up and ran out, expecting him to follow, but when we turned to check, he was still standing, hands in his jacket pockets, watching us and smiling.

We ran, our footsteps soundless on the thick patterned

carpet. We turned a corner, headed for the elevator, Grace leading us. She pressed the button, a bell rang and the lift whirred. The door slid open. Jarrold stepped out.

'Hey,' he said, as if we were old friends with no violent history, no dark angel baggage. He was casually dressed in dark grey combats and white T, his thick blond hair pushed back behind his ears. 'It's been a while.'

Confused, I managed a feeble smile then straight away regretted it.

Ignoring Holly and Grace, he came closer. 'You missed me?' he mumbled. 'I've sure missed you, Tania.'

'Stay away from me,' I warned.

'Relax, don't be like that. I promise not to hurt you.'

Jarrold moved in closer still and for a moment as I looked into his clear grey eyes, I felt the old magnetism. I pictured him at New Dawn – tall and lithe, moody and compelling.

'I saved your life back there by Turner Lake,' he reminded me. 'Doesn't that prove that I cared?'

'Don't do this!' I cried, stepping back. 'I won't fall for it a second time – not now that I know who you really are!'

'Come on, you can't help yourself.' He grinned and took my hand. 'You and me, Tania – we were meant to be.'

'No!' Breaking free, I hurried on.

Jarrold overtook me and blocked my way. His hair fell across his forehead, his breathing was quick and shallow.

I tried but I couldn't get past him, until Grace and Holly caught up and together we shoved him to one side . . .

Slam – the spirit world claims me.

Jarrold morphs. His broad face narrows and darkens, his man's body becomes wolf. He falls on to all fours, his pelt thick and dense. He is sleek and strong, his jaws snap.

Smooth hotel walls melt and we're in a dark forest of tall black trees with wolves all around. We smell their damp fur, their stench.

Jarrold crouches, ready to pounce.

We're in the power of dark angels but for a while Holly manages to rise above the fear. She challenges Jarrold, who lifts her off her feet and effortlessly throws her back into the shadows.

Wolves surround us, their amber eyes gleaming, jaws drooling. They rear up snarling, and morph again into men with faces streaked red and black, carrying axes. I am back by Turner Lake with ancient, Native American warriors, with black flood water rising.

Wolf man Jarrold wields his axe over my head. I try to

escape by rushing towards the lift and I meet no resistance. To my surprise he lets me step over the threshold.

There is no floor and I'm falling down the shaft, dropping like a stone. I am pitched into total darkness, I smell earth and dampness, I hear nothing. And then I hit the bottom with such force that I believe my ribs are cracked and my back broken. I lie in silence.

Please don't leave me.

Silence except for the slow dropping of water into shallow black pools, the broken sound of my breathing – my choking, sobbing despair.

I wait.

I hear distant screams and falling rock. Earth fills my nostrils, eyes and mouth. I scrape it from my face and more falls. Inch by inch I am buried alive.

And now the unseen, tormented spirits of the underground are with me, crowding in. They wail and cry; they are faceless except for dark, empty eye sockets. They have no colour, no shape.

I close my eyes.

'Tania?' It was Macy's voice that woke me.

She'd pressed for the elevator and found me slumped on the floor. She was leaning over me, patting my face.

I opened my eyes, felt as though the weight of earth had not lifted from my chest.

'Here, let me help you,' Macy said. She raised me to my feet.

'Thank God!' I sighed. 'Press the button, Macy. Take us back up to the third floor.'

She did as I said without asking any questions for once. She supported me as we stepped out of the lift.

'My God, Tania!' Holly was there, scared out of her mind. 'Did that really happen? Are you OK?'

I nodded. My ribs were still aching from the effort of drawing breath. 'Where did he go?'

'Jarrold? It was weird; he just kind of walked away.'

'It was a warning,' Grace suggested. Her normally pale complexion had turned completely white and she was shivering. 'Next time it'll be even worse.'

Holly nodded then launched into her next plan. 'Seriously, Tania, we all need to get out of here. We should get back to Bitterroot and fetch help.'

'You can't do that.' Suddenly Macy sounded scared. 'I mean, really!'

'According to who?' Holly wanted to know.

We were four girls in a hotel corridor. Three of us were shell shocked by what had just happened and the fourth was putting obstacles in our way.

'According to Gwen for starters. Weller just informed security that you broke into her room. They're checking right now to see if anything was stolen.'

'So let them throw us all into jail,' Holly scoffed. 'Did security also find out that Gwen Speke is not who she says she is?'

Macy turned her back on Holly and spoke directly to me. 'You can't leave anyway,' she explained carefully. 'Remember there's fifty centimetres of snow out there.'

'Plus, we didn't find Orlando,' I reminded Grace and Holly. Still aching and suffering from the vision of being buried alive, I finally managed to refocus. 'We have to keep on searching.'

Grace took a deep breath. 'Let's take a long, hard look at this,' she murmured. 'Maybe we have to face a few facts.'

'Number one – Orlando went missing at midday,' Holly reminded me. 'It's now six thirty p.m. That's way too long for anyone to survive.'

I felt the hammer blow of each simple word. 'So maybe he's not still out there,' I protested. 'That's why we searched Gwen's room, remember. We think there's a strong chance that he made it down from the overlook.'

'But we don't *know* that,' Grace argued. 'What we do figure is that this time the dark angels have chosen Orlando as their number-one target. So what if they already got what they wanted out of him?'

'Which was to torment you and keep you here for the final battle. You see what we're saying?' Holly asked in the gentlest, kindest tone – so unusual for her. 'There's a chance that Gwen sent Orlando up to the overlook and didn't care what happened to him afterwards because he'd already served his purpose.'

God, no! I wanted to scream and run outside to find him, scream again. Instead, I froze to the spot.

'Maybe he's already dead,' Grace breathed.

Macy shook her head. Her bright-red hair fell forward across her eyes. 'What are you guys talking about?' she demanded. 'Orlando's with Owen in the bar. If you don't believe it, just follow me!'

15

'So Gwen and I are going to get on the next plane back to New York,' Orlando was explaining to Owen when we reached the bar. From a distance he looked completely normal – so much so that I almost hurried up to him, ready to put my arm round his waist and tilt my head for the special brush-of-the-lips kiss that he always greeted me with. But as I drew close he turned and I saw a manic gleam in his eyes and a blank, mask-like arrangement of his features.

'Hey, we were worried about you,' I muttered.

Ignoring me, he turned back to Owen and went on describing his plans. 'As soon as they open up the roads into Mayfield we'll drive to Aspen and then we're out of here, back to the city. Actually, the whole crew is due back there in the new year.'

'Why is that?' Owen asked as he stacked

clean glasses on a shelf.

'From what I hear Larry showed Ryan the rushes and Ryan wasn't happy with some of the sequences in Central Park. Guess whose fault?'

'Don't tell me. Ryan didn't like Jack's performance.'

Orlando nodded. 'He put a lot of pressure on Larry to reshoot. And hey, he's the guy with the money.'

'So,' Holly broke in. 'Now you and Gwen go everywhere together?'

Orlando jutted out his jaw but said nothing so I pulled Holly away from a situation that was leading straight into an argument. 'At least he's still alive!' I hissed as I sat her down at a table. Gwen hadn't punished him and left him to die out on the overlook and there was still a chance to save him.

'And what about you and me?' Macy asked Owen, perching on a stool next to Orlando. 'Shall we go with them?'

Owen held a glass up to the light then polished it carefully. 'I don't work for Starlite, remember – I work for Xcel.'

'Yeah but wouldn't you like to be there where it's happening?' Macy was chirpy and bright as a little robin, puffing out her chest and singing. Her attention didn't deviate from Owen for a single second. 'With the

298

connections you've made here, maybe you can get a part in the movie when they reshoot. And in case you're stressing about the money for a plane ticket – don't. I'm happy to pay for us both.'

Holly frowned and shook her head. 'There she goes again. Would you ever do that – throw yourself at a guy you only just met?'

Grace and I shook our heads. I felt more than uncomfortable. I would say I felt afraid for Macy. 'That's what she does.' She'd told me so herself – first Jack, then Charlie, now Owen.

'Business class,' Macy promised. 'And I know a great hotel.'

'Maybe,' Owen said after a long pause, placing the polished glass on the shelf.

'And before that we have the party here at the lodge,' she reminded him, brimming with excitement. 'I saw Gwen and she told me the costumes arrived before we all got snowed in. She said I could have first choice.'

'Speaking of which . . .' Owen gestured towards the door, to where Gwen stood talking with Charlie.

With a small squeal Macy jumped down from her stool and ran to join them. She and Gwen had a short, animated conversation then Gwen took her off along the corridor. Charlie gave us a wave and strolled out of sight. Before long, Gwen reappeared and came straight to our table.

'So you broke into my room,' she said, sitting down with us. She was laid back and matter-of-fact, not like she was accusing us of a criminal offence.

'So you stole Tania's boyfriend,' Holly said in exactly the same easy, non-aggressive tone.

Gwen smiled across at Orlando, who was watching closely. 'Orlando has free will. He makes his own decisions.'

I was struggling to swallow the irony of this when Holly came back in.

'Anyway, we didn't break in. We used a key,' she pointed out.

'What were you looking for exactly?'

'Not what – who.' Grace decided to speak the truth. 'Orlando was missing. We were worried about him.'

'You thought I was hiding him?' Gwen found this funny and broke into a high peal of laughter. 'Hey, Orlando, come over here. These girls are such big fans of yours.'

He came when she called. He sat at our table. He didn't look at anyone except her.

'They were so scared for you they broke the law to find you. So tell them where you were this afternoon.'

'They already know I was at the overlook,' he reported.

300

'Where you lied to us about Tania's mom,' Holly reminded him.

'Somebody's idea of a joke, I guess.' Orlando shrugged and spoke as if he'd rehearsed well. 'Hotel reception gets a phone call from a kid in Bitterroot saying Karen Ionescu is back in the hospital. I think it could be true – she was real sick recently with blood clots on her brain. When I come across you and Grace on the overlook, I pass on what I hear. End of story.'

'And afterwards?' I asked. 'After Rocky came to tell us Adam was missing, where did you go?'

'I drove down and joined the search. I was with Charlie. Ask him.'

It made sense until I looked at the glances exchanged between Gwen and Orlando – the hypnotic intensity of her gaze and the hooded, drugged submission in his. Then my stomach clenched and my heart hammered. I knew again and with total certainty that she had Orlando in her grasp.

So what now? I'd run out of pleas and arguments, of opportunities to corner him alone and persuade him that he was being possessed by dark forces. I looked across the table at his pale, haunted face and knew that his spirit was draining from him. Soon there would be nothing left.

Then Macy breezed back into the bar in full costume.

'Look what I chose!' she cried, twirling on the spot so we could see her red satin cloak and the matching body suit beneath. The suit was decorated with swirls of golden sequins and the cloak had a hood with a grinning mask attached.

'What the hell is that?' Holly asked as Macy paraded for Owen.

'I'm a Venetian fire eater. Ryan ordered costumes from the old movie *Carnival*, set in Venice. There's a scene with a pageant with dancers, jugglers and all the rest. Come on, guys, you must remember that.'

'You look cool,' Gwen assured her when no one else spoke. Macy had done her usual thing of bursting into a room and clamouring for attention, and in this bizarre fire-eater costume she had no problem holding it.

'What do you think, Owen?' She swirled the cloak and paraded some more. 'I found a matching costume for you, only in black. It has a cloak, a mask in the shape of a bird's head, with a long, white curved beak – everything. We'll be a couple. Promise me you'll wear it.'

Owen kept to his post behind the bar. He went on stacking glasses. 'I never make promises,' he said.

By Friday morning, with snow falling and all the roads

still blocked, Carlsbad Lodge had turned into a prison and everyone was going stir-crazy.

I hadn't slept, lying awake listening to the rustling movements of Grace and Holly asleep on my floor. When dawn came, I'd stolen to the window and peered through the blind to see snowdrifts covering the cars in the parking lot and totally blocking the tree-lined drive.

'We're never going to get out of here,' Grace groaned as she joined me at the window.

'Don't say never!' Holly had woken up and was stretching and yawning in her sleeping bag. 'What are you saying – it snowed again?'

'Come and look.' I stepped aside and waited for Holly to unzip then scramble over the bedroom furniture to take in the view. 'Pretty, huh?'

'Impassable, huh?' Yawning again, she scraped back her blonde hair into a ponytail. 'Grace is right – we're trapped with a bunch of evil spirits out to get as many of us as possible before the snow melts.'

'If you put it like that we may as well give up right now,' I sighed then smiled faintly. 'Honest to God, Holly!'

'Yeah, it's serious,' she admitted. 'And the clock's ticking. But at least there are three of us – one for all.'

'All for one,' Grace added.

We got dressed then and swash buckled down to

breakfast, passing Weller in the corridor as if he was a normal guest and we were ordinary kids excited to be snowed in halfway up a mountain with movie stars to keep us company. He didn't even glance our way and we ignored him.

Likewise Jarrold, waiting in line for coffee in the restaurant, though when I took a sneaky look at his wolf-like amber eyes, I did feel myself shiver. And when Daniel joined him in the queue I had a hard time staying in the real world. The shiny surfaces of the metal domes keeping food warm on the hot plates reflected and distorted my image, the conversation of people around me turned into a sequence of disconnected, incoherent sounds and my head swam as the floor tilted and walls closed in.

'Tania, are you OK?' Grace asked.

I fought the *Alice in Wonderland* moment, regained my sense of reality and nodded.

We got our food and sat at a table near the window looking out on to Carlsbad, then Grace took up where my thoughts had left off in my room as dawn had crept into the sky. 'So as far as Orlando is concerned, we all recognize Gwen is the problem we have to solve before we can get him out of here.'

Holly agreed. 'There's no point hoping we can rescue Orlando with Gwen hanging around doing her spirit-zapping, mind-bending routine. But if she's a dark angel like you say she is, Tania, she's going to be hard to beat.'

'Unless we check out her alter ego,' I suggested, pulling my iPhone out of my bag. 'The name in her passport was Carrie Hall. I'm going to google it and see what we find.'

Holly drummed her fingers on the table and Grace scanned the busy tables, looking for Gwen and Orlando as I typed and pressed Search. A few options came up in the list of results: Carrie Hall – British gynaecologist based in London; Carrie Hall – marathon runner from Sydney, Australia; Carrie Hall – character in a South African soap opera from the nineteen eighties. I checked out and dismissed each one in turn.

'Did you find anything?' Holly asked impatiently.

'Orlando just came down to breakfast with Gwen,' Grace reported. 'Charlie is with them. They saw us but they didn't wave hello.'

'Carrie Hall – Jay Fielding's third victim?' I scrolled down to a name on the list that looked interesting and brought up the relevant information, contained in a feature from the *Denver Post* dated six months earlier.

'Apparently there's a serial killer called Jay Fielding moving around the state,' I told Grace and Holly. 'They're linking the violent deaths of three women – Alisa Jones in

Boulder, Haley Miller in Durango and the latest one last summer in Denver was Carrie Hall.'

'Forget that,' Grace suggested. 'The Carrie Hall we want is still alive and sitting across the room as we speak.'

'Not necessarily,' I said slowly. I looked up at Charlie and Gwen chatting easily while Orlando sat in a daze between them. 'In fact, this might be the proof we need.'

Holly and Grace wanted more. They bombarded me with why, how, when?

I said whoa and went on to explain. 'That's what dark angels do – they search for people just like Carrie. Remember Zoran Brancusi and how he was seriously injured in a car crash? Everyone thought he died but it turned out this was the ideal moment for a dark angel to strike – just when a soul is ready to pass into the next world.'

'And Aurelie and Jean-Luc at New Dawn,' Grace recalled. 'They were about to drown when a ferry sank. Two dark angels moved in at exactly the right moment and from then on they impersonated them.'

We all held our breaths and silently read the rest of the *Denver Post* article.

'This guy strangles his victims,' Holly murmured, leaning over my shoulder. 'He dumps the body and arranges it in a certain ritual position – they don't say exactly what.'

'Is there a picture of Carrie?' Grace asked.

I scrolled down until I found one. There, smiling out at us from a sunnier, more informal photo than the one I'd seen on the passport was the girl we knew not as Carrie Hall but as small-featured, curly-haired, dainty and delicate Gwen Speke.

Holding my breath and staring at the small screen, I remembered my good angel's promise: 'Be brave. Out of darkness and chaos comes light.'

To discover the secret of a dark angel's name was everything – it brought their deadly powers crashing down.

'Malach!' I'd confronted Zoran on the frozen wastes of Carlsbad. I'd yelled out his name. Malach – angel of death who'd stolen a dead man's body. I'd caught the devil by the throat, identified him. Three times: 'Malach. Malach. Malach.' Brutal spirit of the underworld, destroyer of innocents.

Then, on the island in the middle of Turner Lake, with flood water rising. Know your enemy, name him. I'd confronted the wolf spirit who meant to destroy me and I'd spoken out. 'Ahriman!' Witch in wolf's disguise, creature of nightmares. 'Ahriman.' The name pierced his heart, robbed him of his power, defeated his wolf spirit.

'This is a beginning,' I muttered to Holly and Grace. 'Now we know for sure that Gwen Speke entered the body of a girl who lay dying, but what we don't know is her true dark angel name.'

'So it could be anything,' Grace said slowly.

Holly groaned.

'We have to believe we can do this,' I insisted. If I didn't hold faith in us and the power of good to defeat evil, who else would? 'From now on we have to listen to every word Gwen says, watch her every move. Somewhere there'll be the clue we need.'

'Maybe at the party tomorrow night?' Holly suggested.

'Or hopefully before.' In my mind, the fancy-dress party came right at the end of the lethal game the dark angels were playing. There would be music, costumes and a big confusion of shape-shifting, of monsters and death dealers. I dreaded it and the final ritual that would lead Orlando to give himself over to the dark side for ever. 'Yeah, definitely before,' I sighed.

All day we moved round the hotel as if we were treading on eggshells. We expected the worst, fearing to find Daniel and the other dark angel bodyguards lurking round every corner.

'What do we do if they move in on us?' Grace wondered. We were in the elevator, responding to a call from Natalia. Apparently, the medics had ordered Adam to stay in bed and he was bored. 'He wants you to visit,' she'd told me on the phone in that sweet, confiding voice she uses to make people do whatever she wanted. 'You know how much he likes you.'

'If the dark angels try anything, we hold our nerve.' I tried to sound confident, to put to the back of my mind the panic you feel when a carousel horse morphs and comes to life, or when you fall head first down a lift shaft, lie deep underground and feel earth falling on to your face. 'We'll be brave, like our good angel says.'

'We hold our nerve,' Holly decided as we arrived at the penthouse and walked in on a scene of domestic disharmony.

Imagine a typical family falling apart. Dad is arguing with Mom and the kids are crying. They've been cooped up and nerves are already frayed, then a small thing happens – one of the kids breaks something in a play-fight, someone yells, which makes someone else yell back and soon it's chaos. Crying and yelling, escalating threats and accusations. This is what was happening when we walked in on Jack and Natalia.

'You leave right now!' Natalia shouted. She shepherded

Charlie, Phoebe and Adam, all crying, into Adam's bedroom then closed the door. 'Jack, you get the hell out of here before I call someone!'

'Make me.' He noticed Holly, Grace and me step through the door but he was too angry to care. 'Go ahead and call. Who's going to throw me out of my own rooms?'

'I am,' Charlie said. He'd come out of the kitchen into the living room. Unlike the other two, he wasn't shouting, but his body language told you everything – head back, watching Jack through narrowed eyes, stepping right between husband and wife.

'Yeah well, surprise, surprise! Guess who's been hiding and listening to what was meant to be a private conversation.' Jack gave a savage laugh.

Natalia came up beside Charlie. 'Jack, you're drunk. It's bad for the kids to see you like this. That's why I'm asking you to leave.'

'That's a frickin' lie. I haven't had a drink in twenty-four hours.'

'The kids can hear this,' Charlie warned, indicating that the bedroom door had opened again and three tear-stained faces were watching. 'And so can your visitors.'

'OK, girls, you're witnesses.' Suddenly Jack broke away from Natalia and Charlie and rushed at us. 'I'm being accused here. She's keeping me away from my kids for no reason. I arrive back from a meeting with Larry and they're all in Adam's room watching TV. Natalia stands in the doorway and tells me to leave. You're witnesses, OK?'

'Because you're drunk!' Natalia shouted. 'I can smell it, I can see it.'

Jack stuck his face in mine and breathed over me. 'You smell anything?' he demanded.

I shook my head.

He rounded on Natalia and Charlie. 'See – not drunk! And don't think I don't know what you two are doing. You're setting me up here in front of witnesses. If you can't get me on the alcohol charge, you'll go down the domestic violence route. You'll drag me in front of a judge and swear I'm an unfit father. You don't care how you do it, just so long as you can screw me over and keep me away from my kids.'

'Why would I do that?' Natalia appealed directly to us. 'More than anything I wanted Jack to be a good dad. Haven't I tried everything I know? I've kept his drinking away from the media spotlight, I've watched him go through rehab God knows how many times!'

'Yeah, you kept the show on the road,' Jack agreed. 'We were big business – the Jack Kane and Natalia Linton bandwagon. You weren't about to jump off and go into

311

freefall, lose yourself millions of dollars.'

Natalia stared at him like he was something she'd scraped off the sole of her shoe. 'You're despicable, Jack.'

'Not me, baby,' he argued. 'This time it's you – you're way out of line. Tania's my witness: I'm stone-cold sober and you're stopping me from being with the kids. And that's not all. You and Charlie. God knows what you two get up to, and no, don't tell me because if I knew every dirty little detail I wouldn't be able to keep my hands off him. He'd be through this window, there'd be glass and teeth and blood on the carpet and Charlie Speke would be lying outside in the snow with a busted skull.'

'You see!' This time Natalia focused on Grace, who nodded.

'Wait. That's enough.' Trust Holly to take charge. She skirted around Charlie and Natalia and went to pick up Phoebe. 'Hey, baby, everything's going to be OK,' she murmured. 'Your mommy and daddy and Uncle Charlie will stop shouting. It's cool.'

Little Charlie put his arms around Holly's leg and clung tight. Adam shook his head and retreated into his room. 'No,' he said, walking to the window and staring out at the snow. 'No, it's not.'

Out of the mouths of babes. Adam seemed to sense that Jack was losing the fight for his career and family,

312

while Natalia, for whatever reason, was dead set on snatching everything from him, with guard dog Charlie on duty.

Holly took baby Charlie and Phoebe into Adam's room then closed the door. Jack had finished the busted skull tirade and hung his head. He'd gone too far. He'd shown his kids the side of him that wasn't good to know.

Charlie strode past him and held open the door into the elevator lobby. There was no expression on his face as he waited for Jack to slowly turn and walk away.

I felt the only thing to do when you've witnessed raw hatred between a man and his wife is to concentrate on the kids.

Grace and Holly played a hide-and-seek game with Phoebe and Charlie while I sat cross-legged with Adam on his bed.

'How do you feel?' I asked him. 'Did you get hurt when you crashed your skis into the tree?'

'No.'

'Were you scared?'

'No.'

'Jeez, I would've been,' I admitted. 'I hate getting lost.'

'I wasn't lost,' Adam said calmly. 'I just didn't want to be with Charlie.'

'Sshh!' Putting my finger to my lips, I looked towards the closed door. 'How come? Isn't Charlie your buddy? Don't you like him?'

Adam shook his head. 'Not any more.' He looked so serious and alone that I put an arm around his shoulder and squeezed him. 'He's not my friend. He just pretends.'

'Eighteen – nineteen – twenty, coming ready or not!' Holly called as Phoebe and little Charlie wriggled out of sight under Adam's duvet. Grace was hiding behind the curtains with her feet poking out.

'I hear you,' I told Adam. 'I'm sorry you don't like him.'

'I wish Mommy wasn't Charlie's friend. I wish she didn't fight with Daddy.' There were unshed tears in his big brown eyes and his bottom lip trembled.

'Me too,' I sighed and squeezed his hand.

Holly the seeker lifted up a corner of the duvet, making Phoebe giggle. She revealed the two hiders, who rolled off the bed with glee.

'Maybe they won't always fight,' I told Adam. 'Maybe one day it'll all work out.'

Charlie was still with Natalia when we left the suite. They'd been deep in conversation in the living room, with Charlie holding Natalia's hand and Natalia hiding her face from us as we walked by.

'This is unbelievably tough for Natalia,' Charlie explained quietly. 'She's desperate to meet with her attorney and sort out this mess, and she's relying on you three girls to keep everything under wraps.'

'We won't say a thing,' I promised, eager to get out. 'I'll be busy choosing a costume for the party tomorrow. After that, maybe the snow will have let up and Holly and Grace can make it back to Bitterroot.'

'Neat.' Grace praised me as we took the elevator. 'Let Charlie think we're leaving you all alone.'

'We're not though,' Holly insisted. 'We're seeing this thing through with you.'

It was my turn to blink back the tears. 'That means a lot to me,' I whispered.

We hit the ground floor and the door opened. 'So let's pick a costume,' Holly declared, striding ahead down the corridor.

There was a large room on the ground floor of the hotel that was used as a conference room, but today it was stacked high with cardboard boxes containing costumes used in the Starlite production of *Carnival* dating way back to the nineteen seventies. Gwen and Lucy were in charge.

'Owen, look at this!' Macy was in her fire-eater's

315

costume, holding up a weird mask in the shape of a bird's head. 'This is the one I told you about. The mask comes over your head and hides the whole of your face. You wear it with this hat and cloak.'

The black hat was broad-brimmed and decorated with a swirl of white ostrich feathers. Owen took the outfit and tried on the mask with its long curved beak. As he turned his head in our direction, his eyes glittered through the black eye holes.

'Wow, he looks evil!' Holly whispered, while Grace picked up a beautiful silver mask. The face had slanting, almond-shaped holes for the eyes and was painted with elaborate scrolls. A matching headdress rose like a fan to frame the wearer's face.

'You should definitely wear that,' Lucy told her, searching in the box for a stiff lace ruff and a tight-waisted, full-skirted dress to match the mask.

'Maybe. But we're planning not to be at the party tomorrow night,' Grace replied. 'As soon as the snow stops and the graders clear the roads, Holly and I are out of here.'

'No – stay!' Macy cried, dancing across the room. 'It's going to be the best party ever. How can you miss it?'

'We're not exactly flavour of the month around here,' Holly pointed out. 'Even before we went into Gwen's room and she made us public enemy number one.'

'Yeah, that was dumb.' Macy tilted her mask back from her face and frowned. 'I can't work out why you did that. Even if Tania is still feeling sore about Orlando and Gwen, where does breaking into her room get you?'

'You'd be surprised,' Holly muttered.

Seizing my arm and dragging me into a corner for a private conversation, Macy piled on the pressure. 'So tell me. What did Holly mean: "You'd be surprised"? Did you find something in Gwen's room that you weren't supposed to know about? Come on, Tania, you're my buddy – you can tell me!'

What does it reveal about my personality type (gullible, naive to the point of stupidity?) that I was about to share our latest discovery with Macy? 'Gwen isn't really Gwen. She's a dark angel who's possessed the body of a dead girl named Carrie Hall, blah-blah . . .'

But then I caught sight of Owen standing by the door in his cruel bird mask, his head turned towards us. I looked again at Macy and noted that her forehead was beaded with sweat and her eyes darted everywhere as if she was scared.

'No, forget it,' I told her. 'You really don't want to know.'

'But I do!' She sounded desperate and it struck me

that it was Owen who'd sent her on the mission to get me to talk.

I had a sickening, split-second tectonic flash – a vision of him in his black costume towering over Macy and pulling her strings. She was his puppet; he was the evil puppet master. He was a dark angel; she was his victim.

I couldn't believe how slow I'd been. Why hadn't I seen it earlier – the infatuation, the manic behaviour, the total submission?

I stared at Owen with an ice-cold shiver running down my spine. Though I tried to disguise my terror with a fake smile, I was sure it didn't fool him and he straight away made his way towards Macy and me, his face still concealed behind the bird mask.

'Come to my room in an hour,' I managed to whisper to her. I was thinking on my feet, working out a desperate plan to get Macy away from Owen and out of his control. 'Come alone and I'll tell you all about what we found in Gwen's bag.'

'We have to pray that it's not too late.' I shared my latest discovery with Grace and Holly as soon as we'd each quickly chosen a costume and hightailed it back to my room.

'You'll still be here for the party,' Lucy had convinced

Grace and Holly. 'The snow's so bad no one will leave before Monday.'

So they'd picked their costumes and now the bed was piled high with silver and gold dresses, stiff petticoats, big headdresses, masks and matching shoes.

'You're sure?' Grace quizzed. 'You're certain it wasn't just Macy being Macy?'

'Yeah, manic is Macy's natural mode,' Holly agreed.

'Not this time,' I argued.

'So you had one of your visions?'

'I saw Owen literally pulling her strings – you know, like she was a little puppet dangling. Just for a moment, but it was enough. He's definitely on their side—'

'The dark angels?' Holly interrupted.

'Yes, and he'd sent her on a mission to get information out of me. She was scared that if she didn't get it she'd be punished.'

'Did he say anything?' Grace wanted to know.

'Not a word. He came straight over and snatched her away from me. I just had time to tell her to meet me here.'

'What did he do then?'

'He raised his mask and stared at Macy. I guess he was mind-reading to find out if she'd carried out his orders. She kind of crumbled – her face looked white and terrified. Then he grabbed her and dragged her away.'

'So what if he locks her up or doesn't let her out of his sight?' Holly ran through some options. 'Or maybe he'll zombify her, just zap her willpower so she has to do everything he tells her.'

'That's already happened,' I pointed out. 'Owen is in total control.'

'So why are we sitting here waiting for her to show up?' For once it was Grace who wanted to spring into action. 'I think we should go look for her.'

'Then we have the same problem as we have with Gwen and Orlando.' My instinct was to agree with Grace, but my head told me no. 'We can't free Macy from the dark angels by using force. We have to figure out a smarter way.'

'But from what you said we don't have time,' Holly argued. 'Owen was using her as a pawn in his game – trying to find out what we knew about Gwen. You didn't give her the information he wanted so in his eyes Macy failed to carry out orders.'

'He was angry,' I admitted. 'When he pulled off his mask his eyes were intense – burning with anger. She was more scared than I can tell you.'

Trembling, white-faced with terror, weak-kneed with fear, breathless, out of her mind as he dragged her away. 'You're right,' I said. 'Let's go find her!'

Our feet made no sound on the thick hotel carpets. We trod the corridors without any firm plan in mind – only that we knew it was vital to track Macy down before her dark angel exacted his revenge.

We turned a corner and – whoosh! – the wall lights suddenly broke out in flames, like burning torches on castle walls.

Two worlds clash. Reality melts.

The torches cast dark shadows along the corridor; footsteps ring out on stone floors. We flee from the footsteps and come to some steps – a spiral staircase with cold stone treads, taking us down, down into a dripping cellar, a dungeon with a vaulted roof, where the torches flicker and die. A single, weak shaft of light falls from on overhead grille.

We grope our way across the dungeon until we reach the far side. My fingers grasp an unseen metal handle, which I pull. A door opens on to a dark tunnel, nothing like the hotel corridors we have left behind. The floor is cold, hard and uneven. The walls are of rough-hewn rock, with narrow niches containing kerosene lamps. The lights come at regular intervals – I count my steps as we stumble forward up a gradual incline, twenty-five paces between them. We pass five before faint voices start to whisper.

'The way ahead is blocked.'

'Rockfall in front and behind.'

'What now?'

Then silence except for the soft popping of flames as the lamps go out. Soon we are in total darkness.

'Did you hear that?' Holly whispers. Her voice echoes down the tunnel. 'The voices – who's down here with us?'

'We're trapped. We'll never get out of here.'

'Dear Lord Jesus, help us!'

'Nobody,' I told Holly. 'Ghosts. Dead miners, workers on the subway. Anybody, everybody in this whole world who was ever buried in a rockfall, an earthquake – whatever.

The voices multiply. They wail and cry for help. We're suffocated by the lost souls around us.

'You mean this isn't real?' Grace asks in a small, scared voice. 'We're imagining all this?'

'Not real?' The idea offers bold, gutsy Holly our lifeline.

'Help!'

'Help us get out of here!'

'Dear Lord, I don't want to die!'

'Ignore them,' Holly orders us. She focuses and forges ahead through the tunnel. 'Concentrate on what we have to do, which is to claw our way back to reality. Come on, Grace, and you too, Tania. I can see daylight!'

We scramble and fight – the three of us together are strong. All for one. We stumble and cough the dust from our lungs as

322

we break out of the tunnel – Holly first, then Grace, then me.
By the force of our combined wills we overcome the nightmare.

'Fire Exit.' We were back in the muffled corridor, confronted by a green sign over a door leading out into the parking lot. I took over from Holly, pressed a metal bar and heard the door click open. We stepped out into the snow. A hard crust had formed over the drifts, thick enough to support our weight. Gingerly, with the snow creaking under our feet with every step we took, we made our way past the rows of buried cars towards the avenue of pine trees lining the driveway.

'Why are we doing this?' Grace wanted to know. 'Even Macy wouldn't be crazy enough to come out here in these conditions.'

The multicoloured Christmas lights in the trees winked. I followed where they led – towards a silver glow outside the gates which hung with thick icicles almost a metre long. Looking up at Carlsbad, I saw that the peak was hidden by thick grey cloud and that great swirls of snow were blowing in from the west.

'What can you see?' Holly asked me.

'A light. I connect it with my good angels. We have to follow it.'

We walked through the gates out of the hotel grounds, our feet crunching over the frozen crust of snow, a wind howling in our ears.

'Where? I can't see any frickin' light,' Holly protested. 'We're being tricked here; led by the nose until we get lost.'

'It's like searching for Adam all over again,' Grace sighed. 'Only this time I don't think we get a good outcome.'

The wind blew and the snow fell, silent and white, soft and cold, covering our footprints. The silver light beckoned me on.

'Tania, maybe Holly's right.' Grace overtook me. 'We didn't fall for the dark angels' fake dungeon and tunnel trick, so now they create this new illusion – the "good angel light" – because they totally know you'll follow it.'

'You two don't see it?' I asked her and I pointed to where the light was leading – up towards the ski lift terminal.

'No, but I do see a light switched on inside the terminal,' Grace replied.

'Not that. I'm talking about more of a silver glow.' It was the glow that had surrounded Maia when she first explained to me the battle for power between good and evil, the light that accompanied the armies of good angels when they came to do battle against evil and darkness. Zenaida, my mourning dove, had brought the same soft, pure light out of a clear blue sky. She'd perched in the aspens at the end of my garden and told me who she was – my guardian spirit who would always be there for me. And now Adam, with his own pure spirit and a child's wisdom was leading us to Macy.

As I began to run up the mountain, the snow crust beneath me gave way and I sank to my waist. I struggled out of the drift and on up the hill.

The electric light in the terminal went off then on again and the chairlift motor started to whir.

'You were right, Grace. There's definitely someone in there,' Holly cried.

An empty gondola left the terminal and started up the mountain, hardly visible through the thick snow. A second followed – still empty. Holly had reached the foot of the steps leading up on to the platform when Owen appeared at the top.

'Where's Macy?' Holly yelled. She took the metal steps two at a time, closely followed by Grace. But I could see what they couldn't – a third gondola emerging from the terminal, containing a small, slight figure dressed in a bright-red cloak. Macy. It jerked, hesitated then carried her up the mountain out of our reach.

Owen laughed as he stopped Grace and Holly from entering the terminal. He kicked out and landed his foot against Holly's shoulder, forcing her backwards into Grace. Together they slid down the steps.

'Macy!' I yelled her name, got no response. The red figure in the ski lift was turned away from me, gazing up at the white blizzard howling down from Carlsbad peak. The covered chair swung and tilted dangerously. 'Macy!'

Now she heard me and turned.

'It's me – Tania. Stay in your seat. I'll follow you up the mountain on foot!'

She took no notice. Instead, she unlatched the safety bar, and as the gondola swung wildly in the wind, she released the catch, lifted the bar and stood up.

'Macy, don't!' I cried.

She stood and spread her arms. The carmine cloak billowed, the chair tilted to one side.

'Sit down!' I begged. My voice was lost in the howling wind.

The red costume looked like a splash of spilled paint on white canvas as she kept her arms spread wide and tilted forward. She waved her arms like a kid pretending to fly then stepped out of the gondola into the whirling snowflakes.

She plummeted to the ground.

I struggled up the slope and was the first to reach her where she lay on her back, arms flung wide. Her body and legs were twisted like the torso and limbs of a discarded puppet when a child has finished playing. Her eyes were still open.

'Tania, did you see?' she breathed, a smile playing on her lips.

'Don't talk. Don't move,' I begged.

Snowflakes settled on her white face, eyeliner and mascara streaked her cheeks. 'I flew through the air,' she whispered. 'Truly, I did.'

I was there holding her hand when she closed her eyes. 'Yes,' I murmured.

No more breath. No more broken dreams. Macy was dead.

16

'I couldn't stop her.' Owen kept his story short and not very sweet. 'I don't know what cocktail of drugs and alcohol she'd been taking, but she was out of her mind on something. Dude, she was crazy.'

He told everyone how hard he'd tried to talk Macy out of going outside. 'She wouldn't listen. She was wearing the stupid cloak and the mask, said she could fly through the air. I told her no way.'

'Did you actually try to stop her?' Holly asked, her face conveying disbelief.

We were gathered in the main hotel lobby. Macy's broken body had been carried down from the mountain and taken to the medical centre behind the spa and pool, waiting to be driven to the mortuary in Mayfield once the weather broke. Larry and Ryan were part of a large group, plus Rocky and his girlfriend Lisette, Gwen, Charlie and

Angela – everyone except Natalia and Jack congregated in the lobby once the news broke.

'I tried everything I knew to straighten her out, but the second I turned my back she was gone – no jacket, nothing except the costume – running like a crazy girl out into the snow.'

'Owen, it's OK,' Charlie said. 'You're not to blame.'

'You're a big, strong guy. You could have restrained her,' Holly argued, but she was quickly overruled.

'Charlie's right,' Larry decided. 'This was traumatic for you, Owen. Even though you two only just met, you obviously had feelings for her. I guess we all should have realized how unstable she was. We didn't pay enough attention.'

'What about you, Tania?' Charlie turned the spotlight on me. 'You knew her better than anyone. Did you ever imagine she was irrational enough to do something like this?'

I shook my head. 'Macy was a big personality but I never thought she was crazy.'

'So Owen's right – substance abuse is involved and the autopsy will identify the exact cause.' Ryan James cut to the chase. 'Amber, do we have a contact number for Macy? Who should be informed?'

No one, I wanted to tell them. Macy was alone in the

world. But the words sounded too stark and final so I kept my mouth shut.

There was an uneasy silence as the receptionist checked her records. 'Macy has family in Idaho,' she reported. 'An address and phone number for Mr and Mrs Osmond.'

'No, that's not right.' Now I was forced to explain about Macy's recent family history. 'Macy hasn't seen her dad since she was eight years old and her mom passed earlier this year. She died of cancer.'

'Call the number,' Ryan told Amber with steely determination.

She dialled and we waited for what seemed like an age for someone to pick up the phone.

'Mrs Osmond?' Amber began. 'Am I speaking to Macy Osmond's mom?' There was a short pause while Amber listened then spoke what is every parent's worst nightmare. 'Mrs Osmond, I'm calling you from the Carlsbad Lodge in Colorado. I'm afraid I have very bad news.'

Nowheresville turned out to be Darwen, Idaho, so at least Macy hadn't lied about the state. But everything else was pure fabrication.

For a start, both her parents were alive and well.

It turned out that two months earlier Macy stole her

mom's credit card and ran away from home, school and an entire family of mother and father, three grandparents, one sister, an aunt and two cousins all living together in a small town off the beaten track. Her mother reported her missing, the police traced her usage of ATMs and card payments through her home state then in New York. Her phone company provided records of calls and texts. It wasn't long before they tracked down the runaway to her expensive Fifth Avenue hotel.

Her mom flew up to New York on the fifteenth of December, just a couple of days before Orlando and I ran into her in Central Park. Mrs Osmond had pleaded with her and begged her daughter to come home. Macy had told her no, she was already enrolled on a course at a film school and she loved New York – no way was she going back to hicksville.

'None of what she told me was true.' This was the stark fact I was left with after Macy died. Everything shifted and settled into unfamiliar patterns, reshaping the grief I felt over her loss. 'The life she described – her mom's driving phobia, the cancer diagnosis – was total fantasy.'

'So why not cancel the credit card?' logical Grace asked. 'The Osmonds must have known that without money Macy would have had to go home.'

'Not necessarily.' Holly pointed out a few ways Macy could have survived without her mom's card – none of them strictly legal, all of them dangerous. 'I guess that's what the family was afraid of. That's why they had to go on funding her.'

'You know, Tania, back there when I first met Macy I didn't like the girl,' Holly confessed. 'She didn't seem like a good person for you to hang out with.'

'Me neither,' Grace admitted. 'I wasn't certain but deep down inside I thought maybe she came from the wrong side – from the dark angels. Something about the way you two met – just before the mugging, when all the bad stuff started to happen.'

'Too much of a coincidence,' Holly said. 'She drops her bag and draws Orlando away, leaving you all alone. It could've been a conspiracy.'

I shook my head and sighed. 'Well, it turns out you were both wrong. And so was I. To me she seemed genuine. Sucker that I am, I believed her when she told me she was in contact with her mom through a medium.'

'And you felt sorry about all the bad stuff she said had happened,' Grace realized. 'Me too, once I got over my suspicions. I thought the red hair, the piercings, the mascara could all be ways to cover up the big hurt of losing her mom.'

332

'In a way they still were,' Holly said. 'It was just a different kind of hurt. There's a label for fantasists like Macy – bipolar. But then again, Grace, what do I know? You're the one who's training to be a shrink.'

'And she still died out there on the mountain because of it,' I murmured. Nothing took away from the tragedy of Macy falling into the hands of the dark angels or the guilt I felt that I hadn't been able to help her, or the fear that squeezed my heart.

By dusk the snowstorm blew itself out. The clouds lifted and the white peak of Carlsbad glittered under a full moon and a million van Gogh stars.

Orlando! I stared at the sky and it felt like a hole had been carved out in my chest in the place where my heart should be. I remembered that once, long ago, there had been a special, loving place for Orlando and me under the starry night sky.

Later, down in the bar, life-stranded-by-a-snowstorm-in-a-five-star-hotel went on as before. Owen served drinks to Charlie, Orlando and Gwen. Ryan and Larry talked schedules and money. After she put the kids to bed, Natalia came down to join them.

'It's like Macy never existed,' Grace said sadly.

Holly and I agreed. 'One thing we can say for sure is

that Owen doesn't miss her,' Holly muttered.

'Plus, he's going to get away with murder,' I added. 'We know he brainwashed Macy to do what she did, but no one will believe us.'

'They didn't see the look on his face when he appeared at the top of those steps,' Holly reminded us.

'Or hear him laugh, or watch him lash out at us.' Grace swirled the Coke in the bottom of her glass.

'Who could we tell?' Holly wondered out loud. 'Ryan? Larry? Charlie? No, there's no one here we can trust. And now that the dark angels don't have Macy to spy on us, who are they planning to use in her place?'

'Maybe they won't even bother to find out what we know about Gwen,' I suggested. 'They believe they've got way more power than we do, and Macy's death proves it. Besides, they only have to hang on for another twenty-four hours.'

'Until the party?'

'Yes. Then it's end game.'

Orlando, why won't you listen to me? My inner voice grew stronger and louder. Please believe me. Leave Gwen and come back to me.

His back was turned and I gazed at his broad shoulders, the curl of his dark hair on the nape of his neck as I forecast the next day's events.

'There will be a dance, some kind of ceremony or ritual to smooth the way for Orlando. Gwen will be the temptress. She'll look spectacular. He won't be able to resist.' I was surprised how calm I sounded as I said this – maybe it was exhaustion and the shock of what had happened to Macy. Anyway, my words floated across the table without drawing any reassurances from Holly and Grace, and meanwhile we all saw Jack stride into the crowded room.

'Uh oh.' Grace saw him head straight for the bar, lean across it and demand a drink from Owen.

Owen raised his eyebrows and turned to Charlie to check with him if it was OK to serve Jack. Jack took angry exception to the delay.

'What does it have to do with him!' he yelled, so loud that Larry and Ryan broke off their conversation with Natalia and the whole room fell silent. 'What is he – my nanny?'

While everyone else froze, something brought me to my feet and took me across the room to where Jack stood. I did it without thinking, only feeling that I needed to protect him.

'Whisky!' Jack lunged and tried to snatch the bottle of Jack Daniels from Owen. I held him back. Owen flashed me a menacing look and I sensed the army at his side made up of a thousand lost souls.

The mirror behind the bar melts and morphs into an enormous wall of water cascading over a rock face, down into a dark whirlpool that threatens to drag me under.

I blinked, fought the dark vision and reopened my eyes.

With a cynical grin Owen let Jack take the bottle. Charlie did nothing, only watched me and my reaction as Jack raised the whisky to his lips.

'Jack, don't,' I protested. Further along the bar, Ryan had broken away from Larry and Natalia and was heading our way. 'You don't need this,' I told Jack. 'You're not drinking any more, remember.'

Suddenly, from out of nowhere, Jarrold and Weller had shown up. Weller smiled and raised his glass to Jack, drank his shot then slid the empty glass across the bar for a refill. Again I glimpsed the waterfall, the whirlpool and souls being dragged into a dark vortex.

Jack still had the bottle raised to his lips. His head was tilted back and he looked at me from under hooded lids.

'You take that drink and you lose it all,' I reminded him. Kids, career – everything.

He could smell the alcohol, practically taste it by the time Ryan arrived. But still he hadn't downed a drop.

'That's it, you crossed the line,' the movie mogul

declared. He spoke with total authority, confident that no sane person would dare to cross him. 'You already had your final warning, Jack.'

Slowly Jack lowered the bottle without taking a drink.

'He didn't cross it,' I argued. 'OK so he thought about it but he didn't actually do it.'

Ryan made a gesture to bat me away with the back of his hand. 'I saw you with my own eyes, Jack. And you do this in front of your wife. You break a promise to me, to Larry, to her—'

'He didn't!' I insisted.

Ryan shook his head. 'We finish this movie without you, Jack,' he said, firmly closing the book once and for all. 'You're off the payroll. Consider yourself fired.'

Rocky Seaton was the only person in the bar who came across to Jack. All the others – the hangers-on, the good-time drinking buddies, the girls he'd slept with – every single one turned their backs.

'You know what you need to do, Jack? You need to speak with your lawyers,' Rocky advised quietly. 'Get them to check the small print.'

For the longest time Jack didn't reply. It looked to me like he was going to go for the Jack Daniels after all, but then he pulled back. 'Hey, man, if you want to keep your job with Ryan you don't want to be seen talking to me,' he warned with a show of bravado that didn't hide his inner panic. The bottle still stood on the bar within easy reach.

'OK, so Ryan owns Starlite, but in terms of your actual contract there's still a good chance the organization can't fire you for no good reason,' Rocky said.

'How many reasons do they need?' Charlie muttered – his first comment of the evening. He'd split away from Gwen and Orlando and now he picked up the bottle and thrust it into Rocky's face. 'You know as well as anyone here how many times Jack failed to show up, how often he forgot his lines and fell over in front of the camera.'

Rocky kept calm and outstared Charlie. 'Jack gets fired, so do you,' he pointed out. 'Remember, Jack is the goose who lays your golden egg. So if I were you, Charlie, I'd be out there fighting to have him reinstated.'

As Charlie laughed and brushed him off, Rocky blocked him with a grand-standing, in-your-face speech intended to draw maximum attention. 'And just in case you figure you can fill the shoes of the movie actor who's been nominated for three best-actor Oscars and won one for his role in *Reluctant Hero*, the highest-grossing movie of the decade, I'm here to tell you, no way.' Rocky paused to enjoy Charlie's building fury, then he went on. 'The fact is, Jack has as much acting talent in his little finger as you, Charlie Speke, have in your entire over-pumped, fake-tanned, surgically enhanced body.'

It was too much – Charlie lost it and hit out at Rocky, who sidestepped so that Charlie swung off balance then stumbled against Weller, who set him back on his feet and mumbled something in his ear. Charlie drew a deep breath then unclenched his fists.

Rocky shook his head and turned back to Jack. 'Don't cave in without a fight, buddy. Get the lawyers to read through your contract,' he said again, loud enough for Ryan to hear. 'So blacklist me too,' he told him, staring his all-powerful employer in the face as he strode away.

'He's right,' I told Jack. I walked him out of the bar into the reception lobby, where I sat him down on the big cowhide sofa. His hands were shaking badly and his whole body had slumped. 'Ryan can't do this to you.'

'In this industry Ryan James is God,' he muttered. 'He can do anything he wants. Anyway I don't give a crap about my career. I'm done with all that.'

'No, don't talk that way. You're good. Your fans love you.'

'*Was* good,' he contradicted. 'Did love me. Past tense. I was as good as the script and the director let me be, back in the day. What is it – eight, nine years since I was offered a role I really wanted to play? Ever since then, I've taken any crap they threw my way.'

'If that's true, I agree with you – don't do it any more.' Talking to Jack, I waited to see his head come up again and his shoulders to go back. After all, there were other things to fight for. 'Either that, or hold out for a worthwhile project.'

He looked up at me and laughed at my naivety. 'You're a good kid, Tania. I really do like you.'

'Yeah well, just don't offer me a part in your next blockbuster movie,' I shot back at him.

'Why – because your boyfriend would get the wrong idea?' Seeing my smile fade, he apologized. 'I forgot – no boyfriend. I guess you hate Gwen Speke as much as I hate her brother.'

'Which brings me to my point,' I told Jack. 'Charlie. I used to really like him. He acted like a guy who would help out in a crisis.'

'Mister Sensible.'

'Yeah. And reliable too. I thought his heart was in the right place.'

'But not any more?'

'No.' I'd wavered after the incident in Charlie's room and finally changed my mind about him over the Adam emergency. 'It was after Adam got lost,' I confessed. 'I kept asking myself, why didn't Charlie do a better job of taking care of him?'

'You're asking me?' Memory of the incident brought Jack up to a sitting position. 'You saw – if I could've got my hands on the guy I'd have killed him.'

'So what if he lost Adam on purpose?' I suggested without really knowing where I was going with this.

Jack shook his head. 'That doesn't add up, not after the way Charlie wormed his way into Natalia's good books. He wouldn't want to lose face with her.'

'He'd know she would blame him if anything bad happened to Adam?'

'Yeah, right.'

'But did she?' I reminded him.

'No. As it turns out, I'm the bad guy and he's still flavour of the month.'

'Exactly. So if I gave you one big reason why Charlie would lose your son out there on the ski slope, would you at least hear me out?' This was it – I was about to break new ground with Jack.

'Go ahead,' he muttered, giving me his full attention.

'There's a whole world we don't normally think about,' I began slowly, expecting a flare up of cynicism from world weary Jack. 'It's a spiritual thing – dead souls out there in the ether, trying to communicate with the living.

Some of them are good, some evil. No, wait – just give me a chance to explain.'

He'd broken in with a sigh and a grunt then made as if to get up off the couch. But something made him change his mind and he sank back down. 'This had better be good.'

'I have a psychic gift,' I explained. 'It all happened because I was born in a house where a baby girl died in a fire. She was called Aimee. At the moment my mom gave birth to me, Aimee's spirit entered my body. We're twinned souls. I hear and see her whenever I'm in my room. Her mom is called Maia. She was my first good angel, before Zenaida and now your boy, Adam. My gift gives me contact with a reality that most people don't see.'

'I should get up and walk away,' he groaned. 'Why am I even sitting here?'

'Because this is to do with Adam and you know that even if there's a one per cent chance of me not being crazy, you have to stay and listen.' I felt calm and determined, certain that Jack would have to hear me out. 'So, there's good and evil and there's a universal battle going on out there. Dark angels fight to drag fresh souls into hell. Good angels are on the side of light, offering a route into heaven. And some way, somehow Adam is on this earth as a good angel.'

'Wait, you were talking about a kid called Aimee?' Jack seemed not to have heard the last bit and was deeply moved. There were tears in his eyes as he spoke. 'I'm going to share a secret but swear on your life you won't let it go any further than this lobby. Adam wasn't my first son. Before I knew Natalia, before I was famous, something bad happened in my life. I was eighteen years old and living in LA. It was pretty wild. I got my girlfriend pregnant. Eventually she had a baby boy but the kid had something wrong with his heart. He lived two days.'

'I'm so sorry,' I whispered.

'We named him Adam,' Jack whispered. 'I hoped and prayed non-stop for forty-eight hours for that boy to survive. What the hell for? It didn't do any good – we lost him anyway. But I never forgot him and how he had a whole life ahead of him but he never got the chance to live it.'

'It must have been incredibly hard.'

'Worse for Anna than for me. My girlfriend – she went crazy back there. They kept her in the hospital, put her on anti-depressants then she was in therapy for a whole year. She wasn't into me any more. Soon after that my career took off and we lost contact.'

'Then you met Natalia.'

'She doesn't know about Anna or the baby,' Jack said quickly.

'But in a way, the Adam you have now links you to your first baby and what I'm saying about good angels living on through others could be true – this Adam is twinned with the son who died. He did get a chance of life after all.' I took a deep breath and thought of the halo of silver light that protected Jack's oldest son from harm.

Jack bent his head and thought for a long time.

'And if Adam is a good angel, there will always be dark angels wanting to destroy him,' I warned.

'Charlie?' Jack realized what I was saying and sprang to his feet. 'Where is he? When I find him this time, I mean it – I'm going to kill him.'

'But there's a problem,' I cautioned. 'We still can't be sure that Charlie's a dark angel. They shape-shift and trick everyone so that you never know who you can trust. What I've just told you about Charlie wanting Adam to be lost in the snow and the reason why he would want it to happen – good angel versus bad – it's only a theory. But what I do know for sure is that Adam didn't want to be out there with Charlie. He told me so himself.'

'But Natalia trusts this guy!' Jack exclaimed angrily. Changing his mind about seeking Charlie out, he strode back across the lobby towards the bar and, as chance would have it, bumped into his wife, who was on her way upstairs. The two almost collided.

'Yeah, Jack, hurry on back in there,' she muttered. 'It's almost ten whole minutes since you had a drink.'

'It's not alcohol I'm looking for, it's you.'

'So you found me.' Natalia seemed tired. She'd dropped the smiley, sparkly act and her face looked drawn and pale under the up-sweep of red hair. 'Let me by, Jack. Lucy's child-minding for me. I got a message to say that Charlie woke up crying. He had a nightmare.'

'So I can babysit,' Jack offered. 'You go back and schmooze Ryan.'

She looked with disdain at his shaking hands and unshaven face. 'You – babysit?' she repeated slowly.

'They are my kids,' her reminded her.

'Yeah, poor babies.' Drawing herself up tall and haughty, she sidestepped Jack and carried on towards the lift.

Poor babies – two tiny words with giant impact. Jack felt the full force and swayed. 'They're my kids!' he repeated, running after Natalia. 'You can't take them away from me.'

She turned – ice queen without a heart. 'Watch me,' she said and stepped into the lift.

* * *

345

Jack went nuts. He swore and stormed, cried and swore again until Rocky and Lisette showed up and offered him floor space in their first-floor suite.

'You and Natalia need some time apart,' Rocky advised. 'Give her chance to cool down.'

'Cool down? She's already so bloody freezing she can kill me with a single look,' Jack complained.

'I mean, give her time to think things through. She'll have to recognize it's not good for the kids to lose their dad out of their lives.'

'She's got Charlie Speke all trained up as a surrogate, hasn't she? That's been her plan all along – to replace me with that lousy lookalike. Bottom line – this is where I'm at. No job, no wife, no kids.'

'Come with us,' Rocky insisted. He thanked me for being there for Jack when no one else was.

'You were there too,' I pointed out. 'He needs friends like you. So take care of him, OK.'

'You too – take care.'

The three of them walked to the elevator while I decided to head for my room using the stairs, wondering all the while about ice-queen Natalia and Charlie's ever increasing influence.

What was Natalia – victim or accomplice? Was she sleepwalking out of her own life, being sucked into the dark angel vortex without realizing or did she know what she was doing every step of the way? Nothing, I repeat, nothing was impossible.

I climbed the stairs two at a time, stopped at a first-floor window to look out over Carlsbad. Twenty-four hours from now it'll be over, I thought.

I see my reflection in the glass and another figure standing behind me – wolf man Jarrold with amber eyes. His pupils are dark slits, his jaws snap and he smells of sweat and blood. A wolf on hind legs, panting at my shoulder.

I climbed the stairs and reached the window on the second-floor landing.

My reflection – there it is again. And this time it is Weller with a knife in his raised hand – behind me, beside me, morphing and multiplying. He's not extraordinary. He's any punk you would see on every city street, in a multi-storey car park, springing out from behind a civic statue, pursuing you over a bridge, through a dark colonnade. His face is blank. He will strike you dead for your cell phone and the twenty dollars you carry in your purse. There are a thousand Wellers waiting for me round every corner, up every flight of stairs.

I drew a deep breath, held my nerve and went on, came to the third floor and opened the fire door into the corridor leading to my room. Dark angels were everywhere, in each shadowed stretch of carpet between the wall lights, behind each numbered door.

I opened my door with my key card.

Daniel sat in a chair by the window. He acted like it was the most natural thing in the world for him to be sitting there, smiling at me, saying, 'Hey, Tania – I was wondering how long it would be before I finally got you all to myself.'

Like Jarrold before him, he caught me off guard and in desperate need of someone to take care of me.

'You got me all wrong last time around,' Daniel continued smoothly. 'I know it's hard to work out which side people are on. That's the game they play.'

'Who do you mean?'

'The dark angels. You have me nailed down as Zoran's right-hand man, and I don't blame you for that.'

'Are you telling me that wasn't true?' I asked warily. Here he was in my room, handsome and powerfully persuasive. 'You were on my side all along?'

'I'm here now, aren't I? And why else, except to watch your back?' He stood up, one hand in his pocket, leaning against the wall. 'It seems like you need a friend.'

'But not you.' I'd been through this already with Jarrold. No way would I trust Daniel.

'Why not me? Think about it, Tania. Run through everything I did for you back there on Black Rock. When did I ever let you down?'

As he came towards me, I backed away. 'You tried to seduce me, to draw me onto the dark side!'

'Not true,' he insisted.

'Why am I even bothering to argue with you?' I cried. 'We both know exactly what you did!'

'But don't you see? It was all a pretence.' He was close now – near enough for me to feel the heat of his body, to see from close up the clean line of his jaw, the softness of his lips. 'I faked all that dark angel stuff to fool Zoran. All the time I was working to protect you.'

'An angel of light?' I gasped. For a split second it seemed possible, and with all my bruised and battered heart I wanted it to be true.

'Now you get it,' he murmured as he put his arms around me.

Almost surrendering to his embrace, I glanced over his shoulder and through the window. A silver cloud passed across the face of the moon. A thousand warning voices whispered, 'Nothing is what it seems.'

I felt Daniel's kiss cold on my lips. I shuddered and broke free.

Here is Daniel. Daniel my god of the underworld, dressed to kill. He is in the costume he wore to Zoran's Heavenly Bodies party. A bird mask hides his face and a cloak of black feathers hangs like wings behind him. He is naked to the waist, perfectly proportioned, beautiful and strong – my dark lord.

I smell smoke. Flames of a forest fire flicker in the reflection I see in the window. I choke and try to run. Jarrold and Weller stand in my way.

'Death, darkness, suffering.' Daniel speaks through the smoke and flames. 'The more the worms suffer, the more powerful we become.' The flames rise and engulf him.

In his place a huge figure emerges from the smoke. He is hunched over, half beast, crawling out from the mouth of a tunnel, stinking of decay. He stands and fills the room. His face morphs. It is Charlie.

Now at last I am certain. Rocks fall, earth clogs my lungs. Breathe, I tell myself.

In the distance there is the sound of dripping water, muffled, despairing voices and more rocks falling.

'I will survive,' I swear. Charlie appears with the claws and dull, matted hair of a bear, the face of a man. 'This is the third and final test. You won't beat me.'

He smiles. His teeth are yellow, his eyes hollow. 'Too late,' he whispers.

'No. I already know that Gwen isn't your sister. She stepped into a dead girl's body so that she could come back from the dark side and walk in this world and seduce her victim. I'll find Orlando and tell him the truth. He'll have to listen.'

Charlie laughs. 'If only it was that simple.'

'And now I know you!' I protest. 'What you are, what you do.'

He fills the room with the smell of wet earth and decay. Bones lie strewn across the bed; there is a row of skulls on my pillow. 'Who am I?'

'You're a dark angel. You can't hide from me or trick me any more. I know you.'

The smile broadens. 'Name me,' he taunts.

My heart thumps. I search frantically for the exact word I need to destroy my enemy. No sound passes to my lips.

Charlie smiles. The rocks above my head grind together then slide. The tunnel props splinter, the roof collapses. Death.

Breathe. Believe.

'Hey, Tania, what the hell happened to you?' Holly demanded, shoving at the door and turning on the light.

17

'A name – that's all I need!'

All night I racked my brains, sifted through every past conversation with Charlie to find the one word I needed to destroy him. At midnight I stood at my window gazing up at the night sky, recollecting the first time I met him in Central Park – my amazed double-take, his calm reassurance, 'No, I'm not Jack Kane.'

For a while I hadn't believed him.

'Nope, I'm not him,' he'd repeated to the seen-it-all-before carousel worker.

Grace and Holly were also awake, trying to help me work it out. 'I've always wondered how Charlie was in the right place at the right time to save you.' Grace said.

'I don't know. I never asked.'

'But it was Charlie who found you a cab and sent you back to the B&B, right?'

I nodded. 'Which meant he had my Hubert Street address so he could hand over the security passes next day.'

'So he organized for Orlando to meet Gwen and the rest is history,' Grace murmured.

'I should've seen it coming,' I sighed. The stars twinkled harmlessly; the moon cast its serene silver light. Who would believe there was planetary chaos, stars imploding and burning, infinite armies of angels at war?

'Tania, this is not the time to beat yourself up,' Holly warned. She was sitting on a chair, her bare feet resting on the bed. 'Focus on Charlie. He's got to have said something that could give us the clue we need.'

'I'm trying. All I remember about New York is that Charlie was always there for Natalia and the kids. It didn't seem weird at the time. I figured everyone in Jack and Natalia's situation has someone like Charlie – someone they can trust to handle life's daily routine.'

'"Trust" – ha! So the only weirdness was that you couldn't tell one from the other; Jack could've been Charlie and the other way around. Charlie could fool everyone into thinking that he's Jack.'

'Yeah, even Macy made the usual mistake and she was the biggest Jack Kane fan you could find.'

Mention of Macy sent everyone quiet for a while. In my mind I went through a dozen more moments when I should've suspected Charlie's motives: the way he drew Macy in with his talk of the movie-star life, how he dumped her and hit on me when I was aching for comfort – the St Bernard dog slug of alcohol, the star-gazing philosophy, the arm round my shoulder, the dark angel seduction.

'And still I didn't figure it out,' I groaned.

'There's no point,' Holly decided, suddenly standing up and starting to pace. 'We have to stop going over old stuff and start looking ahead to tomorrow's party.'

'Today's party,' I corrected, looking at my watch. It was one in the morning.

'No, wait.' Grace still wanted to go back to the point when she and Holly first met Charlie. 'What exactly did he say? "I'm not who you think." When you spend time focusing on that, it was an obvious clue. But we didn't pick it up either.'

'It's as if Charlie's been playing with us all along, like he gets his kicks out of fooling with us.' Holly got what Grace was saying.

I agreed and saw a glimmer of hope. 'And that's always been the dark angels' weakness,' I pointed out. 'They play with us and get enjoyment out of it. Charlie even said it: "The more the worms suffer, the more powerful we become."'

'Pure sadism,' Grace sighed. 'Remember, he made that stupid joke about having supersonic hearing. It turns out he actually does.'

'So Tania's right.' Holly grew more animated. 'It's because they don't just finish us off, end of story, that we're still alive – we still have a chance.'

'And we have to follow it through to the end – to the party.' To me it was crystal clear that Charlie had set this stage for multiple victims – for me, Grace and Holly, but mainly for Orlando. The script was already written. Lights, camera, action!

'So the grader's out clearing snow from the helipad,' Holly reported soon after dawn when she went down to reception. She came back to the room with fresh coffee and news from Amber. 'If the snow holds off for a few hours, they'll fly in and airlift Natalia and the kids off the mountain.'

'Before or after tonight's party?' I wanted to know.

Holly shrugged. 'It depends on conditions in Aspen, I guess. That's where the chopper's based.'

'Oh God, I hope they stick around,' I groaned. Suddenly, more than anything else I needed Adam to stay.

Be strong. Take my hand.

'Whose idea was it?' I wondered with a fresh jolt of fear. 'Don't tell me – it was Charlie's.'

If he couldn't get rid of my good angel by losing him on the ski slopes in a snowstorm, it looked like flying a helicopter into the side of a mountain would do the job instead.

'I need to talk to Natalia,' I said.

It was nine a.m. when I pushed the button and rode the elevator to the premier suite. Meanwhile Holly and Grace had agreed to warn Jack.

'He's in Rocky and Lisette's rooms,' I'd reminded them. 'Just tell him what Charlie's got planned for Natalia and the kids. Try to keep him calm and focused.'

It was early and my offer to visit the penthouse had taken Natalia by surprise. Stepping out of the lift, I found the kids in their jammies and their mom making breakfast for them in the small kitchen. When she saw me, she came out into the living room and I registered the full effect that the stress of family break-up was having.

'Sorry,' she sighed, making no effort to smooth down her tangled hair. She was paler than ever, without make-up and she looked fragile. 'Hey, Adam, look who came to visit. Aren't you glad?'

Adam glanced up from a book about dinosaurs. He gave me a bright smile then carried on looking at the pictures with Phoebe. Charlie sat in a highchair, chewing on wheat toast.

'I'm sorry I look the way I do but I'm glad you're here,' Natalia said wearily. 'Even if it's only to say goodbye.'

'Yeah, I heard you were leaving.'

She nodded and sank down on to a sofa. 'They're preparing the helipad. I have to get out of here.'

'But is it a good idea?' I asked. 'Will the pilot even fly out of Aspen?'

'All he needs is a three-hour window – no snow, no wind. The local forecast is good.'

Finishing the dinosaur book, Adam turned to Phoebe. 'You want to play superheroes?' Soon they were busy with invisible cloaks and light sabres, jumping off sofas, flying through the air.

'Ryan said I should wait until the roads are clear,' Natalia confessed. 'It was Charlie's idea to bring in a helicopter.'

'I agree with Ryan. Why the rush?'

Natalia winced. 'You want the truth? It's because I can't stand being in the same building with Jack.'

I did what I could to put the record straight. 'Yesterday he stuck to his word. He didn't drink that whisky.'

'So what? It doesn't really matter, does it? The fact is, he and I are through and the faster I get out of here, the sooner I can get on with the rest of my life.'

'It matters,' I insisted. 'Jack had all the reasons in the world to stretch out across that bar and drown his sorrows but he didn't do it.'

She gave a faint shake of her head. 'Too late,' she insisted.

I pushed harder. 'You know it was Charlie who kept the Jack Daniels flowing for Jack these last few months?'

If I'd told a born-again Christian fundamentalist that God didn't exist I couldn't have got a bigger reaction. Natalia jumped up from the sofa, startling little Charlie and making Adam and Phoebe stop their game. 'Tania, that's a mean, mean thing to say,' she told me. 'After everything Charlie did for you, how can you believe that?'

'I'm warning you – don't rely too much on Charlie,' I went on. 'Lately I've learned things about him—'

'And how do you know that it was Charlie who supplied the whisky?' she interrupted.

'Jack told me himself.'

'Hah!' Rushing back into the kitchen and out of sight, Natalia acted like I'd just proved her case. 'I thought you were smart,' she shouted. 'I guess I was wrong.'

'No, Natalia, listen. Don't go in that helicopter. I know

the weather round here. If a storm gets up in the mountains behind Carlsbad, it blows in without warning.'

'Charlie tells me it's safe, so it is.' She reappeared in the kitchen doorway, lips trembling and voice breaking. 'You don't understand. It's dangerous here. I feel trapped. This hotel is a prison.'

'I do – I understand.'

'No.'

'Why? What are you afraid of? Jack loves Adam and Phoebe and Charlie. There's no way he would harm them.'

Fiercely Natalia swept the tears from her cheeks. 'You don't know him. You don't know that he was here in the middle of the night, standing in the lobby banging on the door and swearing the way he does, yelling for me to let him see his own kids. If I didn't open the door he'd break it down.'

'You're sure?' I asked. 'Really certain that it was Jack and not Charlie?'

Now she was furious. 'What kind of stupid question is that?'

'There's one way we could check. Rocky invited Jack to share his suite. Why don't you call him now and ask him where Jack was at three o'clock this morning?'

'You're saying it was Charlie pretending to be Jack?'

Natalia laughed. 'Oh grow up, Tania. Just because you tried to hit on Charlie and he turned you down flat—'

Now it was my turn to laugh in disbelief. 'He told you that?'

'Add to that the fact that your beloved Orlando is now sleeping with Charlie's beautiful, talented little sister . . .'

'I came here because I care what happens to you, Natalia. There's stuff going on here that's too big for you to get your head around in the time we've got, but all I'm saying is – for your kids' sake, don't use the helicopter.'

It made no difference. She reached for her phone and spoke into it. 'Charlie, I need you,' she said. 'Tania's here and she's paranoid. Come up as soon as you get this message.'

I didn't hang around in Natalia's suite waiting for Charlie – what was the point?

Instead I made my way down to the first floor in search of Holly and Grace, only to have one of my shuddering, juddering elevator moments when the door slid open and I came face to face with Orlando.

Not quite face to face, actually.

He stood in the corridor carrying his costume for that night's wrap party. There was a black tunic and a cloak hanging over his arm and a white mask with ornate silver decoration, which, when he saw me emerge from the lift, he held up to hide his face.

Too surprised to say anything, I took his free hand in mine and felt how cold it was. Slowly he lowered the mask and stared at me.

Don't scare him. Don't make him run away. My reaction was to act as if I was dealing with an untamed, wild creature in a forest – to hold my breath, not to make any sudden move. It gave me time to study his face for any small sign that my old Orlando still existed. Recognize me. Remember what we had, I pleaded silently.

His hair seemed darker and duller, his eyes a paler grey and it felt to me that though he'd lowered his carnival mask there was still an unnatural smoothness and stillness to his features.

Remember me. Realize what's happening to you.

'How are you doing?'

'Good,' he murmured. He seemed hardly to breathe, his face was fixed in a blank stare. But when he looked full into my eyes, I saw a flicker of dark fear.

'I've missed you,' I whispered.

He frowned then almost imperceptibly he nodded.

'More than I can say.' Please remember our starry nights, our dreams. You are me and I am you. 'Orlando, come home with me.'

The fear in his eyes flared up. 'I can't,' he mumbled. 'It's too late. I just can't.'

'But you do remember what we had?' I pleaded.

He nodded again.

There was so much pain, so much loss – neither of us could bear it. 'Hey,' I breathed, still holding his hand. 'You found a costume.'

He nodded slowly while I ran my hand over the shiny black fabric.

'Where are you taking it – to Gwen's room?'

'No.'

'Where then?'

'I'll show you.' Turning away from the elevator, he pushed through the fire door and took the stairs to ground level. When I didn't follow him, but remained where I was standing, he turned to wait.

'You want to find somewhere for us to talk?' I asked.

This time he didn't nod but he didn't say no either. He waited.

I knew it wasn't right. His movements were slow and stiff; his expression didn't change. 'OK, I'm coming.' I followed him down the stairs.

We made it to the ground floor and Orlando led the way down a corridor showing arrows to the swimming pool and spa, with a temporary sign saying 'Closed for

Maintenance' hanging from a hook. I hesitated again.

'What's wrong?'

'Nothing.' Everything.

'Don't you want to see me try on my costume?'

'Yes.' No. I want to talk to you. I want to save your life.

'Come on then.'

Again I followed. As we passed through a large tiled area I smelled the jasmine fragrance from the oriental spa to the left, the scorched cedar wood of the sauna to our right. I saw white towelling robes and towels piled high on a reception desk, heard soft piped music played through invisible speakers.

'Orlando, talk to me,' I begged, overtaking him and blocking his way into the pool area that opened up ahead of us. 'Don't you see what Gwen has done to you?'

Tiny muscles twitched – under his eyes, around his mouth.

'You do! Somewhere, deep down, you still know what's happening to you.'

'Shall I try on my costume?' he asked in a monotone.

I thought he was still talking to me then in the split second it took me to understand that he wasn't, Gwen stepped silently through a changing-room door with Weller, Daniel and Jarrold. I gasped and tried to run. Daniel stopped me – stood in front of me and thrust me back with enough force to send me stumbling and sliding along the wet tiles to the very edge of the pool.

'Orlando, don't leave me!' I cried when I saw him turn and walk away.

'Don't waste your breath,' Jarrold snarled. I remembered the snap of his wolf jaws, heard water lap against the sides of the pool.

They'd sent Orlando to lead me into this trap and now he went away silently and they stood over me, united in their evil intent. They looked down on me as I lay sprawled on the limestone tiles.

'What's it to be this time, Tania?' Gwen asked in her high, childlike voice. 'Do you choose death by drowning over suffocation in a rockfall, or burning in white-hot flames over both of those? Which is quickest, I hear you wonder.'

'Rockfall,' Weller grunted. 'Underground, in total darkness.'

'Fire,' was Daniel's choice. 'Not quickest but for sure the most painful.'

'Water.' Jarrold dropped to his knees and pushed his face close to mine. I recoiled from him.

'And you believed you could win a victory over me,' Gwen sighed. Her breath seemed to fill the vast pool area with thousands of butterflies – gold, scarlet, iridescent blue – all beating their fragile wings against the glass canopy, soundless and desperate. 'Didn't you know that I could see every move you made?'

The butterflies swarm around my head. They fade and fall into the water.

'I watched your pathetic attempt to discover my name. It amused me.'

I closed my eyes and took a deep breath, rose to my feet, stared her in the eye.

'Look,' she invited, and she unwound the sky blue scarf she wore to show me bruises – deep thumb marks, areas of broken skin like a cruel necklace around her slender neck.

I couldn't bear to see it so I closed my eyes again.

Butterflies fall in their thousands, like autumn leaves on the surface of a pond.

'Carrie died slowly,' she whispered. 'I watched. I chose my moment with care. But knowing what you know, seeing what you now see – the proof of how she died, you must realize that the name Carrie Hall gets you nowhere.'

'One step closer,' I argued.

'But not close enough.' Circling behind me and coming to face me again, Gwen savoured her moment. 'Zoran Brancusi equals Malach. Jean-Luc and Aurelie Laurent equal Ahriman. Carrie Hall, Charlie Speke – they equal . . . what? That's the key.'

'I'll work it out,' I promised. I gritted my teeth, held my breath to ward off the dark angels who surrounded me.

Jarrold springs forward. He leaps at my throat. I stagger, I fall. I hit ice-cold water and sink to the bottom of a lake amongst drowned corpses, decaying houses, the rusting iron cross from a church steeple. Slimy weeds pull at me and hold me down. I look up at rising bubbles of air, light shining on the surface. The light will save me. I kick free and rise.

Daniel and Weller hooked a hand under each armpit and dragged me out of the water. They manhandled me and walked me down the length of the pool, out through a back door labelled Medical Centre. They pushed me into the centre of a windowless room, then before I was able to resist they backed out through the same door and turned the key in the lock.

The room was stark and cold under an ugly strip light. Its white walls were lined with locked cabinets, there was a desk with a glass top, a large white leather chair and a cubicle screened off by a floor-to-ceiling white curtain. Rings rattled along the supporting rail as I whisked back the flimsy fabric and found Macy's body lying on a doctor's examination bed. She was covered in a stiff, pale-green sheet with only her head and feet showing. Her toenails were painted brilliant red.

Shuddering, I whipped the curtain closed and rushed for the door. I wrenched at the handle. 'Help!' I cried. 'Somebody, let me out of here!'

I shouted for what felt like for ever, until my voice went hoarse. I didn't cry or cave in but gradually my energy drained away and I sat on the leather chair with my head in my hands, trying not to imagine the last time Macy had painted her nails, ready to party.

Over and again inside my head I heard her gush, 'Owen is a fascinating guy, he's going to be a superstar!' And I recalled my own private, unspoken opinion about the brash wannabe who had once auditioned for a Spielberg movie – that he was a nobody who had hooked gullible Macy with what turned out to be his dark angel charms.

I thought of the things I could have done to keep her alive.

I grew cold in that room, following the long red second hand of the wall clock as it ticked through the morning. From time to time I made a half-hearted search for a hidden phone or intercom – some way of communicating with the outside world – but of course Gwen had been thorough; the landline phone had been ripped from its socket and thrown into a wash basin in one corner, and the computer cables were trashed.

OK – she'd done a good job. It was a great example of her enjoying my pain, to lock me up here knowing from the hands on the clock that the time for the big party crept closer.

But even Gwen had overlooked one secret weapon in my armoury – or, to be exact, two.

At two thirty p.m. I heard faint voices echoing through the pool area. Holly and Grace had ignored the Closed for Maintenance sign.

'Help!' I ran to the door. 'I'm in here!' I picked up a metal chair and banged it against the door.

'Holly, I hear a noise.' Grace's faint voice grew louder. Then there were footsteps on the tiled floor.

'It's me –Tania. Get me out!'

'This way,' Grace told Holly.

Soon they were shoving at the locked door, looking for ways to force it open, disappearing for a while then returning.

'Stand back, Tania,' Holly commanded. 'I ran to the gym and found some weights. I'm going to batter my way through.'

'Hurry,' I urged. I heard a heavy thud and saw the door move, another blow and it moved again. Three times and the door frame began to split, a fourth and finally Holly succeeded. The frame shattered and the door crashed in towards me.

'Come on, what are you waiting for?' Holly cried.

I took a running leap over the debris into Grace's arms.

'Everyone's getting ready for the party,' Grace told me breathlessly as we sprinted past the pool and spa back to the main hotel. 'The Starlite lighting guys are setting up in the bar. There's going to be a giant screen with videos of the Venice carnival, there'll be music, the whole deal.'

'Where's Jack?' I asked. 'Did you get to talk to him?'

Holly shook her head. 'He wasn't with Rocky and Lisette. They said he needed to clear his head so he went hiking up the mountain.'

'Bad idea in these conditions,' I groaned. Snow drifting over hidden crevasses, threat of avalanche, wind chill . . . I ran through a list of dangers. 'When exactly did he leave?'

We'd reached hotel reception and could see the techie guys in the bar, hard at work setting up for tonight as Grace had said. Behind her desk Amber was already wearing an elaborate costume of pink lace with huge white flowers in her hair. She spoke on the phone as we passed.

'Early this morning,' Holly told me. 'We didn't get to him with the message about Natalia's plans.'

'So he can't still be hiking,' I decided. 'He has to be back in the hotel somewhere.'

As if on cue a familiar figure emerged from the bar. The stumble and slurred greeting gave him away.

'Hey, girls. Let me buy you a drink.'

'Jack!' It felt like a kick in my guts. I hurried towards him and tried to grab the whisky bottle he held in his right hand. 'You swore you wouldn't . . .'

As he snatched his hand away, the liquor sloshed on to the bearskin rug. 'Too slow!' he laughed, then made a display of raising the bottle to his lips and taking a slug. 'See – there's nothing wrong with the old hand–eye coordination.

'Jack, if you carry on this way Natalia will never speak to you again,' Holly warned.

He laughed again; took another drink.

'She's threatening to fly out of here with the kids,' I told him. 'It's crazy in this weather. You need to stay sober, talk to her – persuade her not to leave.'

'Too late,' he sneered, veering towards the cowhide couch and slumping down on to it. 'The chopper flew in and they already left.'

I swallowed hard. 'They can't have. I warned her not to.'

'When did my wife ever listen to advice?' Suddenly Jack's drunken bravado collapsed and he started to sob. 'I didn't get to say goodbye. They already left on guess-who's advice.'

'Charlie Speke,' I said faintly, aware that Holly and Grace had kept a safe distance and stayed close to the reception desk.

'Right first time.' Jack sniffed and drew the back of his hand across his mouth. 'Charlie cleared the helipad. Charlie talked to the pilot. Charlie told him to fly right back to Aspen.'

'So where are they now?' I asked, trying to control my racing heart with long, deep breaths.

Jack took another drink before he answered. 'It's all over,' insisted. 'Right now they're in the air over Carlsbad.'

'Jack totally lost it,' I told Holly and Grace. Time was racing on. We were running up the stairs to my room to put on our costumes. 'The second Natalia and the kids took off in the helicopter with Charlie, that's when he fell apart.'

'Wait.' Grace stopped on the landing between the second and third floors. 'Jack is under the impression Natalia flew to Aspen with Charlie?'

I nodded. 'He just told me.'

'So how come Amber was just talking to Natalia on the phone?' Grace asked. 'Honestly, Tania – Amber told Natalia she'd send a room-service guy to collect her bags. The chopper isn't due to leave until four o'clock.'

'Say that again – this time slowly.'

'Watch my lips,' Grace insisted. 'Amber talked to Natalia. Natalia is still in the hotel.'

Holly was set to take more stairs. 'Come on, we're wasting time.'

'No.' I insisted on staying where I was, gazing out at the helipad and the parked chopper. It confirmed in my mind that the girls were right and Jack's version was wrong. I watched a pair of grey doves alight on a tree in the grounds. As they landed they shook snow from the branch. The snow dropped and dislodged more snow from the branch beneath, and so on until it thudded to the ground.

'Come on, Tania,' Holly repeated.

'No. If Natalia is still here then so is Charlie.'

'So?' Grace stayed with me while Holly took the stairs.

'So who was that I just spoke with – was it Jack or was it Charlie faking it, making me think it was Jack?' However hard I tried with the deep breathing, my pulse raced like an express train.

'Why? What reason would he have?'

'Don't you see?' I cried, making Holly wait on the next landing and peer over the banister to listen to what I was telling them. I saw from the shocked look in Grace's eye that she was already halfway there. 'Jack confronted Charlie over my dark angel theory—'

'Wait. Hold on just a second,' Holly demanded. 'Run that by me again. Jack knows about the whole dark angel thing?'

I nodded.

'How?' Grace asked.

'I told him,' I said quietly.

'And somehow Charlie found out and saw the need to eliminate Jack from the picture.' Grace was ahead of me, fitting the pieces together.

'Maybe . . . probably. One thing I do know – Charlie played a good drunk back there in the lobby but he wasn't totally into the role.'

'Meaning what?' Holly had come back down to our landing to demand an answer.

'His hand didn't shake enough; his coordination was too sharp.'

'So where is Jack?' Holly wanted to know.

Deep breath. Stay focused. 'Dead or dying,' I guessed. 'The body double just took over the starring role.'

18

There was no time for us to do anything except sprint to my room and grab thick jackets to go and look for the real Jack.

'How many hours of daylight do we have?' Grace asked as we ran out into the snow.

'Three, maximum,' Holly told us.

We reached the gates at the end of the drive then paused to look over our shoulders at the chopper resting on its giant metal rails.

Grace picked up on what I was thinking. 'Let's split,' she decided. 'You and Holly go look for Jack. I'll backtrack and find a way to stop Natalia.'

'Report a freak storm over Aspen. Stop that chopper from flying out,' Holly agreed.

Which left two of us searching for Jack on Carlsbad.

'He could be anywhere,' I sighed.

Holly took a deep breath then set off at a run towards the ski-lift terminal. 'If Charlie did kill Jack, where are the most likely places he would dump the body?' she demanded, only stopping when she reached the base of the metal steps leading up to the platform. 'Not in the hotel – it would be too easy for someone to find. It has to be out here on the mountain.'

'Climb up and take a look inside,' I gasped. 'I'll go on ahead.'

I heard Holly take the steps two at a time as I struggled up the smooth slope, heading into a vast white space. I stumbled and sank into a drift, went down on to my hands and knees to haul myself out and when I looked up again I saw Holly emerge from the terminal in a gondola.

'There's no one inside the building!' she yelled down at me. 'But there was a fight. There's a smashed partition and a rip in one of the seats – looks like it was slashed with a knife. Oh, and there was this!' She held up a pair of shades with a missing lens. 'Who wears this style of Oakleys?'

'Charlie does,' I yelled back.

'OK, so maybe this is where it happened.' Holly's voice grew fainter as the gondola carried her up the mountain. 'It looks like Charlie used a knife on Jack then took him up the mountain and dumped the body on the overlook.'

'It's worth a shot,' I agreed. 'I'll carry on towards the old mine. That's another possibility.'

'OK, and I'll get to the top then make my way down. Whatever we find, I'll meet you halfway, OK?'

'Gotcha.'

The cable car carried her smoothly over my head while I fought to make progress through the drifts. It's hard to make out landmarks after recent snow fall and it was harder still not to be awed by the smooth, sparkling whiteness of my surroundings. The sun was low, already casting long violet shadows. There was no wind.

'Look for something you recognize, I told myself as Holly's gondola rose higher towards the overlook. Keep the cables and towers of the ski lift to your right, the red and white poles bordering the dirt track to your left. The mine entrance lies a few hundred metres straight ahead.

I held to this route, climbing out of late afternoon sunlight into shadow as the sun vanished behind the peak. Eventually I spotted the canvas awning used by the film crew – the place where Holly and Grace had found Adam after his ordeal. It still stood despite the weather, though the roof sagged and supporting poles were buckled under a weight of snow. I reached it and stood a while to catch my breath.

What next? Say I made it to the silver mine – would I be brave enough to face my demons and step inside? And if I was, and this was the place where Charlie had dumped Jack's body, what would I do then? Wait for Holly, call for help, take the corpse down off the mountain and announce to the world that Jack Kane was dead?

'Yeah, right,' I muttered to myself. 'Like Charlie is going to let us go ahead and do that!'

I faltered. My legs and lungs ached. No part of me wanted me to go on.

Only the prospect of the look on Holly's face if I turned back stopped me from turning and trudging back to the hotel.

No, I couldn't turn round now. I could see the mine entrance a hundred metres from where I'd taken shelter – a dark tunnel into the rock. I set off towards it, picking up the first signs in the snow that someone else had been here recently – faint scuff marks, a trampled area on a flat ledge and then a dark, shiny fragment of glass from a pair of sunglasses. I picked up the broken lens, turned it between my fingers then slipped it into my pocket.

Then I saw blood – real blood in the snow, not fake blood from Gwen's box of special effects. This time there were no cameras rolling, no actor wielding a gun and running out of the mine, no one spouting lines from a script.

I stooped to examine the crimson patch. It was about ten metres from the entrance and there was a trail leading into the mine – a trickle then a few specks, then another bigger area, where a serious amount of blood had been lost.

Don't stop now! I fought a second, even more powerful urge to run away as I stood at the entrance to the tunnel, smelling the old animal stench. Hold your nerve, walk forward one step at a time.

I bent my head and entered the mine.

It was almost dark – just enough light to make out the unravelled coil of razor wire and the branches dragged in by bears then left to decay. The dull yellow skull of the wolf caught in the wire reminded me that this wasn't the first time that someone or something had come here for shelter, only to die.

The smell of wet earth and death was so strong that I cupped my hand over my mouth. It was sharp and bitter at the back of my throat.

Wolf spirits materialize. Their eyes shine amber in the dark. They slink towards me, tails raised, bodies close to the ground. I reach out to steady myself. Then there are creatures worse than wolves, seeping through the rock. They have no name, no recognizable, fixed shape. Pale and bloodless, unseeing, they are in pain. They howl and wail, twist and writhe as they fall over a ledge into a vortex, fall for ever and drag mortal souls to hell.

I resist but there is no air to breathe, no exit into the world of the living. I am close to the edge, looking into darkness. I say again, there's no air and my knees buckle. I get ready to fall.

Be brave. Look for the light. Adam, Zenaida and Maia are at my side.

Gathering together every scrap of mental energy, I resisted and lurched back from the spiritual precipice, stumbling over a decaying branch and falling to my knees. I made contact with something solid and investigated with my fingertips – touched the cold metal line of a zipper, soft fabric, cold flesh.

I jumped. My breath became shallow. I leaned forward again and made out more detail. The flesh I'd come into contact with was a hand, the fingers curled tightly around a small plastic object – a child's toy, a superhero. Instinctively I tried to ease the hand open to retrieve it.

The fingers resisted. The hand would not let go.

Gasping and trying not to sob, I felt for a pulse – very faint and uneven.

Quickly I took off my jacket and threw it over the

injured man. I leaned in to listen for breath. His eyes opened slowly and tried to focus.

'It's me – Tania,' I murmured.

The eyelids fluttered closed then open then shut again.

'Don't die on me now,' I pleaded. 'Jack, please don't die!'

Between us Holly and I knew enough first aid to stem the flow of blood from the knife wound in Jack's arm. He was unconscious as we raised the arm and improvised a tourniquet then talked about how we could get him back down to the hotel without causing more problems.

'It's good that I showed up,' Holly told me, carefully trying to work Adam's little plastic toy out of Jack's grasp.

'No, let him keep hold of it,' I said quietly, noticing his eyelids flicker open for a moment as if to say thanks.

'No way could you have done this alone,' Holly went on.

I worked with numb fingers to tie a knot in the strip of fabric. 'Yeah, thank God you got here fast,' I muttered. I'd just had time to discover that Jack was alive and to apply pressure to the wound before I'd heard Holly yelling my name. I'd run out of the shaft entrance to see her plunging down from the overlook, running part of the way but mostly sliding on her ass and raising a wake of powdery snow.

'I came as quick as I could,' she told me now, having helped me ease Jack out towards the exit from the mine. 'I could see from the gondola that no one had been on the overlook in twenty–four hours – no tyre marks, no footprints. So I jumped out and headed straight down to you.'

'So do we carry him?' I wanted to know. 'How do we do it?'

'We make a stretcher,' she decided, and went back into the mine to choose two sturdy branches from the bears' old den-making stockpile. 'Let's hope they'll take Jack's weight,' she mumbled as she took off her jacket and ordered me to do the same. 'We zip them together and use the sleeves to attach them to these pieces of wood, so we have a hammock. OK, get ready to lift him. Easy now.'

Jack groaned as we eased his weight on to the makeshift stretcher.

'He feels pain – that's a good sign,' Holly insisted.

I sighed. 'We hope.' There was a hell of a lot more blood on the floor of that tunnel, I'd discovered.

'Come on, let's go.'

Holly and I took the strain and lifted Jack. Clumsily

we made our way down the mountain – Holly in front, me behind.

'Tania, you did good,' Holly told me as we drew level with the ski lift terminal. 'I know how hard it was for you to step inside that old mineshaft.'

'You don't know how close I came to wimping out.'

'I totally do,' she insisted. 'I admire what you did. What are we gonna do when Jack wakes up and the shit hits the fan?'

'As in, Jack gives a blow-by-blow account of how dark angel Charlie stabbed him in the arm then threw him in the mineshaft and left him to die?'

'Exactly.' Sliding and slipping, we carried our heavy load down the final slopes and through the gates of Carlsbad Lodge, where Holly came to a sudden halt. 'Uh-oh,' she grunted.

She'd heard it before I did – the churning of a chopper engine. 'Looks like Grace's plan didn't work out,' I gasped.

The noise of the helicopter's engine grew louder and soon we could see its blades rotating, preparing for take-off.

'That sucks,' Holly groaned.

'No, no – it's all good! Quick, Holly, move!'

'Which way? What are we doing?'

'Hurry. Carry Jack towards the chopper. This is a big emergency, right? They'll have to fly him to the hospital.'

'Out of Charlie's grasp.' Changing course, Holly cut between the trees festooned with Christmas lights and across the snow-covered lawn. 'Look, there's Natalia and the kids coming out of a side entrance,' she reported.

I spotted them too, Natalia carrying Charlie with Adam in his sky-blue ski jacket carefully holding Phoebe's hand and following close behind. The wind from the chopper blades made them bend forward and keep their heads down.

'Natalia, wait!' Holly called.

The noise from the engine meant she didn't hear. We saw the pilot come down a short ladder and shake her hand. Then he stood aside for her to carry the baby up the ladder.

Jack lay senseless as we struggled to heave our makeshift stretcher. We saw the pilot hand Phoebe up into the chopper then turn to Adam.

'Wait!' I yelled.

Adam pulled back from the stepladder. He turned, saw us carrying his dad on a stretcher and started to run towards us.

The pilot followed while Natalia reappeared in the doorway.

'Daddy!' Adam reached us as we were two thirds of the way across the lawn. His eyes were wide, his face pale under the mop of dark-brown hair. He grabbed his father's hand – the one that carried the plastic toy.

'Who's this?' the pilot wanted to know. 'What happened?'

'This is Jack Kane. He's hurt bad, he lost a lot of blood. You need to get him to the hospital,' Holly explained.

The pilot took one look, nodded and quickly retraced his steps, telling us to follow.

'Daddy, Daddy, Daddy,' Adam chanted under his breath, running as fast as he could to keep up, refusing to let go of Jack's hand.

Natalia descended the ladder and hurried across the helipad to meet us, just as Charlie came striding out of the hotel.

'Girls, I need you to lift him up to me,' the pilot instructed as he scrambled up the ladder.

Holly and I prepared to shift position and hand over the stretcher to the pilot. Charlie had arrived, his face set in an expression you couldn't read – eyes narrowed, teeth gritted, black hair blown back from his knitted brows.

'Oh, God – oh Jack – what happened?' Natalia wailed, ignoring Charlie and standing in our way. She reached out to stroke Jack's cheek with the back of her hand.

'I'll handle this,' Charlie told her.

For once Natalia still wasn't listening. 'He isn't going to die, is he?' she begged. 'Tania, please say he'll make it.'

My hand was shaking as I prised Adam's fingers away from Jack's hand. 'It's OK,' I whispered. 'They'll make your daddy better in the hospital.'

'Thank God,' Natalia breathed, eagerly accepting my promise to her son. 'You hear that, Adam? Daddy isn't going to die.'

'I said I'll handle it,' Charlie repeated sternly. 'Natalia, you stay here with the kids. I'll go with Jack to the hospital.'

No! I resisted the urge to spring forward and stop this from happening.

'Why would I do that?' she asked.

'Because you two are through and everyone knows it. And because you have to stay for the party tonight to secure the new movie deal with Ryan.'

'I don't care about deals right now!'

'I know – you're traumatized. And it's hard to let go when you see Jack like this. The old feelings kick back in. Believe me, I know.'

'No, you don't.' With one final shake of her head Natalia turned away from Charlie and gathered Adam in her arms. She handed him into the chopper. 'Please help me up,' she asked the pilot. 'I'm coming to the hospital with my husband.'

'Interesting.' Charlie watched the helicopter rise into the darkening sky. The first stars had already appeared and a full moon sailed from behind the jagged mountains to the east. He swung round towards us and his sinister eyes flashed in the moonlight. 'That wasn't on my radar. The plan changes.'

We shuddered as we stood with him on the helipad, partly from fear and partly because we were almost freezing to death without our jackets.

'So now you're going to zap us to hell with your superpowers?' Holly challenged and I remembered never to underestimate Holly's ability to put on a brave front. I bet any money that underneath she was shaking and trembling as much as I was.

I mean, I was stunned by the strength of evil emanating through every ice-cold pore.

'Not yet,' Charlie sneered. He stood tall and powerful as the helicopter disappeared down the narrow pass between Carlsbad and Mount Evelyn. He stared at me with cold, cruel eyes, his good-guy disguise long gone. In its place was a dark, vicious and violent force that made me shudder and stagger back. 'No, Tania, not yet,' he repeated with a laugh. He'd done with us for now, turning again and striding towards the lodge. He paused, turned and smiled again. 'Later, maybe.'

'We look forward to that,' Holly muttered. She held the bravado until he'd finally swung in through the side door and disappeared. 'Why not now?' she asked me in a sudden show of panic. 'Why didn't he destroy us on the spot for spoiling his fun?'

'It's not the right time. He's making us wait until the party.' I gave a big sigh as I pictured the scene. 'That's the highlight. It's where I lose Orlando to the dark angels. Charlie wouldn't want me to miss that, now, would he?'

19

Grace's costume was pure white, with the silver headdress covered in fantastic scrolls. A silver mask covered her face.

Holly was dressed in a magenta gown and a hat festooned with black ostrich feathers. Her mask was white, with enormous almond-shaped holes for her eyes and a rosebud doll's mouth painted in red to complete the effect.

They both looked as if they were about to step out of a Venetian palazzo into a gondola that would take them across the shimmering blue lagoon to the doge's ball.

'Tania, get dressed,' Grace urged.

I was sitting on my bed, desperately wishing I could stop time.

'Put on your costume,' Holly told me.

It was seven thirty pm. The party was due to start. I

wasn't ready. I would never be ready to face what was about to take place.

Grace held up my dress of black and white silk. She made me step into it and hold still while she closed the back zipper. It had a nipped-in waist and a stiff, corseted bodice. The skirt billowed over a wide, hooped petticoat.

'Now your mask and hat,' Holly said.

The black hat had a wide brim and big silk flowers. The mask was white, decorated with delicate pink flowers. It felt weird for my face to be hidden behind a painted plastic shell.

'OK?' Grace checked.

I shook my head. This was what Marie Antoinette must have gone through before they carted her through the streets of Paris to the guillotine. She had ladies-in-waiting to clothe her in fine linen, to lace her into her embroidered gown and dress her to impress the crowds as she faced her executioner.

Grace squeezed my hand. 'The beauty of this is that no one will recognize us. But you know what Orlando will be wearing, right?'

'Black cloak, black tunic with silver decoration,' I recalled. 'White mask with a kind of cowl hood and a broad-brimmed hat.'

'Good,' Grace murmured. 'We pick him out from the

crowd and do whatever we have to do to get him out of here.' When I didn't respond she grew more insistent. 'What! You've done it before, haven't you? You got Holly out of New Dawn and me out of Black Eagle Lodge.'

'That was different,' I whispered. This time it was Orlando.

'Right.' Holly stood by the door in her spectacular red costume. 'So, Tania, this is it. We really have to go.'

A white screen covered one entire wall of Owen's bar. Projected on to it were images of Venice – waterside palaces, piazzas, white church spires and narrow covered bridges spanning the canals. The music playing through the speakers was stately and classical.

The plan was for Holly, Grace and me to enter separately and mingle with other guests. That way we wouldn't be so easy to identify. We'd agreed on a place and time to meet and update – eight thirty in reception. Beyond that, none of us knew what to expect.

'Find Orlando. Get rid of Gwen.' Holly's parting instruction couldn't have been clearer.

I focused on those six short words to cut out the fear. I reduced it to two – find Orlando. Then I added two of my own: Breathe. Believe.

Find Orlando. Breathe. Believe. In preparation for

the final battle, this was my mantra.

I went in and mingled. The music was loud, the room full of Ryan James's excited guests. Ryan himself was easy to recognize – a tall figure dressed in a long dark-blue velvet cloak with a high collar, his fair hair visible beneath his hat. I guessed that the person next to him was Larry King and the girl to his left must be Lucy Young, listening so intently that she failed to move out of the path of three jugglers who had just entered the room.

The juggler who collided with her was dressed in a green and red tunic with matching jester's hat, complete with bells. He and his fellow performers darted through the crowd throwing balls high into the air, leaping to catch them, adding more balls, magicking them out of their long, bell-shaped sleeves, even out of their mouths and ears and from under the hats of astonished guests.

People behind their masks laughed in surprise and began to applaud.

Then a team of nimble fire-eaters appeared, all dressed in the figure-hugging, flame-red, sequined body suits that Macy had chosen as her costume. There were six of them, jumping on to the bar and parading along its length. They carried flaming torches, which they threw into the air. The torches twirled, flickered orange and yellow, tracing crazy circles, arcs and zigzags in the air, until the performers caught them and thrust them into their wide-open mouths. There was a series of soft pops as the flames went out.

Onlookers gasped. There was more applause.

The sound of hands clapping. A fire-eater leaps down from the bar brandishing a flaming torch, a red devil. His fingertips are alight, he breathes out fire, flames dart from his eyes as he throws his arms around me to claim and destroy me.

'Tania?' Grace peered at me from behind her silver mask. 'How are you doing?'

The fire-eaters' performance had ended. Wreaths of blue smoke hovered over the bar. 'I'm doing good,' I lied, and Grace carried on by.

Then with a swish of his cloak Ryan broke away from Larry and Lucy. Guests made way for him as he strode to greet a band of musicians – the signal for live contemporary music to take over. Guitar players, drummers, pianists and singers all took their places under the giant screen.

'Fabulous party,' a woman close to me said to her partner.

I recognized the voice and body of Angela Taraska. The body was draped around her companion as only Angela knew how.

It took me a couple of seconds to work out who her dance partner was – a guy of middle height but stocky, wearing a surreal white bird mask. The beak was sharp as a curved knife. Weller.

The backdrop video image of narrow waterways seemed suddenly real. To the rapid, urgent beat of a drum, Weller and Angela transmuted on to the screen. He danced her along a colonnade, under a bridge and out of sight. I told myself to get a grip, to ignore the image of Angela being swallowed into unreality.

Two more dancers whirled by. The woman shrieked and her hooped skirt billowed upwards as her partner lifted her off her feet. Then I glanced at the musicians by the bar. They wore grotesque, ugly masks with black gaping holes for eyes and contorted, down-turned mouths.

The mouths tell me they are in agony. They are the wailing, tormented creatures of the underworld. Their guitars screech, the piano thunders as rocks fall. My chest feels crushed; I can hardly breathe.

Grace watched from a distance as Holly caught up with me. 'Do you see Orlando and Gwen?' she murmured. 'Over there, by the door. Is that them?'

Bracing myself, I studied a couple who had just entered the room. Yes, that was Orlando's black costume with silver trimmings. It was definitely him behind the white mask, under the wide-brimmed hat.

Gwen held his hand, dressed all in silver. The bodice of her dress was straight and stiff, coming to a point below her waist and she wore a thick sash over one shoulder. Her hat was formed from a tall column of embroidered silver satin; her mask was plain white.

A tall figure in black approached them. He spoke to Gwen, who turned her head sharply to look over her shoulder. Then she and the messenger quickly left the room.

'Now's our chance,' Holly decided. 'Come on, Tania – Orlando's alone!'

There was no time to think or plan. Gwen could be back any second. We threaded our way through the dancers, signalling for Grace to join us.

Silk dresses brushed against us, satin-shoed women and cloaked, grotesquely masked men blocked our way. There was a whirl of shiny fabric and soft feathers, glimpses of suspicious eyes behind masks with painted smiles.

'Orlando, it is you, isn't it? I came to say hi,' Holly began in her everyday voice.

He didn't move or react in any way.

I stepped forward. 'It's me – Tania,' I told him. 'Grace is here too.'

He turned his head away.

'We're leaving this party,' I told him. 'We want you to come with us.'

The floor tilts. We're not on firm ground. We're in a boat, a narrow gondola, and the boatman is Weller in his cruel beaked mask. We're way out in the lagoon. There's a whole city beneath the waves – crumbling palaces, broken bridges, churches where silver fishes swim.

'Come with us,' I beg.

Orlando takes off his mask. I scarcely recognize the lost face beneath. It's as if the mouth has never smiled, the eyes have never shone. He looks at me and he doesn't even know me.

A wave sweeps the boat off course. Grace, Holly and I sway and clutch each other. Another wave slams against us. The boat overturns. We're in the cool, clear water and sinking to the bottom of the lagoon, our skirts ballooning around us, clouds of tiny bubbles rising to the bright surface.

'Orlando has to wait for Gwen,' a bystander explained above the wave of sound – drumbeat and guitar, keyboard and a rising babble of voices.

'Why? Where did she go?' I asked.

'Who knows? But I hear there's going to be some sort of an announcement about her and Orlando. Watch out, here she comes.'

Gwen crossed the lobby with the tall figure in black. I

could tell by the walk that it was Charlie hiding behind a plain white mask. Before they came back into the bar, Gwen caught Charlie's arm and spoke urgently. They were about to hurry on when a third figure crossed the lobby behind them.

At first I didn't believe my eyes, but the slight figure and cascade of beautiful red hair was unmistakable – Natalia Linton was back. Unable to think straight and stick to plan, I left Orlando and ran out into the lobby.

'How come?' I cried, tearing off my mask.

Natalia put up both hands as if trying to stop the express train of events. 'We ran into a snowstorm the other side of the pass. The pilot had to turn round.'

'And Jack?' I cried.

'He's OK, Tania. The Xcel team has a medic permanently on call here at the hotel. Amber paged him the moment she heard we couldn't fly Jack to the hospital. The doctor's with him right now. She's sutured the wound and given him fluids.'

'Is he conscious?'

Natalia nodded.

'Does he remember what happened?'

'It's too early for him to talk about that. The doctor wants to sedate him so she sent me down to the medical centre to fetch diazepam.' Natalia held up two packs of sedatives with a wry smile. 'But you know Jack – he's fighting the medics' advice.'

'So, everything's good?'

'Yes, everything's good,' Natalia echoed, but with a rising inflexion like a question mark at the end of her sentence. She held me back as I got set to run back into the bar. 'You don't need to go back in there, you know.'

'Yeah, I do,' I sighed.

'You'll only torture yourself watching Gwen and Orlando party together.'

'I still have to be there.' I could spot them now, arm in arm against the video backdrop of St Mark's Square. Music and guests spilled out of the bar into the lobby.

I was about to fight my way back into the bar when Natalia stopped me again.

'Tania, do I get the impression that you know more than you're saying about what happened to Jack? Who else did you and Holly see up on Carlsbad?'

'Nobody.' My focus was back on Orlando. This had to wait, I told myself and I pulled away. The action was sudden and it made Natalia drop one of the packs of pills she was carrying. I saw it skid across the polished floor and under a couch. 'Sorry,' I muttered. 'It's under here somewhere.'

'It's OK, I have enough here,' Natalia decided, in as

much of a hurry to get back to Jack as I was to find Orlando again.

I bent down and my fingers closed over the pack of diazepam but when I stood up she was already on her way.

'Let's talk tomorrow,' she said as she ran towards the lift.

'Tomorrow,' I agreed.

Should I have left her in the dark about what Charlie had done? Should I have stolen the drugs? I didn't have time to consider my answers as I ran back to the party.

20

Find Orlando, get rid of Gwen. I'd never needed my mantra more as, clutching the diazepam, I plunged into the crowd of dancers.

Breathe. Believe.

I took a moment to inhale. On screen I saw a beautiful image – the dimly lit interior of an Italian church with round arches and decorated marble columns, a vaulted roof that soared towards heaven. There was a carved wooden screen leading through to an altar covered with a cloth of gold. On the walls and ceiling were faded frescos of angels and cherubs and in one cool, quiet corner there was a life-sized marble statue.

I am there in the church – a pilgrim kneeling on the cold black-and-white mosaic floor. I look up at the smooth face of the Virgin Mary carved in sparkling white marble. The face is serene and compassionate like Maia's; the folds of her long cloak and dress fall softly to the ground. She cradles an infant in her arms. The stone seems to give off a mysterious silvery light.

I am drawn into that light. I hear high, pure voices singing. A grey dove flutters from the rafters and alights on my shoulder.

Breathe again. Have faith. My good angels are with me.

The screen faded on a close-up of the pietà – on Mary's loving face and the gentle, sleeping Christ child. The focus softened then the screen was blank.

'Hey, everyone!' Ryan had waited for the musicians to come to the end of a slow, romantic number played on Spanish guitar before he stood on a chair in the centre of the crowded room and called for silence. 'I want to take time out to tell you guys what a great job you've done here in Mayfield. I recognize that we've had some setbacks, but I also know that *Siege 2* will be huge when it hits the screen in spring next year – bigger than anything in the whole thirty-year history of Starlite!'

Ryan let the applause run just long enough for Charlie to join him. People enjoy congratulating themselves, after all. I saw the two men exchange a few words before Ryan nodded then spoke again.

'As we all know, movie-making is all about team work every inch of the way. Each one of you here has played a vital part in making *Siege 2* the great movie that it's going to be. And I'm not bullshitting here – at Starlite we totally place the same value on every member of the team, from runners through technical crew members, extras and stand-ins to our major stars. We love you all!' This time he raised his hand to halt another outbreak of smug clapping and whooping. 'So enough from me. Enjoy the rest of the party, but before we really let our hair down, Charlie Speke wants to say a few words.'

My stomach lurched as Ryan stepped down and Charlie took his place. I'd lost sight of Grace and Holly but had a clear view of Gwen and Orlando standing arm in arm by the bar.

Glasses shake and rattle on the shelves – a small earth tremor, a warning. Bottles crash to the floor, the mirror cracks.

Charlie stood on the chair and took off his mask. For a split second I saw him as I'd seen him that first time in Central Park – the angular jawline, the cheekbones: overwhelmingly handsome. Then his face and figure morphed. They melted and reformed as Weller, my stalker in the park then as wolf man Jarrold and finally Daniel, god of the underworld – all in less time than it took me to take a sharp breath. I reeled, closed my eyes then forced them open again. Charlie was back to his human self, smiling across at Gwen and Orlando, beckoning them forward.

'OK, guys, I hope you won't mind me holding up the party for a couple more minutes,' he began, as if embarrassed but quickly gaining confidence. 'I have an announcement. You all know my little sister Gwen through her great work in the make-up department. What you may not realize is that one of those really neat, story-book things has happened during the shoot.'

'Yeah!' Someone gave a shout of approval and a couple of people clapped.

'So Orlando Nolan is a newcomer to our team – he's a design student in Dallas. But during a visit to Manhattan he came on set as an intern. That's where he met Gwen. What can I say? It was love at first sight.'

There were more whoops and cheers as the crowd eased aside to let Gwen and Orlando through. Some people patted them on the back, others took off their masks to say hi and congratulate them. The walk across the room went on for ever. My face ran with cold sweat. I struggled for air so badly that I had to rip off my mask and hat and throw them to the floor.

'It's a romantic story of true love in a tough, hard world,' Charlie continued, smiling broadly and enjoying every moment of his dark angel victory. 'So, to cut a long story short, I persuaded my little sister that this party was the perfect opportunity to set the seal on their romance and announce their engagement.'

Yeah! All around me guests were clapping and cheering. Party time.

I try to deny it. It can't be true. Then suddenly I'm under attack. Masked creatures crowd in on me. They are misshapen and cruel. Their bird beaks peck at me. They thrust flaming torches into my face.

They morph from human into beast, fall on all fours and prowl out of the light into darkness. They are lean hounds herding me into a forest, they are wolves stalking me between ancient trees, driving me into more danger.

I fought them off and returned to the moment when Gwen and Orlando reached the centre of the room and took off their masks. Her pretty, porcelain face shone with triumph. His was void of emotion.

One step more and he'll be gone, I realized. He was at hell's gate.

Kiss! Kiss! Kiss! A demand went up – one or two voices, then more until there was a general shout for action. They wanted the Kodak moment, the Romeo and Juliet balcony kiss when the loved-up couple seals the deal.

Gwen turned to Orlando and drew him to her. She

put her arms around his neck, pursed her lips and tilted her head.

No way! I wouldn't let this happen. With the ghost of an idea taking shape inside my head, I pushed people aside, waiting for the dogs and wolves to pounce.

I didn't notice Jack at first – not until after Charlie had spotted him from his vantage point on the chair and signalled for Daniel and Jarrold to move in and stop him entering the room. Startled, Gwen let her arms drop to her sides.

Jack came in and it was like the waves of the sea had parted – people gasped and fell away to either side as he advanced unsteadily towards Charlie, one arm heavily strapped, hair dishevelled, his face whiter than the masks worn by Ryan's guests.

Charlie himself was skewered and wriggling under the point of his own dagger.

'Hey, man.' Jarrold minus his mask, was the first to step across Jack's path. 'Whatever it is you're planning to do, wait until the party's over – OK?'

Jack paused, muttered under his breath then with his free hand he shoved Jarrold sideways against the bar.

The wolf man roars. His jaws open and snap shut. He is ready to pounce.

'This won't wait,' Jack told the whole room. Unsteady

but dead set on achieving his goal, he walked on towards Charlie. 'It's between me and you, buddy. We have unfinished business.'

As Jarrold fell to one side, Daniel stepped in. 'Later,' he challenged Jack, ready to manhandle him back the way he came.

Placing the flat of his hand over Daniel's face, Jack used all his strength to push him away.

Zoran Brancusi's god of the underworld falls to the floor then rises. He hovers with his hawk-like beak, a black shadow above our heads.

Again without stopping to think, I fought my way through the throng of people until I reached Jack. 'What are you even doing here? You nearly died up there on the mountain!'

'But I didn't,' he muttered, shoving me away too. 'Unlucky for you – huh, Charlie, you sack of shit!'

'Jack,' Charlie began as he stepped down from the chair. 'I don't know what's happening inside your head—'

'Sure you do,' Jack argued.

It was weird to see them – mirror images, except that pain racked and twisted Jack's features while Charlie's face was cold as steel. I noticed Gwen grasp Orlando's hand and back away from the action towards the giant screen.

405

'You had your turn, Charlie. Now shut up and guess what announcement I'm going to make! No, on second thoughts don't say anything – let me do the talking.' With the help of the nearest bystander, who turned out to be Rocky minus his mask, Jack struggled to stand on the chair that his rival had vacated. 'This is it, people. I'm back from the dead to tell you the truth about Charlie Speke.'

As Charlie lunged forward to topple Jack, Rocky stopped him with a swinging punch to his jaw, bone against bone. Charlie staggered against Ryan, who put him back on his feet.

Jack grimaced then gave a short groan as he raised the injured arm. 'Back from the dead to point the finger – watch closely, Ryan – at the guy who did this to me. Yeah, that's right – it was Charlie. Who else?'

In the chaos that followed, Gwen abandoned Orlando at the bar and rushed to join her brother while Grace and Holly struggled towards me.

'He's out of his head.'

'The guy doesn't know what he's saying.'

'Charlie? No way!'

'Tania!' Holly was the first to reach me. She had to yell above the chorus of dissent. 'This is our last chance!'

'I know it!' And suddenly I also knew what to do. I

took the lead, with Holly then Grace hard on my heels, shoving people aside in our desperate push to reach Orlando, who seemed totally out of it, leaning against the bar for support.

'What happened?' he mumbled. 'Where's Gwen?'

'It's OK. *You're* OK,' I told him. 'We're here for you now.'

In the centre of the room, Charlie had recovered and was protesting his innocence. Gwen was there to back him up, gesticulating and shaking her head. Rocky had helped Jack down from the chair then had taken on Daniel, Weller and Jarrold single-handed.

'We're getting you out of here,' Holly promised.

Orlando shook his head. 'No. I'm not going anywhere.'

'Yes,' Grace pleaded. 'Orlando, come with us!'

While they argued with him, I snatched a bottle of water from the bar and popped out three tablets from the foil wrapper, at the same time quickly reading the label: 'One to be taken three times daily.'

'Listen to me,' I told him, uncurling his fingers and making him hold out his hand. 'You have to swallow these.'

I don't know what made him obey – maybe the sound of my voice stirred up memories of the time we were together, or maybe his brain was only programmed for the engagement, the slow romantic dance and the moment of crossing over to the dark side. Now that the plan had suddenly veered off course he had no direction and was thrown into confusion. Anyway, Orlando hardly looked at the three tablets in the palm of his hand before he threw them into his mouth and swallowed them down.

I didn't know what triple the recommended dosage would do to him but we quickly found out. As Daniel and the others launched themselves at Rocky, I watched Orlando's head tilt back then slump heavily forward. One hand went to his head while his legs buckled and Grace and Holly stepped in to support him.

'What the hell was that?' Holly grunted.

'Tranquillizers.' No time for explanations so I shrugged an apology instead.

'Jeez,' Grace sighed. She sagged under Orlando's dead weight. 'What now?'

'Get him out. Hide him in a safe place.'

'Like where?' Holly wanted to know. But she and Grace began to drag Orlando towards the door.

Fine, I told myself. No one except a dark angel is going to stop them – a guy who looks like he's had too much to drink and two good buddies taking care of him.

Charlie, Gwen and the other dark angels were still

occupied in trying to control Rocky and convince Ryan that Jack had finally lost the plot.

All good. This was going to work out. I'd reached the door and sent Grace and Holly ahead with Orlando, turning one last time to make sure.

Old Venice is back on the screen. Monks in black cloaks and hoods file into church. The candles that surround the Virgin Mary and baby Jesus flicker and die; smoke rises in thin grey wisps. The monks throw back their hoods to reveal domed skulls, black eye sockets, grinning jaws.

I flee into the street, into a procession of fire-eaters, jugglers and masked revellers. I feel the heat of a flaming torch close to my face. Masked men surround me. I push through them and run again over a narrow bridge. Jesters and jugglers block my way. I climb on to the parapet of the ancient bridge, look down into the grey canal water, prepare to jump.

Across the lobby the doors of the elevator slid open and Natalia stepped out with Adam. He ran towards me, arms outstretched.

'Jack disappeared,' Natalia told me hurriedly. 'He pulled out his drip feed when the nurse left the room. Adam saw him stagger towards the lift.'

'He's in the bar.' I said, crouching to hug Adam and feeling a surge of energy as he flung his arms around me. 'Go with Mommy,' I whispered.

They hurried on and I ran after Orlando, Holly and Grace.

'Where's safe?' Grace wanted to know. 'Come on, Tania, what are you thinking?'

'Not in the hotel.' Charlie and Gwen would find us. They would send Daniel and the others to search us out.

'Ski-lift terminal?' Holly suggested as she shifted Orlando's weight and hooked his arm more firmly over her shoulder.

I shook my head for the same reason as before.

'Where then?'

I led the way out of the lobby on to the driveway festooned with silver Christmas lights. I glanced at the cars in the parking lot, all still submerged under half a metre of snow. Then I looked to my right and spotted the chopper parked on the floodlit helipad. 'Over there,' I decided.

We crossed the frozen lawn to moans and slurred words from Orlando. 'No way,' he protested. 'Not leaving. Gwen . . . not leaving.'

My heart sank, and for a moment I despaired.

'God, I hope we don't have to tranq him again,' Holly groaned.

'And who's going to fly this thing?' Grace wanted to know.

'The pilot's right there, look.' I pointed to the figure leaning over the instrument panel, checking data then setting the giant blades in motion. 'It looks like he received the all-clear to fly out.'

'Finally we got lucky,' Holly sighed.

A black eagle flies over Carlsbad. The sky is crystal clear, the sun is high. The bird circles then hovers directly overhead.

'Let's hope,' Grace added.

Together we manhandled Orlando towards the helicopter.

'No, not leaving. New life,' Orlando muttered then opened his eyes but failed to focus. The chopper blades had raised a flurry of snow that blew straight into our faces.

'You're safe with us,' Grace explained as I hurried ahead, afraid that the pilot would raise the ladder before we got there.

Icy snow stung my cheeks as I stepped on the bottom rung and the blast from the chopper blades almost flung me back down. But I made it up the ladder, yelling at Grace and Holly to hurry after me with Orlando.

'He's a dead weight – we can't lift him,' Grace called back.

'Wait. I'll get the pilot to help,' I promised.

I saw him from the back, hunched over the instruments,

pressing buttons, consulting an array of small screens. The ladder started to telescope up into the body of the machine and the door to slide shut. 'No, wait!' I protested.

I heard Holly yell my name from below, saw her, Grace and Orlando disappear in a cloud of whirling snow.

The door closed. The pilot raised the chopper from the ground.

'Wait!' I rushed forward and put my hand on the pilot's shoulder. 'Wait for my buddies. We all need to get out of here.'

He shook his head. The chopper swayed as it rose to roof level and turned away from Evelyn Pass directly towards the summit of Carlsbad.

I looked down on the parking lot, the line of twinkling trees and ahead at the yellow light of the ski-lift terminal. And I knew without having to see the pilot's face: Charlie.

'Hey, Tania,' he replied. 'Your time is up. This is the final deal – just you and me.'

My dark angel flew over Carlsbad. There was nothing I could do or say, nowhere I could go.

Through the glass roof of the chopper I could make out constellations of stars – Aquarius and Pegasus, Orion with his chariot.

'You never truly believed you would beat me,' Charlie mocked. 'Not this third and final time.'

We rose high up the mountain into the dark night.

I still believe! Don't let go of the last thread of hope.

'I couldn't let you do that, Tania. There was too much to lose.'

'You haven't won – not yet,' I told him. Not while I had breath.

'Think about it.' Enjoying being at the controls, he flew straight at a sheer rock face, only pulling away at the last second, tilting the machine at a crazy angle and climbing again. 'What did we leave back there? Jack sounding off about me trying to kill him, but who's going to believe a burned-out movie star with a drink problem? No one. And people won't listen to Holly and Grace either. Who are they? Just two deranged girls trying to hijack a guy to stop him marrying a talented make-up artist. And for what reason? Because the guy fell out of love with his childhood sweetheart, who happens to be their best friend. A case of misguided loyalty, obviously. Talking of which, the childhood sweetheart went missing. People are going to find her frozen corpse and say she lost her mind and threw herself off the mountain.'

Again I had nothing to say. Let him enjoy the moment because what difference did it make?

'You're quiet, Tania.' He wheeled the machine back

towards another rock face in a second game of chicken. 'Scared?' he laughed.

'Holly and Grace won't hand Orlando back to Gwen.' This was me, hanging on to that last thread.

'They won't have a choice. What are they going to do – unwire his brain and reprogramme him? Forget it – you don't know my sister!'

'Gwen is Carrie Hall. You don't have a sister.'

The laugh changed. It grew higher and childlike, and when I steeled myself to look at Charlie at the controls he was transformed into a fragile, golden-haired girl. I groaned and looked away.

'But who is she? Who am I?' he taunted.

My stomach lurched as we flew straight at the cliff. To die like this, crashing into the frozen mountain, to be found months later in a pile of mangled wreckage . . .

He pulled back and steered into a deep crevasse with white cliffs to either side. The cliffs closed in. Charlie steered the helicopter through the narrowest of gaps and came through the other side.

'You see?' he smiled. 'This was your last attempt to defeat me and you failed.'

Still I had to hope.

'You know the problem?' Charlie said, as if he was an accountant called in to run through details of a failed business venture. 'This time your good angel didn't come through. He didn't deliver.'

'It's not ended,' I argued, looking up through the roof at the stars.

'What do you expect when goodness shows up in the shape of a five-year-old child? Oh yeah, and the dove – what was her name: Zenida, Zenaida? And before that we're talking about a grieving mother and a baby, an infant.'

'Aimee.' My twin, my own alter ego. Saying her name out loud gave me the strength to argue back. 'You don't understand goodness. Not the first thing.' I was talking about the pure spirit of a newborn baby, the freedom of a dove, the blazing, blinding light of a child who died and was reborn.

Charlie raised us high above the snowy cliffs, straight towards the moon. 'Convince me,' he sneered.

'Goodness is love, pure and simple. You, Gwen, Daniel, all of you – you live without love in total darkness.'

'Where life is more interesting. Come on, Tania – you have to admit that. Wouldn't you rather be out on the campaign trail with me, scouting for innocent souls. lusting for power? Like now – nothing in your bland, boring world beats the way I feel.'

'No way,' I groaned. 'You can't seduce me and God

knows you've tried. So what do you do instead? You target the only guy I ever loved. You steal him from me but it's me and my psychic power that you still really want.'

'One way or the other, it doesn't really matter,' he argued as the moon seemed to grow larger and we saw all the craters, the mountains, the dried oceans and river beds. 'Either way, it ends.'

The moon glows silver. It radiates eternal light. We're a speck against its pitted surface. We're surrounded by stars.

'I trusted you for a while, until I found out the games you were playing with Jack and Natalia.'

'Yeah, that was fun.'

'Until I understood Adam and followed my own instincts.'

'You know what disappoints me about goodness, Tania?' Throwing up his hands, Charlie lost interest in steering the helicopter. He left the engine on full speed and let it sail towards the moon. 'Goodness is so predictable. There's no subtlety.'

A wind whipping off the mountain destabilized us and we lurched to our left then fell into a sudden, deathly drop.

'Whereas there's no telling what I will do,' he laughed. Then, without warning, he leaned across and wrenched open the door.

The helicopter dropped through a layer of cloud. Icy mist rushed into the cockpit.

'Ready?' he asked.

Without waiting for an answer he flung me from the helicopter into free fall.

I'm falling through the night sky, spreadeagled. I need wings.

Charlie falls with me. These are my last thoughts.

Who are you? What's your name? You morph and shift. You're Daniel, Jarrold and Weller. You're Gwen. Everyone and no one.

What did you say to me that first time in Central Park – tall, dark-haired, too handsome to believe? 'I'm Charlie Speke, Jack Kane's stuntman double.'

What did he tell everyone the first time he met them? 'I'm not him. I'm nobody.'

We fall through the air. I look up and I see the moon and stars.

You morph and shift. You're everyone and no one – my dark angel's last, twisted trick.

He's a black eagle, soaring on the wind. He's a beast rising from the water, a monster of rockfalls emerging from his stinking cave.

'I know you,' I say. 'You told me yourself like you always

do but I didn't hear you. I looked in the wrong places.'

We fall together. He doesn't believe that I've learned his final secret.

'This time you don't have a name or an identity. You're everyone. You're nobody.'

No name. I know I'm right.

We fall and he lets out a long, agonized sigh, as if all the air has left his body. He goes limp, his handsome features start to lose definition and disintegrate. High above our heads there is a bright explosion then shattered glass and fragments of metal from the helicopter rain down. Charlie morphs. I catch glimpses of Gwen then Zoran, of Aurelie and Jean-Luc, Daniel, Owen, Jarrold and Weller – split-second changes as all the dark angels struggle to exit Charlie's doomed body. He keeps on falling through the black night.

And what's left after the final transformation? A shapeless, insubstantial being screaming out in terror, burning up, turning to smoke, gas and cosmic dust. Nobody. Nothing.

'Take my hand,' Adam says. So simple and inevitable.

He lifts me out of the abyss and carries me from star to star, across the face of the moon. Gently he sets me down on the side of Carlsbad and walks with me back to the hotel.

21

Ours was the calm *after* the storm.

I returned to Carlsbad Lodge with Adam and handed him over to his relieved parents. Then straight away Holly and Grace took me to see Orlando. Instinct told them that I had finally defeated my dark angel.

'We'll talk later,' Grace said.

Orlando sat in the deserted bar amongst party debris – half-empty glasses, the giant blank screen, abandoned musical instruments. He looked dazed, like a soldier staggering from the battlefield unable to believe that he had survived. Unscathed, but the horror of what he'd been through still gripped him.

I sat facing him and waited.

He took deep, shuddering breaths. 'Where's Gwen?' he gasped.

'Gone. They're all gone.'

'Really?' He gazed around the room, startled by a guitar propped against a chair when it slid to the floor, by the movement of the drapes as the wind blew through an open window.

'Really and truly. Charlie and Gwen – all the dark angels.'

'Gone,' he sighed.

We cried then and held each others' hands.

'We're free,' I told him gently. 'Just like you always wanted.'

Of course, Jack and Natalia kept their promise. We had official invites to the New York premiere of *Siege 2* when it launched in the spring, but we chose to stay home and watch it on late-night TV – me and Orlando, Holly and Grace at my house on Becker Hill.

'Why won't you come?' Natalia had argued over the phone. 'We'd love for you to be here.'

Too many bad memories, Orlando and I agreed.

I stayed away mostly for Macy's sake. She couldn't be there and I didn't want to watch Jack launch *Siege 2* without her.

Orlando understood. 'Besides, we're enjoying our freedom too much,' he added.

Eventually Natalia had seen it our way. 'So, Tania,

you'll visit us in Nassau instead,' she'd decided. 'Adam wants you to come. And Jack – he particularly mentioned it.'

'Tell them I'll be there,' I'd said.

So we saw them on the screen – Jack Kane and Natalia Linton, the world's most glamorous couple and now our personal friends. They walked the red carpet, flashlights popping. We saw Rocky Seaton – one good memory amongst the bad.

'That guy's cool,' Holly sighed.

'If you ever need someone,' he'd vowed. And he'd meant it and acted it out, taught me never to lose faith in the goodness of your fellow man.

Now he walked the red carpet with Lisette.

Angela Taraska came alone. She wore shimmery, strapless, cut-away Versace.

Ryan James had a better haircut, I noticed. They filmed him after the show, promoting the next sequel, *Siege 3*. When you've established a global brand, why change the name?

I'm not overlooking Jack's alcohol addiction and the marriage split, I'm only saying that Jack was four months into a rehab program and he and Natalia were both in long-term counselling. Brick by brick they were rebuilding their damaged lives.

'For the kids,' Jack had told me when he and the Starlite team flew into Aspen in February for more reshooting. They hadn't found a body double to replace Charlie so Jack had to do the scenes himself.

It was a huge deal at the time – the disappearance of Charlie Speke and his sister, Gwen: a forty-eight-hour wonder involving mountain rescue teams and police investigators. Eventually they discovered small pieces of wreckage from a helicopter that had slammed into the side of Carlsbad. No bodies were ever found but the educated guess was that Charlie had been the unqualified pilot and Gwen his passenger.

They never knew the reasons why the brother and sister had made that final tragic journey but there was plenty of rumour and speculation, none of it accurate.

'We should have been there in person,' Holly sighed as she stretched out on the couch watching the TV. 'We should have hired the dresses, walked the walk.'

'No thanks.' Grace agreed with me. She chose not to be reminded that she'd once upon a time flown too close to the dark angel flame. And tonight she was the one who suggested to Holly that it was time for them to leave.

'Orlando flies back to Dallas tomorrow,' she reminded her.

'What? Oh yeah.' Holly raised herself from the couch.

'Lucky you have one sensitive, socially aware buddy, Tania. Not like me, huh?'

'I love you both,' I laughed as they left the room through the French doors and strolled across the garden.

'This is our last night together,' Orlando murmured, his lips against my hair, arms around my waist.

'Yeah, six whole weeks without you.' Him at college, me taking a study trip to Eastern Europe and then maybe schmoozing in the Bahamas.

'I really don't want to get on that plane.'

'Yes, you do,' I kidded. 'You love what you're studying. You're driven by an unstoppable ambition to reach the top.' It was back to normal, long-distance loving for Orlando and me.

Only, nothing was normal and ever would be again. Everything between us was special.

You know the weird thing, the one tiny detail he got hung up on after the cosmic battle was over and the dark angels were gone?

'Diazepam?' he'd queried three days after the party. 'Jesus, Tania, you gave me enough to tranquillize a horse!'

'On a need-to basis,' I'd argued. 'No time to look up dosages on Wikipedia – what else could I do?'

I promised never to repeat anything like that in the future. I forgave him for Gwen the way he'd forgiven me for Daniel – stuff that was beyond our control.

'And that's it – they're gone for ever?' It was Christmas Day before Orlando fully recovered from his dark angel ordeal enough to finally believe that it was over.

'We are free,' I insisted. 'Now it's time to move on.'

I'd been with him constantly since Adam and I had arrived back at the lodge, never left his side, even after my dad drove out to Mayfield to bring us home to Bitterroot.

By mid-January he was fit and healthy again and I could bear to let go of his hand. Four months later we were like we were before any of it happened.

We'd had fun watching the premiere. Holly and Grace were gone. We followed them into the garden, where we walked hand in hand between the aspens.

'Does the sky look different?' Orlando asked.

'No it's the same.'

'There are more stars.'

'That's not possible – there's a fixed number.'

'No. New stars are created, old stars die.'

'So anyway, don't look at them. Look at me.' I turned his face towards me. 'I need to remember you. When you're in Dallas, I want you in my mind, just like you are now.'

God, his eyes were beautiful behind those dark lashes – big and clear, totally focused on me. His mouth was wide and soft. The moon cast a silver light.

'We'll Skype,' he murmured.

'It's not the same.'

'I'll be back in June.'

'Promise?'

Orlando nodded and held me close. Our dream of loving and living a life together was all I ever wanted – moment by moment, one step at a time.

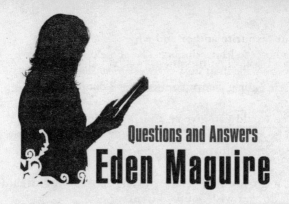

Questions and Answers
Eden Maguire

Where do the ideas for your books come from?
My ideas come from a mysterious region of the brain – the 'What if' part which must have a neurological label, but which works something like this: 'What if the world really is split between supernatural good and bad forces? What if we can all be tempted on to the side of shape-shifting, terrifying dark angels to fight against the angels of light?' With this basic idea, I can create a setting, a heroine and a whole cast of characters, plus a plot so full of twists and turns that even I don't know how it will end until I get there.

Who would your dream cast be if *Dark Angel* was made into a film?
Actors in a film of *Dark Angel*? Most of the ones I can think of are a few years too old (sorry!), but how about Natalie Portman for Tania (she's the right physical style and can play sensitive, tormented souls) and Robert Pattinson for Orlando (dream on!).

Who do you relate to more – Darina from the *Beautiful Dead* or Tania in *Dark Angel*?
I think Darina has more of the rebel in her – something I can relate to from my own teen years. I don't have Tania's psychic powers, but do share some of her thin-skinned sensitivity.

If you could invite five people to dinner who would they be?
Top of my list for ideal dinner guests are: Marilyn Monroe, Shakespeare, Catherine Earnshaw from *Wuthering Heights*, John Lennon and Atticus Finch from *To Kill A Mocking Bird*.

Where is your favourite place to write?
I can only write in one place and no other – it's my first storey office overlooking a river and a wooded hillside. No other room will do.

Who is your favourite author and why?

Favourite author is so hard – this time I'll choose one who is alive – it's Annie Proulx who wrote the short story *Brokeback Mountain* which they turned into a great film. Everything she writes is strong and disturbing.

What advice would you give to aspiring young writers?

People who really want to write don't need my advice. They're driven by some inner compulsion. It turns out right if they stick to the truth of their imaginations.

What book do you wish you had written?

A book I totally admire is *The Kite Runner* by Khaled Hosseini. I wish I could write something so moving and powerful and true.

How does it feel when you see your books in a bookshop?

When I see my own book on a bookshop shelf I have a mixed reaction. There's a big temptation to position it so that customers can see it more easily, but there's also an unexpected panic and a need to run and hide!

Tell us one thing your readers won't already know about you.

I once fell off a horse high on a mountain with no other riders around. My horse didn't run off – he stayed and waited for me to get back on my feet, thank heavens. Not many people know that!